Ann Schlee was born and brought up in Greenwich, Connecticut. After schooling in the United States, Egypt and England, she studied English Literature at Somerville College, Oxford. Since then, she has done various kinds of teaching, both in the United States and in England, and currently teaches creative writing to adults at Morely College, London. Ann Schlee lives in London with her husband and four children.

The Proprietor is Ann Schlee's second novel.

'I have seldom read a novel which, in style and detail, was so convincingly grounded in fact and period'
Sunday Telegraph

'Realized in startlingly vivid detail'
Times Literary Supplement

'Subtle and impressive'
Sunday Times

'Written with a great fluency and insight, creating a close weave that really begs a slow, attentive read'
New Statesman

'Passion gleams through a surface of carefully modulated prose . . . The magic here is in Schlee's ability to create a felt world in the past and to give it substance . . . a delight to read'
Books and Bookmen

'Fine Murdochian symbolism and dazzling prose: a subtle, striking novel'
The Kirkus Reviews

Author photograph by Jerry Bauer

Also by Ann Schlee

RHINE JOURNEY

THE PROPRIETOR

a novel

ANN SCHLEE

BLACK SWAN

Acknowledgements
I should like to thank Ron Cooper and
Malcolm Cole for generously sharing their
knowledge of the period in which this
novel is set.

THE PROPRIETOR

A BLACK SWAN BOOK 0 552 99099 X

Originally published in Great Britain by
Macmillan London Limited

PRINTING HISTORY
Macmillan London edition published 1983
Black Swan edition published 1984

Title page illustration from Lady Sophia Frances
Tower's *Sketches in the Isles of Scilly* c. 1849.
By permission of The British Library

This book is set in 11/12 California

Black Swan Books are published by
Transworld Publishers Ltd., Century House,
61 – 63 Uxbridge Road, Ealing, London W5 5SA

**Made and printed in Great Britain by the
Guernsey Press Co. Ltd., Guernsey, Channel Islands.**

To James and Gilli Wright

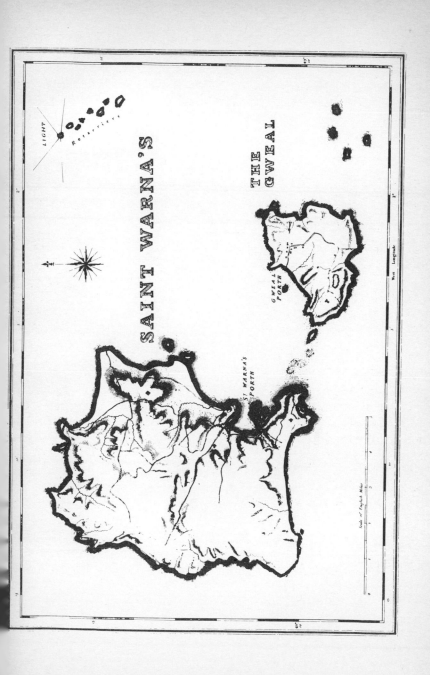

SAINT WARNA'S

THE GWEAL

LIGHT

Retarriers

GWEAL PORTH

ST WARNA'S PORTH

West Longitude

Scale of English Miles

The documentation on Augustus Walmer is slight. There is a journal kept fitfully during his early years on the islands. There are the letters to his agent in which he discussed the day-to-day matters of running his estate while he was on the mainland. There are the letters written to Amelia Pontefract over the long years of their friendship and his rancorous correspondence with the Duchy over the terms of his lease. That is all.

Some information exists about his background. He was born the year before Trafalgar, the second son of a London banker. Death swept through his family like an epidemic, taking forms particular to that time. His elder brother was killed at the age of nine by a fall from a horse. His mother died of puerperal fever after giving birth to a little girl, Fanny. His father, worn out by amassing a fortune, died when Augustus was eighteen. A younger brother lived to manhood only to succumb to the cholera in India. His sister Fanny contracted a chill in her fifteenth year from which she never recovered. By the time Augustus purchased the lease of the islands, at the age of thirty, he was the sole survivor.

His motives for going to so remote a spot are obscure, but it would seem he intended to devote his life to the conducting of an experiment to restore the islands' economy along utilitarian principles and to promote the greatest happiness among the greatest number of his people.

1

Time cannot have affected the sensations of seasickness. Then as now that complaint could thrust itself upon a man like Augustus Walmer, whose health was flawless; who need never, in that long interval of peace, and as he eschewed the hunting field, feel any bodily weakness until his health finally broke; who must seek out violent physical exercise for the supreme luxury of lying down at night certain that the body's fatigue could drug the mind's activity.

So the whole passage, from ten in the morning when the *Lord Wellington* passed the sheltering Lizard and put out to sea, was passed by him in a semi-conscious state in the captain's cabin: the consciousness being only of that most abandoned of miseries, the rest merciful periods of sleep. Even the cold cabin's one advantage of privacy was wasted; so lost was he, lying waking or retching, to any sense of who he was or why he had come. Only when a boy came to the door with a jug of hot water and told him that the islands were in sight did he venture to sit, still huddling his travelling cloak around him, and then cautiously to stand as upright as the cramped cabin would allow. He washed, and rinsed out his bitter mouth with brandy from his flask. He was shaking with cold which neither the brandy nor the burning sensation at the pit of his stomach could dispel.

He had no idea how long he had lain shivering in the dimly lighted cabin, and had not roused himself sufficiently to ask the boy the time, so it surprised and confused him to see a patch of faded evening light ahead as he

11

hauled himself up the ladder of the narrow compan-
ionway. All the more to find the islands so close. They
floated ahead of the little cutter like a shoal, low and sullen
in the water. It angered him to find himself unable to tell
one part of his possession from the next. He had made a
point in his first month of ownership of studying his map
night after night, until every rock seen during the day's
tour of inspection was named and committed to memory.
But now, at the sight of them, all that was confused. With
every plunge of the deck they altered their alignment one
with another, so that the very rocks seemed to change
shape before his eyes and he sensed something hostile,
evasive, conspiratorial in them, which an instant later he
told himself was not among the properties of stone.

To his relief there were no more than three or four
passengers on the deck, none of whom he recognized or
who appeared to know him. He crossed the deck and stood
beside the master, who turned at his approach and said,
'Good evening, Mr Walmer.' Respectful and contained.
Silent now, perhaps because he did not know how to
express sympathy without alluding too openly to the Proprietor's weakness, but then men in their element must
always feel a contempt for those who are not.

'Will this be the last tack?' Augustus wrapped his cloak
around him trying to sound indifferent. He thought the
cold affected his voice.

'I trust so. You'll be glad to be back in the islands, sir.'
There was ambiguity there, amusement perhaps at his
plight. Perhaps kindness. It could not be helped.

'Indeed I shall,' he said, clapping his arms against his
body inside his cloak. 'It was good of you to let me have
your cabin.'

'My pleasure, sir.' Their soft voices could be quite
expressionless. After only three months on the mainland he
had to strain after some of the words. He walked a little
way apart and stood leaning over the rail. It was twilight.
Stars had appeared. The breeze was damp and chilly,
making him shiver the more. Now they were close enough
to see a solitary light on the dark hillside. Then,

12

unbearably, the helmsman cried, 'Ready about,' and the cutter flung out again into the dark sea.

On the return tack he found his mind had cleared. The long low outline ahead of him was the main island. This final tack had fetched them up to the entrance of the sound. Now dim shapes of land surrounded them. They rounded a headland and there were the lights of the town raised up behind the bobbing masts and shrouds of ships. He named everything now. He apprehended it. But then the lights flickered behind the masts. The dark line of the hill heaved up and down. The very land seemed unsubstantial.

He stayed by the rail, watching the half-obscure activity on the water below. Slackened sail set up its racket; the anchor rattled down. Oars splashed. Voices called out of the darkness: 'Anyone for St Warna?' 'Anyone for the Gweal?' A boy's voice called out, 'Is Mr Walmer there? I have his boat.' He looked down and saw the clustering boats make way while his own was manoeuvred to the base of the ladder. The master called across the deck, 'Mr Walmer's luggage to his boat!' He gripped the man's hand and thanked him again. Then he made his way down the ladder, his legs so stiff with cold that he feared the final indignity of falling. Looking down once, he saw a boy hold up a lantern from the dinghy at the ladder's foot.

'Welcome back, sir,' he said with a formal politeness. Augustus settled himself in the rocking boat. The rays of the lantern set up a haze of bright light around the boy's face, which so flattened and altered his features that Augustus, peering from the darkness, did not know him. When, in the next minute, he set the lantern in between the thwarts to reach down the two portmanteaux, Augustus said at once:

'Mrs Traherne's boy, isn't it?'

'That's right, sir. I'm John Traherne.'

'Who told you I was coming?'

'Mr Wills, sir. He said he'd gladly have come with me only you had said not.'

'No,' he said. 'That's right. I'll see him in the morning. I'm good for nothing tonight.'

They sat in silence as the boy steered the little boat

between the heaving hulks of anchored ships towards the quay. Then Augustus said, 'Where's Walter Webber, then?'

'Broke his arm, sir. It's ruined him for rowing. I have his place. Mr Wills gave it me.'

'Poor fellow. I hadn't heard.'

'It was since you left, sir.' He heard in the boy's voice the great gap in time that three months could establish.

'Who's taken his place in the gig?'

'I hope to, sir, if they'll have me. Only there's been no wreck all winter. So I've not had the chance yet.'

'You're young for that,' he said reprovingly, but saw now that the boy must be seventeen or eighteen at least and pulled as effortlessly as a man. He had turned his head away to steer the boat in under the dark shadow of the quay. A moment later he shipped his oars and jumped onto the bottom step to make them fast. The old structure towered solid above them. Augustus could see the outline of the crane and the flat lighters piled with stone tied to the base of the new extension, but all that could wait until morning. The boy's hard hand helped him onto the steps. He clung to the rail as he climbed. The only sensation that his legs conveyed of return to his property was a faint jarring as they struck at the stationary land.

The quay was crowded with men, indistinguishable in this light, made the same shape by their dark working clothes. They waited for this weekly moment of contact with the half-forgotten mainland. The boat following his brought ashore some crewmen and the few passengers. He heard gruff greetings. A bundle of newspapers was untied and passed among them. He saw John Traherne easily shoulder his heavy portmanteau and clasp the smaller one under the arm that held the lantern. Then, as if with one movement, the little crowd began to tramp down the quay towards the town.

He let himself be carried along with them, at pains not to glance about for recognition, and if they watched him it seemed they did so furtively. But of course he was known. Even in the dark his height, the shape of his cloak,

14

proclaimed him a different breed. He seemed to feel the current of apprehension and excitement his return sent among them. He thought he heard his name muttered – Mr Walmer . . . Mr Walmer – just beyond the range of certainty, whether in greeting or comment he could not· tell. He made no response other than a nod of the head, which they might take as they pleased.

He would not have it otherwise. He relished the secrecy and separateness of his arrivals. In his cold and discomfort it amused him to think himself some god alighted, his fiery messenger sent on ahead, striding over the land with his cloak of invisibility tight about him. Then, when his presence was perhaps still unknown, his sense of ownership was at its strongest and most satisfactory.

In the spring of 1836 he was still living in a house on the main island of St Warna at no distance from the harbour and overlooking the main street of the town. There, later that night, he sat in his dressing gown by the bright basket of coals in his bedroom fireplace, waiting for the cold to recede and the shivering to cease. He drank some more brandy from the flask. He was, for once, too tired to read or write. When the maid came to tend to the fire and take away his linen he did not attempt to speak, but felt oddly comforted by the sight of her tucked hem swaying against the floor as she poked and clattered with the coals. She had a pleasant smell compounded of sweat and soap which, combined with the coal fumes, breathed of childhood. Her great calm shadow on the flickering ceiling drew on memories too indistinct to harm. When she had gone he blew out the lamp and climbed into bed. He lay drowsily watching the movement of the firelight and listening to the close crowded sounds of the men's boots going to and fro on the street below. He heard their deep wordless voices. His strength, his brief illusion of deity, had gone from him.

It seemed that after thirty years his life, with its sad freight of early bereavement and early inheritance, veered

15

out on an unseen current and swung at a distance until he might find the strength to recall it.

In the morning he woke quite restored to himself. It was later than he had intended. Sunlight imprinted the pale birds and garlands on the drawn curtains. Gulls carried their restless complaints back and forth above the house. A cart passed on the stones. The place was awake and alive before him. He resented that, as if something of his own had been taken from him. He begrudged the three months' intricate living that had kept pace with his time away and was now gone beyond his reach. He felt all the bitter irritation of one who has allowed things to slip from his hands through absence and drew on his clothes with a speed that amounted almost to anger. Still, as he tied his cravat, his fingers felt too clumsy and slow to achieve all that must be done in that day. The latest letter from his agent lay with the contents of his pockets on the top of his chest. He snatched it up without folding it and carried it downstairs in his hand.

Alone at the long table in his dining room he read and re-read the letter and rehearsed in his mind what he would say to Wills when he arrived. He took out his watch. Wills would come punctually at nine-thirty. Ten minutes. He sipped tea. Re-read the letter. Listened for the front door bell. The agent was prompt as always. He must wait in the road, consulting his watch so as to ring the bell on the stroke of the minute. It was a waste of time, but of Wills' time, not his. It showed dedication. He could hear the young man's voice in the hall.

'Come in. Come in,' he called, and as Wills appeared in the doorway, 'won't you join me?' With one hand he dabbed his handkerchief vigorously at his lips, with the other he waved Wills to any one of the nine empty chairs around the table. 'Won't you sit down?' For he was genuinely pleased to see him: the only man on the island who troubled to be punctual.

The young man remained smiling, standing, approaching only to grip the back of the chair nearest him, repeating in his gentle voice that he hoped he was well and that the crossing had been tolerable.

'I was wretchedly sick,' said Augustus.

'I am sorry to hear that, sir,' he said as if he meant it. He was remarkably pale for one who had seldom left the islands since birth. His slight delicate hands shifting along the back of the chair were white as a girl's. Poor fellow, he must cling to these signs of gentility. His beard was trimmed, his black coat neatly cut but showing the rusty tinge of the sea air which made even the black cats of the place shabby. His quick eye was caught by the sight of his own handwriting on the paper on the table.

'Well, what first?' Augustus said.

Wills said, almost apologetically, 'There is a meeting of the magistrates called at eleven this morning. I thought you would want to be present.'

'The church, I suppose,' They looked at one another.

'Yes.' But by an indefinite lengthening of the word he knew there would be something else.

'We have time for the quay first, then,' said Augustus, rising and pushing back his chair. He rubbed his fingers hard on the napkin, tossed it on the table, picked up the letter, clapped Wills briefly on the shoulder as he passed him. He held up the letter and said over his shoulder, 'I debated whether or not to answer this, but decided not as I was coming so soon.' In the hall he took his stick from a stand and his yachting cap which he pulled firmly down over his eyes.

They walked side by side along the narrow grey stone channel formed by the paved street and the closely fronted cottages on either side. Overhead the sky was all activity; high clouds were blown rapidly by a cold east wind and gulls circled the harbour. Wills walked deferentially in the road; Augustus, a full head and shoulders taller, swinging his stick and raising his cap to the people he passed, kept to the narrow pavement. He felt an excitement he would hold in check. He said to Wills, 'The storm must have set them back.'

'They have it up as high as it was. They lost three courses.'

'Yes. You said. No further than they were?'

17

'A little,' said Wills. 'They've faced the outer wall now.'

'How long do you think? October?'

Wills shrugged. 'It depends,' he said, 'on the weather.' The scepticism in his voice implied all the vagaries of the place. Augustus gave a snort of collusion partly through his nose, partly at the back of his throat. He liked Wills, who was intelligent and, being not too profoundly of the islands, shared his impatience.

'Do you find McPherson adequate?'

'He drinks a bit. Cash is his main problem. He gets behind in his payments to his men. Then they drift off.'

'Ah,' said Augustus, staring speculatively at his agent. 'Yes, I imagine they would. None back to the Gweal, I hope?' But without noticing Wills' hesitation he went on, 'I heard about Webber's arm. Can we find him something?'

'They'll have him in the shipyard. It's his left arm.'

'Good.' He walked with his brisk mainland stride, consuming the short distance to the quay at a prodigal rate.

Already he could hear the masons' hammers ringing in the stoneyard on the beach, but the harbour wall still masked the sea and the outer islands. Almost he feared his first sight of them. In the clear washed light, the sharp focus of new return, he feared he might become severed from himself, as if in admitting the beauty of the place he might also give access to its terrible passivity. 'It looks all much the same,' he said to Wills, as if it displeased him. And coming through the gap in the sea wall he looked angrily at the sight which at that time he most loved: the Gweal, innocent, contained; and the uninhabited islands floating in their turquoise sea. He would not let them distract him from the task at hand. He turned his eyes to the workings on the quay.

2

In the February of the previous year he had written in his journal:

Wills agrees that the most immediate advantage to the islands' enonomy would be gained by the repair and extension of the old quay to accommodate a deeper draught of shipping and so to provide opportunities for repairing and revictualling such ships as seek shelter within the islands. The new church must wait upon this quay.

This work was now entering its second season. Augustus strode to the very edge of the old granite structure, stepping impatiently over rope and scattered tools, raising his eyes when he could to watch the next block hoisted up from the waiting lighters. Below him the men standing on the half-filled shell of the extension moved to catch at the dangling facing stone and guide it to its place. Their deep soft voices shouted directions up to the man on the hoist. Augustus tapped on the edge of the old quay with his stick and called down to them, 'A little to the left.' The workmen stopped at the sound of his voice, strange in its intonation, but familiar enough to them all by now.

'Morning, sir.'

'Good day, sir.'

They stood looking up at him, shielding their eyes while the block of granite dangled.

'Good day to you,' he called down, waving with his stick. 'Don't let me stop you.' The little exchange pleased him, as did the alacrity with which they set about edging and rocking the stone into its place in the wall. He was intensely pleased with the brightness of the sea, the men's willing activity, the busy ringing of the hammers from the beach. For this was how he had intended it and even in his absence it had been accomplished.

The Scots contractor scrambled towards him up the piled stones of the half-filled core. 'It's coming on,' Augustus said, holding out his hand to him. 'I heard about the storm. You've done as well as you could in the time.' In the clear light he searched the man's face for signs of recent drunkenness, but there was nothing noticeable. He seemed decent enough – eager enough to get the job done and get back to the mainland. Augustus told him he'd loan the money for the next wages, if it didn't come through in time. He said that if the men weren't paid on the very day it was bad for morale.

McPherson said, nodding towards Wills, 'I expect he's told you we had trouble with Pender.'

'I only arrived last night,' said Augustus, but shot a fearsome look at his agent who had kept his back from him.

'Was it his wages?'

'The man was no damn good. More trouble than he was worth.'

'What happened to him?'

'He shouted a bit. Then put off in some damn boat. I don't know where he went. He hasn't been here since.'

'The Gweal?' Augustus said to Wills.

Wills nodded.

'That's everything, then,' Augustus said curtly. He turned, pulled out his watch, polished the glass with the heel of his hand and put it away. Then, with Wills half a pace behind him, he walked quickly back the way that he had come.

The magistrates met in a room on the upper floor of the Customs House. Augustus and Wills were not the first to arrive. As they climbed the stairs, they heard men's voices in desultory conversation fall silent entirely. It annoyed him that they were there. He would have liked to have caught them out in tardiness.

Their three fellow magistrates had taken up formation on the far side of a mahogany table set in the square, rather bleak room. An open fire scarcely warmed it. 'Can't you build that up a little?' he said to Wills. He walked over to the far side of the table with his hand extended. By nature he had always been quiet and serious beyond his years; his few close friends would have considered any show of heartiness or geniality a sign of danger. The three men who knew him less well than they supposed rose uncertainly: General Veitch, who commanded the garrison, Augustus' chaplain Peters, whom he had found when he came and not troubled to replace, Captain Hall of the Coast Guard. With Wills they made up the island gentry.

'I hope you are well,' he said to the General. To Hall, 'I am very pleased to see you.' To the chaplain he felt bound to speak the truth and said more gently, 'Wills tells me it has been a mildish winter. I hope your wife's health is improved.'

Without waiting for any answer, which indeed they scarcely offered, he walked vigorously past them and took up his position on the opposite side of the table. Wills remained kneeling by the hearth, feeding lumps of coal onto the flames. 'Not too much coal there,' Veitch called out. Wills ignored him.

'Well,' said Augustus, slapping Wills' letter on the table and his hand flat on top of that. 'Wills says you thought it best to meet sooner rather than later after my arrival.'

'This is something in the nature of an extraordinary meeting,' said General Veitch. He invariably put up a show of running these occasions. His command of the islands' garrison of five Napoleonic veterans gave him untold importance.

Augustus said quietly, 'Then I assume you have extraordinary matters to raise.' There was a silence from which he made no attempt to lead them.

At last the chaplain said, more it seemed from social embarrassment than from any premeditated wish, 'Well,

21

this matter is hardly extraordinary. In fact it is a question which I have put to you again and again. What explanation can there be for the delay in restoring the church?' He paused for a moment, watching Augustus, but the younger man stayed as he was, face impassive, leaning back in his chair, his hand resting on the letter on the table. Peters went on, 'I understand that it was part of the agreement, when you purchased the islands, that the church be restored.'

'Or rebuilt,' said Augustus, nodding as if in perfect agreement with him.

'Rebuilt!' exclaimed Hall. 'Surely, with everything else you might be doing, you do not intend to tear down a perfectly good structure?'

'Would you describe the present church's condition as perfectly good?' Augustus asked. He had never moved his eyes from Peters.

The chaplain, on whom the need for absolute solidarity had clearly been impressed, now stammered slightly, 'Certainly not in the condition in which it has been left.'

'I would agree with you,' said Augustus heartily. 'I can see no other explanation for the small congregation in such a God-fearing community than a very reasonable fear that the roof might collapse during the service.'

He smiled agreeably at Peters, but he felt angry with himself at the meanness of the gibe when he held the man's livelihood at his whim.

'Then what do you intend to do about it?' said Veitch. His manner was habitually bullying. Augustus detested him.

It gave him pleasure to watch the fixed resistance on Veitch's face as he said, 'As soon as the quay is complete and the schoolhouse on the Gweal put in good order, I intend to commence work on a new church more convenient to the town. I have drawn up the plans myself. I hope to have it consecrated in two years' time.'

'Why was I not told of this?' said the chaplain.

'I have just told you,' said Augustus evenly, and added in a darkened tone, 'There seemed little point in troubling you with an event two years distant – until, that is, you asked.'

'I have asked frequently.'

'Now you have your answer,' said Augustus. It surprised him to look up and see white gulls wheel against the blue arch of sky in the window.

Veitch said, 'The real reason we called you here is to tell you our feelings about your agent's treatment of Georgy Pender.'

'I thought as much,' said Augustus, and turned his mind with reluctance to the Penders, who could not be built stone upon stone. Wills came from the fireplace and drew back the chair next to him. 'Thank you,' said Augustus, glancing around at the flames. 'That's better.'

Veitch said bitterly, 'No doubt you and Wills have settled the poor fellow's fate between you, but you must realize that there is very little you can do without our authority.'

'Indeed,' said Augustus and fell silent again, forcing Veitch to continue.

'What do you intend to do?'

'I have had no time to think the matter over, but there is clearly only one thing that can be done.'

'Well?' said Veitch, leaning across his two clenched fists which he had set side by side on the edge of the table.

'Well,' said Augustus carefully, pitching his voice so as not to appear to imitate this angry ageing man. 'What course would you say was open to me?' In the silence he watched them, looking from one to another, wondering how long he need endure their opposition. Poor Peters he could be rid of whenever he chose. Veitch was in his seventies, very heavy; his scarlet complexion never varied from summer to winter. When he died he would not be replaced. Hall was still in middle age and would outlast the others, but it was well known in the islands that in the three years he had been stationed there he had greatly extended his circle of enemies beyond the fishermen whose smuggling activities he had been sent to curb. He was too much disliked to carry any weight. None of them spoke;

23

none of them wanted to be drawn into stating Augustus'
policies for him.

Finally Hall said unpleasantly, 'I think it is only fair to
say that Pender has approached us direct in your absence.'
It was clear from the sudden raising of Peters' head that it
was he in fact who had been approached, but that he
thought better of saying so.

'Appealing to you gentlemen to protect his poor old
mother from eviction.'

'You may not be aware,' said the chaplain quickly, 'that
Mrs Pender has been very ill since her bereavement.'

Augustus ignored him other than to say to them all, 'And
what was your reply to Georgy?'

'It was to call this meeting,' said the General. They had
come full circle and it seemed pointless to fence with them
any longer. Augustus said, 'I think you are well aware of
my intentions for these islands. I am sure you agree that
they have been shamefully neglected for centuries.' There
were sounds of protest, but he went steadily on. 'That they
can no longer subsist on the fruits of smuggling and mainland charity. No man can continue to live on the islands
unless he can fully support himself and his family. They
are overpopulated. The soil is overworked. The cottages
must come down and keep coming down until there are
few enough people for the land to support.' He thought as
he spoke with a kind of physical pity for the thin layer of
black soil glittering with flecks of silica from the granite
which so closely underlay it – fed on to exhaustion.

'And what will you do with the poor old soul when you
turn her out?' said the chaplain. 'Will you build a work-
house next?'

'I have made no mention of turning Sarah Pender out,'
Augustus said coldly. 'She is old and ill and I can afford to
wait.' He avoided Veitch's eye as he said this. 'But Georgy
is quite another matter. He must go.'

'How is she to survive without him?' said Peters.

'She survived well enough without him for the six
months that he was employed on the quay,' Augustus said.
'Even if she never saw a penny piece of his earnings, she

was still free of the burden of keeping him. He cannot stay. He has had his chance of earning his living within the islands; he has thrown that away. He understands what the circumstances are, better, I think, than you do; it was made quite clear to him. The naval recruitment officers will be in the islands within the fortnight. I shall give them his name.'

'And if he refuses?' said Hall. 'We'll have no pressing here. Nor have you our authority to evict him by force.'

'If he refuses then the cottage must come down over both their heads. I believe I do not need your permission to pull down my own property.'

'You would be hated from one end of the islands to the other,' said Hall.

'I can bear hatred,' he said, looking slowly from one to the other but letting his eye rest with a particular irony on Hall.

'I feel, in view of your newness to the islands,' said the chaplain, 'that you might be wise to make a compromise in this one instance. I am surprised that Mr Wills, on whom you must depend for information, has not advised you better in this. Sarah Pender is much revered in the islands.'

Augustus put out a hand to silence any defence his agent might set up. His deep voice menaced with the control he set upon it, but he was flushed now. His eyes were very bright and moist. 'You do not seem to understand that in this one thing there is to be no compromise, not now, not ever. Every able-bodied man in the islands is to earn his own keep. He is not to live upon his parents' land. In cases of my choosing, an elder son may take over the lease; in all other cases they must find work on the main island or make their way at sea. I will not be crossed in this. Is that clear to you?'

When they remained silent he stood upright, placing his hands so heavily on the edge of the table that he might have been thought to strike it. 'There is no man, be his cause a thousand times more worthy than Georgy Pender, will make me move one inch from my intended plan for the well-being of all the islanders. Each may be called upon to make sacrifices, but in the end it must be apparent that this is the only course to take and unless it is pursued without discrimination it is scarcely worth pursuing at all. I hope I have made my position clear to you. Gentlemen.' He nodded abruptly and turned towards the door. Wills, who had risen with him, followed at his heels. With his hand on the door Augustus said, 'I forgot to mention that in future our meetings will take place in my house. This room is too large for our purposes. I intend to transfer the infant school here.' He shut the door on silence and heard the babble of their dismay raise behind it. He ran heavily down the stairs to be in the street where his anger might expend itself upon the open air. At the door he gripped Wills by the hand and said, 'Order the boat for ten tomorrow morning, then.'

'No sooner?'

'He knows I'm coming. Let him wait. I'll walk now. It will relieve me.'

He climbed the hill with his back to the harbour and resisted turning to look at it. Now that he was outside, he did not wish the energy of his anger to dissipate too quickly, nor the beauty of what he owned to confuse and distract him from his purpose. He guarded instead his detestation of Veitch and Hall and poor Peters. Rigid, stupid, with no thought beyond clinging to their wretched shreds of self-esteem. They were all that he had fled from. And Georgy Pender and his kind were little better, dreading nothing so much as change, passively waiting the next assault of the weather, caught in their deep scepticism of any human action that did not subject itself to the natural course of some wind or tide. He would fight them in that. He would build structures against these things: the structures of his deep conviction, the quays, the schoolhouses, in good time a church as sturdy and functional as he would have his faith. Behind them he would live as he chose. No one could check him.

He climbed rapidly upwards. A deer jolted noisily away through the bright dead bracken. Its startled eye turned back at him. He carried in his pocket a small bag of gorse seed and stopped now to loosen the string which bound it. He filled his hand with seed and, walking more slowly, began to scatter it about him as he had seen Pontefract do to improve his coverts for foxes. He planted for a better purpose. In time the woody complex roots would grip the soil to the land. He felt its hardness jar through the long bones in his legs. Only when the bag was empty and he stood at the summit did he face the prospect of what he owned.

The tide was high. The mass of uninhabited islands and isolated rocks were drawn in upon themselves; held separate. Below him, on the main island, he could see the ruinous church and its crowded burial ground perched on the edge of the sea, as if exhaustion had only permitted the drowned to be dragged just out of its reach. Beyond he saw the paler stretch of water that covered the sand flats between St Warna and the Gweal. In another week, at the neap tide, these flats would lie exposed, but now they lay hidden under the slow bright movement of the water. The Gweal floated free.

Already he found his sense of remoteness eroded. In that one morning the mainland had become so lost to his imagination that he seemed drawn against his will back into the centre of things. Other places interrupted his line of vision. There on that outer island, where the sloping land faced up to the sun, it seemed he might escape to the very edge of his shrunken world: the eye would be free.

9th of March, 1836:

Have spoken firmly with G. Pender regarding his future in the islands and heard today from Wills that he has seen the recruiting officer and will be gone from here within the fortnight. A good riddance. His mother will remain where she is until she dies, at which time the cottage can be pulled down. Have resolved to build myself a house and garden on the Gweal.

*   *   *

27

4th of November, 1837:

Last night, at approximately midnight, the steamer Severn *struck the western ledges. Despite brave attempts since first light to save her passengers and crew, she broke up and sank in clear sight of the men of St Warna at 10 a.m., taking all with her save four women, one of whom subsequently died, and a child. One of our boatmen, John Traherne, was drowned, swept overboard in the act of securing a line from the doomed ship. I feel his death most bitterly. Have recommended most strongly to Trinity House that a light should be raised on the ledges.*

22nd of April, 1839:

Three farmers from St Warna's came together to request the loan of my young horse during the forthcoming season to improve the island's stud, their only stallion having died over the winter.

2nd of March, 1840:

Severe gales. The barque Ariel *which last week put into St Warna's, her carpenter being dead on board, parted her cables and was driven onto Crow Rock, the sea breaking over her. Her crew of twenty-two men were brought safely away in heavy surf. Her cargo of tea, within easy reach at low tide of the men of the Gweal, gives cause for concern.*

26th of May, 1842:

Went this day to the Gweal to inspect the school, and more especially Mr Davies, the new schoolmaster brought over here new last month from Exeter. Everything appeared satisfactory. Davies satisfied with plastering of ceiling and Mrs D. with the new cooking range. Lessons in English, History, Navigation and Carpentry have commenced. As I was leaving, looked into the room where the younger children wrote their task for Mrs D. and saw there Adela Traherne, bent over her slate in just such a posture as I remember my poor Fanny bent over her little volume of poems in the schoolroom at Longridge. Just so the child gripped her pencil in her tight fist. She has grown very pretty. About nine years old as far as anyone can surmise, with dark hair that fell behind her sweet face, so that I was doubly reminded and must have made some sound, for Davies, very nervous at my presence, asked if something were amiss and I affected coughing and quickly left the room. But later after discussing with him other matters, I brought the talk around to Adela Traherne and he assured me that she is one of his most promising scholars and that the old woman is most circumspect in bringing her to be catechised and promises to put her forward for confirmation in two years' time. Most gratifying. Poor lovely child.

22nd of February, 1843:

Completed the plans for the new church to my own design. Most pleasing in its simplicity and perfect utility. The corner stone to be laid as soon as better weather allows the foundations to be completed. Some difficulty in obtaining lead at a reasonable price.

3

There is a path running along the eastern side of the Gweal, the smaller island that Augustus contemplated on that afternoon in the spring of 1836. It runs from the village to the rear gate of the domain he established there a few years later. Now, one hundred and twenty years after his death, its very texture is different. Where it dips there are accretions of soft dark earth composed of decayed pine needles and slurry from the entrance to the Hill Farm. It holds the rain and bears the wide plaited imprint of tractor tyres and the neat incisions of cows' hooves. The woods to the left, which he planted, are rotted and devastated. Even creating their own soil year by year they have achieved only a shallow stand on the granite core of the island. The winter gales uproot them. Last winter five hundred were felled in a single night and the woods above the lake have taken on a look of destruction like a fleet of hulks left to rot.

Along this path, early one morning in the August of 1843, a woman and a child walked side by side. Then nothing interrupted the brilliant line of the sea. Clear, unfiltered light fell on the path, which was as bare and stony as the hillside above it.

The woman was a diminutive person, ageing, with a defiant bearing, although nothing in all that benign scene would seem to offer any threat. She walked briskly, but the path was rough and her progress was slow. The little girl, though slight, was scarcely smaller than she. She delighted in this walk, which was her favourite, and kept at bay thoughts of the different end it would have today.

She moved about rapidly, crossing from one side of the path to the other, staying behind to look intently at something, hurrying ahead, but always keeping within the sphere of the woman's steady progress. Once the child paused by a stunted bush, waiting quite still until a bird blundered through the twigs and flew past her. Then she carefully parted the leaves and stared into the minute nest where four pink eggs fitted like petals.

The woman, failing to hear her for a minute or two, called out 'Adela'. Slowly the child withdrew her hands so that the twigs sprang back and hid the nest. Then, lifting her skirt, she ran back to the woman's side.

'I was looking at the nest,' she said.

'Are they hatched, then?'

'No, still eggs.' When her companion made no comment she said shyly, 'Shall I bring her here and show her the nest?'

'Oh, spare the poor robin,' said the woman. 'She doesn't want anyone meddling in her affairs.'

'I'd tell her to be quiet.'

'You'd tell *her*,' said the woman ironically. 'She'll tell you, more likely. Besides, you'll not play out here. You'll play in the garden or the house.'

'What do you play in a house?'

'Anything you like. Anything *she* likes.'

They had been bidden early. The sky, though perfectly clear, was still far paler than the intense blue sea. The day's hushed promise of perfection seemed almost a burden to the child. There were so many hours to be sustained yet, in which nothing must go wrong. She would have liked the path to extend itself forever but it would not. Already the lake was in sight, glittering through the haze of reed beds; behind it she could see the raw stone battlements of the Proprietor's new house.

They came to the gate no one might go through.

'Is it all right?' the child asked anxiously.

'He asked us, didn't he?'

But it seemed strange to open the gate and fit through the gap her Aunt Traherne had left her, when the lesson

31

not to go there had been so recently learnt.

'We used to come here, didn't we, to pick berries?'

'There used not to be a gate nor a wall.'

The path went on and on. Adela could just remember it opening out without warning like the sequences of a dream. 'There was an echo,' she said.

'Don't you go shouting out and drawing attention to ourselves,' said Mrs Traherne.

Excitement and apprehension made Adela walk at her aunt's pace now and hold her hard safe hand. At the end of the lake they joined the broad path that led through bracken to the entrance of the house. The child leant so suddenly against the woman that she nearly caused her to stumble.

'When will you come for me?' she asked anxiously.

'I've been told at six.'

'Can't you come sooner?'

'We must do as we are told.'

'Don't you want me to go?'

'I've little choice in the matter.'

It was as if every time the child tossed up one of her questions the woman struck it down with her flat ironic tones. It confused Adela that she spoke so, for she had seemed eager and even excited, bathing her last night and dressing her this morning. But for all her aunt's sudden grimness the child was quite fearless of her. Now, as they walked between massive stone gate posts and climbed the rise beside the granite walls of the house, she held more tightly still to her Aunt Traherne's hand and felt the loose skin slide over the round swollen knuckles.

'Where do we go?' she whispered.

'We'll go to the back,' said Mrs Traherne. 'To the kitchen.'

When they reached the kitchen door she reached up and pulled a metal handle. A bell jangled hollowly somewhere inside and a moment later the door was opened by a house-keeper in a dark dress.

'Well, Mrs Bateson, I've brought the child.' She freed her hand and pushed Adela gently forward.

'Were you not meant to take her round by the front, Mrs Traherne?'

'I was not told to.'

'Oh well, perhaps best not.'

'Yes,' said Mrs Traherne.

'Will you not come in and see him?'

'There's no need.'

'But he might expect it.'

'He'd have said.'

'Well, as you wish, Mrs Traherne.' She added awkwardly; 'Will you come in and have a cup of tea with us in the kitchen?'

'Not today, thank you, Mrs Bateson.'

'As you wish. I'll take her, then.'

Adela turned back to her, but Mrs Traherne gave a shake of her head which forbade farewells. She was too proud to say to the child 'Mind your manners', or 'Be good', because that would imply a less than perfect trust in her own training, but seeing the child's anxious face turned back towards her she felt the full intense force of her desire to protect this one being from all of life as she knew it.

'What can I be doing?' She asked herself, with a kind of inward passion that forced her to keep her face rigidly without expression; for her mistrust of the rich was absolute, and here she was delivering Adela into their careless grasp. What could she do but turn and walk away erect across the yard.

The housekeeper stood for a moment watching her go, then, putting her shoulder against the heavy door, she pushed it shut and said, not unkindly, to Adela, 'Come along, then. We'll find Mr Walmer, shall we?'

Adela stood in confusion. Never had she faced separation from her aunt for an entire day. Immediately she reached out her hand to this other woman, who took it awkwardly, for it was the gesture of a much younger child than Adela was assumed to be.

The housekeeper led her across the big kitchen where a row of three or four maids stood chopping food at a long table. They looked at Adela and smiled in their different ways. They all had faces that she had seen, but not here.

Another door was opened and Adela was pulled through it into a dark corridor. She had supposed the big kitchen to be the entire house, the woman whose hand she held to be the lady visitor with whose child she was intended to play, but now it appeared that there was more. All along this passage were other doors and from behind them the sound of voices or things being moved about. When they came to a heavy door at the end of the passage the housekeeper turned and said to her, 'You will remember to curtsy to Mrs Pontefract.'

Seeing the child's face stiffen she said anxiously, 'You have been taught to curtsy?'

'No,' said Adela.

'Well,' said the woman coaxingly. 'You can manage a little bob for the lady. Really, you should.'

'I shake hands.'

The housekeeper regarded her, head to one side. 'Here, do me a bob. Just a little one before we go in. I'm sure you can. Like this – look.'

Adela took her hand and tried to do as she had done, but all her Aunt Traherne's contempt rose up in her as she did.

'My, but you're a stiff little thing,' said the housekeeper. Then, seeing Adela's eyes suddenly brighten with tears, she said hastily, 'There now, don't go upsetting yourself. She's a pleasant enough lady. She won't mind.'

She opened the door and they came out into a central hall with polished flags. The doors at either end were open to the sunlight. Through one of them Adela saw the blue line of the sea, which already seemed like something out of reach and in the past. Two dogs lay stretched out, absorbing into their flanks the cool of the stones. The door to a room stood open beyond them. The housekeeper paused for a second to tap with her knuckles on the open door, then, pulling Adela forward by the hand, she announced, 'It is Mrs Traherne's child, sir, come to play.' From inside the room she had sensed a restless movement. Now a deep man's voice said, 'Ah, bring her here, Mrs Bateson.'

There was no other lady, no child in the room and for a moment the Proprietor himself seemed unfamiliar to her. She had only seen him hatted and part of the distance, looking through the schoolroom door, smiling and frowning at once, standing among the men who built the wall and planted the trees and pointing with his stick. She had no fear of him, but watched steadily the thick gold watch chain that hung across the wrinkles of his waistcoat as he advanced rapidly upon her. The room bewildered her with its inclusion of light and its stillness. His footsteps made little sound on the coloured carpet. The curtains were of too soft a stuff to flap, although they streamed into the room like pennants from the open windows. Outside, when they fell back, she saw the sky beat with its bright expectancy. She wondered where the child was waiting. Whether she hid somewhere in this room and might spring out.

He went down on one knee when he came up to her. She watched his mouth as he spoke. 'Will you like to come and play here?' Some words like that. He looked over her head, and Adela heard the quiet click of the door as the servant withdrew. Then he took her chin gently between his thumb and forefinger and turned her face fully into the light from the window to what he saw.

Adela was not at all alarmed by him. There was nothing to fear from grown people, as there might be from the hidden child. Besides, his hand on her chin carried the cold exciting smell of dog. She could hear the sound of a dog's claws moving about the room somewhere behind her, but did not twist away to look for it. Instead, she reached out and slid her finger very lightly along the links of his watch chain. It was that, rather than his face, which interested her. Still, she was acutely aware of an alien substance set opposite her. She sensed his hardness and a strained quality which had seemed audible in his boots as he knelt down.

Undoubtedly he impressed her. She always carried some recollection of that room. Although she never entered it again, she could have told you late in her life where the window was, where the sofa; that there were blue and

35

white plates hanging on the walls and a tree in a china pot. Perhaps at that moment the boundless region that was Adela met its end and met the outer boundary of another existence, out of sight and inaccessible. It was no sort of impression she could have carried away and shared with her Aunt Traherne. As soon as she was away from him she forgot his existence and would scarcely have recognized him as anything other than the figure he had by now become: identifiable all over the islands as the Proprietor, with his hat and his stick and his loud voice.

A woman in a grey dress who had come into the room now said, 'What will become of me, Mr Walmer? I make for a chair meaning to sit quietly' – laughter seemed a part of her voice – 'but then I must rush to a window again and look out.' The swiftness with which he rose to his feet startled Adela.

The woman had crossed the room and caught one of the flying curtains in her hand. Now she cried out, 'Oh, each prospect is more lovely than the last. I shall become quite distracted with looking!' Then, turning back and seeing Adela, she said, 'Why, who is this?'

'The child I have sent for to play with Harriet.'

Quickly she advanced towards them, smiling at him over Adela's head before stooping and extending both hands which Adela shyly reached out and held. She felt the warmth and excitement of that grip and the pressure on her own fingers of the woman's rings. Her face she scarcely noticed, beyond an instinct that its pleasantness might for the moment be trusted.

'Ah,' said that person, almost sadly, 'you have found us a little beauty.'

He said, 'I chose with care.'

Adela stood, knowing herself to be the subject of this talk, but no more a part of it than if she were out of the room. She was used to hearing herself remarked upon in just this tone, that seemed to imply what was said was no concern of hers. And scarcely it seemed so. Still firmly rooted in Eden, she carried her slight body all unawares unless she felt cold or fell and was bruised. Her Aunt

Traherne allowed no glass in the house to tell her what she was.

At that time she had long black hair which Mrs Traherne had her wear loose about her shoulders, although the trouble this caused was endless, with its being constantly tangled by the wind and becoming stiff and matted in the damp salty air. The woman spent hours, which the child patiently endured, washing it in precious rainwater and brushing it out. She felt all this worthwhile for the protection it seemed to provide Adela's pale little face, now beginning to show the first random signs of that beauty that the visitor had noticed.

'And who are you?' she asked again, this time in a voice for Adela.

There was an habitual hesitancy in Adela's manner, a tendency to hang her head even when she spoke. Her aunt had done nothing to draw her out of this reticence. Like the dark mass of hair it seemed to provide cloudy protection. Besides, this was not an easy question to answer. She thought, and then said so quietly that they could only just make out the words, 'I am an Island Child.'

'Why, that is something that I should like to be,' said the woman, and she gave Adela's hand a quick grip of pleasure so that the rings were almost painful. 'Come,' she said, 'you shall help me to keep still by sitting with me and telling me about your island.' As she spoke she led Adela to a little sofa and settled her at one end of it before she herself sat down. Adela sat there dumbly. She lacked the required words.

'Tell me your name,' said the lady.

'Adela.'

'Why, that is a lovely solemn name. I think you are a very solemn child. Shall we teach her otherwise, Mr Walmer, while we have her with us?'

'I think you must,' he said. 'I am quite as solemn as she.'

'Oh, I cannot believe that,' she said, laughing upwards over her shoulder. 'This is far too lovely a place to be solemn in.'

'Perhaps you will teach us both.'

37

She said quietly, 'The genius of the place must teach us all.'

Adela sensed in an instant that attention was withdrawn from her, but continued to sit patiently waiting for its return, only half listening to the Proprietor's deep tones and the lady's quick light replies. So long had she lived at the centre of her Aunt Traherne's undistracted concern that she believed, without ever giving it a thought, that even in this silent and withdrawn state she naturally commanded interest and sympathy. To seek either openly, by any attempt to charm or entertain, would have seemed an absurd risk to take. Besides, she would have thought it – had she thought – quite unnecessary.

As presently it was proved, for the lady, tugging at her hands which she still absently held, said, 'What is your father, Adela?'

'He is dead.'

'And your mother?' said the lady gently.

'She is dead, too.' She spoke the words without pain. They were her credentials in the world. Unfailingly they drew warmth. The fine skin between the woman's eyes had creased sharply with concern. 'Who cares for you, then?'

'My Aunt Traherne.'

The lady smiled. 'There is true refinement here,' she said, freeing one hand and moving it lightly before Adela's cheek as if she would brush something aside. 'What will you make of my Harriet, I wonder?'

'Where is she playing?' asked Adela.

'I scarcely know,' said the lady. 'I have not seen her since we arrived. I imagine she is somewhere in the garden with Miss Christian.' She referred this upward to the Proprietor, who said, 'I believe so.'

'And Mr Walmer will be anxious to be out in his garden. Will you go with him and find your new friend?'

Without a word Adela went behind the sofa and took the Proprietor's hand expectantly. But he stood for a moment where he was.

'I had delayed going out. I hoped that you and

Pontefract might come with me. Is he recovered?'

'Oh no, I fear he is not.' Laughter was inherent in the words.

So that he said quickly. 'Oh, it is no laughing matter, I assure you. I suffer myself quite dreadfully. Poor fellow.'

'It is just that I woke feeling so very well,' she said, as if to excuse herself. 'I must go to him.'

'You will not come into my garden?'

'Later,' she said. 'Oh, please, later.'

In the hallway the dogs jolted to their feet and fell in behind them. Adela could hear the rattle of their claws on the stone flags; one of them came close and pressed its cold nose against the base of her neck and sniffed alarmingly. She shrank a little against the Proprietor, but he disregarded her now and dragged at her arm in his haste as he walked out on to the bright terrace and down the wide flight of stone steps that divided the hillside from top to bottom. On either side were the raw boulders blasted out to form the foundations of the house, still waiting to be grouped into rockeries.

The garden is his one memorial. It is a strange place now, with its giant palms and Eucalyptus whispering and clattering where most English gardens heave and sigh. The weathered stones are now almost entirely hidden by a green profusion of creepers and succulents, as if all their outer layers had erupted into minute tumerous swellings. The crowded exotic blooms come and go, some simply and regularly, some in so hectic and infrequent a manner that the whole plant dies with its flower. The place is alive with birds. Their reptilian dartings and rustlings are perfectly suited to it. The leaves they constantly disturb are as dry and as stiff as feathers. How immobile the blue line of sea appears among the dry incessant business of the place: so reminiscent of his restlessness.

It is impossible to tell how much of this he intended when he first began to plant the stiff roots and cuttings of sub-tropical plants and trees that he had never seen growing. When he died, nothing of all this strange proliferation was more than twelve inches high. On the

day that Adela first saw it there was little more laid out
than the long flight of steps that the gardeners were just
beginning to flank with Agaves. At its foot, by the arches
of a ruined abbey, he himself had laid out with string two
rectangular beds in the shape of Union Jacks. It was without terrors then: the sunlight still scoured it like a tide. He
had planted nothing that would shed its leaves. No flowers
offered themselves up for violation. It had no voice. There
was no suggestion that people walked invisibly along the
next path. No fear yet that leaves might impersonate the
breathless hidden voices of children. Nothing of the deep
damp cycle of growth and decay inseparable from English
gardens, and holding for him especial images.

He now strode down the steps pulling Adela behind
him, calling to the gardeners that he would be presently
with them. At the bottom of the slope Adela could see an
awning. Under its shade a young woman sat with her
knitting fallen idle in her hands and a child at her feet
playing, without enthusiasm, in a heap of sand.

At the Proprietor's approach, heralded by the busy dogs,
the governess sprang to her feet, quite forgetting her knitting, and then, as it fell, stooped in confusion to retrieve it.
The little girl rose to her knees and regarded the Proprietor
and Adela steadily and openly. Children meet as animals
do, intently watching one another for signs of threat. Perhaps in those first cautious moments they also watch for
promises of pleasure, but Adela was too unversed in
friendship to be able to imagine these. She looked directly
into the other child's eyes for the flicker of hostility and
noticed at the same time that the front of her smock was
silvered with tiny particles of sand. The give and take of
adult voices passed overhead. The Proprietor's deep voice:
'I have brought you a playmate, Harriet.'

The governess's, light and mournful: 'Miss Harriet has
been waiting for her, sir. She is very grateful to you. Are
you not, Miss Harriet?'

'Yes,' said Harriet, without altering her steady stare.

'Say good morning, Miss Harriet,' the governess now
prompted.

'Good morning.'

'Good morning, Mr Walmer.'

'I *know*,' said the child with an oddly commanding frown. She had a slow, almost gruff voice.

'Will they suit one another, do you think?' said the Proprietor over their heads.

The governess said, 'I am sure they cannot fail to be happy in such a beautiful place. Everyone must, sir, and I am sure both the children and I feel most fortunate to be here.'

'That is the intention,' he said gravely, 'that you should all be happy.' He had freed his hand from Adela's as he spoke and with that stricture he left them.

4

To refer to Adela as the Island Child, as everyone at the
Abbey quickly fell into the habit of doing, was not strictly
accurate. Nor, in fact, was she Mrs Traherne's niece. Her
arrival in the islands, six years previously, was already
part of their mythology. At the same time, the appearance
of the child walking through the village to school, or crossing with Mrs Traherne to the main island for some special
purchase, was so familiar that she herself had become
divorced, in most people's minds, from her own legend.
Mothers, telling their children of the little child being held
aloft in a last despairing bid for life on the drenched deck
of the *Severn*, found it easier to give the tale its true drama
if they did not think of so daily an item as Adela herself.

Even the small group of men who carried pictures of
that terrible dawn, and circulated them in their talk as
they drank, trying still to make some reality out of what
they had survived, found it easier to remember what they
had seen as elements of a legend they had been told. There
had been the huddled mass of people on the deck of the
broken steamer. They had managed to bring the boat close
enough to distinguish the recruits in their scarlet coats
soaked black by the sea. There had been the young lady
who had clung to her father until to save her life he had
thrust her from him. There had been the two stewardesses
chosen out of the little group of common women with no
claim to make for their salvation. And that one woman
who held up her child above her white face and arms, and
that little wrapped form that was in fact Adela.

These visions came and went. The men were half blinded

42

by spray and driving rain. The cries of those poor souls whom they could not reach were only occasionally distinguishable from the wind. Certainly they heard no sound at all when their youngest member and most recent recruit, John Traherne, was dragged from the boat by the first line thrown from the steamer. They were too numbed, too exhausted, to grab him back in time or even comprehend his sudden absence and the terrible instantaneous closing over of the sea. Only they struggled with a fury that carried them way beyond the limits of cold and fatigue to secure the second line and drag along it first the young lady, then the two stewardesses, and last, before the turn of the tide made matters hopeless, the woman and the child lashed to her with rope.

Then the rising tide had caught at the severed quarter-deck and dragged it slowly from them, with the people on it shouting and waving, convinced that they were being carried to the shore and safety. While the men in the boat knew well enough what current it was that drew them, and that all were doomed. They watched it turn and tilt and vanish almost as suddenly as John Traherne had done, except for the mast and the two recruits who still had strength to climb it. In another moment they too were gone without trace.

The men of St Warna's had, with their last strength, managed to row back towards home. Finding some shelter between the rocks they had anchored there, unable to go on with the extra weight of the vomiting women in the boat and John Traherne's oar lost to them.

There they had sat exhausted, staring out at the empty space of heaving sea as if they could not accept the absence of that broken shape on which all their endurance and concern still concentrated. Within half an hour they were taken in tow by the coastguard steamer. The women and the child were taken aboard and the journey back to the main island begun.

The quay had been packed tight with men and women waiting. Most, despite the bitter weather, had climbed the hill at

43

dawn and stood hour after hour staring at the leaning, threadlike spars of the wreck and its narrow smokeless funnel. The boat carrying their own men had disappeared from their sight shortly after leaving the island and, when a squall of violent wind and snow struck, a great wail had come out of the black knot of women watching from the hill. Hours had passed before the boat was sighted again, being towed behind the steamer. Then, with one movement, the watchers trooped down to the quayside. Only when it was very close in was it apparent that one man was missing; even then there seemed a possibility that he might have been taken aboard the steamer.

As the boat drew in the crowd, who had kept dead silent, shuffled apart, leaving a narrow pathway for the men and any survivors there might be. As the first of the boatmen, John Hicks, was handed silently up the stone steps, Mrs Traherne was observed, tiny, black and solitary, making her way towards the quay steps. No one attempted to stop her. They said afterwards that her face was quite calm, but set, as if some force beyond her urged her forward. Without a sound they watched her approach John Hicks and watched him soundlessly convey to her that her son, her only child, was gone. Some said they saw her stoop and kiss his raw hands, as if to exonerate them from the blow they had delivered. Then, erect and composed, impelled surely by some strange prescience, she walked past him and took up her solitary post at the foot of the gangplank, just as the survivors were being supported down it.

Leading them was the master of the steamer carrying the little girl. When he reached the quay there stood Mrs Traherne directly before him, holding out her arms. Death had given her a terrible authority. He said afterwards he felt he had no choice but to hand the child over to her. But how had she known it existed? John Hicks swore he had not said a word about it. Yet there she stood with the wretched little thing clasped to her in a grip that no power on earth could loosen, calmly giving orders for the mother to be brought to her house. Then, turning, she led the grim procession back to the town.

The poor woman to whose body Adela had been lashed had not regained consciousness since she was dragged from the sea. One of the men from the steamer carried her into Mrs Traherne's small stone cottage. She pointed them to a room which had probably been her son's, though little enough trace remained of him; only his land boots were noticed, placed side by side before the fire, and these Mrs Traherne quickly removed from sight. The fire was ready laid to warm him on his return. She knelt to light it. The neighbours whom she permitted to help her nurse the poor woman had never seen the inside of her home before. Even in the stress and awe of the moment they made swift note of its sparse signs of a past gentility. But that must be stored. Now all their efforts must be to bring some warmth and comfort and, if possible, life to the poor soul on the bed.

The woman showed no signs of returning consciousness. Her skin was the very colour of bone, drawn so tightly back across the cheeks and nose and teeth that the small stiff face looked a death's-head already. Only her harsh breathing told them she lived.

Mrs Traherne meanwhile sat by the fire, on which she warmed a little oil. Carefully uncovering the child's limbs one by one from the rough blanket that had been wrapped about her, she began gently to rub them with oil. Still holding the child in her arms, she went to a cupboard and drew out a little flannel nightdress which might once have been her son's. She sat down by the fire again, first pulling the nightdress over the child's head, then raising her plump arms one by one and pushing them up the sleeves. The child had not uttered a sound but lay slumped against her in an accepting torpor.

Next, still encumbered with the child, whom she now rode on her hip, she began to pour milk into a pan to warm that too.

'Can I not hold the little one?' Mrs Toms said softly to her. 'It would be easier for you.'

'No,' said Mrs Traherne. Awkwardly she poured the milk into a cup and, resuming her seat by the fire, leant the child back against her own body and tilted the cup to her lips. The child drank eagerly and then quite suddenly grew heavy and slept. Mrs Traherne sat rocking her. She stared into the fire, humming a rough tuneless air and quite ignoring the two neighbours and the sick woman. The power of her unexpended grief frightened them so that they scarcely dared whisper to one another. They could hear heavy footsteps going to and fro in the street and the restless moaning of the wind in the chimney. Mrs Traherne's chair creaked painfully as she rocked. The sick woman's breathing was louder in the room than any other sound. The child's breathing was so gentle that Mrs Traherne bent her head several times to assure herself of the miracle of her continued life.

When for very peacefulness Mrs Toms began to nod, Mrs Traherne startled her by saying, 'You may go home now, both of you. You have been very kind but I can see to them now.'

The two women exchanged glances. They had watched her covertly for the past hours and it seemed impossible that she should not suddenly break out into some wild exclamation of grief or lose consciousness and drop the child, who might strike her head or burn her cheek against the range. Then there was the poor thin body in the bed with scarcely life enough to raise the blankets. Could Mrs Traherne be trusted to rouse herself from her trancelike state if she called out?

'I'll have a little nod where I am,' said Mrs Toms soothingly. 'Then you can wake me if you need me.'

'You are very kind,' said Mrs Traherne, almost bitterly they thought, but, as they were to say, death takes different people in different ways. Some people cannot stop laughing. At least Mrs Traherne did not laugh.

At the very darkest hour of the night they were all three startled by a weak but entirely clear voice, saying, as calmly as after a pause in conversation, 'I know that I should care for the child, but I feel that I am floating.'

For a moment it was impossible to connect the words with the woman in the bed. They all sat quite still where

46

they were and heard the voice repeat in the same rather surprised tone, 'I am floating.'

Then all at once they were on their feet, including Mrs Traherne with the child held from her as if she meant to place her in her mother's arms, but when she had come close to the bed she quickly withdrew, for the woman's head had fallen sideways, her jaw slackened, her eyes held open but unmoving. It was apparent that without a word to God or any mention of the child's name she had died.

Mrs Traherne went quickly into the adjoining front room, tended the fire there and sat beside it with the child. Mrs Reed, lifting her shawl from her shoulders to cover her head, followed and quietly let herself out into the street to go in search of the chaplain, although there was no question that the poor soul had fled his ministrations.

Mrs Toms, when she had straightened the narrow body in the bed and pulled the covers across it with an unnatural tightness, closed the door of the bedroom behind her and, moving over to the parlour fire, took the chair opposite to Mrs Traherne. She eyed the elder woman sadly and cautiously, knowing that she must trespass upon the chair in which, night after night, the son had sat reading to his mother as she knitted, or playing upon his flute to amuse her. Quiet sounds through their adjoining walls had revealed this.

Shyly the neighbour reached out a hand to the child's warmly wrapped back and said, 'The poor little soul. What will become of her?'

'Why, she will stay with me,' said Mrs Traherne sharply, as if she had caught her neighbour out in an error or even an impertinence.

'Perhaps,' said Mrs Toms with increasing timidity, 'there will be some name in the clothes, or the survivors can give some account of them. She must have people somewhere.'

'No,' said Mrs Traherne, with the same fearsome certainty that she had shown since the boat drew in at the quay. So that Mrs Toms thought grimly to herself that the old woman's heart must break itself a second time through very stubbornness.

But in the event Mrs Traherne proved right. The surviving women from the *Severn* had been in no condition to take notice of the one who had died. There was no one to confirm that she was the child's mother. One of the stewardesses remembered seeing the little girl stretched out asleep on what looked like a bundle of bedding in the crowded cabin but had no idea in whose charge she had been, and anyone, of course, could have snatched her up in hopes that compassion for the child might ensure her own rescue. The stewardesses remembered that in the last moments of embarkation a number of women of the commonest sort had come aboard connected presumably with the recruits. Of course there was no record of their names. Learning that the *Severn* had put out from Belfast, the Proprietor wrote off, during the next weeks, to a number of priests in the city, and to others in the country where the regiment had been based, but no answer to the child's identity was forthcoming.

The child herself, although about four or five, was unable to help: the trauma of the shipwreck had erased any memories of her former life. Because her little dress had been new and finely sewed, although the woman's had been patched beneath the arms and at the hems; because the child was plump and the woman half wasted away, a conviction grew in many minds – for there was the rest of the winter to go over and over these events – that the dead woman was not Adela's mother at all, but some servant accompanying her to an unknown destination (a convent in Spain was a favourite choice) from which an inscrutable God had snatched her.

But had He really intended to give the child into the arms of Mrs Traherne? For Mrs Traherne's position on the island was an ambivalent one. She had appeared there ten years previously without explanation. Her son was then about nine, a handsome boy and well educated. He might have risen to a clerk or a schoolmaster, yet in spite of her obvious pride in the boy Mrs Traherne seemed to have no ambition for him. She was quite content to apprentice him to the shipyard, where his skill with figures and general aptitude made him very useful. His ignorance of the minutiae of information concerning the islands made the old men in the yard condescend, but no one could dislike him. He was goodnatured enough, though seldom able to join in their laughter. He worked harder than most, but gave himself no airs and, for all his cleverness, accepted that his ignorance of the names of rocks, the position of sandbanks and the very direction from which the wind blew upon him placed him far below those old sages. Immediately the day's work was over the boy had always left for home and was seldom seen about the place, unless it was walking with his mother arm in arm on Penninis Head on the summer evenings, shortening his stride solicitously, for he was very much taller than she, and bending his head in eager amused conversation as they paused to watch the men fishing from the rocks.

The cause of their separateness soon became understood. They attended neither church nor chapel. At first there was much speculation about this. Almost anyone but Mrs Traherne would surely have brought upon her the suspicion that she dare not, for reasons unthinkable, enter a holy place. This and her apparent cleverness in anything she set her hand to might all too easily have brought down upon her the envy of her neighbours in some pernicious form or other. As it was, they found themselves able to tolerate her. She faced the world with a defiant probity in which the minutest siftings of her neighbours could find no fault. She was generous in undemanding ways, and unfailingly courteous, but her pleasantness threw out no grapple. She asked nothing of anyone. Even that could have been taken as a haughty conviction that her new neighbours had nothing to give, had not she carried herself with an unconscious humility which could not give offence.

Of Christ, when questioned, she would say, with unexpected emotion – even with tears in her eyes – that he had been the only good man to walk the earth. Why not go to church then, when many who felt less strongly went with great regularity? Because, she would say in her bitterest tone, it seemed an hypocrisy to do so when we had killed

49

him for his goodness. She spoke as if she had been personally involved in these events. There was no reasoning with her. In time her godlessness came to be accepted as a harmless foible which she did not really mean, and that of her son as a sign of filial loyalty.

True, there had been some murmuring, when John Traherne first began to volunteer for the lifeboat, that he might bring bad luck upon them all. Yet he had proved fearless and a stronger rower than his gentle ways had led anyone to believe. The fact that he alone of all the crew had been dragged so suddenly from life did not go without comment, and this especially at the time when men and women of any standing in the island must ask themselves whether it was right to leave the poor foundling in the care of Mrs Traherne, when the community abounded in motherly women who were also good Christians.

Meanwhile, on the day after the storm, which was one of exceptional beauty, the boats put out at low tide to search for survivors, knowing quite well that there could be none. In fact they went in search for those bodies which the rocks had snatched and held for burial on land. They found sixteen in all, lying scattered barehead and barefoot over the black ledges of the reef: the soldiers still distinguishable by the remnants of their scarlet. Lying upturned among them was the only face that the searchers knew, that of John Traherne.

All day the men in the shipyard and any available carpenter had worked at making sufficient coffins. A mortuary was set up in the Customs House on the quay and a single coffin carried to Mrs Traherne's house to receive the dead woman.

On the third morning every person on the island followed the procession of coffins across the hill to the old church. It was wondered whether Mrs Traherne would appear at all on this occasion, but as the first cracked sounds of the bell reached the town she stood like all the others on her doorstep, dressed as always in black and clutching in her arms the child, swathed so that she was scarcely visible, in a thick black shawl.

One by one the coffins were carried past. John Traherne's

led the procession, carried by the men who had rowed with him out to the wreck. It was hard to conceive that they had all wakened untroubled in their beds only two days before. The men still looked wretchedly haggard from their ordeal and as they climbed Penninis Head two dropped out, and their places were promptly taken. Chief among the mourners were the young Proprietor, more pale and drawn than anyone could remember seeing him, the chaplain and the other two magistrates. The islanders themselves hung back to let them pass and allowed a gap to appear. Then they thronged into the road and by gentle steering contrived to place Mrs Traherne and her inseparable burden at their head.

It was a position she did not desire, yet she would not argue, but walked where they wished with her stern and suffering face held upwards above the child's head. Something in her bearing conveyed that her only purpose in being there was to perform a duty towards the child. Unfalteringly she climbed the hill. No one dared now offer to relieve her of the child's weight. The sky grew steadily darker and by the time they reached the churchyard it had begun to snow. Snow clung to the bowed black shawls of the women and caught in the men's blowing hair. It picked out the texture of the upturned earth all around the great trench dug beside the track leading to the church porch. When the first spadeful of earth rattled down on the coffin lid the child began to cry. Perhaps it was the sudden harsh sound, for how could so little a child grasp the thing that had befallen her, except through a frightened awareness of adult grief? Or perhaps again it was the bitter dispiriting cold that made her cry out. When the chaplain tried gently to lift her from Mrs Traherne's arms – for he feared she must be exhausted – he found that the child clung as tenaciously to the woman as the woman held to the child. Who was to separate them? A struggle of such a nature by the very graveside was unthinkable.

That evening, at prayer, a suggestion formed in the chaplain's mind which he found profoundly comforting. On the following day there was a meeting of the magistrates called to discuss Adela's future if no one should claim her. The Proprietor at the last moment sent word that he was unable to attend, but wished to be informed of the outcome. He was ill, perhaps. Certainly his absence enabled Mr Peters to rise with confidence and suggest that God had made his will abundantly clear in these events. The other two agreed that He had left them very little choice. And what possibly could His purpose be, asked the chaplain, other than that the child should effect a gradual softening of Mrs Traherne's heart, and, as she grew older, draw her protectress gently back to God? There was an audible breath of relief, for this surely was the explanation. The customs officer and the General concurred the more readily that each acknowledged in his heart a considerable amount of time must pass before this theory could be judged true or false.

5

The storm which had snatched Adela off her vanished track had intervened with other projects. The roof of the Proprietor's new house on the Gweal, being not yet plastered against the beam, was ripped off, and it was several months before the weather was settled sufficiently for the builders to undertake retiling it. The following summer therefore found him still living on St Warna's, when he had intended by then to be settled on the smaller island. The delay filled him with impatience. He visited the site two or three times a week, pacing out the proposed garden and frequently arguing with the master builder who, it seemed to him, delayed out of some obscure malice. As soon as the packet arrived he was down at the new quay, poking with his stick among the barrels and parcels as they were rowed ashore, in search of various consignments from the mainland: lead for the window frames; bell wire; marble slabs for the fireplace. All were delayed, one way or another. He planned now to sell his present house on St Warna's; it plagued him to think that he might not be able to transfer its contents to the new house before he set out for the mainland in November.

One morning, in the late spring following the storm, he sat in the study of the old house with the plans of his new one spread out on the tables under the window. Carefully and lightly, with pencil and ruler, he sketched in the formal beds where the slope levelled on the site of the Abbey ruins. It was a wretched morning, else he would have found something to do out of doors. Rain seemed thrown in spiteful handfuls against the windows and the glass rattled irritatingly in the constant wind. When the door bell clattered in the hall he felt surprised that anyone should venture out. He stood leaning across the desk and looked askance at the front porch, where he saw the black erect figure of Mrs Traherne with the child standing at her side and gripping her hand.

He drew back abruptly. He could have explained to no one the particular discomfort this woman provoked in him, though he understood it well enough as rising directly from his own troubling part in the events of the shipwreck.

On that similarly bleak November morning he had heard the maroon go up as he was dressing. A few minutes later the front door bell had jangled with unusual violence. On going downstairs he had been informed that a wreck had been sighted. The servant's voice as she said this had been so filled with the drama of death that, without questioning her at all, Augustus had seized up his hat and cloak and rushed out into the street, with an immediate and powerful impression that some action was required of him.

In his haste he had never even asked the whereabouts of the wreck. Now, seeing groups of people hurrying along the track to the hill above the town, he began to stride in that direction himself, overtaking one group after another. To each he said a curt good morning but did not stop until he stood at the top of the hill among a growing crowd of townspeople. He sensed their sober exaltation at being caught up in some great event. It seemed, as he stared at the crazily tilted spars of the steamer, that all the cruel movements of the sea affected these people directly. He believed he could not feel as they did, and this sudden sense of isolation impelled him to involve himself in some way in the disaster. He hurried down, therefore, onto the beach below, where he had seen another group gathered. Only when he came close did he realize the full nature of the drama, for efforts were being made to fill a boat to row out to the stricken ship.

Four men had volunteered already and stood beside the boat staring directly into the crowd, which stood back a little apart from them. John Hicks could be seen to shout; although the wind obliterated his words, there could be little mistaking what he asked.

But no one more would come forward. They shouted back and pointed to the north where the black formation of the snow squall was already visible. Augustus, running towards them as best he could with his boots sinking into the drenched sand, determined for an instant to join them. It seemed suddenly infinitely desirable that he should be taken up in the storm with his senses baffled and numbed by the din and cold. That he should hurl himself and feel at last the full measure of his strength in an ultimate exhaustion. Perhaps he simply wanted to be in among them: to be of use to them in a way of their choosing. His words as he struggled forward were snatched and dissipated by the wind, but his intention must have been clear enough. He thought John Hicks looked at him with contempt before he turned his back and continued to harangue his neighbours. He was neither needed nor wanted. Realizing this, at the very height of his wanting to go, filled him with fury against those who might have gone and yet hung back. All the force risen in him must drive them. He had no understanding of the intricate balances of poverty, nor the complexities of knowledge of wind and tide that operated on their deeply cautious minds at that moment, and fought against their powerful compulsion to cheat the sea of anything they might.

As he dressed he had put into his coat pocket a small leather bag of gold coins, the second year's rent money, which he had been going to send that day by the packet to his backers in Penzance. He went in among them, holding out the bag and shouting at the top of his powerful lungs, 'A gold piece for every man who goes in her.'

Whether it was the temptation of the gold or the dominance of his bearing towards them, in a very few moments the boat was filled and was already at sea when the force of the squall struck. He supposed at first that he had sent them all to their deaths, but had discovered that only his own boatman, John Traherne, was lost. The boy's bright face lit by lantern light haunted him.

Afterwards John Hicks came to him and asked that the gold pieces be handed over as promised to the men who had rowed out to the wreck, for they intended to present them to Mrs Traherne in her need and to help her care for the child. The rumour that went around the town was that Mrs Traherne accepted them, but had declared to John Hicks that they were not coins she could ever find it in her conscience to spend. Instead, they said, she had them linked one by one to her dead husband's watch chain, which John had sometimes worn on Sundays, and kept this as a necklace for Adela to wear on her wedding day, in memory of the men who had saved her.

He could not remember, out of all the din and confusion on the beach, whether or not John Traherne had joined the boat after he had proffered the money, and there was no one to whom he could bring himself to ask such a question. The thought of the necklace somewhere in Mrs Traherne's possession, holding as it must that one particular coin that might represent to her the force that had directly driven her son to his death, troubled him deeply in his few dealings with her.

Indeed the necklace did exist, and often at night, when the child slept, Mrs Traherne would take it out and, reaching towards the firelight, run it for comfort through her fingers. She would stare then at the small coins with a kind of wonder, seeing them as a row of shining souls in a world she had ceased to trust, or at the very least proof of a shining moment in the existence of that group of souls who, all but one, still went about their daily heartless business. Nor did it ever cross her mind to single out one coin as her son's. Rather she took comfort from the thought that his soul was indistinguishable from the rest; that he had found a companionship in death which she feared she had robbed him of during his short manhood. She did not once connect the necklace with the young Proprietor, so that if she noticed his deference and his slight shrinking from her it meant nothing to her. She had no need for his liking. Nor, until today, for any consideration from him.

Now, though, she had brought the child out in the rain to ask for his favour towards a plan which had formed in her head during the previous night. She had lain, as she often did, wide awake, listening to the rain drag on the roof like the coils, it seemed, of a giant serpent; conversing with her own mind as she must, for now there was no adult to whom she spoke, apart from her formal pleasant remarks to her neighbours about weather and sickness. She lay very still so as not to disturb the child, who slept beside her in a kind of restless abandon, throwing out an arm or leg, muttering, even laughing in her sleep, as if sleep were a place where she played free from the gravity and regularity of the waking life they shared. At such times Mrs Traherne would listen, fearful lest in a dream the storm would strike again at the child and terrify her, or, more selfishly, that in sleep Adela might find her way back to that previous existence of which her guardian was passionately jealous.

For always at the back of her mind was the fear that someone would appear to claim Adela back, or the more invidious fear that this enemy, this parent, compounded of ignorance, crudeness, depravity, might lurk even now inside the child, a tiny unformed thing, that would grow as she grew and one day leer out at Mrs Traherne in defiance of all that carefully nurtured innocence.

During the day, by force of her formidable will and by crowding her mind with schemes for Adela's protection, she kept these thoughts at bay, but at this most vulnerable time, lying helpless, with the world dark, having surrendered those familiar forms the mind can control, others almost unimaginable came in their place.

Lately Mrs Traherne had grown to fear, or so she told herself, the attention that Adela drew from their neighbours. No one could deny it was kindly meant. But even in acknowledging the existence of this kindness she felt her view of the world, as a relentless place, dangerously weakened. Then, surely, their behaviour grew out of the false sense of romance surrounding the child's circumstances.

They were forever touching and stroking her as if there was something of her they would take for themselves. 'What hair, Mrs Traherne,' Mrs Toms would say, feeling deeply the soft heap of curls. And then, with a vein of shrewdness through the pathos of her tone, 'It makes you wonder.'

And what, pray, did they wonder? Some crude fantasy that Adela was the child of an Irish nobleman, who had dispatched her with the scullery maid and neglected to ask for her back again? It was absurd and intrusive, for what if, when the child grew older, they filled her with false ideas of who she might be until she grew restless and resentful of the fate that had tied her to an old woman of no significance? It had seemed rash enough to bring a child into the world by natural means, but what extraordinary audacity had inspired her to step forward and claim an entire life? What had she meant by it? At such times the thought of what she had done appalled her.

All the more essential that she ensure Adela be protected from a false vision of herself; that she learn to see herself with the unsparing eye of truth, as a creature whose existence in this time and place might be beyond commonplace explanation, but who, all the same, must endure her time with patience.

For a long time she had entertained a dream of removing her few possessions to a cottage on the Gweal. Because the idea had seemed a whim, more especially because there had been no employment there for her son, she had resisted it. But now, with him gone and no one but the child to consider, would there not be wisdom in such a move? Adela's story would be known there, and at first she was bound to be identified in its terms, but none of the men of the Gweal had been directly involved in the rescue. Memories of it would be less immediate there. Besides, it was a simpler place. There was no town there such as had developed on St Warna's, with its worthless hierarchy, its mimicry of power and wealth, its incitements to greed and vanity. Her lips moved without sound as she discussed the matter long and earnestly with herself in the darkened room. The island itself, she was convinced, had an undisturbed virtue. It was there that she had always wished her existence might be, and now she could tell herself it was to the child's advantage to remove there.

Yesterday, buying a length of ribbon in the crowded store in the High Street, she had heard of the death of the widow Pender of the Gweal. 'He'll have her cottage down before the week's out. You watch him,' the woman in the shop had said. But Mrs Traherne knew all at once that he would not; that she would go to the Proprietor and beg, if need be, that she and the child might move there. She knew that he had razed a number of cottages on the off-island over the past year, but then too he was building on that same island for reasons of his own which might bring him within the reaches of her understanding. I shall go to him in the morning, she thought.

As the room began to resume its daylight shapes she fell into a deep sleep and so rose late and was hurried in her preparations. Haste and anxiety made her clumsy in brushing out Adela's hair. Twice she scraped the bristles over the stiff rim of the child's ear so that she cried out, and then asked fretfully, 'Where are we going?'

'To see a man.'

'What man?'

'A man who may give us a new house.'

'Why?'

'Why, to live in of course.'

'We have a house to live in,' said the child slowly, turning to study Mrs Traherne with her round serious eyes.

'You will like this new house better.' But she should not have troubled her with so confounding a thought: that there might be such a thing as another home, when this one now lay at the very centre of the child's world. That there could be two of anything whispered of separation and might frighten her.

'There,' she said, turning over her wrist to do up the button of her glove. 'There. It may never happen.' But she was determined that it would happen. To distract the troubled look from the child's face she gave her her little

59

beaded reticule to carry and the child came willing enough at her side, swinging the weighted purse by its chain.

When they were shown into Augustus' study she whispered to Adela, 'Go sit by the window there. See who goes by in the street.'

The child obeyed instantly, out of what Augustus saw was a deep trust. Only when she had seated herself on the low window sill did she glance shyly back at Mrs Traherne, who gave a quick nod of approval, and then, as if in spite of herself, a sudden deep smile of almost frightening intensity.

He said to Mrs Traherne, 'She looks happy and in good health. You have cared for her well.'

'She has been very good to me,' said Mrs Traherne, aware that her words were oddly chosen, so that, searching in her mind for others, she became distracted from what she had wanted to say. He watched her sit there silently, folded like a little black bird, her veined hands with their swollen knuckles gripping her knees.

'Can I help you?' he said at last.

'I have come, sir, to ask if you might consider allowing the child and myself to exchange our cottage here for Sarah Pender's on the Gweal. That is, of course, if you have no other plan for it.' She sat a little forward on the chair as she delivered this speech and then sank back as if prepared to wait indefinitely for an answer.

Augustus was silent now. She watched him open and shut the hinged half-lid of a silver penholder, lifting it each time just before it clicked back into place. He seemed to consider. In fact he needed a moment to collect his thoughts, which almost unconsciously had gathered to resist the accusation he felt this woman must, in time, hurl at him. It took him several seconds to turn his mind to the widow Pender's cottage.

He said, 'I had intended to tear it down,' and instinctively his hands moved about the littered desk until they rested on the note he had written Wills that very morning, ordering its destruction.

'That is your decision,' said Mrs Traherne quietly, but not by the slightest movement did she hint that she would ever leave.

He rallied himself by lifting the piece of paper and pretending to read from it, as he recollected the condition of the cottage. The thatch was in poor repair but the beams not rotten. There had been no cause to destroy it other than to reduce the number of people attempting to subsist on the island. Mrs Traherne, he knew from Wills, had means of her own, however scanty. In time she would die. Adela would marry. The cottage could see out both events for only a small expenditure.

Then he turned and studied the child, who now knelt bolt upright at the window with her small hands spread on the glass. She was engaged in obscuring the street with her breath and then making peepholes with her tongue, through which she peered intently before leaning back to watch all fade away. She was quite indifferent to the voices in the room behind her. Still, instinctively he lowered his voice when he spoke of her. 'Why do you want such a thing? Will it not be very lonely for the child?'

'Lonely,' repeated the old woman sharply. She seemed to make some wild observation on the human condition as a whole.

The child started and turned towards her, but seeing her position unchanged turned back to the window. Mrs Traherne began again. 'It is for the child's sake that I go.'

'How is that?'

'I cannot find the words to explain to you, sir.' She looked at him earnestly. Her eyes were a profound blue, showing very brightly under the parched wrinkled lids that partially hooded them. 'But the attention she receives here will turn her head. I know it will.'

He smiled at her earnestness but was frowning too between his eyes, trying to make out if some motive underlay her simplicity. He did not think so.

She repeated, 'I cannot find the words to explain to you, sir.'

'Yes,' he said. 'Yes.' For he could not doubt she had

61

explained some instinct as well as she was able. 'But it is a remote spot for a child.'

'There are other children there. There is a school. I will send her to the school.'

'Yes,' he said. 'You must send her to school.'

She had meant to resist him in that, but even having given her word so casually now would not. And further. She would go further. 'I shall send her to Mr Peters, when he sees fit, for the confirmation classes, although, as you may know, that is a painful question of conscience with me, but all that I swear to you I shall do if you give me my way in this.'

He said, 'I am only thinking of the child.'

'But whatever thought but that is constantly in my mind?' she said to him. Her voice seemed to have penetrated to some deep welling emotion that affected the rhythm of her words. 'And you, sir, though you say that we should not, have the same desire to go there and build yourself a house in which you mean to live and perhaps raise children. How can you deny us what your own heart wishes for yourself?'

She had his attention. His eyes were fixed and bright. She had no idea why he was affected by her words but knew instinctively to go on:

'Do you not feel that there is a virtue in the place?' As she spoke she saw it very clearly. Her son, she told him, had taken her there once. They had stood on the central hill and had seen the wild sea held at a great distance by the rocks, forced to expand its power in great plumes of spray so that only calmed water could reach the smooth white beaches. She had seen the long lake with the light upon it and the white swan vanishing into the reeds, and although she could find adequate words for none of this she thought, by his intent look, that he shared these sights. Something she sensed had sorrowed his youth and the accusations that he was without a heart were not perhaps entirely true.

He said quietly when she was through, 'So you think it is a safe place?' He never took his eyes from her. 'Even for a child?'

'Why, what harm could come to her there?'

'Nowhere can be safe,' he told her.

She sensed some train of thought that was his and not hers and said stiffly, 'That's as may be, sir. I only ask for the cottage.'

'Well,' he said. 'I must put the matter first to Mr Wills.' But she knew that she had succeeded.

It proved far easier to complete the few repairs to the widow Pender's cottage than those to the new house. Immediately after his interview with Mrs Traherne Augustus gave orders for the thatch to be renewed and the earthen floor to be boarded over. Finally the whole place was given a thorough clean out and whitewashed. These attentions did not go without notice. It was two years since he had forced her son Georgy into the navy and it was well known that since then the Proprietor had made every effort to persuade the old woman to remove to the main island, where she might be better cared for. The widow, known for her canniness, had not so much resisted as delayed. She had mentioned that there were a number of things she must see to first, namely her pig. There was nothing to lose through patience with the old. The pig fattened in consequence over several seasons, grew immense and domineering. As the widow weakened – it was said that she pined for her son – it moved into the cottage and lived there on all but the balmiest days. On her death it was promptly killed and two joints used to furnish the funeral feast with the rare luxury of roast pork. Although the meat was pronounced tough and the taste of fish that permeated all the local pork unusually strong, it was a cheerful occasion. The general opinion was that both pig and widow had held on to the last in stout defiance of their natural predators. It was assumed by those present that the cottage, like several others in the same condition, would be pulled down within the week, and when the contrary proved true it was inevitably rumoured that Mrs Traherne had some hold over the Proprietor and that he had taken her and the child under his protection.

In August Mrs Traherne began to pack her few possessions into potato baskets for removal to the island. She covered each basket carefully against the day when they must be carried through the streets to the quay. Adela watched with awe as each treasure was moved from its fixed place and wrapped and put away: the button hook and shoe-horn with the matching tortoiseshell handles, then the embroidered linen runner on which they were laid. Finally the mahogany chest of drawers and the stool set before it were carried out. The rooms were desolate now. Their voices sounded strangely. Even their clothes had gone. Mrs Traherne locked the door behind her without regret.

The neighbours stood on their porches watching, partly as a token of respectful farewell, for they had nothing against her, and partly too in a last attempt to spy out her secret, if she had one. John Traherne's tin trunk, which proved exceptionally heavy, caused excited speculation. Gold bars were suggested, or some other form of loot. When the returning boatmen declared it had been filled with books that seemed scarcely less suspicious, for what innocent purpose could an old woman possibly have for a load of books?

Still, she had escaped them and their like. The new cottage was on the lane that ran from the village to the new estate. It stood isolated, on a rise above the coast-guard cottages, with a fine view of the sea. The nearest neighbour on the other side, a tenant farmer called Jenkins, was out of sight over the crest of the hill.

Mrs Traherne had seldom been so happy. She moved about the little house, humming roughly and abstractedly under her breath, while the child followed at her heels watching in wonder the home reassemble itself in this strange place: the chest, the runner, the button hook, the shoe-horn. 'You see,' said the old woman, almost reproachfully, 'it is all just as it was.'

But, of course, it was not. It was all quite different. For a day or two Adela could not be persuaded to venture outside unless she held onto Mrs Traherne's hand. The weather was warm. The child stood leaning against the open door, staring out at the new place. A green hill rose up to the sky. Cows from the Hill Farm stood on it eating the grass. Then she grew bolder, and after solemnly bidding her aunt goodbye she would walk all around the house, coming in with a delighted look through the door she had left. Within a week she chose to play outside all day until her aunt called her in to eat. She found mussel shells from a pile thrown behind the cottage in the widow Pender's day, and set them on the ground and called them cows. Mrs Traherne could hear her through the open window chattering absorbedly to herself.

That autumn, true to her word, Mrs Traherne took Adela to the school in the village and paid her weekly penny to have the child taught. It was soon discovered that Adela could read already and write with some proficiency. When asked who had taught her the child looked puzzled, and finally explained that her aunt liked to be read to as she knitted in the evenings. She made no special friend. The other children ignored rather than tolerated her. Always, when the schoolroom door was opened at the end of the day, Mrs Traherne was waiting for her. Adela ran to her with relief and clung to her hand. Once home she would run out behind the cottage and, with Mrs Traherne watching from the window, would line up her mussel shells, give them the village children's names and teach them what she had learned during the day.

It took the whole of the following summer to complete the work on the Proprietor's new house, and then it was decided to leave it empty over the autumn and winter for the plaster to dry. The stone wall that bounded the northern end of the estate was finished, too, and although a child could have scrambled over it and the gate was never locked, the idea that a whole portion of the island had been enclosed was irksome and difficult to understand. A year ago Mrs Traherne and Adela, following a procession of island women and their children, had filled a basket there with blackberries. The following autumn the blackberries were left to ripen and wither, although some of the village boys crept over the wall at dusk and ate their fill. The sandy ground where the thickets stood were rife with rabbit warrens, and these too were now out of bounds. The older boys still ventured to set snares and visit them by stealth, but often they found the bracken trampled and their snares torn up and broken. Two gamekeepers had been brought over from the mainland and patrolled the hillside with water-spaniels at their heels. In summer their full white shirt sleeves were clearly visible among the tall bracken. Sometimes with slow arrogant gait they walked into the village, cradling guns in their arms, with pheasant feathers nodding from their hat bands. In the early evening the guns could be heard echoing on the far side of the hill and again in the spring, when the eastern gales blew woodcock over the island.

The Proprietor was late in returning to the islands that spring. By the end of March he had still not arrived. Perhaps there was disappointment when the promise of extra employment and the mixture of excitement and dread his returns occasioned after the dreary winter were withheld. Perhaps they wished him gone for good and the islands given back to them. On Walpurgis night, after the celebrations for the early potato harvest, a gang of boys went over the wall and ventured up the slope on which the house was built. There was a bright full moon and the dogs began to bay in their kennels. They lay panting in the bracken, seized by that particular terror that can overtake anyone at night: this night of all, when to some the spirits abroad were more menacing than the gamekeepers.

When the dogs gradually fell silent and no one seemed about, they crept up onto the front terrace, feeling themselves exposed in the moonlight. Under the tall front windows they found dark heaps of little birds. A large flock of starling had been seen over the islands a few days before. Deluded by the sunlight, motionless in the empty rooms, they had flown straight against the glass to their death. Here and there the dusty imprints of their outstretched wings were visible on the panes. Now moonlight fell into the empty enclosed spaces of the house. Either fear

66

prompted some kind of destructive rage, or perhaps they felt a more primitive instinct that the spirits should be free to come and go as they wished. They began to gather up stones and retreated below the parapet of the terrace to lob them at the windows. They had shattered at least a dozen before terror overcame them and they fled back to the wall and safety.

In the morning, when the violence was reported, Wills rowed over to the island and visited every house in the village. No one would admit that any member of their family had strayed from their hearth the night before. On his return to the main island he wrote indignantly to the Proprietor, promising that he would get to the bottom of the matter, but he knew well enough that he never would. By the time the Proprietor arrived on the islands three weeks later, the windows were reglazed; the stones and glass and the dead birds carefully swept away.

Within a week of his arrival boatloads of furnishings began to arrive daily on the island, and were carried or transported by cart from the quay: barrels of china, hampers of cooking pans, pierglasses and portraits swathed in canvas sheets, a vast mahogany dining table, no less than seventeen bedsteads and mattresses. Most of the village women were employed, one way or another, in getting the place ready. In early June he took up residence, and by July the first batch of summer guests had arrived and could be seen in their strange clothes travelling about the island in the cart or on horseback, waving and smiling indiscriminately at everyone they passed.

Into the complicated pattern of their various harvests from land and sea the islanders learned to fit his comings and goings. He usually spent Christmas on the mainland at his family place, returning in February. Then he spent the season in London and would be back in the islands with his visitors for August and September. When they left he would remain working at one project or another, until the weather broke and he returned home for Christmas.

Adela was nearly nine when he recorded his approval of her progress at school. It was the following summer that he

wrote to Mrs Traherne requesting Adela's daily atten-
dance at the house to play with a young visitor he was
expecting shortly.

Mrs Traherne accepted. There had always been certain
ambiguities in her attitude towards Adela. True, she felt
her hair afforded her some kind of protection, but was she
not more than a little vain of its beauty? True, she had
never wished to send Adela to the village school, intending
to educate her herself, yet in her heart she took great pride
and satisfaction from Adela's unprecedented progress
there. And now, amidst all her fears for the child's first
encounter with wealth, there may have lain a natural
enough ambition that Adela might find in that household
appreciation, even affection, at the very least a friend
more suited to her natural gentleness than the rough island
children.

6

With the stricture that they were to achieve happiness the Proprietor left them. The governess sank back on her chair. Adela and Harriet continued to stand facing one another. The heaped sand pressed against the instep of Adela's shoes. She noticed that the poles supporting the canvas were oars and saw the sun burn in a bright yellow speck through the canvas.

The governess said impatiently: 'Will you not play in Miss Harriet's sand?'

Obediently Adela sank on her knees and began to dig a hole. It had rained recently. Beneath the fine glittering surface the sand was damp and cool. Adela began to pat the sides of her hole and smooth its edges to a thick round lip. Her little hands worked purposefully. She scraped the dry surface sand into mounds and drew complicated sinuous paths between them with her fingers. At some point she became aware that the other child had knelt beside her and was building up the hills. For a moment Adela felt an intolerate irritation, for they had been silver and now dark wet sand was flattened clumsily on top of them. She did it wrong. She did it wrong. But she knew to say nothing.

They worked in total silence, watching each other's hands but not their faces. Adela was aware, as she squatted to her task, of the sun on her back warm through the awning and the smell of her own person scrubbed with soap on the previous night. The other smell was Harriet's, warm, wholesome as sun on straw.

By a sweep of her hands in the sand Harriet suggested that they have a lake. They began to work together scraping back the sand like dogs. Water was needed. Perhaps she said so, for Harriet got to her feet and was gone. Adela, scarcely feeling her absence, worked on. In a moment Harriet returned with water in a can and poured it without warning over Adela's hands, so that she looked up and laughed. 'More,' she said at once, for all that water had sunk darkly into the sand. Harriet ran. The governess called sharply after her, 'You should not run errands, Miss Harriet.'

Adela did not look up. Fiercely she patted the sand at the base of the lake and waited for the cool rush of the water over her fingers. When it came she crowed with laughter and shouted for more.

The governess said, 'You must fetch it yourself. You are not to order Miss Harriet about.' It was the enmity in her tone that gave pain. Adela crouched on the sand without moving.

Harriet said, 'Don't be foolish. I go because I want to go.'

But the game was instantly over. 'Let's do something else now,' said Harriet. But they had not finished this. Adela sat back on her heels. They stared at one another. She knew then that Harriet would go whether she came or whether she stayed, and got slowly to her feet although the unfinished roads and hills dragged at her will. 'Come on,' said Harriet, and set off along the path without glancing back to see if she followed.

In time it became a garden that might frighten a child with its choked complexities, its exotic births, its sudden deaths, its air of secrecy, but then Augustus had not complicated or much altered the place. He had merely laid out the paths of his labyrinth. Nothing had yet grown near to the height of the little girls' heads. To clamber about as they did now was an assault on a mountain rather than a jungle. Their shoes pattered on stone. Their two heads, Harriet's fair and Adela's dark, were everywhere visible, and they could easily see Miss Christian toiling up the path without mystery behind them.

'Quickly,' whispered Harriet.

'Why?'

'To get away from her. To hide.'

Adela glanced anxiously behind her. 'Will she be angry?'

'I don't care.'

'At me?'

'What is it to do with you? Come on.' Their path was intercepted by another. Harriet turned and ran down it. Adela followed. They hid side by side among the freshly blasted boulders.

When in the late afternoon a servant led Adela back through the kitchen passages to the door, Mrs Traherne was waiting for her. She captured the child's hand and held it tightly as they walked in silence past the lake. The birds were very active on the fresh water at that hour, coming and going, changing shape and colour as they wheeled in flight, into the low direct sunlight. Woman and child stopped for moments at a time to watch, but did not exchange a word until they were through the gate of the estate. Then Mrs Traherne drew the child around so that they faced one another on the path and scrutinized her deeply, as if to detect the very faintest sign of change or damage.

'Well,' she said, and when the child had no answer, 'Well, did you enjoy yourself?' There was something mocking in her voice, as if she had given way to the child's pleading to taste something she would not like and now would have her condemn the experience out of her own mouth. 'For if you do not like to go, no power on earth can make me send you there.'

'Oh, please let me go again,' said Adela, almost passionately, her brow suddenly lined with anxiety like a much older person's.

'Very well. Very well,' said Mrs Traherne, and Adela could not have told whether she were pleased or disappointed.

On other days Mrs Traherne would ask, 'Well, what did you play with the other little girl?'

'We do not exactly *play*.' For she herself was unable to

71

understand, let alone explain to her aunt, how the days passed. It did not seem that they differed from one another at all. She had a recurring impression of walking down the cool hallway towards the brightly lit rectangle of the door open onto the terraces. It was an exceptionally fine summer. People referred to it for years afterwards.

Then they walked along the paths, not hand in hand but sometimes with their shoulders pressed hard against one another's. They knew these paths and the individual rocks that lay scattered about them with an intimacy that adults, with their sudden increase in height and their various distractions, lose. Adela found that she could without effort think of names for the rocks. This ability seemed to please and impress Harriet. In this one thing Adela was allowed to take the lead. Otherwise she followed where Harriet led, as unresisting as a shadow.

So she could only repeat to Mrs Traherne, 'We do not exactly *play*.'

'Then what do you do with yourselves?'

'We go for walks.'

'And where do you go for walks?'

'In the garden.'

'Garden,' said the old woman scornfully. 'What garden does he have there? Nothing can have grown in the time.'

'It is a rock garden,' said Adela.

She has been told that, thought the old woman, for she seemed to speak in some other person's voice. 'Does he grow rocks in it, then?' she asked the child mockingly.

They were pressed side by side between the rocks. Adela's heart thumped at the base of her throat. She ached with running and the fear of Miss Christian's anger, but the thick dusty smell of Harriet's hair comforted her. Harriet's breath whispered warmly, explosively against her ear, 'I hate her.'

'Why?'

'She's horrid. She's mad.'

'She's not.'

'What do you know? She says horrid things.'

'What things?'

72

'She says that Papa is ill, when he's not. He pretends to be ill because he does not like it here. He wants to go home. She says Mr Walmer killed his sister.'

On another day Harriet led her up to a rather old gentleman who was sitting in a wicker chair on the terrace with a checked travelling rug across his knees. The terrace was then so exposed that he was able to survey the surrounding scene through a telescope propped on a table in front of him without rising to his feet. They watched him for a little time before Harriet went up to him and leant against his leg. Without a word he drew her in between his knees and held the telescope in front of her eye, at the same time laying his long rosy cheek against her hair.

'Can you see it?' he said. 'Can you see the big ship, my darling?'

'Yes,' said Harriet, but Adela could tell from her voice that she could not.

'And what have you been doing?' asked the old gentleman. When he spoke Adela thought him less old and saw that his thin hair lifting in the wind was colourless rather than grey. 'I never see you here.'

'Playing with Adela.'

'And who is Adela.'

'Adela is an Island Child,' said Harriet.

He turned then and looked slowly at Adela. 'Why, yes,' he said, 'I can see that is exactly what Adela is. I can see it at once. An Island Child. Come here, child. Admired Miranda come here.'

Adela took a step forward out of pity, but sensing that he wished to touch her kept out of reach. It pained her that he was aware of this and sighed. 'Well, well,' he said. 'You will want to go on with your play.'

'Who was he?' said Adela, when they were among the rocks.

'He is Papa,' said Harriet, shocked at her ignorance.

'Is he old?'

'Rather old.' She added, 'Mr Walmer is not Mama's friend. He is Papa's friend. That is why we came.'

73

'I thought he was old.'

'He's not dead,' said Harriet. 'Your papa is dead.'

It was as near to quarrelling as they ever came.

'Harriet is not Mr Walmer's little girl,' Adela told her aunt. 'She has another rather old papa.' For though she must have known this, the matter needed more affirmation.

The old woman let out one of her scornful crowing laughs. 'I should hope so too,' she said. She was cleaning out the pan in which she cooked their porridge, rubbing sand around the inside with an angry circular motion. The anger, the laughter, were troubling.

Adela said in a low unsteady voice, 'Don't you like me to go there?'

'So long as you like it,' said Mrs Traherne crossly. 'It's nothing to me one way or the other. You say you like it there.'

'Yes,' said Adela.

She could no longer conceive of a day when she would not eat her breakfast and then set out along the path to the big house. For Adela that month lay outside the normal delineation of time. In later years the residue of memory, the actual events gathered at the bottom of the clear floating days in which she played without loss of interest with Harriet in the garden, was so slight that it seemed they scarcely filled one afternoon. She had an impression that these few happenings had all been crowded in at the end of the visit and had been the actual agents that disrupted it, but that may not have been so.

Miss Christian, from the start, had taken it upon herself to brush and plait Adela's hair as soon as she arrived, tying the plaits with two ribbons produced from the depths of her knitting bag. Adela resented this ritual less than she might have done. The alteration of herself, the different names they called her by, freed her of any comparison between the two lives she was leading. Once the ribbons were tied, the day might begin.

Often the governess would lead them through the high

74

sweet bracken to the beach and there they would walk along the black line of stranded seaweed methodically collecting shells.

Miss Christian gathered the pale shy cowries, wearing her spectacles, bending almost double, frowning fiercely over the bright sand until, with a little cry of triumph, she snatched at one and secreted it in her embroidered pocket. She hoarded these little shells and counted them with something akin to avarice.

Adela collected the thin worn outer rims of broken mussels which her grandmother called onion rings. She threaded these diligently onto a length of blue knitting wool which Miss Christian, in a lapse of disapproval, had broken off and given her. Shaken on the wool the shells made a pretty ringing sound, and for all their ordinariness they had the precious quality of being worn so frail that they might at any moment break. Besides, the particular beach where they were to be found was now forbidden to the islanders as a part of the newly walled off estate. A certain streak of practicality warned Adela to gather her treasures while she might. She loved the places where they were found, broad shallow channels carved into the sand and catching light in a curious way so that each appeared to contain a loose golden plait in which the shells were entangled. The sand around these channels was ribbed in places like a smooth ancient landscape, and often patterned with the sharp fresh prints of horses' hooves set there between one tide and the next.

Harriet was less intent in her gathering than either of her two companions and far outstripped them down the length of the beach, although she often stopped to look about her or ran to the water to launch a bit of driftwood or fling a stone. Nevertheless, before Miss Christian had uttered her second cry of discovery, she had half filled a black holland bag with the commonest shell of all: the big white serviceable scallop.

Once all three heard the muffled thud of horses' hooves rise from the sand as they bent over it, and all looked up together from their various positions along the line of seawrack. At first the change of focus from their minute searchings to the great bright expanse of sea and sky was almost blinding. Then they made out two riders, a man and a woman. You could see the black veil fluttering out behind her hat as they urged their mounts up the soft inner curve of the dunes. Their hooves slipped back and sent down sand like puffs of smoke, but the riders crouched forward with their pale gloves patting their horses' necks and eventually reached the line of stiff grasses at the top. They could all three hear laughter.

'Wave to your mama,' called Miss Christian to Harriet, who was far ahead of her up the beach, but she could not have heard for although she faced the riders she stood stock still as if without recognition.

The next day Harriet, holding her bag of shells, led the way up to their pile of boulders. Miss Christian sat below in its shadow with her knitting.

Harriet, with an urgency unusual to her, set out the shells on the flat surface of a rock, saying in a whisper, 'One for you, Mrs Briggs, and one for you, Mrs Bloggs. I am afraid you must take your tea very quickly for Pontefract is ill in his room and I must go out riding.'

Obligingly Adela supped at the edge of her scallop, which smelt and tasted of the sea. She wondered if she were required to speak, but thought that she was not.

Harriet said in the grown up woman's whisper. 'Of course I go riding to fetch the doctor to Pontefract. If you don't know that you're useless.'

One afternoon she sat cross-legged on that same beach below the house, with her shells spilled into the dip of her skirt, restringing them onto her piece of the blue wool. Every movement of Harriet's down by the water's edge conveyed itself to her. Clink went the shells as they struck one another. The sea made a sound, voices made a sound. Harriet's mother, sitting somewhere near but out of her line of vision, talked to Mr Walmer. Of him she was more aware. A current of restless movement always ran through him. He paced about. He sat down a little way from them.

He rattled his stick on his boot, so that the dachsund was kept in a constant state of expectancy and panted as he sat watching him, poised at any moment to dash away after him. He would not go. He would not stay. There was something demanding of attention in his very silence. And when he spoke the deep tones of his voice were still strange enough for Adela to hear them through her other preoccupations. The low still light warned her that soon she must go home; that Mrs Traherne might be kept waiting for her.

He was saying, 'You go so soon.' Adela looked up, but of course he did not speak to her.

'Do not even speak of it.' He so sad. She so bright.

And then the woman's voice again. 'Is it possible to walk to those rocks?'

'At the neap tide you can cross to St Warna's.'

'On foot?'

'At that one tide. They drive the cows over here for fresh pasturage.'

'Oh, I should so like to go.'

'You will.'

'Not now.'

'Next time.'

'Next time.'

When they stopped talking it was very quiet. Occasionally tall jets of spray burst against the outer rocks, but that violence was so remote that no trace of it reached them. Ripples like long narrow shadows approached and broke on the pebbles with an exhausted sound that echoed down the length of the beach more and more quietly. It was an effort to speak into such a silence.

'Harriet,' her mother called, 'Harriet.'

Adela listened. Harriet came towards them, solid against the bright sea, scowling in earnestness, plodding in the sand. Adela watched the mother smile, and then the smile set as Harriet came towards her, watched the quick motion of the ringed hand as it reached out to push the stiff fair hair from Harriet's face and rub for an instant at the frown between the child's eyes. 'Well,' she said, 'show me your shells.'

She watched Harriet test with a quick look the truth of her mother's interest and then begin to work loose the neck of her bag with square intent hands.

'Will you show them to Mr Walmer?'

'No. They are for you.'

'I think he would like to see them.'

But she would not look at Mr Walmer. 'Will you take tea with me?' she asked her mother.

'If we may take it all together.'

'I will pour for you and then perhaps take some myself. Adela does not want any.'

'Have you asked Adela?'

'She told me.'

He sighed then, so that they all heard, and walked rapidly away from them down the beach with the dog bounding after him. Adela could see him picking his way carefully over the stones. He was one black shape with the sea behind him. His head was bowed. She understood the pain he felt at not being asked to tea. He climbed the rocks of the headland. They could still see him.

'You will spill your tea,' said Harriet reprovingly.

'I think you were unkind to Mr Walmer not to share your tea with him.'

'This is your plate,' said Harriet insistently. 'You must say what you want to eat. Quickly. Say.'

'What do you have?'

But already Harriet was placing smaller shells in the big one. 'They are cakes.' She poured sand in the cup. 'That is your tea. You must drink your tea and then you must be Papa and talk to me.'

Mr Walmer stood in front of Harriet's mother, silently holding out his hand. He had walked quickly. The dog had gone off somewhere. They had not heard him come. Adela stood up and came closer to see what he held in his hand.

Harriet's mother said, 'Look, Harriet. Mr Walmer has brought us an egg.' Quickly she brushed the shells and the sand from her skirt. 'Hold it. Mr Walmer will let you hold it. Here, put your hands together.' Harriet's square hands held the egg, but did not want it.

He said to Harriet's mother, 'It is for you.'

'For me?' Adela would have been the last to notice the candour of her smile and its sudden access of caution.

'I thought you might like to collect them.'

She dusted the sand from her hands and held them out. 'It's still warm,' she said.

'There were three others.'

'She won't grieve?'

'She won't know.'

'You are sure?'

'I promise you that.'

The unaccountable bulk, the endless continuance of adult conversation is something which children learn to ignore. Really Augustus' dog, if he had not found something to distract him by the shore, would have picked up as much of the adults' conversation as Adela did. But something sad and precarious in the mood of that occasion, as well as the first disturbing mention of departure, made her remember it as coming towards the end. Surely it was that afternoon, when she ran to the gate of the courtyard to take her aunt's hand, that Mrs Traherne said with scarcely concealed interest, 'Well, have you done, then? Have they bid you goodbye?'

7

'No,' said Adela, and then, when her aunt fell silent, 'why should they not want me?'

'Didn't they tell you that there were other children coming to stay? They won't need you now.' She spoke almost quizzically, but did not relent to the anxious face turned up to her. 'Did the child say nothing?'

'Nothing that I wasn't to come. Besides,' she added eagerly, 'there is to be a picnic.' For it had been promised that as Mr Walmer was to visit the workings on the light-house they would all picnic on an island nearby.

'No one told you that his sister-in-law is to come to stay? She has children.'

'Oh yes,' said Adela, recollecting suddenly, 'she told me that.'

'Well, they won't want you as well. You were just there while there was no one else to play with her.'

'He said we were *all* to go on the picnic.'

But Mrs Traherne was not to be convinced. She so feared the child's rejection at the hands of these people that it had become a reality to her. How casually had they swept Adela up, and how carelessly at any moment they might discard her! She did not even trust to Augustus' permanence in the islands, but regarded him and his con-stant flow of visitors as little better than a troupe of play-ers, sweeping in with their bright disruption of normality; posing unanswerable questions about the drabness and inevitability of life; stealing away the innocent hearts of children. She cursed herself for succumbing to the tempta-tion of wanting them to take an interest in Adela. For what could she have actually hoped for the child?

She could tell from her careful questioning of Adela that little enough interest was taken. The child scarcely saw the adults and was no more than a plaything. She could not let the matter rest, although she saw she was causing pain, but said, 'Well, I do not think they will want you any more. I shall come with you to the door and make sure.'

Accordingly, in the morning, she led Adela to the kitchen of the Abbey and rang. Adela, accustomed now to running in and out at will, waited uncomfortably beside her. Already her innocence was so far damaged that she could perceive that her aunt belonged nowhere here, neither among the island women in the kitchen, nor among the family in the drawing room. Aware of this, perhaps, she had a sudden instinct that her own sense of belonging was an ephemeral thing, whereas before it had all the permanence of the present succession of warm summer days.

When the housekeeper came to the door her aunt repeated bluntly, 'I came with Adela because I was not sure that they would want her, now that Mrs Walmer and her children are here.'

The housekeeper shook her head slowly from side to side. 'There's been nothing said to me.'

'What had I best do, then?'

'Would you not come in, Mrs Traherne, and ask him yourself?'

'No, I would not. Thank you, though.'

'As you will. What would you have me do, then?'

'Take her,' said the old woman bitterly. 'I'll wait a little by the gate,' she told Adela, 'in case they send you back.'

Adela darted from her and without hesitation vanished into the kitchen and down the long passage to the hall.

Coming out onto the terrace she saw Harriet, sitting on the top of the flight of steps with her elbows on her knees and her fists dug into her cheeks, staring downwards. The pleasant clinking of the gardeners' spades floated up the hillside. That morning they had commenced digging the two beds laid out like Union Jacks on what had been

81

the nave of the old Abbey chapel. Two of Augustus' little dogs raced each other up and down the long flight of steps yapping frantically. Nothing had changed.

Without a word Adela went and stood with her back to Miss Christian and presently felt the first assault of the hairbrush. No one told her to go away. Harriet did not so much as look around. But she could not let it stay so. She must ask: 'Have they come?'

'Yes,' said Harriet indifferently.

'Where are they?' She looked reluctantly about the terrace, so that Miss Christian jerked her head painfully back into place.

'Upstairs somewhere,' said Harriet.

A moment later the sound of the pony's hooves and the grinding of the cart's wheels came through the open hall. The day would not stand still but must gather pace.

'We are to go in the cart with Miss Sarah,' said Miss Christian.

'I want to walk,' said Harriet.

Footsteps and adult voices could be heard descending the stairs inside the house and presently a boy and a girl came out onto the terrace, frowning in the sun and looking about them.

Harriet turned then and, lifting her feet onto the step she sat upon, laid her cheek on her knees and scowled as steadily at them as she had at Adela when she first arrived.

'Say good morning to Miss Sarah and Master Alfred,' said Miss Christian in her endless sing-song of admonition.

Adela kept her head stiffly in place and said nothing, but she watched them covertly.

The boy said, 'When do we go?'

'I don't know,' said Harriet. 'When the cart's ready.'

'I'm not going in the cart,' he said. Alfred was thirteen that summer and already growing tall. Adela, watching him from inside the boundaries of childhood, saw that already he had crossed into an adult world where unfamiliar rules applied. He was too unknown either to trust or mistrust.

She noticed his beauty rather as she might have noticed

82

something remarkable that he held in his hand. His skin had taken sun smoothly. His hair was fair. Already the sea wind had defined each curl and made it stand up brightly from his head. His face had that instinctive stillness that such children seem to acquire long before they can understand the nature of their gift.

The girl sat beside Harriet on the steps and whispered in her ear, keeping her face pressed to the frill of Harriet's sunbonnet, but rolling back her eyes towards Adela. She threatened in familiar ways, so that Adela felt her body a hollow comfortless place. She could feel it was a different substance from what was around her. She was aware that she could be seen. She seemed to swell and felt herself distasteful to these people. She stood with her back to Miss Christian, looking to see which of them watched her.

The boy had gone inside but reappeared leaning in the open doorway with a gun broken over his crooked arm, staring quietly, sometimes at the sea, sometimes with a cold attention at Miss Christian plaiting her hair.

Now Mr Walmer came out onto the terrace. Moving without a glance at any of them he called down to the gardeners, 'How is it going?' They could see the men straighten up from their digging.

'Not too bad, sir,' one called up. 'There're plenty of those tiles to clear.'

'Yes,' shouted Augustus. 'There would be.'

Now a woman followed him out of the house and, bracing her arms on the parapet, looked briskly this way and that as if to set about some task.

'What are you going to do with all this rock?' she said. 'You'll never grow anything.' She had a loud voice and shouted slightly as if she were used to speaking with him from one room to another.

'Oh, in time,' he said.

'At least they've done the steps.'

'They're digging the formal beds at the bottom today. We'll see them as we go.'

She had turned to look at the Proprietor as he spoke, and now her glance fell on Adela, whom Miss Christian had just released after a final tug at her ribbons. 'Who's she?'

'I had her in to play with Harriet.'

'What, she's local? But whose?'

'An island woman.'

'Oh.' Her voice was loud and brisk again. 'Do we go now? Are we ready?'

It was time to get into the cart. Harriet's papa was to go in the cart and Sarah, the new girl. The boy Alfred was to walk with Mr Walmer. Harriet, who had said a moment before that she did not want to go in the cart, now said that she did.

'Does *she* have to come too?' said the other girl as she was lifted in. She meant Adela.

'She can if she wants,' said Harriet, but there was no more room in the cart. Miss Christian said that Adela should walk with her. She walked beside Miss Christian down the steps past the gardeners, out between the stone gate posts onto the path that led to the beach. The boy Alfred walked ahead with the Proprietor. Harriet's mama and the new lady followed, talking so that their parasols touched and jerked away from one another.

'Wave, Adela,' ordered Miss Christian. The pony cart went faster than they did. She waved. They waved. They shouted, too, but when she shouted no sound came out.

Miss Christian said, 'You must put yourself about to play with the other little girl too.'

It was bright on the beach. It hurt her eyes.

In the boat Sarah and Harriet knelt in the stern and trailed their hands in the water and laughed.

Miss Christian said, 'Why can't you sit still like Adela?'

They turned around then, but they did not smile at her.

When they were on the little island where the picnic was to be, Harriet and the other girl began to walk away along the beach.

'Do you want to come too?' said Harriet over her shoulder.

Adela shook head.

The Proprietor said, 'Why don't you take Adela?'

'She can come if she wants to,' said Harriet reasonably,

84

'but she doesn't want to.' The girl called Sarah lolled her head onto Harriet's shoulder and stared at Adela. She sat on a rock under the awning. She could not move. She wanted to cry, but could not. All around her voices were talking.

'Fetch my glass,' Mr Walmer said to the boy called Alfred. And he ran to the boat and back with the glass. Mr Walmer stood on a rock and looked at the sea through the glass.

When the other boat came back they carried the cook onto the beach.

The old papa shouted, 'Three cheers for Cook!' He had his gun on his shoulder. They would shoot at the birds. 'Hip, hip . . .'

She tried to shout hurrah, but no sound came out.

'Hip, hip . . .'

'Hurrah!'

'Hip, hip . . .'

'Hurrah!'

She would have shouted but no sound came out.

'Adela is very quiet,' said Miss Christian. 'I think the palm must go to Adela by default.'

And the old gentleman pulled her to him and kissed her hair. 'And why is Adela so quiet?' he said, but she held away from him.

'She is a wicked woman,' he whispered in her ear, so close that his voice boomed like water.

Who is wicked? she thought. Am I wicked?

Miss Christian said in a whisper, 'You must come behind the rocks and do your business.'

The girl called Sarah squatted down and watched her, but she went behind another rock where that girl could not see her. She stayed there a long time, looking out to sea.

When she came out Miss Christian was walking away holding the other girl by the hand. Sarah's mother was standing on the sand between the rocks. She sank down on

85

her knees in the sand and put her hand around Adela's wrist.

'You are Adela, are you not?' she said. She smiled but her face did not change. 'Do you know who I am?'

'You are that other girl's mother. I think you are that boy's mother too.'

'Yes,' she said. 'And I think you are a very pretty little girl.'

Adela looked at the sand.

'Tell me, Adela,' and very slightly her hand tightened so that Adela twisted her wrist to free it. 'No,' she said. 'Keep still a minute. Tell me. Where is your father?' She looked closely into Adela's eyes from under the brim of her hat.

Adela said, 'He is where he has always been.'

The mother waited a moment and then said, as if she did not care, 'And where is that?'

'He might be in the churchyard,' said Adela, almost in a whisper. 'And he might be under the sea.'

'I know, I know,' said the woman impatiently. She stayed holding Adela's wrist and looking at her as if she scarcely knew what to do with her. Then she brought her face closer still so that Adela could see the beads of sweat standing on the little hairs on her lip. She said slowly, 'And have you any *other* father than the one that drowned?'

'No,' said Adela. 'Only that one.'

'Oh well,' said the woman. She let go Adela's wrist and stood up, brushing the sand harshly from her skirt. 'Run along then,' she told Adela. 'You will be late for your food.'

There was stew on her plate and she must eat it although she was not hungry.

'Eat it while it's hot,' said Miss Christian. 'Just because we eat out of doors, Miss Harriet, there is no need to eat like a savage person. See how carefully Adela eats.'

'Is Adela a servant's child?' said the other girl.

'No, she is not,' said Harriet.

Mr Walmer said, 'We'd best go.' He made the glass fold up small. 'They'll set out in a minute.'

86

But the new children's mother stood in between them, saying, 'No, you are not to take him out there. I will not have it.'

'Well, Alfred,' he said, 'will you come?'

The boy stood between them on the sand.

'No,' said the woman, who was his mother too. 'It's absurd to take such a risk.'

'I take it. It's perfectly safe. It's dead flat calm.'

'No,' she said.

'Very well, then. I thought it would interest you,' he said to the boy. But the boy walked up the beach away from them.

Then he said, 'Adela will come with me, won't you, Adela?'

'Nonsense,' said the mother. 'You come and talk with me, Adela.' And she held out her hand so that Adela quickly reached up and held to the Proprietor's. She felt his hand close about hers, moist and slightly shaking.

'It would be madness to take her out there.'

'What's that to you?' he said. 'She's my concern.'

'You must love it here,' she said, 'with no one ever to say nay to you.'

They stood on the beach, in the hot sun, angry because of her.

'Adela's not afraid to go in a boat,' he said in his loud voice.

'No,' she said. She liked going in the boat. He would go to see the men build the lighthouse. He would take her with him.

The mother stood in the sand and said: 'It is too dangerous. What if anything happens to her? Think what your position would be then? Very well,' she said, 'but don't say I didn't warn you.'

'No,' he said. 'I would never say that.' He did not like her. 'Will you come with me in the boat?' he said, leaning down. 'Will you come to see the men building the lighthouse?'

'Yes.' She held his hand and ran to keep beside him, but she looked back at the mother walking away with her head down and her feet going deep into the sand.

'Keep your sunbonnet on,' shouted Miss Christian.

But they could do nothing. They must all do exactly as he said.

She sat in the stern between the Proprietor's knees while he spoke to the helmsman. She felt happier then.

The helmsman was Harry Sumpter.

He said, in a soft shocked voice, 'Whatever are you taking her for, sir?'

'It's safe enough today.'

'Well, that's true. It's safe enough today for an hour or so.'

It was very bright. The light off the water was in her eyes. Behind them the big island and the little island were tossed up and down, up and down. She could see the smoke from the cook's fire and the shrunken figures moving about the beach.

The Proprietor sat with his glass to his eye, moving it this way and that. 'There's the tender,' he said to Harry Sumpter. 'Will they have put out yet?'

'The tide's on the turn,' he said. 'Any minute now, sir.'

When he spoke the men at the oars nodded. She knew all their names too, but it was as if she did not. They did not speak to her nor she to them.

He moved the glass about. 'I can't see the rock yet,' he said to Harry Sumpter.

'Any moment now she'll show, sir.' One arm rested on the tiller. He held the other to shield his eyes from all the brightness in the direction of the lighter. Adela could see a still black shape.

'There it is, sir. They're lowering a boat.'

The glass swung round. Augustus said, 'Shall we give them a run for it?'

The boat went faster in the water. Their teeth were white in their dark faces. All around shaking saucers of light rose and fell. The world was in too many pieces ever to come together again. The men began to grunt at their oars. Their lips went tight and grim. The small boat had put out from the tender and they could see those figures drawing back and leaning forward.

The tide had turned now. They said that. 'Look there, sir,' said Harry Sumpter, and there in the sea was the black surface of the rock and a square black shape raised upon it.

'That's the forge,' he told Adela. 'That's the anvil. Do you see? That's the forge and that's the anvil. They're ahead,' he said to Harry Sumpter. 'They're winning. Ease off,' he shouted a minute later, 'they're there. They had less far to go,' he said. 'We'd beat them in a straight race.'

'There's not a seaman among them,' said Harry Sumpter. 'Tinners, the lot, but they've learnt to row over the summer.'

She could see the workmen landing on the rock. One after another they jumped out onto its shining surface. They stood with the water about their feet, waving, standing together in a little group right out in the middle of the sea.

They were very close in now. The men in the boat shouted back. Pickaxes were being handed up from the boat. 'That's the bellows,' he told her, and she saw the great black shape of the smith's bellows, and the men bunched together to drag it out of the boat.

They were in close now. The men had beards and bare feet. The rock rose a little out of the bare sea and the waves washed around it. Now you could see that it was not black at all, but pink and shining like the inside of a lip. A little wisp of smoke went up. The smith had his fire alight.

'Look,' the Proprietor told her, 'there's the fire.'

They saw the great bellows heave up and down and the men working it; and the blacksmith in his apron, standing with his bare legs apart. Then the clear sound of chisels cut across the slapping of water.

He could not promise that they would let her land on the rock. She might have to stay in the boat.

'They might not like it, sir,' Harry Sumpter said. 'They're a rum lot, tinners. Very superstitious.'

He jumped onto the rock first. The men in the boat put down an anchor and the men on the rock threw them a rope and they had pulled in close to the rock so that the boat heaved up and down. There was more pink rock showing now. Each wave lifted the boat up level with the surface and then it sank down again. 'Jump,' they shouted when the boat rose level. The first time he did not jump, but the second time he did, and they reached out and hauled him onto the rock.

The men on the rock stared down into the boat and she stared up at them. The Proprietor spoke to a man in a jacket. He went among the men speaking to them, then he called out, 'Yes. Hand her up to me.'

Harry Sumpter held her and the men called, 'Jump,' when the boat rose. The second time he said in her ear, 'Now,' and tossed her forward and one of the men caught her and set her down on the rock out in the middle of the sea.

All around the men continued working. They looked at her and smiled but they must not stop working because there were only four hours left before the tide rose again and covered the rock. The man in the jacket explained that to her, bending politely down.

One man squatted, holding the chisel. Another man swung the hammer over his shoulder and brought it down so that the sparks flew, and each time her eyes shut without her wanting them to. Another man crouched at the side and cleaned out the hole with a sponge on a stick. Some men worked with picks making the hole bigger and when their picks blunted or their chisels bent they took them to the forge to be mended. The blacksmith told her that. They all came to him. He was the most important man there, he said.

The man in the jacket showed her all these things and the Proprietor prodded into the holes in the rock with his stick and they talked about how many inches deep they were and about how many inches must still be chiselled away.

When the holes were made they would put iron bars down into them and wedge them in tight with pieces of wood, so strongly that the great waves coming in off the sea in the winter storms wouldn't shift them. She had seen them, she told him excitedly. Big waves, and she lifted her arms over her head as he smiled down at her, bursting against the rocks.

'They'll get up to no tricks like that here,' he said. 'There'll be nothing to burst against. They'll just pass right on through the legs of the lighthouse and waste themselves far below the light and the man tending to the light.'

They smiled at her in an odd feeling way as if her being there mattered in some way that she did not understand. She stood holding the Proprietor's hand and looking about her at the great shining shaking circle of water, thinking how far away the islands looked and how strange it was to stand here where the sea did not want them to be.

The man in the jacket said to him in a quiet voice, 'Should we give it to her, sir? Would it upset her, do you think?'

'Oh, I think not,' he said looking down at her. 'It cannot mean anything to her.'

He said, squatting down, 'This is for you. Do you know what it is?'

On his hand was a small round button, rough and green. It had been in the sea for a long time.

'Do you know what it is?' he said again. She shook her head because she did not know why he gave it to her. He said, 'It is a button. We found it there, look, wedged between those rocks. Take it,' he said kindly, moving his hand closer.

'Take it,' said the Proprietor.

'Take it and put it in your pocket,' Harry Sumpter said. 'Your aunt will tell you what it is.'

She smiled at him. He was being kind. He winked his eye at her. She put it carefully in her pocket.

They lifted her back into the boat. They must go back though the day was not nearly done. All around the big island and the little island you could see the black rocks that the water covered when it was high. They were not meant to be seen. The bright water was meant to hide them, but it went down, down until you could see all the black rocks and it seemed it would go down and down and never come back to cover them up again. She did not want

91

to go back to the picnic. She would have liked to ask if she might go home but she did not dare.

When he lifted her out of the boat he let go her hand and walked away.

Harriet wanted to ride in the cart with the other girl. Miss Christian said, 'It is Adela's turn to go in the cart.' But Adela said she would walk. Harriet's mother said, 'Everyone must go ahead. I walk slowly.'

Adela walked behind the Proprietor. When he looked back once she went up to him and took his hand. She pressed his hand to her face and began to cry. A hard ring on his finger prodded against her cheek bone.

Then he took her by the shoulders and held her a little away from him. He said, 'What is the matter?' Harriet's mother was there. She wiped Adela's face with her handkerchief. The hand went away then. Adela opened her eyes and saw that he had taken it and held it against his lips. It was very silent apart from the warm murmur of the bracken. 'No,' Harriet's mother said. 'No.'

Adela said, 'I want to go home now. I do not want to come again.' She began to run, pushing the bracken away from her face. The air was full of its broken smell. She grabbed at her hair and loosened it as she ran. The ribbons she threw away and left dangling from the bracken.

So great was the din she set up in the bracken that she only heard the cry very distantly. How could she interpret it other than as someone calling angrily after her to come back? It made her run on the faster, although now her panting ached in her ribs and her breath tasted thick and strong in her mouth. When she heard other footsteps running rapidly behind her she did not even look back, but scrambled over a low stone wall that ran along the edge of the track and crouched down behind it, trying to quiet her painful breathing. A moment later the footsteps crashed past her hiding place. Only then did she dare peer over the stones to see who it might be. What did she expect? The Proprietor himself? It was in fact one of the gardeners, which one she could not be sure as she never saw his face. Still, she supposed he had been sent in pursuit of her and it was some time before she dared come out onto the track again and make her way back to Mrs Traherne's cottage.

8

Adela had gone. In a sense she had come close to Augustus. The little sister whose death had most appalled him remained with him as a living child. For those few weeks, distracted as he was, he was free of that ghost. He could attribute to Adela, who slightly resembled her, those cruel assaults on his senses to which his imagination often betrayed him: the sense of being spied on from hidden places, stifled laughter, the heavy fall of children's feet, the sudden seizing of his hand were all sensations which Adela for a time made real for him, and so she greatly relieved him. Of course she understood none of this.

As for Amelia Pontefract, for all Adela saw of her, she might have been one of those lifesized figures in tin, painted to represent some motionless attendant. She was certainly Harriet's mother, but all functions of what she understood as motherhood were taken over by Miss Christian.

If it were impossible to imagine that young woman removing or putting on her clothes, or performing any of the bodily functions other than eating, it also was quite out of the question for Adela to imagine Mrs Pontefract waking on that same morning: just aware of the sun in the room, but unable for the instant to imagine who she herself was. It had rained in the night. The washed clarity of light playing on her open eye forced her to assemble herself, even to the point of knowing that tomorrow she must leave this place and return home.

The light made her think, lying there, of the hotel in Bognor where she and Cissy had had beds like white tents side by side. The maid had awakened them by opening the curtains. There had been a storm. They had watched the lightning through a small arched window on the landing, then, in the morning, the same brilliant light as now, with its nervous assurance that all was well. Had she been seven or eight? Eight perhaps, and Cissy six. She had been very happy in that place, but then she had expected happiness. It was strange to find again that child, with whom she shared the opposite ends of her life, alive and clamorous to start upon the day, when she in her thirty-eighth summer knew well enough the wisdom of lying where she was, crouched about her own warmth, with the day kept at bay for as long as one's duties might permit.

She had been happy here, too. But immediately she thought the word she moved restlessly in the bed and would not accept happiness but cast about for some other term: well-being or good health. In that first letter to her sister from the island she had written:

> . . . I am able to tell you the one thing you are most anxious to hear, that I am recovered. How shall I describe it to you? It is as if I had been trepanned in sleep and some beneficial oil poured into my poor fretful brain so that when I woke all worked smoothly – no grating, no jangling, no pain. All is as it once was and with that bygone health and vigour restored. Why, I walk again and ride each day! It is this place that has restored me.

Sea air had always suited her. And why not call it happiness? When it was of so short and clear a duration, it could be in no way suspect: need not be thought of as a loan on stern interest to be repaid in due course with all the rigour of number. She sat up then, and very slowly, as a child will scrape minute portions onto the edge of her spoon, began upon her day.

'Pontefract,' she called softly. 'Pontefract,' and tapped on the dividing door so gently that it seemed she wished to prove that he slept rather than to rouse him. No answer. She opened the door only enough to know that the room stood empty of all but the clean dry smell he gave to places.

He had gone down and left her sleeping.

She dressed. Watching in a glass she loosened her plaits, then brushed, gathered, twisted and deftly pinned her hair. She saw her eyes, dark and round, stare steadily with the look of slight surprise she turned upon the world. The strange configuration of blue veins in the soft skin just beneath them that passed from generation to generation in her family was the only mark of beauty she would allow herself. Her mouth was large. Staring solemnly in the glass Amelia never saw or understood the charm of its mobility. In the same way a certain quick lift and turn of the chin, always the prelude to the gentle force of her attention, was quite unknown to her.

When all was done she sat still for a moment, took little steps in the passage, dragged her hand on the stair rail. So by moving very slowly she kept time in command. She would not let it pass. The day would be warm. The doors at either end of the hall were flung open. Sunlight fell at an angle. Harriet ran shouting from the terrace. Sarah ran after her, the troop of dogs yapping at their heels. It was the last day. It was that which gave everything its slow and conscious quality.

Mr Walmer stood in the hall with his knuckles raised to the barometer and the stiff dachshund caught under his arm. He did not see her.

'Good morning,' she said, but did not watch him turn.

'Good morning.' He walked behind her. The dogs knew to wait by the door. The children sat stiffly at the table.

In that first letter she had written to her sister:

'And Mr Walmer?' you will ask me when I see you, 'What of him?' Perhaps I shall have forgotten what of Mr Walmer by then, so I shall describe to you now what little I am permitted to see. I do not know that we should like him, Cissy, left to our own judgements in these matters. Is he not altogether too stiff and too important in his own eyes? I wish he might laugh more. It is such a serious business, all this enjoyment we are having. Yet Pontefract swears by him – declares him a sound fellow, and vastly knowledgeable – but not of our Knowledge, Cissy.

'Good morning,' she said to her friend Euphemia Walmer.

'Good morning, my dear,' to Pontefract, laying her cheek briefly on the warm crown of his head.

'Ah, ah,' he said, smoothing the white napkin tucked into the divide of his waistcoat. Through the top of his head she could hear him crunching his toast.

The sun was very bright in the room. She straightened her fork. Very slowly she slid her napkin from its ring and spread it across her knees.

'Did you sleep well?' she asked Euphemia, when she had sipped her tea. She had no appetite.

'No, I did not,' she said, and then called out as her brother-in-law came in from the hall, 'I was attacked, Augustus, by a simply enormous moth.'

'I hope you fought back bravely,' said Pontefract, and dabbed demurely with his napkin at the corners of his mouth.

His wife arched her lip and laughed when he said that. Mr Walmer, standing in the doorway with his head leaning against the door post, laughed too. Then time endured a soft explosion. She felt it inside her. And if other such moments were to occur might not the day expand rather than diminish, and there be no fear in its passing?

The boat was ordered on the Abbey beach for noon. From the breakfast table his deep voice could be heard discussing with the boatman. He was to go out to the rock to see the work commenced that summer on the lighthouse.

Our pleasures must be fitted around that, she would write to Cissy. *Even Mr Walmer must wait upon the tides, not they on him. For compensation we are allowed to take a picnic to a nearby rock.*

'Why must he hurry a man so?' said Pontefract, through the open door between their rooms. 'It seems no time since I ate breakfast.' They prepared themselves to go in the boat.

She tied a scarf over her bonnet and said to her

reflection, 'The rock is only uncovered an hour or so. He cannot waste the time.'

'He seems to rush about so.'

'Well,' she said, looking about, for she could hear by his voice that he had come to the door, 'it is only a little time now and we shall be at home.'

She saw him then detachedly, could have found the words to describe him. He was a neatly contrived man. To say he was small was true, but would in some way mislead. There was precision in his making. Everything about him had a fineness. His fingers were long and delicately shaped. He stood very straight. His features too were fine, his eyes direct, his nose narrow, the ridges and hollows of his cheeks discernible under tight ruddy skin. His hair was pale and straight and lay close to his skull. He seemed designed like certain terriers to slip through the world about some authoritative but obscure purpose. Perhaps his wealth confused people's understanding of how they felt about him. But small women in particular thought him handsome. Everyone loved him for his charm. He was courteous to everyone, thanked everyone, remembered everyone's name. To her knowledge life had never thrown up at him a moment when he had been at a loss for what to do or what to say. No doubt had ever assailed him about any past action of his. Only with dogs and young children did he show any sentimentality or need for affection.

'Tomorrow will be bad enough,' he was saying a little plaintively. 'Could we not be left in peace on dry land today?'

'You do not want to come?' She watched her mouth in the glass speaking the words.

'I do not like the water.'

'But it is never rough between the islands,' she said, turning quickly to him. 'We are not to go far. Only Mr Walmer means to go to the rock.'

'The waves seem devilish high in those small boats; I do not care for it.'

'Tell him, then.'

'No, no, no. Poor fellow, he is so anxious to entertain us all.'

'I am entertained.' She sat sideways on the dressing table chair. He stood holding the open door by its handle.

'Yes, yes. I can see.'

'You have not enjoyed it here.' She spoke out of fear for the future, not for the past weeks: concern for herself and not for him; feeling the certainty, like a failure in the blood, that when they were asked again he would find a reason not to go. The extent to which she was unable to act outside his will occurred bleakly to her. He was saying, 'Come, we will delay them. There is some hurry about the tide.'

The trap was drawn up to the door. They waited in the hall and listened to the pony's desultory stamping and to the Proprietor giving orders. Miss Christian could be seen on a chair on the terrace dragging the Island Child's hair tightly behind her passive unhappy face. Euphemia's boy stood quite still in the doorway leaning on his uncle's fowling piece and solemnly watching the child's hair being plaited. His sister and Harriet sat side by side on the top step. Now it was all arranged. Pontefract was to go in the trap with little Sarah Walmer and Harriet, who would not be separated from her. All about their feet were heaped the day's necessities, a shrimping net, the basket of specimen jars, her watercolour box and folding stool, the guns and the game bags.

All this, she wrote in her mind to Cissy, *he must supervise.*

Between them they mocked whatever troubled them.

What an opportunity for Mr Walmer to point with his stick where each separate item must go and then to reach into the cart and rearrange all himself.

'Have you everything you need? Have you your scarf?' she called to Pontefract when it was too late, when the pony had already lowered its head and allowed itself to be led forward. 'You are going in the boat. You know it can be cold in that boat.'

'Yes,' he said in a brave voice. 'Yes.' He clung to the side

99

of the trap as if he had already been cast adrift.

But the rugs had been forgotten. At the last, a servant girl ran out of the house with a pile of them folded across her arms and these too were packed away. The pony clattered across the courtyard. The trap ground past the open door.

We wave, she told Cissy. We shout goodbye as if they set out for the ends of the earth. 'Shore party advance,' calls Mr W. and we raise parasols and fall in obediently enough. Mrs W. and I. Miss C. and her remaining charge. Mr W. very martial with his gun on his shoulder and his dog and his nephew to heel. And Cissy, dear, I ask you would it not be a more sensible way to eat a meal to spread a cloth upon a table and sit down to it upon a chair?

But once outside she was beguiled by the day. She would put aside her letter until tonight and see it all as she was intended to. Side by side she and Euphemia Walmer walked in their slow skirts down the long flight of steps, past the toiling gardeners, through the open gate in the garden wall. Because it was obligatory to talk, they talked. Amelia asked of the new vicar who had arrived in their mutual parish while she was away. Euphemia allowed him to be a spiritual man but thought him boorish. He had preached at too great a length the Sunday before their departure. Could not Pontefract remonstrate with him on their return? She doubted her husband would break him of the habit but she would ask.

And what to talk of now?

But there was no need. As they set out along the sandy path through high bracken towards the dunes, the pony trap appeared travelling smartly along their crest. Augustus hoisted his gun in salute. The groom raised his whip. Pontefract and the little girls could be seen to be waving.

'It is warm,' said Euphemia. 'I hope he will not be too long at the lighthouse.' And she poked at a cloud of gnats with her parasol.

As they walked on they could see the pony cart drawn above the beach and the groom helping Pontefract down, and then lifting out the little girls. The climb up towards them took attention and again removed the need to talk, for their feet slid backwards in the yielding sand. By the time they reached the crest and stood ankle deep among the stiff grasses the pony cart had turned back to the Abbey to fetch the cook. She watched it go and felt, with a catch in her breathing, the day progress and diminish.

'You have brought your sketching things, I trust?' said Euphemia, who walked beside her now down the steep incline of sand.

'Oh, yes,' she said. 'I am never without them.' The day was brilliant. She lifted the glittering sand on the toe of her boot. All around them the sea splintered into light. 'It is impossible. I shall never achieve it,' she told them all, laughing. 'I need heavy grey days where everything keeps still. On a day like this I am beside myself,' and taking Pontefract's arm she slipped cautiously down the dunes and walked towards the waiting boats.

The boatmen were splashing to and fro in the water, loading the equipment into one boat and carrying the little girls aboard the other. There they sat, quite still in their sunbonnets under the flapping awning, awed at setting out to sea. The Proprietor directed it all. The ladies were to go in one boat, the gentlemen in the other. But no. He would accompany the children, and the Pontefracts and Mrs Walmer would go together in the other boat. What matter: in either case Euphemia Walmer was her lot and so she might sit with Pontefract and be of some comfort to him.

Mr Walmer helped her up the little wooden plank into the boat. She felt the hard unvarying pressure of his hand, and again when they landed, but he said nothing to her. And perhaps would not. Though in the shifting formation of such days there come a few moments when you walk beside each person in turn and find something to say. The pattern breaks and reforms. She would find time to thank him. She might wait. Portions of the day were left. Harriet

101

and Sarah went arm in arm down the beach. One boat went back for Cook. The other waited to take Mr Walmer on to the lighthouse.

She would sit in the shade of this rock and reduce it all to harmless words:

And all is taken up with his establishing his right over this new rock in the sea, and it calls upon all his powers of resource to assemble us behind a cluster of rocks where there is shelter from the wind. For he must impress on us all that he owns the winds here and understands, quite as well as the boatmen, which way they blow.

The voice in which she wrote to Cissy was that of good sense: the best of her voices.

She watched the boatmen carry four oars across the beach, and here, he directed them, prodding the white sand with his stick, and here, and here, and here. And then, over the top, the awning. How cheerful the men seemed, and he so serious. Already one of the boats sped back to collect the cook, while the barefooted boatmen continued to wade back and forth from the other, carrying the strange equipment: the guns, the boxes, the nets, the basket of specimen jars, the folding stool.

'But never mind those,' shouts Mr W. For an awning must be erected so that the ladies might be sure of the shelter from the sun. For we might think the shade of our rock sufficient, but it will move. It appears he cannot order it to stop. What disillusionment, Cissy! And poor me come to think he must own the sun too.

So she defended herself with her letter.

And now, Cissy, there is the problem of the siting of Cook's fire. It should be here, so that the wind blows the smoke away from the ladies clustered under the awning, says Euphemia, who is quite as accustomed to having her own way as he is. But the wind will alter at noon, says her brother-in-law (who, you may remember, owns the winds). 'Does not the wind change at noon?' he calls to the boatman. 'Yezz, zurr,' says he, nodding his great bearded head slowly as if every such statement needed the gravest consideration. Yes. Very often the wind changed at noon. At least you could never be sure that it would not. So that decides it. The fire will be here and not there, and poor Euphemia must make the best of it and retreat to her throne beneath the awning.

Oh, but she went too far. She would make amends: *For in his way he is an admirable man. We should not mock, Cissy, we should feel some compassion. For he has had a sad time of it. Mother and father dead when he was still a boy. His elder brother fallen from his horse when only nine years old. All this I have had from Euphemia. Her husband, the younger brother, as you may know, dead of the cholera in India some years ago. And, cruellest of all, his sister Fanny dead at fifteen, the result I am told of overtaxing her strength walking with him. The cause she says of his bitter grief and his coming here, and my not meeting him before.*

Enough, enough. Euphemia Walmer by a gathering of her skirt indicated that she was willing to share her rock. What choice was there but to sit beside her, watching the shadow of the awning dart on the sand? The boatmen moved about the highwater line collecting pale driftwood into the crooks of their arms while Euphemia said, 'He is intolerable, always has been, but coming here has made him more so.' What could she say? and so spoke silently to Cissy:

And now he climbs upon a rock a few yards away and now shouts 'Where is my glass, Alfred? I must have left it in the boat. Look in the boat, boy. Here, boy.' And poor Alfred like the dog goes this way and that, obedient to his master. A very well-trained obedient boy. And it is sad to see in his worship of his uncle how he must miss his father.

'Here she comes,' Augustus cried, and following the direction of his glass they could see the boat carrying the cook come rapidly in to land.

Two of the men carried her ashore and she, good soul, laughed and waved and Pontefract, who had his fowling piece already in his hand, raised it above his head and shouted, 'Three cheers for Mrs Watson.' Everyone cheered then.

His wife called across the sand to him, 'Would you find my sketching box?' For by now the pile on the sand was increasing every minute with hampers and boxes as Cook's equipment was unloaded. The alacrity with which he laid down his gun and did what she asked still had the power to touch her. 'And my stool,' she called after him.

When he returned with these she slid her hand under his arm and asked gently how he felt, but did not entirely listen to his answer. For at that moment Euphemia whispered in her ear, 'And I should very much like to know where that child came from.' She stared intently at the Island Child, who sat perched on a rock at the very edge of the awning's shadow.

'But were you not told?' said Amelia, and would have recounted the Island Child's story, when the significance of the remark struck suddenly so that she said, 'Oh, no,' and looked about her quickly under the impression that she had cried out.

But the child did not turn. On the next rock Miss Christian absorbedly counted her cowrie shells one by one from the lap of her skirt into her little bag.

Pontefract said quietly, 'Miss Christian's bride-price increases every day. Who can afford to take her off our hands?' So that Amelia must cover her mouth with her hand and look away.

He rose then, out of contrition perhaps, and stooped over Miss Christian, with his long hands turning slowly about each other behind his back.

'No, no,' he was saying, 'don't think of rising. You will spill your pretty shells.'

He lowered himself onto a rock and Miss Christian, with a graceless crablike movement, transferred herself to one beside him.

'What do you mean?' Amelia whispered to Euphemia.

'You do not see the likeness?'

'To whom?'

'To Fanny.'

'I only saw her once. Oh, years ago. She came to our wedding.'

'Well, it is very slight. Or probably it is a coincidence.'

'But surely he would not . . .'

She shrugged.

'Not, I mean, have her in the house if it were so.'

'Perhaps not.'

'I will not believe it.' And would not. Would put the whole thought from her mind. But her eye was drawn irresistibly to the little group at the shadow's edge.

'Now, tell me, Miss Christian,' Pontefract was saying, 'which of your charges has been the most virtuous today?' Her habitual brightness intensified as she spoke to him.

'I should like to be able to tell you Miss Harriet, sir, but she is turned quite the hoyden since her new friends arrived, as witness the hem of her dress. Miss Sarah's, too. And Master Alfred is already too much the young gentleman entirely to heed *me*. Adela is very quiet today. I think the palm must go to Adela – by default,' she added.

'And why is Adela so quiet?' Pontefract said, extending his long red hand to the child, who looked, indeed pale and unhappy.

'She is an only child,' said Miss Christian, as if by adopting a tone of confidentiality she cleared herself of any damage done to Adela's feelings, without in the least attempting to speak so that the child might not hear. 'I think she has little idea how to play with other children.'

He had the child pressed close now. He kneaded her thin arm. He put his lips to her hair but she would not yield to him. She stood at his side rigid with misery.

'You come from a large family yourself, Miss Christian?' he was saying over the child's head.

The governess leant towards him, brightening further, 'As it happens, I too am an only child. But wisely brought up by my mother who saw that I was constantly in the company of others, and would not permit me to withdraw into myself. Some,' she said, laying her finger along her round red cheek, 'might call it sulking.'

'Your mother is from Derbyshire, is she not?' If the child had wounded him, he was restored. He could still comfort himself with the power of his own charm.

Like some eager dog she was after his stick. 'My mother's people come from Westerby. Do you know Westerby Lodge, sir?'

Well, he did not, his wife suspected, but long ago had learnt a deferential movement of the head that implied he did or at least conceded that he should. It quite sufficed.

'She was a Miss Westerby,' and with this announcement all brightness faded and her little face altered quite with dignity and sorrow at the quirk of fortune that had brought her here.

'Indeed she was, my dear, indeed she was,' said Pontefract, patting her on the knee.

His wife watched him. Even as he spoke he turned his thin face towards her and said as surely as in words, 'Was it wise of us, my dear, to take on anything so grand as a Westerby down on its luck?'

And she must smile at him and nod her head and know that they were in perfect agreement at least about Miss Christian. 'No', she said to Euphemia, 'I would not believe such a thing against Mr Walmer.'

The fire was well alight. Cook's pot hung on a tripod over it. Through the area of disturbance above the flames, they watched her sturdy form: her sleeves pinned up, a spoon at her lips. It was hot enough. They might eat. The two little girls had returned. Miss Christian and Euphemia shepherded them all behind the rocks, but Amelia had been schooled in restraint and might wait. They gathered again under the awning. The food was served. They ate cautiously from plates. He was restless, seeming neither to sit nor eat, but going busily to supervise the fire or stand on the rock with the glass to his eye.

The gulls, drawn by the smell of food, drifted on the currents overhead, crying like cats but more relentlessly.

How the sun burned through their wings. The day consumed. The tide had turned. He would be gone now to inspect the lighthouse.

'Will you come with me?' she heard Augustus say indifferently to Alfred. He looked through his glass and did not lower it from his eye or turn around. She saw the boy move awkwardly, unsure whether he had been spoken to or not, waiting to be asked again, frowning up at his uncle in the bright sun.

'Can you see them?' he said, so eagerly it hurt the heart. Pontefract too had wanted a son.

'They're ready on the beach. Are you coming?' he said, crushing the eyeglass down and turning his bright demanding stare onto the boy. 'We'd best go if we are going.'

Beside her Euphemia said sharply, 'No, it is absurd to take such a risk.'

She did not wish to hear them quarrel. She did not wish the day spoilt. Euphemia had risen from her rock and was saying so that everyone could hear: 'No.'

'Very well, then. I thought it would interest you,' he said to Alfred, who flushed harshly and turned and walked away.

The little girl watched with a child's steadily unguarded stare.

'Adela will come with me. Won't you, Adela?' and he shot out his hand to her. How trustingly she took it. But there was nothing there. Nothing. Euphemia had no right even to suggest.

'Not out to the rock,' said Euphemia Walmer. 'You must love it here,' she was saying, 'with no one to say nay to you ever. It would be madness to take her out there.'

He said in his loud voice, 'Adela's not afraid of going in a boat, are you, Adela?'

Amelia would not watch but stood up and reached for her box and her stool. For some men are built by their anger and others you can see it disintegrates. She had seen something full and defenceless in his lips when most he

seemed to domineer. It had upset her. She could not see
him so clearly as she had. The voice of good sense had
deserted her. When she looked back Euphemia stood her
ground on the beach between her brother-in-law and the
sea and was saying, without hiding the anger in her voice,
'It is madness. What if something happens to her. Think
what your position would be then.'

'It's dead flat calm,' he said, glaring at the sea with
hatred inspired by this woman who tried to thwart him.

'As you wish,' she said, 'but don't say I didn't warn you.'

'No,' he said, 'I would never say that.'

He strode now angrily to the boat with the child holding
his hand, having to run in the trampled sand to keep up
with him.

The discomfort of the quarrel had scattered them all.
Pontefract had shouldered his gun and set out across the
island. Harriet and Sarah, arm in arm, dwindled down
the bright beach, to hunt again for shells. The boy had
gone off somewhere by himself. Euphemia and Miss
Christian had withdrawn in whispers under the awning.
She would be gone beyond the range of what they said. She
set out towards a path worn into the grasses at the edge of
the beach and followed it up onto a narrow turf isthmus
between the two rocky ends of the island.

She walked rapidly, for some unpleasant thing had
intruded on the day as a small cloud can darken and
deaden an entire landscape between one cleaning of the
brush and the next. Yet nothing had changed in the day
itself. On every side was the bright agitation of the sea.
The black reef where the lighthouse would stand was just
visible above the falling tide. There was the boat moving
rapidly towards it. She could make out the boatmen's figures and Mr Walmer, erect with his projecting glass, and
the child's head just visible.

She was standing by a pile of rocks, shaggy with pale
green lichen and bent all in one direction, as if they had
once been pliant to the wind. Beyond them the land fell
away again to the shore. She set down her box and her

stool at their base; but still was too unsettled to begin.

A little way below her a pool had been left between the rocks by the sinking tide. She climbed carefully down to it. Once there, being quite alone, she knelt and stared profoundly into the miniature concave landscape made up of pebbles and weeds, like some island in reverse, impressed below the water.

For it was not the present distaste that threatened. Rather it set a definition on the morning's pleasure she could not accept. 'What am I doing?' she said inwardly, 'what has become of me?' but continued where she was, staring fixedly into the pool as if some tiny self might appear walking between the wavering trees and provide an answer. Then, as if she feared that answer, she reached down her hand into the warm water and stirred it all about. It became alive with tiny darting fish that had lain still and invisible among the weed. She withdrew her hand suddenly and, shaking the water from it, rose to her feet and climbed briskly back to the rocks. There, setting up her stool and lifting the lid of her box, she resolutely faced the open sea.

It flickered, a great expanse, in all directions until it touched on the motionless sky. Nothing was visible except the black reef and now a plume of white smoke above it. The forge was alight. They must have arrived. She turned abruptly back to face the island and began to draw things grown familiar to her: a white beach, curving dunes, a row of cottages, gorse, the tormented rocks for a foreground. So had she every day from different vantage points recorded. She was meticulous in her work. She ceased to look about her, but only down at her drawing. Once or twice shots rang out near at hand and sent the sea birds racketing up into the air. She felt time pass by a stiffening between the shoulders. She dipped her brush into the metal water bottle and watched with a mixture of satisfaction and impatience the painting grow more and more to resemble other paintings she had made. When she looked up again the island floated in a haze of sunlight, quite still in the sea's activity. How easily it had evaded her. She laid her open book on the grass and weighted it with a stone so that it might dry.

When she turned back there was no sign of the boat. He might be back. She stooped to pack up the contents of her box and climbed down to the encampment. Cook had already left. The boy stood by the water throwing stones. The rest sat in the trance-like attitudes of people who have finished with a place and await removal. The boat could be seen returning. She began to walk quickly across the sand until she might reach out and touch her husband's shoulder and from habit incline her head towards his so far as her bonnet would permit.

'What view did you choose?' asked Euphemia. 'I could not see you.'

'You know I could not go far,' said Amelia, opening the clasps of her box.

'Ah,' said her friend with apparent kindness, 'may we see?'

'Of course.' She fumbled as she undid the tapes of her book. 'It was impossible to capture.'

'It is delightful,' said Euphemia with her particular deadening emphasis.

Pontefract said, 'I cannot help myself. I think of the terrors of that crossing.'

'It is calmer returning,' said Augustus, who paced about, speaking from behind people's backs.

'And shorter,' said Amelia. 'Returning is such a rapid affair compared to going anywhere.' But her own voice struck a chill inside her.

'None of that can be true,' said Pontefract forlornly.

Certainly it seemed not to take a fraction of the time to dismantle the day that had been needed to set it up. The encampment was soon undone, the pile of possessions transferred back to the boats. They climbed in. The men pushed off. The island was deserted.

When they had climbed the beach on the Gweal, the little girls were lifted back into the cart. Pontefract, as if to celebrate the existence of dry land, declared he would

110

walk and, taking Euphemia's arm, set off along the path to the Abbey. Miss Christian followed a few deferential paces behind. Then came Mr Walmer, with the Island Child clinging to his hand. The boy strode morosely ahead of them all, while Amelia, with as little taste for company as he, followed in the rear. Slowly she pushed her way between the fronds of bracken that overhung the path, allowing the space between herself and the others to increase. It seemed that the whole glittering passage of the water still crept at the back of her eye. Her sudden transference, merely by climbing up through the grasses from that bright mineral world to this expanse of quiet green – warm and sheltered, as if it were held in the palm of a gigantic kindly hand – left her sleepy and stupid. She saw when she looked up that Mr Walmer stood in the path and must wait for her, although he seemed not to watch her approach. She had wanted to speak with him and now could not avoid doing so.

He stood back, holding the child to the edge of the path so that she might brush past them and said, as she did, 'Were you pleased with your sketching?'

She must answer, and forced out words she did not greatly care for. 'I am defeated. I cannot capture your island.'

'Is it not enough to have captivated it?'

Her scarf rattled against her ear. She would not interpret the tone of these words but said, without looking behind her, 'Did you succeed in landing on the rock?' and heard her voice sound just as she would not have had it do, as if it said something else compliant and kind.

'Yes.'

'And the child?'

'Yes.'

How he pressed upon her, walking noisily behind. At any moment it seemed she might feel the prod of his stick between the shoulder blades, driving her forwards.

Pauses occurred between their words. She did not care to feel clumsy. On other days they had spoken freely enough.

'Did she enjoy it?'

'I believe so. Did you enjoy yourself?' he asked the child, who burst suddenly into tears.

111

She turned then and saw him go down on one knee. 'Why, what is this?' he said to the child, who was incapable of answering.

'Gratitude?' she suggested. For gratitude was on her mind, and, fumbling in her cuff, she produced a handkerchief and reached it out instinctively to do away with the intrusive tears. Then in confusion felt both the child's tears and his mouth on her hand and drew it swiftly away, saying 'Oh, no,' as if threatened. For she had wanted nothing of that, which must bring everything to an end.

The child, sensing their distraction, broke away then and began running from them through the bracken. He rose abruptly and, walking a few paces ahead, waited on the path by the gate post for her to join him. She stood still, watching the child's raised arm force a way through the fronds of bracken that reached across the path.

It was a rare instance of a single moment defining itself between the one confused impulsive action and its consequence.

But in fact the burden of speaking was taken from them. At that very moment a sound intervened at once too unfamiliar to name and too appalling to ignore. Mrs Pontefract was aware of the alarmed clatter of flight and saw the birds lift and wheel off the surface of the lake. She saw Augustus run rapidly through the gates towards the house before she would accept that what she had heard was a single human scream issued from somewhere inside the garden.

She was left all alone. The sense of her own contained life which had been so powerfully with her throughout the day was now almost painfully intense. Her skin seemed drawn tight into it. Everything, the warmth of the sun, the nodding bracken, the steady unbroken hum of insects, the confused wheeling of the birds, the dwindling echo of that strange cry continuing inside her ear, all seemed to pertain directly to her, and she stayed quite still, hardly aware that she breathed, waiting for the mystery to reveal itself.

When she heard the sound of footsteps running rapidly

on the far side of the garden wall she supposed it to be Augustus returning. Hearing the steps blunder and stumble in their reckless haste she imagined there would be brought to bear on her a force which would somehow free her of the necessity for thought.

But it was one of the workmen who broke through the gate and ran so recklessly towards her that she was forced to step back into the bracken to avoid collision with him. His panting was louder than his clumsy running. His eyes when he looked at her were ringed with terror. He blundered on past her in the direction of the village. No one came in pursuit of him. For a moment she watched his violent progress, then she stepped back onto the path. Gathering her skirt in both hands violently she shook the bracken from it before she walked through the gates into the Abbey garden.

The rest of the picnic party had been some way ahead and had some time before entered the garden and begun to climb the steps towards the house, the boy leading the way two steps at a time. He was followed sedately by his mother and Pontefract. Meanwhile the pony cart containing Harriet and Sarah had drawn up at the front door on the far side of the house.

Miss Christian, toiling up the steps at the rear of the party, heard its distant clatter and hastened on, fearful that the girls might arrive before she did and escape her altogether.

She was therefore already flustered when the unearthly scream floated up the blasted slope. It was too formal a sound to be termed a scream, rather it seemed a single phrase from some ancient lament held and drawn out intolerably. The sound was quite devoid of age or sex. Her first instinct was to gather up her skirts and run upwards, calling in a faint but dramatic voice, 'Miss Harriet, oh, Miss Harriet.' All in an instant a number of nameless threats against the child seemed realized and she, charged with excitement, became the child's only true protector.

In the next instant she saw Harriet and Sarah appear

113

hand in hand at the top of the steps, staring apprehensively, not at her, but beyond the boy who now bounded down again.

She turned in time to see the figure of a man break from the group of gardeners working in the ruins and run distractedly away, throwing aside some tool which could be heard to fall with a clatter. Fragments of his cry still echoed off the hillside and had startled a flock of birds who flapped overhead, adding their own strange yells.

Then, after a moment's silence, the voices of the remaining men could be heard calling out. It was apparent that they had discovered something among the ruins and there could be little doubt as to what.

Miss Christian's first concern was towards the children who, still hand in hand, were running down the steps past their respective parents towards her. She barred their way, catching successfully at Harriet's plump arm and Sarah's thin one, with an almost vicious desire to protect.

'What is it?' said Harriet, in her gruff peremptory voice. 'I want to see.'

'Nothing of any interest,' said Miss Christian with a patent dishonesty. The whole hillside still echoed with irresistible adult agitation. One of the younger gardeners could be seen bounding up the hillside towards the house, but at that moment the Proprietor appeared through the garden gate and at a shout he began hurrying down again. The men could be seen to point, the troop of dogs raced past yapping frantically.

Then, with total inconsistency, induced maybe by all this noise and confusion, Miss Christian, never releasing her fierce and painful hold on the children's arms, began to propel them towards the very thing she had a moment before forbidden them absolutely to see.

And after all, what was it?

A long yellow bone laid out on the freshly turned black earth which glittered with particles of silica. Bones are only tolerable when they are bleached. The earth adhering to it here and there was horridly suggestive of decay. The children shuddered at the sight of it but scarcely knew

114

why. Only Alfred was able to stare at it without flinching.

Harriet said, 'It's a person's, isn't it?'

'Hush,' said Miss Christian, and began to cry painful furtive sobs that seemed to have been with her all along and to have found in this commotion a suitable moment for release. Indeed, they drew no attention to her. In reaching for her handkerchief she forgetfully let go of Harriet and Sarah, who pressed forward among the legs of the men and more closely regarded the bone and the broken earth which was perhaps more frightening than the bone itself in the promise of what it still held.

Most disturbing of all was the subdued wretchedness of the gardeners. They stood fingering the edges of their hats in front of their bodies, making no sound other than the faint shiftings of their discomfiture.

The Proprietor's voice was loud and angry but shaken too. 'Well, cover it up then. I'll send for Mr Peters to do whatever's necessary. For God's sake, what has got into you? Cover it up then and be off with you.'

He turned and strode furiously past them all, including Amelia, who had come slowly through the Abbey arches and stood watching the scene from the foot of the steps. He passed her without a word, so changed in those moments that he turned upon her the baleful glare of some ghost who cannot forgive the living and the unobtainable.

9

Augustus had used the now abandoned diary to record the small vexations which can plague a lonely man, unable to expose them to another's sympathy or humour, or proportioning indifference. Never did he make a similar use of his correspondence with Mrs Pontefract, although it was after her departure that he first felt the full weight of his isolation. That autumn was particularly sad for him. The end of Euphemia's visit, which normally he would have greeted with relief, he dreaded as a final severance with the summer's pleasure. When she and her children left he found the house strangely altered. Voices, doors slamming, the din of the staircase, gave way to the incessant aimless rattle of the dogs' claws about the bare hall. Every movement he himself made seemed to set up an exaggerated sound which would cause him to question the action he had embarked upon. The wind in the islands is seldom silent. Indoors and out it is heard like the traffic in towns, rather as a stifler of sound than a sound in itself. Now, even on nights when it had no voice, he was aware of its penetration of his house, its suggestion of footfalls and doors being tried.

By day he was disturbed by the strange variety of animal and human cries with which the gulls filled the air. So assiduously had he shown her about the island that there was almost no part of it he could visit without being reminded of her. But these memories were haphazard and fugitive. He could not control them. He could not, even in the act of reading her letters, recall her face clearly or the sound of her voice.

His constant straining to do so, combined with an unaccustomed depression of the spirits, left him particularly susceptible to his private images of death: the gardeners running on the gravel path, holding by its arms the wicker chair in which the body slumped, hair and hat awry, the groom coming from behind the dark hedge with the boy in his arms and the riding boots dangling stiffly as he ran, while somewhere out of sight the horse was heard being led back to the stable. These unwanted objects, excluded carefully from his mind for years, troubled him constantly and added to his distress.

None of this is apparent in the tone of his letters. In the April of 1845 he wrote:

My dear Mrs Pontefract,

On Wednesday last the new church was finally consecrated, but look as I might among the press, I caught no sight of you, whose interest has been so material in the planning of it. [She was, of course, at her home on the mainland, but the charming conceit that he might at any moment catch sight of her in that remote spot persists in his letters.] *I have since been, one might say, In Bishop. Endeavouring to play host to that most crustaceous of his species. His retinue stayed partly here and partly with Wills and taxed somewhat the limits of our cramped hospitality; his Grace showing no marked eagerness to leave as the cholera, they say, has appeared in Exeter.*

All I think went well. Their arrival in the islands caused no little sensation. Old Mrs Penwith, on seeing them rowed ashore with their white canonicals fluttering in the breeze, declared they put her in mind of a band of angels – you would have thought an acceptable body to bless my poor church on St Warna's. Yet this morning, returning with Wills from a visit to the shipyard, we passed poor John Trevethick, attended by two or three of his neighbours, carrying on his shoulder the coffin of his infant son. The sight afflicted me sorely. We stood bareheaded to allow them to pass and did not intrude upon

117

their sorrow, but later I sent Wills to enquire and found
that no power on earth could have persuaded Trevethick
to consign his poor scrap of humanity to any but the old
burial ground. So much for the sanctifying powers of a
mere bishop and a band of angels.

Tell Miss Christian, who I am sure is more enlightened
in these matters, that the skeleton (which I shall always
think of as 'hers') was finally interred with all episcopal
pomp in the new churchyard. There may it rest. I am
filled with compunction as I send you this funereal letter,
but it has eased my mind to write it. Will you accept it
then as a token – albeit a selfish one – of my esteem for our
friendship?

Yours sincerely
Augustus Walmer

Even this 'funereal' letter, for which he apologized, obscured several practical worries. Since the moment of its discovery, two years previously, the skeleton had continued to cause him endless trouble. At the time he had been severely shaken to find that such a thing could lurk within the sacred precinct of his garden, waiting its chosen moment to leer out at him. Once he had recovered from the shock, he could see that it was scarcely surprising for an area which had been the floor of an ancient Abbey to yield bones. He imagined them as ancient as the crumbling arches, with no trace of remembered life clinging to them. Nevertheless, he sent a message to Peters that very evening by his boatman, informing him of the discovery. Then, considering the hysteria produced in Miss Christian, he decided to leave the matter for another twenty-four hours, arranging for the bones to be decently covered over – a task which he had to perform himself in the end. When all was done, he had Harriet's awning dismantled and fixed around the spot, so that even the sight of disturbed earth should not cast any shadow over the Pontefracts' departure.

By the time that Peters kept his appointment on the following day rumours were already rife that Augustus did

118

not mean to reinter the desecrated bones at all, but rather to keep them for his own nameless practices. The chaplain deemed it necessary that he should be seen to bury the bones with all due ceremony forthwith. He suggested a public, rather grand affair. But here Augustus took one of his perversely stubborn stands. He considered the old graveyard grossly overcrowded. The superstition surrounding this one corpse disgusted him, all the more when he recollected the number of unmarked graves that had been disturbed when the trench was dug for the victims of the *Severn*. He took it into his head that these remains – the only ones other than his own over which he could be sure of having any say – should be the first to be buried in the yard of his new church. He was pleased with the plan. It would free others of the onus of burying their dead in solitude, though it surprised him that they should be reluctant to. Did they suppose the dead to commune with one another in the night? He thought of the family vault at Longridge, stirred by whispered recriminations. He would never be trapped among them. His own burial plot he had already selected, in that corner of the churchyard overlooking the Gweal. The monk at least could be trusted to keep him silent company.

But, though the burial ground was marked out in the open field behind the church, it could not be consecrated until the building was complete and the bishop made his visitation. In the end, until the bishop could complete the job properly, the wretched bones, in a handsome coffin provided at Augustus' expense, were laid to partial rest in the new ground; Peters, Augustus and the faithful Wills being the only attendants. The brief ceremony was held early and attracted little attention, but the whole affair continued to be discussed endlessly, much to Augustus' detriment. He found himself oddly upset at one tale that the bones were not those of a monk at all, but of the body of a young man washed up on the island during the late wars and taken to the base of the arches as to a spot where the last vestiges of holiness might linger. Undoubtedly, from the moment that it was found he never had the same purity of pleasure from his garden. He continued resolutely with his plans to expand it, but always with the fear of some further discovery that death had possessed it before he did.

Nothing of this you would have guessed from his outward appearance. He had many visitors during those years. Word of his achievements had spread on the mainland and a steady stream of philanthropists, economists and progressive landowners came to see at first hand the miracle he was reputed to have wrought in so few years. They noticed the wealth of shipping in the shelter of the new quay, the activity in the shipyard, the signs of prosperity in the narrow stone street of the town. There was a dressmaker's establishment now, a milliner's, and three shops instead of one. They visited the three new schools, in which the standard of teaching and discipline compared very favourably with anything they had seen on the mainland. Walking about with him they were struck by the health of the islanders, their open courtesy, the marked lack of rural idiocy among them. He told them that a regime like this could not make him loved.

'But surely they respect you for what you have done?'

'Oh yes,' he would say. 'In time they will respect me for it.'

He was in his element then, showing them around. The stiffness that had marked him in youth was to a large extent gone. He was a genial and considerate host. Most of these visitors liked him personally and were to return as friends on other summers. They were all impressed by what they saw, and after a few days went away again feeling that Mr Walmer was performing admirably the slightly eccentric task he had set himself.

In truth, the task which had once absorbed and delighted had begun to weary him. He was happy enough showing his visitors around; through their eyes he would be briefly reassured of the utility of his measures. Once they had gone he must face the fact that most of what there was to do of a practical nature he had accomplished in a remarkably short time. He had built the buildings. He had

120

reformed the system of land tenure. He had stamped out the old habit of smuggling. His restless mind cast about for some new venture, but his fortune was depleted by all that he had done before. He could not afford to undertake projects merely for his own amusement. Besides, his days were irritatingly full of those coercive duties he had always found the most distasteful.

The completion of the church, two years after the laying of the corner stone, meant that a number of young men were thrown out of employment. There was no other building project planned, and for some of these there was no alternative but to go to sea. When, on the day before the bishop's arrival, he had gone over to St Warna's to supervise the final arrangements, he heard for the first time that a youth called Edward Jenkins, on being paid off the previous week, had made his way immediately back to his father's farm on the Gweal. It occurred to Augustus that he had heard nothing of Jenkins' return because he had not been intended to. Accordingly, when his business on the main island was done, he told his boatman to take him not to the Abbey landing but to the harbour. From there he set out walking briskly towards the village. The matter of Jenkins must be dealt with at once, and if his authority were being flouted he would have as many of his tenants as possible see him take the track up to the farm.

It was a few days past Easter, which had fallen early that year. The day had held still and enchanted since early morning. As he climbed the hill with his back to the afternoon sun he felt the first touch of warmth between his shoulders. The hamlet lay in a hollow of land below him. It, too, seemed dazed by the promise of warmth. Smoke rose idly above the crowded thatched roofs. He had recently given a field adjoining the village as allotments for the cottagers and was gratified, as he descended the hill, to hear the ring of hoes and see a number of men stooped over their patches of earth. 'Good,' he said to himself. 'All to the good.'

The sight of him advancing down the hill still had power to draw the women to their doors, and now they would see him at his most relentless. The high cloth of his cravat and the low visor of his cap held his head at an attitude of arrogance which was not perhaps his own. The quick dark eye looked out to the right and to the left as he strode along the muddy street, provocative in his assertion that he would have his will; that he had the strength to outwear their hatred. For he knew himself to be hated; could bear that. In his way he relished it. The thread of violence just perceptible in his dealings with his tenants still excited him.

The women leant, as if carelessly, against the door posts with their shawls drawn to their faces. Little children clutched up handfuls of their mothers' skirts and peered from behind them. They had all at one time or another been threatened with him and each believed the stick he raised in curt salutation had been especially brought for someone's chastisement.

Augustus reached the end of the village and set out to climb the stony track to the farm. He had no need to look back to know that they would come from their doors and cluster in the road to watch him go. They knew well enough what he was about, as he intended them to.

The farm lay on the ridge of land above the path that Adela and Mrs Traherne had taken to the Abbey. He passed their silent cottage and took a path off to the right, which skirted around to the rear of the house and avoided the slurry of the farmyard.

There was a pause when he knocked. He waited, trying to distinguish, above the absentminded clucking of hens about the yard, some sound that would reveal whether these people were inside the house. He thought they were. Thin smoke rose from the chimney. There was, besides, an almost tangible sense of close furtive life withheld from him behind the door. When he knocked a second time there would be anger in the hand that held the stick. He had raised it impatiently when he heard the drag of a slow step and the rattle of the wooden latch.

The woman who opened it looked out at him with a still, pallid face and bright dark eyes.

122

'Good day, Mr Walmer.'

'Mrs Jenkins,' he said.

Without a word she turned and walked ahead of him, leaving him to close the door and follow. The clear spring light had so affected his eyes that at first all he could see of the crowded room into which she led him was a poor fire of coals glowing in a grate. From the mantel above it came the slow hesitant tick of a clock. Gradually he made out a table with a dark cloth and sitting behind it, with his back against the wall, a man square and motionless, his legs, massive in their sea-boots, jutting out on either side of the table leg. His fist out of his dark jersey was clenched on the handle of his tankard.

'Good day,' said Augustus gravely. This was his tenant Jenkins, who he heard had been ill. Though he thought the malady to be drunkenness, he said civilly enough, 'I hope you are better, now that the weather has turned?'

If the man answered at all it was with some movement of the head that was lost in shadow. He had aged suddenly. His silence was unnerving.

Mrs Jenkins gestured Augustus to a wooden chair by the fire, but she remained standing, quietly staring down into the coals. The grace of her stillness, the thinness of the grey plaits circling her head, now troubled him. He had noticed before the particular immobility of the poor in their homes. It seemed to constitute a primordial claim to be left as they were.

But of course he could not. He said, 'You know why I have come, Mrs Jenkins.'

'I do.'

He asked her then: 'And why is that?'

'You have come to move me on, Mr Walmer. After the many generations of my husband's family that have had this farm, you have come to take it from us in our old age and our need.' She lifted her head to glance mournfully at her husband.

Augustus said, 'You do me less than justice if you think that.'

'Do I?' She was content to say no more, but stood with

her head bowed, looking into the smouldering grate.

'I have come about Edward. I know he is here.'

'Do you now?' she said without impertinence, in the same clear speech. Then she raised her head and looking steadily at him said, 'Perhaps you can tell me, Mr Walmer, how the farm is to be run without him, with Mr Jenkins as he is and the boy with his affliction. You'd as soon turn us out and be done.'

'I have no intention of turning you from it. Billy has farmed it well enough this last year, with Edward away on St Warna's.'

'He's slow,' said the mother. 'He's less strong than Edward.'

'He works hard,' said Augustus. He was aware that a curtain at the side of the room had parted slightly and that one or both sons might listen. It made him hesitant to speak of the younger boy's slight deformity. He said, raising his voice, 'I spoke to Edward in the autumn and he did not seem adverse then to going to sea.'

'And what if he never returns out of that world of great risk and I am left with the other? What is your answer then?' She raised her face to him and he saw that she wept slow tears that she made no effort to wipe away and that this was no question, but a lament on the whole casting of her life. Tears fell in dark spots on the bosom of her dress, but her face remained curiously unaltered by them. He had touched on something he did not wish to know.

He said sternly and rather loudly: 'But you do understand that Edward may not stay here with you?'

The young man came out then from between the dark shapeless curtains, saying, 'It's no good, Mother. He'll do what he wants with us whatever you say.' He came past his mother and stood opposed to Augustus with an angry expression which, because of his youth, seemed close to tears.

'I'm glad you see sense,' he said to Edward Jenkins, and got vigorously to his feet so that the young man might not stand over him. He had said all that needed saying. They must come to terms with it as best they might. He would be gone now and drawn in no further.

The boy had turned back to his mother and now said, 'Why, Mother, he has made you cry.'

'He says you are to go.'

'Well, I've told you he says that.' He had gone to her and put his arm about her quite regardless of Augustus' presence in the room. That gesture, and the easing of the mother's face as she looked at him, defined to Augustus the thing he had come to sever, and at once the rectitude of what he did hardened inside him.

'But can he make you go?' the woman said to her son.

'You know he has power to turn people from their homes if they do not do what he wishes. Is that not so, Mr Walmer?' He turned to Augustus at last, defiantly, with the colour high in his face.

'Yes,' said Augustus, watching him steadily. 'Yes, it is.'

'You leave us very little choice,' the boy said bitterly.

'I leave you none,' said Augustus.

'By rights it's mine. I'm the eldest. My father intended it for me if I saw Billy right.'

All the time the old man sat motionless, except that he had drawn a corner of his long moustache into his mouth and sucked on it with all the semblance of thought.

Augustus said, 'It's of no matter to me which of you takes on the lease. I've nothing against either of you. But both of you cannot. It cannot support two families. One of you must go; as Billy's leg unfits him for a life at sea, I think it must be you.'

'There's little justice in it, then,' said Edward Jenkins bitterly.

'There's good sense in it. I think you were not adverse to going to sea when I spoke to you before.' For it was absurd to hold to this patch of land, this old woman, when the world was offered to him.

'And what if I go and he dies and Billy cannot manage as you wish? Do you turn them both out then? Do you turn her out and me come back some day and find them driven off the island and left to rot in some ditch on the mainland? What promise have I?'

'You have my word she may stay here so long as the farm is well run.'

'What's that worth?' turning from him with contempt as if he spat with the words.

Augustus watched him. He thought the boy might turn back and strike him and held to his stick behind his back. He was well built and hardened by his work on the church, but young yet. Not grown to his full strength; weakened, not strengthened, by rage. He did turn now and leant a little towards Augustus, swaying slightly on the balls of his feet, drawing his lips back as he spoke. 'Because if I come back and find you've harmed one hair of her head, I'll kill you, Mr Walmer. You see if I don't.' The old woman reached out hands that hovered about his shoulder but knew better than to restrain him.

'Go right ahead,' said Augustus coldly. 'You'll only hang for it.'

'I mean it,' said the boy.

He does, thought Augustus. He never will, but he thinks he will. He said, 'Can I take it you'll go?'

'Yes, damn you. I've got no choice, have I.'

'Then I shall give your name to the recruitment officers when they are in the islands in a week or so.'

'Do what you bloody will.' He broke away from his mother then and pushed his way back through the curtains.

'See what you've done,' said the old woman to Augustus. 'See what you've done now.'

'I've done my best for both of them,' he said, and abruptly took his leave. For none of this concerned him. He had accomplished what he had come to do.

He might have rejoined the track he had come by and followed it over the crest of the downs to the wall of his own estate, but the rapid thought that the brothers might wait for him in the farmyard made that seem like a retreat. He walked slowly through the yard therefore, swinging his stick at his side. Undoubtedly they watched him from some vantage point or other. He was quite fearless of them: he only wished he knew the elder brother's exact

126

whereabouts, and went cautiously through the slippery mud to avoid the indignity of falling.

He could hear a sound of scraping and made out Billy Jenkins shovelling dung into a wooden cart at the door of the cowshed. Dung had been hurled at him before. The gate to the lower track lay just beyond the shed. He went on.

'Good day,' he called out to Billy Jenkins.

The boy stood upright. 'Good day,' he said, sullenly perhaps, but Augustus thought him ignorant of what had just passed and judged then that the elder brother had stayed in the house. The younger leaned on his shovel, staring at him without enquiry. Well, he stands to gain by it, Augustus said to himself. He should have been as handsome a lad as his brother and had no very apparent flaw when he stood still. Only when he moved his shorter leg afflicted him with a lurching ungainly walk and it seemed, now that Augustus watched him closely, that the same imbalance echoed itself in the cast of his features and the set of his shoulders. Standing there, squinting in the sunlight, his clothes caked in the soil he worked in, he seemed a rooted thing. It had been right to free the other from all of this.

The arrival of the bishop on the following day distracted Augustus from this incident, but when, after his departure a week later, he and Wills sat drinking port in the agent's parlour, Augustus said to him, 'Edward Jenkins offered to kill me.'

He looked acutely at Wills who merely grunted, but watched him too to see how he had intended this remark to be taken. His voice had given no clue.

'Do you think he might?' Augustus asked dispassionately.

Wills said, 'They say his grandfather killed a man.'

'I dare say. Well, we'll have to wait and see,' said Augustus.

'He's only a boy,' said the agent, and then, smiling at him, 'you've been threatened before.'

'Many times,' said Augustus. He could not explain that

never before had he felt so drawn to an adversary. He perversely wanted, perhaps for the sake of his faith in the boy, that the threat be known at least by Wills and taken, in part at least, seriously.

10

For some years before Edward Jenkins was sent to sea, Mrs
Traherne and his mother had enjoyed a close friendship.
They were neighbours and set, like their dwellings, a little
apart from the village. If asked about this, Mrs Traherne
would have revealed little, beyond tersely conceding that
'We do take tea together.' (A wreck in the spring of 1840
had conveniently provided the island with a wealth of this
commodity, and an excuse for these meetings to become
regular.) In fact the two women loved and needed one
another, although neither would have cared to admit that
this were so. Each felt the continuance of the friendship
through seven years now to be the fruit of her own toler-
ance. Mrs Jenkins had chosen to ignore Mrs Traherne's
oddity, her poverty, her scepticism. Mrs Traherne generously overlooked her friend's social inferiority, though
from what elevation was never clear to anyone but herself.
The friendship throve on these mutual sensations of goodness and broadmindedness. Like any other pair of island
women they exchanged gossip about their neighbours and
discussed the vagaries of the weather, but they were both
intelligent women, and each as they talked presented to
the other a picture of life that differed in its individuality.
They were able to spy at their confined world through
each other's eyes as if through altering panes of glass,
which gave them that modicum of variety, of intellectual
space, that otherwise both would have unconsciously
pined for.

Besides, they were both good to one another in their
talk. There was no rivalry between them. Mrs Traherne

had accepted her defeats with fortitude, holding now only to the fact of Adela's cleverness as a source of any future hope. For the child had come to her so unmistakably as a recompense and with her life still lying ahead of her, the extent to which she might compensate seemed boundless. With no daughter to defend from Adela's advantages, Mrs Jenkins was free to feel a warm pity for the child and to take an altruistic pleasure in watching her grow up out of such great misfortune. Her own two sons were pride enough for her. As for her husband: to whom could she confide better than to this austere woman, who would be too proud to relay her sad disloyalties to the island gossips? It seemed tact on Mrs Traherne's part that she never mentioned her own dead husband, neither to reproach Mrs Jenkins with her past happiness, nor to vaunt greater sufferings. So it became possible for Mrs Jenkins to talk, during these visits, about the farmer's failings in a particular low rhythmic monotonous tone which Adela, set to play on the far side of the room, soon learned to distinguish, although never once had she contrived to hear a word that was said, beyond the general statement that Mr Jenkins was greatly altered since the day on which Mrs Jenkins had accepted him.

The front room in which they sat on these occasions had been throughout Adela's childhood her touchstone of warmth and normality. Her brief glimpse of an infinitely richer life at the Abbey had been too swift, too distant now to rival it. Abruptly that world had closed its shutters. The Pontefracts had not returned to the islands. She had never again been summoned to the house to play. She could scarcely imagine it now.

But Mrs Jenkins' front room never lost its glory. In winter lamps were lit when Mrs Traherne and Adela arrived, but in summer sunlight, of a quality that seemed distilled through the long day into something thick and sluggish, penetrated the room through its one deep square window.

It drew gold from the little ornaments on the dark mantelshelf and from the painted plates crowding the two glass-fronted cupboards by the fireplace. In winter the room smelt pleasantly of burning coals and in summer of the sweet bruised leaves of geraniums that crowded on a shelf below the window: odours of well-being. Early on, however, Adela sensed that this well-being had limits: it seemed hollowed out of a crowded existence that was both threatening and exciting. Sometimes men's boots sounded heavily along the path by the door, and their deep gruff voices disturbed the quiet room through the thin panels dividing it from the kitchen. Sometimes without warning these voices would grow loud and angry:

'Don't you tell me what to do.'

'No, I never.'

A door might bang. Mrs Jenkins and Mrs Traherne would exchange resigned contemptuous looks, but Adela noticed their eyes were bright with interest on these occasions.

In a distant undemonstrative way she loved Mrs Jenkins, who was big and possessed of a melancholy acceptance, whereas Mrs Traherne was small and fuelled by anger against wrongs and sorrows and injustices she would never mention.

The two women sat facing one another across a table by the window, their heads, in the white caps they donned for these occasions, extended towards one another, eager for the release of their own and each other's voices. Adela had her own stool by the fireplace where she sat savouring the well-being and contentment around her.

At the base of the glass-fronted shelves were cupboard doors with small round glass knobs cut into a mass of facets which, late in the day, cast uncertain rainbows against the yellowing walls. One of these cupboards Adela was allowed to open. The thick accretions of paint which blunted the edges of the door stuck in the humid air. Both knobs must be pulled outward at the same moment and shaken a little to part them. As she grew older she could still feel that minute fear that this time the cupboard might not open, and relief at the soft crack as the doors did part and release the cupboard's particular enclosed smell.

In it were games: wooden boxes with lids that slid

131

forward from grooves or opened on brass hinges no bigger than her fingernail. There was a box with ivory dominoes, yellow and lined with cracks which the eye could see while the fingers could find no flaw in their uncanny smoothness. There were shining draughts in black and red; a box filled with ivory jack straws carved like farmers' tools. Most beautiful of all was a round wooden tray in which were set, in rows of different length, marbles like solid drops of water containing brilliantly coloured spirals.

The very idea of a game filled Adela with excitement. To do something for no purpose was in itself a token of great luxury. She did not know how to play these games, nor did anyone ever offer to play with her. If Mr Jenkins and his two sons returned from milking before the visitors left, they kept to the kitchen. Nor was Adela capable of inventing anything like a game of her own. She merely handled and looked at them. She was allowed only to take one at a time from the cupboard. This was her aunt's rule, imposed across Mrs Jenkins' kindly protests that the child was far too careful to harm anything. But even as a little girl Adela appreciated her aunt's rightness in this. She could see that each game was a very separate and distinct thing to be relished on its own.

With the dominoes, houses and roads might be built and precarious towers. When she replaced them in the box they must be fitted just so, some on their ends, some on their backs, so that the long wooden lid slid back without interruption. The draughts made towers, too, and the two colours could be arranged in a great many different ways. On the board their circles just fitted the squares, touching them here and bending away from them there in a way that was most satisfactory to her. Then there were the jack straws to be set out and thought about separately, as words and implements, and the marbles to be lifted one by one into the light and turned this way and that until the strange unobtainable spirals spun inside them. Very early their existence convinced her that the glass spheres had been at some point penetrable. It would be impossible to say at what age she no longer entertained the idea that she

132

might find power to grow smaller, to a size so infinitesimal that she might enter the sphere herself and climb the frail green filament, passing other minute beings on other strands, the red, the yellow, the blue: perhaps the invisible Mr Jenkins and his sons, whose distant voices so disturbed the room, or the vanished people from the Abbey, ascending and descending, as angels did, from heaven to earth. Her mind at one time was full of such fancies, which she had been unwilling to surrender or share; for she had observed early that the adult world, if turned to for the magic solution, could only destroy.

Now, of course, as she grew older she put these fantasies aside, but still on these visits she crouched on the same little stool, felt the resistance of the cupboard door and breathed in the air it released with the same tremor of pleasure. From long habit she took the games out one at a time and set them on the patch of ginger-coloured carpet in the same way, but her attention was no longer entirely subdued to them. Half consciously she used them as a screen of normality between herself and the two ageing women: to shelter her from their observing that she had grown quite different. Seeing her sit where she had always sat, going through the same apparently absorbed motions, they never thought, except when speaking of Mr Jenkins, to lower their voices nor alter what they said on her account.

Whereas Adela's need had once been for the games, and the women's talk had merely lapped the edges of her interest like an incessant sea, now her hunger was for what they had to say. They talked to one another frankly about things which Adela would never dare to ask her aunt: like Mrs Sumpter at the Palace cottage, and why her daughter and Billy Beckford were brother and sister, and why Sukie Watson and John Bishop who everyone knew really were brother and sister, coming to school hand in hand, had different names in the school register. Why Mary Bayliss had shouted at poor Charlie Bayliss when he broke the jug, 'You always were a little bastard and always will be'; so enraged that Adela passing in the lane had heard, and struck by the vehemence and ugliness of the word had asked her aunt its meaning. The effects had been startling, but not enlightening. Yet, listening, in time she made out that Henry Bayliss was not Charlie's father and that this was a source of shame. But why shame? She had no father. That had always been a source of melancholy pride. There was some knowledge as central to the understanding of things and as unobtainable as the spiral at the centre of the marble. That it spun together the lives of men and women she was well aware, and was content to listen patiently until it might reveal itself.

When Adela was thirteen she had been made a monitor in the school. The other girls with whom in the last year she had made the cautious beginnings of friendship had gone on: Sukie Watson to be a housemaid at the Abbey, Elly Bayliss to be apprenticed to a dressmaker on the main island. Adela had stayed behind in the schoolroom setting out the exercise books, sharpening the pens, standing beside the master's desk trying not to meet the children's eyes, not knowing often whether to smile or not, taking the blackboard cloth home to wash on Friday and bringing it back on Monday. It shut her away from the other girls she had briefly known, but that did not greatly trouble her. She was accustomed to being alone and liked the schoolroom where she had had nothing but praise, especially when it was empty of children in the early mornings and when the day was over and she remained behind to sweep the floor. Now she was most usually seen in the village, walking alone an hour before the school children ran past in the morning and an hour after them in the afternoons, hurrying always on a Wednesday so as not to be late to take tea with Mrs Jenkins.

On one such Wednesday, shortly after Adela's confirmation at the hands of the bishop, Mrs Jenkins opened the door with her face distorted by weeping, her eyes painful and swollen, a strand of her faded hair fallen and seemingly pasted to the side of her cheek.

'Ah, my dear,' cried Mrs Traherne, in a tone of affection that was rare to her. She seized both her friend's hands

134

and, turning, drew her into her own parlour and settled her at the table, saying, 'It is certain, then? He must go?'

Mrs Jenkins nodded wretchedly, catching at her trembling lower lip with worn yellow teeth. Adela slipped swiftly to her stool. They talked of Edward, the eldest son who must go to sea.

'He came here,' said Mrs Jenkins. 'I can tell you I wept before him.'

'Indeed!' said Mrs Traherne, indignant that her friend had been reduced to this.

'I'd as well shed my tears over a stone.'

'He'd never wring a tear from me,' said Mrs Traherne, 'I'd not let him.'

'Oh, he's a very devil,' her friend cried out.

'I've had little enough dealing with either gentleman,' said Mrs Traherne, 'but I daresay they resemble each other well enough.' She spoke like this when she was moved, very tart and short: the voice gathered up like an angry fist.

Her friend answered in the voice reserved for Mr Jenkins, but forgetting in her distress to lower it, 'He'll not bear it. It will drive him from his mind.'

'The farm must go to Billy, then?'

'What else,' said Mrs Jenkins bitterly. 'They'd never take *him* as he is.'

'Well, he's a fine boy for all his affliction,' said Mrs Traherne. 'He works as hard.'

'Ah, but you know what Jenkins is,' she seemed to plead with her friend. 'He dotes on that boy. All his heart was in the farm being shared between the two of them.'

'Edward was always his favourite,' said Mrs Traherne grimly. 'He's your favourite, too. You should admit it.'

'Well, well, and if he is, it needs the two of them to run the farm with Mr Jenkins being so altered.'

'Altered, altered,' said Mrs Traherne. 'He's been altered ever since I knew you. Why not call it the same? Billy is the steadier of the two.' And then, fearing perhaps that she had gone too far, she took her friend's hand in hers and asked more gently, 'How does Edward take it?'

135

'Oh, he had a go at him. I've never seen him so. Said he'd kill him if his father or I came to harm. And he would. I think he would.'

'But he agrees to go,' prompted Mrs Traherne a little drily. This it seemed was the unendurable part. Mrs Jenkins snatched back her hand and, pressing her handkerchief against her eyes, wept again. 'It is as if he wanted to go.'

'And there you are,' said Mrs Traherne. 'It is for the best, I tell you it is. Here. You've made the tea and have everything prepared. Won't you take a little and feel better?'

Mrs Jenkins drew in a little shuddering breath and shook her head as if some tormenting insect were trapped beneath the white cap. 'There,' she said. 'I mustn't give way before the child' – for so they both still designated Adela. 'It is a mercy, Mrs Traherne, that he cannot take her from you, and to think that in my birth throes I prayed for sons and now this comes upon me. But at least he will not touch her. That one human being can have such power over the lives of others, my dear, that is what I cannot accept.'

'There, there,' said her friend. 'Pour us out some tea now. You will have a fine son at sea and a fine son at home to comfort you if you will allow him. I could wish for the same.' She altered her voice, for death was now the topic. 'It was my greatest dread that when I was gone he would turn her away out of the cottage. She without a soul in the wide world but me.'

'He will not,' said Mrs Jenkins staunchly. 'Not with her so useful to him.' And then looking around at Adela abruptly they lowered their voices.

She was useful to Mr Walmer because she was monitor at the school and rose at six and made her way through the drowsy village where the first few fires were lit and smoking. In the schoolroom she must fill the inkwells and set out the exercise books and pens. He came sometimes to the school and stood restlessly while she asked the children their spelling.

A fly climbed buzzing up the window pane. Though the door was open the thin odour of sweat hung in the room. She watched the children's hands as they wrote. Some were as big as adults' hands, some were small as a child's. She watched Charlie Bayliss' white anxious knuckles staring through the dark skin, for he feared to do it wrong, and she too felt sweat prick in the tight sleeves of her dress and on her lip while Mr Walmer watched her so gravely and acutely. But when he had been from desk to desk he had smiled at her, with his back to the children whom he did not wish to see him smile, saying, 'That was well done, Adela.'

'Why is she so silent?' Mrs Jenkins once asked that summer across the tea table, as if Adela's silence placed her entirely beyond the pale of words.

'It is because she is so much alone,' said the old woman mournfully, and she added, with a bitterness which made Adela cringe, 'I am no company for her.' She had seen, long before Adela would have admitted such a thing to herself, that the old childhood intimacy could not last forever. Why must she talk so, thought Adela angrily, as if I were unkind to her, as if I were deaf? She was unaware of her silence, absorbed so in what others were saying and in her own bright fantasies that her mind was full of words which remained unspoken. So that now when the old women's talk ebbed into less interesting channels or sank to whispers about Mr Jenkins, other voices came to replace theirs. That of Edward Jenkins, the elder and handsomer son, who would go to sea, returning at some time so remote that she would be transformed into a woman in full possession of her beauty. Then, walking home with him from Evensong, she measured exactly the quality of fading light along the path, with certain details of her imaginary dress and the arrangement of her hair. Only he seemed a little indistinct, drawn deeper into the dusk than was quite consistent with his being so close, when suddenly he would fall on his knee in the sand and grab at her hand and kiss it. Now she watched the clock on the wall of Mrs Jenkins' parlour, hoping that her aunt might forget to leave before she heard the heavy fall of men's boots in the scullery and

137

their deep voices behind the door. But when, towards the end of that summer, Edward Jenkins knocked on their cottage door to say goodbye, for he must set out for Portsmouth in the morning, she felt very little beyond the immediate drama of the occasion. It was a part of her plan that he should go and remain away for some time; indeed, her awareness of this young man was so largely constructed of dreams that his actual presence on the island was hardly important to her.

That winter Edward Jenkins wrote twice to his mother, once from Plymouth and once from Tangier. From the Abbey on the Gweal Augustus wrote on January 17th, 1846:

> *My dear Mrs Pontefract,*
>
> *In the past week the winds have wrought havoc along my central path, dealing most cruelly with the Ixias, Sparaxises and Mesembryanthemums. It is my good fortune that roots of these have found their way to Tregilly, and the thought comforts me that if the parent plant perishes the child shall thrive with you. We are very gay here when the weather permits us to leave our own firesides. I am sure no rout in London was half so grand as that at Mrs Hall's on Thursday last. Tonight I heard the wind complain in my chimney that he and I must spend the evening alone in one another's company, but I was not displeased, knowing that I might pass the time in silent conversation with you, and in labelling the eggs with all the pleasure of knowing that next summer or perhaps the next after that they will meet with your inspection. Affectionate greetings to Pontefract and Miss Harriet.*
>
> > *Yours sincerely,*
> > *Augustus Walmer*

And in April of the following year:

> *My dear Mrs Pontefract,*
>
> *Zepherus was kind to me this morning. Your letter was borne in early with its glad tidings that you and Harriet*

138

will accompany Euphemia and her children on their summer visit. Antholyza Ringens blooms the brighter for the news and my quiet house has come alive with preparation. My only sorrow being of course that a recurrence of illness must be the cause of your coming and that Pontefract's current rude health seems reason for his lingering on the mainland. Still, the joy must outweigh the sorrow. I send by return this offering of woodcock to Pontefract as some poor sort of recompense for depriving him of your company.

Yours sincerely,
Augustus Walmer

The following month Edward Jenkins wrote that by autumn he would be in home waters, stationed for a time at Plymouth before putting to sea again.

It was by now, as well as could be calculated, the summer of Adela's fifteenth year. The days were full of bright distractions as she walked from place to place. On Sundays she walked alone to the harbour to take the boat to St Warna's for church. Her aunt, though still through conscience unable to attend herself, was determined that no slur should fall on the child's character that would disqualify her from the job which she was convinced secured her future. With Adela's wages, and the savings made from her eating her midday meal with the schoolmaster and his wife, Mrs Traherne was able to buy a length of muslin on St Warna's. She was clever with her needle. Adela had learned to sew even before she went to school and between them they had made a dress as fine as any on the island. There had been enough to buy a little straw hat with ribbons and so dressed, if the weather were fine, she cut across the field above the village. If it were wet she wore her aunt's old cloak over her finery and went by the road, falling in occasionally with girls she had known who were home for a day or two from work or service. But this on the whole she avoided, and they perhaps shunned her, out of no particular ill-will, but rather as if the sense of separateness, so real to Mrs Traherne, had in time impressed itself on the villagers and upon Adela herself. She bore her isolation patiently enough and could not have put a name to the loneliness which, as she grew older, more and more dominated her life. She was, not without reason, generally fearful of other people, even of the Jenkinses when they met outside the ritual of the weekly tea party, and carried herself with a wariness that might easily have been mistaken for pride and was not entirely free of it. For if you had asked Adela outright, 'Which is right, you or they?' the girl would have answered unhesitatingly, 'I am,' and never questioned the distinction.

11

One Sunday in August the sky was bright and clear from dawn. The day held an excited quality; its light even penetrated the dark cottage. Its air of stilled expectation had Adela dressed and ready for church an hour before she needed. This was an occasion she always looked forward to. She liked to see the people altered by Sunday and name them over to herself as in pairs and groups they gathered for the crossing to St Warna's. She liked to feel a part with them when everyone spoke the service together, and when they smiled and bowed to one another at the end.

'You don't want to be going yet,' said Mrs Traherne, but she could not help feeling pleased at the sight of Adela grown so tall and neat in the white dress, with the little hat perched above her plaited hair.

'May I go now?' Adela asked, eagerly enough for her aunt to be instantly fearful of some new element in her life – some friendship which might threaten the child. As always she was too proud to question.

'As you wish, then,' she said. She stood in the door watching Adela climb the bright green field. When she reached the top of the hill she quickly disappeared behind its crest without once looking back.

Just on the far side of this ridge was a stone which Adela had always designated her throne. It lay at one of the few points on the island where the sea was visible on every side, still and brilliant between the sheltering islands and beyond them tossing up white rags of foam where the black fragmented rocks first intercepted the roll of the ocean. From here she could watch for the procession of families moving slowly towards the quay. Dark men and pale women with children walking stiffly at their side. She hurried down the slope and followed them to the harbour. In the boat it was cheerful and people laughed and talked to one another, but when they all climbed out on the quay at St Warna's a Sunday gravity descended on the people of the Gweal. They processed in a body up the grey stone street to Augustus Walmer's new church, aware of their best clothes and their separateness from the people of this other island. The church bell had an anxious tinny sound. It seemed to fear that no one would obey it.

Adela went to her accustomed place on a bench near the back and knelt and prayed politely to God, for her aunt's health, for her own labours at the school, and then, with a guilty sense of intrusion, for Edward Jenkins' safety at sea. As she prayed she heard the deep booming voice of the Proprietor in the church porch. 'A splendid day,' he would shout to his chaplain. 'Good day to you.' Everyone in the church could hear him.

In summer he never came to church alone. There were ladies and gentlemen, young and old, sometimes children. On several Sundays she had seen stout Mrs Walmer and the boy who had wanted to go in the boat and the little girl who had been unkind: both taller and indefinably older, but unmistakable. She seemed to watch them at a great distance, never supposing that they might recognize her.

This morning there was a passage of wide skirts down the narrow aisle, a whispering and rapid fragrance. When she looked up from her prayers she only saw the backs of the ladies' dresses covered by flowery pointed summer shawls. As they turned to file into the pew at the side of the altar they bowed their heads and their faces were hidden by their bonnets. Only the Proprietor turned, before he knelt, to frown directly over the congregation and note whether it had grown or diminished since the previous Sunday. When the service was over he stalked between the pews, turning his head this way and that to see who was there and who was not. Adela knelt and heard him pass, then a moment later she felt a sudden pressure on her shoulder, and looking up saw what was unmistakably Harriet's face, grown larger and plainer, smiling curiously down at her. Adela felt the sudden movement of her heart. She had wanted this without knowing it. Harriet whispered, 'We have come back. Do you remember me? I saw you while we were singing the hymn.'

'Yes,' said Adela shyly, and felt her own smile pull at her cheeks.

'I'll wait for you outside,' said this different Harriet. It was necessary to wait some minutes while the people in the front of the church filed out. Usually it was interesting to be able to look at them so openly, week after week, and to notice their little changes and their sameness: the agent still stooped from his crouched position at the harmonium, the customs officer, the schoolmaster and Mrs Davies, all became quite other people. Today she fretted, sure that Harriet must by now be gone.

But when she finally reached the sunlight outside the church porch she saw that Harriet was still there, standing a little apart from the chaplain as he spoke to people by the gate. She wore a very pretty blue dress. There were flowers on the brim of her bonnet. Adela moved timidly to meet her but in her heart she felt the same fearless liking she had felt for Harriet as a child. Nevertheless so unaccustomed was she to break in on the otherness of people that the sudden wanting to and the not knowing how left her quite stupid. They stood facing each other at a loss for words, until Harriet in the same rather deep voice asked, 'Well, how are you?'

'Very well, thank you,' said Adela, but at a little frown on Harriet's smooth shaded face she thought the thank you had been an error. 'And you?' she added politely, but felt all the more anxious that it might be impossible for them to speak to one another in their new guises.

'Oh, I am well,' said Harriet. Then she added hurriedly and it seemed with all the old secrecy, 'Only there's no one to talk to here but Sarah, and she is so lacking in seriousness I cannot feel at ease with her. I hoped that I might see you. I asked Mr Walmer and he said that you would be here.' It was almost as if she had come back after all this time to deliver some particular message. 'Will you walk back with me? We could go by the shore.'

'Yes,' said Adela, but as they began to walk side by side she was more and more oppressed by a fear that she must fail to convey her pleasure in words. She was confused, too, by the sudden onrush of recollection. Her mind was quite congested with memories of the rocky surfaces of paths, the warm stone where Harriet had balanced the unsteady mussel shells and whispered so fiercely in her ear, of Mrs Walmer's tightening grip on her wrist. All these were revealed with the sharp newness of things put away, not handled nor allowed to gather new associations. They destroyed the cautioning sense that time had passed, so that when Harriet began to speak in a low and earnest voice it was difficult to grasp that she was saying, 'Did you not find the service comforting?'

'Yes,' said Adela, smiling uncertainly. 'I like to go to church on Sunday.' But she felt that a response had been expected of her which she had been unable to provide, and that perhaps, so early in their meeting, she had been tested and failed. 'Did you like it?'

'It comforted me. I do so miss our church at home, but the words of course are the same and I could imagine them being spoken there at the very same moment. Do you think they might have been – as if by the same voice?'

She seemed so earnestly to want assurance, and the frown between her eyes was so powerfully reminiscent of her child-self, that Adela said quickly, 'Oh yes, I expect it was.' Then, for she would have liked to sympathise, 'I expect you do get homesick, being away. I have never been away from here or I should too.' She ended wistfully, as if she asked a question, 'I expect you miss your friends.'

Harriet said gravely, 'I do not have a friend at home. No close friend, except of course Miss Christian.'

'You did not like her when you were little,' said Adela. She felt shocked and pained.

'Did I not?' she said, turning her steady eyes towards Adela. They seemed empty of all recollection.

144

'No,' said Adela. Her own memories seemed betrayed. 'You said you hated her.'

'Did I?'

'You did. Don't you remember that?'

'Do you remember when you used to come and play with me?'

'Oh yes,' said Adela.

'I thought I remembered it. The house and the garden. But when I came this time it all seemed different. Have I changed?' she asked Adela suddenly.

'No, no. You have not changed to look at. I thought when I first saw you that you had changed, but now that I talk with you I do not think that it is so.' But even as she spoke she felt a wretched questioning of her own words.

'You have grown very pretty,' said Harriet quickly.

Adela felt her face flush and her wretchedness increase lest her own answer had been too niggardly. She looked down at the path and said awkwardly, 'And you too. I thought when I saw you that you were the prettiest lady I had seen in church.'

But the answer gave no pleasure. Harriet frowned and said impatiently, 'But there is no change in me?'

It occurred to Adela that she must speak the truth, but she was fearful of doing so and scarcely knew what it might be. She said, 'You are changed in yourself. Like you saying that Miss Christian is your friend now.'

'She is my dear friend,' said Harriet. Then, seeing Adela stare at her with a return of puzzled disbelief, she said kindly, 'And I think you are my friend, Adela, so I can tell you that I think I am closer in spirit to her – to Miss Christian – I call her Molly now when we are together – than I am to Mama. Even though she has had such misfortunes and is so poor, she is able to understand me more than Mama does. She often says she wishes I might have been her child. I think she used to frighten me when I was little, but now that I am older and understand more what she has suffered I am very close to her.'

Her voice, as she spoke, took on a strange inner, rhythmic quality. Never had Adela been spoken to in such a way before. The intensity and absorption of Harriet's talk half repelled her, but at the same time she found it compelling and flattering to be allowed so close to anyone as to seem to hear them thinking aloud. She felt chosen and trusted. Harriet had confirmed the magical quality she held in memory as being the friend whom daily life had so signally failed to provide. She wished she had the courage then and there formally to ask Harriet to be her friend, but felt it was not her place to do so. She felt solemnly that she had been given a gift, and cast about her bare life for something to proffer in return. She said, 'When I am eighteen Mr Walmer says he will send me to London to train as a teacher. Then, if I do well, I can be assistant to Mr Davies.'

'Would you like that?' asked Harriet, with the same rapid frown gathering between her eyes.

'Oh yes, I should. It is a great opportunity for me.'

'Someone has told you that,' said Harriet almost absently.

'But I think so too. I should be sent to London.'

'Oh,' said Harriet slowly. 'Should you like London, Adela?' She had stopped a little ahead on the path and turned back to look levelly at Adela with the brown steady eyes that had seen London.

'I don't know. I think I should like it. I want to go.'

'I hate to go there,' said Harriet almost violently, then, as if she saw that she might do damage to the eagerness on Adela's face, she said more gently, 'You will feel quite lost there. I always do. I don't know anyone and it's so difficult to talk to people.'

'You don't find it so,' said Adela, almost laughing.

'Oh but I do – to gentlemen. You always feel you must say something particular and cannot think what it is. Don't you find?'

'I only speak to Mr Davies.' Suddenly ashamed of the poverty of events in her life, she added, 'Now that Edward Jenkins has gone to sea.' She did not know why she had felt the need to lie. Perhaps it was the brief luxury of having someone to whom she could say such things, even if they

146

were not true. She was surprised that Harriet seemed to believe her. She said, 'Who's he?' too quickly to pretend indifference. They were walking on the track above the shore, side by side, looking down now at the progress of their dusty boots from out their light hems, now at one another.

'Oh, he lived here,' said Adela carelessly, 'only now he's at sea.'

'Did he like you? Like that, I mean?'

She might go on questioning coolly until the lie was discovered. Adela said, 'I don't know him very well.'

'Oh.' But the seed had been planted. Harriet was impressed. There was no one she could ask could say otherwise. It corrected a little a great imbalance. Still, Adela felt she had turned the talk along ugly lines. She would have liked to set things right by finally disclaiming Edward Jenkins, but did not know how.

Harriet now said, 'I must come out in London when I am eighteen. Mama says I must, but I don't want to.'

'What's that?'

'Oh, go to parties. Dance. I don't want to,' she said again. Then she looked at Adela and smiled. 'It's nice to talk.'

'Yes.' She found it strange and perilous, but she wanted it.

Harriet said, 'I have not been entirely truthful with you, Adela, and I have sworn always to tell the truth now. I have a friend, a very dear friend, and it is to him I have sworn this.'

So soon Adela could feel the jolt of jealousy and the humiliation of her foolish pretence. The imbalance held: became law. She watched and listened to Harriet in total acceptance of her authority in these matters, just as, a child, she had followed her along the paths of Augustus Walmer's garden. 'Will you tell me who he is?' she asked, almost whispering in her awe.

'I'll tell *you*,' said Harriet. '*You* won't tell anyone.'

'No,' said Adela deep in humility. For whom would she tell?

'I have not told Mama. Miss Christian even does not know entirely how I feel.' She stopped and turned to scrutinize Adela without hurry or embarrassment. How complete she was in herself. How sure of the truth and interest of what she spoke. 'He is our vicar at home,' she said.

'Isn't he old?'

But that brought contempt. 'He isn't my friend in *that* way. He is my true friend. My friend in Christ. It doesn't matter how old he is.'

'No.'

'I can speak my soul to him in a way that I cannot speak to Miss Christian or even to you. Do you understand that?'

'Yes,' said Adela, who, even if she did not, believed that she should.

'But it is a very great secret between us. Do you understand? If Mama were to hear she would not let me go to him. She does not like him, I think, but then she is very different to me. Besides, he loves me in a way that she does not. Do you swear?' she said, with the old peremptory frown.

'I swear,' said Adela, so earnestly that Harriet who, a moment before, had been so caught up in her own intensity, laughed, and left her confused as to how she was to sympathize. They had come within sight of the quay and could see the islanders filing down the steps to the waiting boat. She said uncertainly, 'I must go ahead or the boat will be kept waiting.'

'Can we talk again? Can I meet you?'

'Oh yes,' said Adela, but now the thought of how her aunt would react to this, and the burden of moving between two persons, settled upon her imagination.

As if Harriet had caught her uncertainty, she added, 'If we stay.'

'I thought you had just come.'

'We have been here a week. Mama will not say how long we are to stay.'

'Yes,' said Adela, who would have liked to reach for her hand but merely smiled.

'One afternoon. We might walk. If I can.'

148

'Goodbye,' said Adela, and she hurried ahead along the path towards the quay.

All week in her imagination she talked to Harriet, not to the child but to this new person who wanted to tell her secrets. At times she became Harriet and went to parties and talked to gentlemen. The parties held no terrors for her, who knew in her heart she need never go. She wore a white dress, very wide, and one gentleman after another danced her round and round. Edward Jenkins was one of them, but there were many others. Soldiers in red coats. She watched herself go round and round. She smiled and moved her lips. She was talking. She could not know now what she would say when she was eighteen.

When she told Mrs Traherne of her meeting with Harriet, the old woman seemed pleased. 'Did she say she would meet you again?'

'She said she'd try.'

Mrs Traherne said nothing harsh to that although Adela had feared she might. Nevertheless, she found it difficult to ask each day when she came home from the school whether a message had come. She did not want to be seen to care. Mrs Traherne said nothing. She would tell me, surely, Adela thought, but when the days passed she could not help questioning, 'Did you meet anyone today? Did you talk to anyone?' But there had been no message from the Abbey and a guarded pity in Mrs Traherne's replies seemed intolerable.

On the following Sunday she set out very promptly and waited in the churchyard until the bell stopped ringing and she must go inside. The first hymn was begun before she accepted that only the servants had come from the Abbey and that the family must have come early to communion. They might come again in the evening, but she dared not ask her aunt's permission to go twice to church in one day.

Another week began. On the Wednesday Charlie Bayliss was taken sick in the schoolroom. 'Take him home, Adela,' said Mrs Davies when the sick was cleared up.

'Make sure his mother's there to look after him.' She took Charlie Bayliss by the hand. He was quite subdued by his wretchedness and came along like a little child, causing her no trouble. Only as they approached the door of his cottage did he twist his hand roughly from hers and run inside shouting, 'I was sick, Mam. I was sick.'

She heard the woman's voice inside the cottage and thought she need not follow. It was a brilliant day. She did not want to return to the close classroom where the smell of sick would linger all morning. She would go just to the harbour and back. She began to walk quickly on past the row of cottages, down the roadway of smooth sea stones set so steeply into the track that in places they formed shallow steps. Over the thatched rooves of the harbour cottages she saw the Trinity House cutter riding at its anchorage. She watched the Proprietor's boat rowed into the quay and at the same time heard the sound of the pony cart and its sharp echoes from off the hill behind her. It jolted towards her as she came out onto the harbour road. The groom stood shaking the reins and behind him ladies sat on the benches with their scarves fluttering. She saw the Proprietor stride along the sea wall at its side. The young man behind him was Alfred, as tall as he now. She stood back in the deep grass by the foot of the stone hedges.

'Why aren't you in the school?' Mr Walmer shouted, and the young man, halting behind him, stared.

'I took Charlie Bayliss home, sir. He was sick, sir.' But she did not think he listened, so abruptly did he turn and keep pace with the cart. She looked quickly to see if the young man still looked at her, but he too had turned and walked on. Only the ladies smiled and waved. Harriet was among them, seated on one of the benches with her hand on the brim of her hat. She turned and waved and again when she climbed down onto the pier. Although Adela could no longer see her face she knew it must be Harriet, still holding on to her hat with one hand while she waved with the other. She too waved and waved in return while they were all helped down the quay steps into the waiting boat, which immediately began to move away in the

150

direction of the cutter. It had all taken only a few minutes. She wondered how long she dare stand and watch for the cutter in its turn to move. But there was little purpose to standing there watching, and less to waving when no one could see her. She dropped her arm and began walking back to the schoolroom.

12

'Is that not the Island Child? Is that not your little Adela?' asked Mrs Pontefract in the back of the cart.

'Yes,' said Harriet, throwing the word over her shoulder towards the harbour. She had stopped waving. Her mother overstated everything. Sarah and Mrs Walmer had turned to stare.

'Have you seen her? Have you spoken to her?'

'After church on Sunday before last, we walked back to the quay.'

'But you never said.'

'I did not think you remembered her.'

'How charming she looked,' said Amelia vaguely.

As the cart came out onto the harbour they all turned to stare at the Trinity House cutter, large and alien in that world of small familiar things, lying at anchor in the bay: shortly they were to board her. The day was to be spent inspecting the work on the lighthouse. It was five years almost to the day since they had last seen it. Euphemia sat between Harriet and Sarah in the cart. Augustus, with Alfred behind him, strode beside it along the top of the new sea wall, pointing out with his stick the new shed for drying nets, the new fish store, the new hoist at the end of the quay; sternly, as if he might catch the boy out in inattention. But Amelia at least could never have enough of looking and continued to ask, 'When was it completed?' and 'Have they salted the first catch yet?' though the contents of his answers she barely listened to.

Since her arrival two weeks ago she had seemed to move through recollection. Time had slowed. The cows stood like wooden toys on the green hill pegged down to their shadows. On the outer rocks great columns of spray flung up into the air: distant and powerless as childhood's rage. Nothing might harm her here.

I am better, she had written on the second day to Cissy. *Immediately I am here I am better. There is as you may imagine great pointing of the stick, and this is new and that is new, but nothing of what is new is half so dear as what remains unchanged. There's some beneficence in the air. Of that I am sure. Pain withers at its touch.*

Two weeks were gone already but she would not think of leaving.

By day she walked along the terraces with Euphemia Walmer. Harriet rode with Mr Walmer and the young people but she did not. She had been ill. The crossing had weakened her. But now she was restored.

At night she slept and woke without fear of wakefulness, seeming to float on currents of clear thought that led in time to sleep and daylight barred and bright behind the curtain. Her walks alone gave her most pleasure. They seemed conducted along some inner route: turns in the path and glimpses of the sea appeared to be portions of herself. In the evenings she took the path to the beach: down the garden steps, out through the wooden gate, along the sweet-smelling bracken path, where it pleased her to remember that still young and unguarded he had kissed her hand. The lake reflected a colourless sky. Once a swan and two black coots progressed slowly across the dark water, drawing after them long triangles of light. They made no sound. A strange soft clatter seemed to have no source. Then she saw the swan's mate rear up against the reeds on the far bank, stretching and flapping his wings. The reflected sun was pale and lemon yellow, and here and there where the broken water crossed its path brilliant facets flashed on its dark surface. That was past. Their friendship was secure, constructed now of their letters. If this path lay along a vein of sadness, that must be the quiet light in which it was set, or the silent motion of

153

the white folded birds searching without urgency the edges of the dark lake. For nothing but the letters could have continued. So she told herself. Nothing might disturb her peace.

On the quay, when they had arrived, her face, like Euphemia's, must have been as white as cheese. She had looked at Augustus and not looked, taking sips at a potency of which she was wary. But she need not have feared. His person was now less real to her than his absent voice. He had grown stout in five years. The short dark jacket stretched tight. He wore his cravat untidily but high and tight against his leathery jowls, as if restrictions of cloth must compensate a neglect of mind or person. She sensed the hardening of his solitude. His booming voice bore down on them as they stood in a little group on the quay, wrapped round by a cold wind. The language of the letters, the language of ease and intimacy which she had imagined lifted into speech when they met, could not survive its natural element of silence and distance. She must leave before it might return. But she would not leave yet. No term had been set on the visit; Harriet did not seem discontent. And she, once more in possession of the islands, was happy.

At dinner on the previous night he had said to her, 'If you sketch the light I must claim it of you. I am so modest in my demands, but this one I shall press home.'

'Perhaps,' she said, smiling down at her hands. 'If I have time to be satisfied with it before I go.'

'But you shall not go yet.'

He should not speak so. It was the quality of his voice created a privacy which she would avoid. The captain of the cutter, who dined with them, sat at her left. She asked him. 'Are we to be roused from our beds at dawn?'

'We expect you on board by ten. We must take advantage of the low tide to effect a landing on the rock, but the men are able to work considerably longer there now that they are raised up upon the structure.' He was a small man. Stern. She thought conceited. A Captain Robarts. She did not know the name. She would turn from him

154

now, for he must talk to Euphemia, and Alfred Walmer must be freed to talk to Harriet.

'It seems so prodigal,' she said to Augustus, 'and so delightful to lay the blooms directly on the cloth.' Each night the heads of flowers were so arranged in patterns. Tonight the red ensign was set out in red and white geraniums.

'You realize,' Euphemia was saying to the captain, 'that tonight they are in honour of your visit.'

'I am deeply honoured,' he said, but he was a humourless man even when he smiled. 'Is it you who arranges them?'

'No,' Euphemia told him. 'It is the head gardener. Augustus brought him over from Longridge. It is astonishing that his taste can be so relied upon. I should never dare to interfere, although while I am here Augustus does permit me to do the flowers in the drawing room. In my own home, of course, I see personally to all the flowers.'

In the slight loosening of attention this declaration produced, Augustus said to her, 'Once a bloom is picked it seems foolish to preserve it. The more prodigal, the quicker one knows they will die, the greater the pleasure they give. Do you agree?'

'I had not thought,' She would not look at him when he spoke so. She thought of the cloth lifted at the edges and all the flowers jumbled together and thrown out somewhere.

They would go into the cart to the pier. He would give her his hand to descend and again going down the steps into the boat and again as they boarded the cutter. On the deck she would sketch and he would stride about and talk to the captain. He would stand behind her and reach his hand past her shoulder to point to something in the drawing. All day the distance between them would expand and contract and alter in its nature. Their voices would come and go, as disconnected as gulls'.

'Have you visited the rock before?' the captain asked her.

'No. When we were last here it was scarcely begun.'

'There have been many setbacks,' he told her. 'They

should have completed it two seasons ago.'

The servant reached in and out between the conversations with a swathed bottle of wine. When a glass rang instinctively she reached out her hand to her own. And saw at the same moment that Alfred Walmer reached out to Harriet's glass and laughed. Why did she not laugh with him, when he was so pleasant?

Euphemia was saying, 'When will the light be shown?'

'By next season. The structure will be complete this autumn. They should install the light in the spring.'

'And the lightkeeper, when will he take up his strange life?'

'In the spring,' said the captain. 'He will come with the light.'

'How do they live?' Amelia asked him. 'Do they not go mad in all that solitude?'

'Often they do,' said Augustus. She turned quickly at the anger in his voice.

'Very occasionally,' said the captain. 'No doubt the same number go mad on the land.'

Augustus said abruptly, 'I hear you have been recruiting for the post among islanders.'

'Do you object?'

'I should rather have been consulted.'

'Indeed,' said Robarts grimly, and turning to Euphemia continued, 'We have a great many requests for these posts.'

'How odd,' she said, and glanced uneasily past him towards her brother-in-law.

'Why so in a place like this? The pay is good. The men are less separated from their families than if they were at sea.' He turned his head a little. 'There was a young man yesterday called Jenkins . . .'

'Surely not,' said Augustus.

'He was most pressing.' He told his tale apparently to Euphemia. 'The parents are ageing. There's a brother forced to go to sea. If he could find some other occupation in the islands, his brother could return and have the farm.'

'This is iniquitous,' said Augustus. His face coarsened when he was angry. He braced his arms on the edge of the

156

table and leant forward. His voice shook with the effort to keep it steady. 'This is interference of the most intolerable kind in lives of which you know nothing.'

'I only repeat what he said to me.'

'Well, he shall be dissuaded then.'

'By yourself?'

'Damn it, by his own better judgement. No young man would choose that life unless he were deluded. The same circle of water day after day? My God,' he said, pushing his chair abruptly back from the table, 'the soul would rot.'

'It is curious,' said the captain to Euphemia, 'that there is a certain type of man who prefers that kind of life, at any age. Natural solitaries, I suppose. We've had cases of men who have to be persuaded to come ashore when their duty is ended.'

'Then their minds have turned,' said Augustus with contempt.

She felt shaken with his anger. Euphemia had caught her eye. The young people had fallen silent.

It was necessary to intervene. For they must not quarrel with this man who was to be their host to the lighthouse. She said, without knowing what prompted such words, 'At least if they are solitary, there their solitude has some purpose and disguise. It is respected.'

Even as she said it she realized of whom it was she spoke and saw by the expression on his face that she endangered him beyond enduring.

'That is nonsense,' he said without looking at her. He tapped the end of his knife with his finger repeatedly on to the table, giving the words a bitter punctuation. 'It is an unnatural thing. It must be fought against, not indulged. Stamped out. They only come because they are young and lured by offers of paid idleness. Near to their wretched home. Their mothers. Good God. I shall not permit it.'

'It is surely not in your hands.'

'Well, we shall see. I have some influence here.'

He rose abruptly from the table, taking out his watch and saying, 'I will call for the cart. You wished to leave early.'

They all rose, then the ladies, gently smiling, as if nothing were amiss, lowered their heads as they gathered their skirts away from their chairs.

'No, no,' said Robarts. 'I look forward to the walk. My men are at the quay.'

'I'll accompany you.'

'Not at all. The host's duties are with the ladies.'

'Alfred will go with you then. I'll see you to the gate.' And he strode ahead of him from the room.

'I have annoyed him,' said the captain evenly, as if it were of no consequence. 'Will you excuse me?' he said to Euphemia, bowing as he took her hand. 'I have my reports to write tonight and we must make an early start tomorrow if we are to be ready for you. Until tomorrow, then.'

'Charming,' he said to Harriet and Sarah.

To Amelia he said, 'We sail to Plymouth the day following. My ship is at your service if you and your daughter would prefer a swift passage to the packet crossing.'

'How kind of you to offer,' she said, but it was clear that she had not answered him.

'Perhaps you would care to consider it?' He gave his stiff little bow.

'Thank you,' she said again. 'I shall see you tomorrow.'

The granite steps of the quay were slimy with submergence in the sea. The boatmen helped the ladies down. They could see two officers leaning on the rail of the cutter. As the boat drew near they waved and then stood upright: Robarts and his second officer, young enough perhaps to amuse Harriet if Harriet would consent to be amused. On the scrubbed deck the ladies walked up and down, stepping over ropes, catching at their scarves, excited by the vibration of the engines and the distance and wild isolation of the place they were going to.

'Is this not pleasant?' she said to Harriet, encouraging her with a squeeze of the arm to say it was, and wondering if she might encourage the young people to walk together. As it was, all the gentlemen walked counter to them, so that when they met they must part ranks and allow the ladies to pass between and smile as if executing some figure in a country dance. Wicker chairs were set out for their comfort under an awning but it was unthinkable to sit yet. The anchor chain rattled on the deck. They watched it come dripping from the water. The captain and his officer excused themselves; the cutter began to move up the channel towards the sea.

They stood for a while at the rail, watching the familiar shapes of the island alter and pass. The crest of drab wild moor and the long green fields scooped from it on the slopes that fell towards the shore were followed by great rocks, which trailed out among the breakers to form a final promontory.

Around its tip the motion of the cutter quickened. Even with the distant sea calm there is an endless turbulence among the scattered rocks that ring the islands. A hundred years can have made no visible difference to their shapes. For the most part they are square, like wooden chopping blocks blackened by submersion, cut with deep straight fissures through which the broken waves burst upwards like jets of steam. Some rear proudly out of the sea. Others, even at this state of the tide, only arch their gleaming backs in the troughs of the waves. For one instant they show black, with the foamy water streaming from them. Then they vanish. The most treacherous do not reveal themselves at all except by the pale turbulence of the water that washes above them, and the bitter spray flung backward from their hiding place. It was on that rock like a tooth that an entire fleet had perished in one night, taking with it two thousand souls. Captain Robarts pointed it out to Amelia. And there on that hidden reef not many years ago the *Severn* had struck with the loss of fifty or sixty, mostly young militia men. He told her with a gloomy satisfaction, as if the poor dead added up to some personal score which made his own survival the more significant.

She sat in one of the wicker chairs on the deck. He stood between her and the sea: a stocky man with prominent unreflecting blue eyes. Perhaps his short stature had taught him to stand with his head tilted back, so that he

159

seemed to look down his nose from under his lids and point with his trim beard.

'And the light will put an end to that?'

'Oh yes,' he told her, as if he had arranged it all. 'We are very fortunate to have you to record it at this stage of its progress.'

'I have never drawn so mechanical a thing,' she told him. 'I never achieve straight lines.'

But he had swung around. 'There it is, there! Do you see it?'

She rose and followed him to the rail calling, 'Harriet, quickly! The lighthouse.' She shaded her eyes with her hands and watched the bright sea, still in the distance as hammered metal. There was no limit to it. Nothing to hold the eye, but that single frail filament at the hazy join of sea and sky.

'It looks so fragile,' she said. 'How can it survive?' But the captain had moved away. Augustus leaned brooding on the rail and did not answer. Alfred, in the same position exactly, kept a certain distance from him. As if he dared make no greater claim to being his companion.

She said to Harriet, 'Will you not speak with Alfred? He looks so glum.'

'Oh, he does not want to speak with me.'

'Of course he does.'

'He does not. We have nothing to say to one another.'

'Well, you are a guest here. It is up to you to make the effort.'

'He is a guest too,' said Harriet unhelpfully.

'Oh very well,' said Amelia. She would not have the day spoilt. She took Euphemia's arm in hers. They walked along the deck, watching their joined skirts blow before them. Now, when she looked up, her eye went without hesitation to that narrow line which grew steadily more distinct.

At one minute Augustus was at their side. At the next he had wheeled away as if summoned. The boy watched him, uncertain whether to follow or not. He strode to the rail and raised his glass to his eye, as if by that movement he must discover some tiny particular of the structure ahead of them. He contracted the glass abruptly as if he had made some decision. He strode past them in the opposite direction. The deck was too cramped to contain him. She felt surrounded by his restlessness and discontent. She could not put it from her.

Now they passed him sitting in one of the chairs, his elbows on the wicker arms, his hands folded, his chin resting on them, staring straight ahead of him. His eyes, as penetrating and restless as they had ever been, seemed to look with resentment now out of an angry ageing intellect.

Euphemia, pitching her voice between secrecy and the sound of the wind, said, 'Really, he becomes impossible. He is too much on his own. He should have married.'

'Surely he may still?'

'Do you think so? I think not.'

'I had not thought at all,' she said, making to look for the lighthouse.

'It is the uncertainty,' Euphemia said a moment later.

'What do you mean?'

'Why, Alfred. If Augustus does not marry. He will inherit.'

'Of course,' she said. 'I had not thought. Is that what Mr Walmer intends?'

'I should be the last to know his intentions. I thought perhaps he might confide in you.'

'Why, no.'

'I suppose not,' she said with a little laugh. Then, lowering her voice, 'Perhaps he is less alone than we suppose. For what do we know of this place when we are gone?'

'Look,' Amelia said in mockery of an answer, 'you can see it more clearly now.' They had rounded the stern deck as they talked and could see the lighthouse now, not as a single upright, but as a central column supported on all sides by metal struts.

'Is there to be no more to it than that?' she called to the captain, compelling him to join them, for she would have no more confidences. 'Could anything so frail withstand a heavy sea?'

'That is the cunning of it,' he informed them, with such importance that surely the whole structure was of his own devising. 'It dissipates the force of the sea. A solid construction that would confront it without yielding must feel its full brunt and surely be destroyed. That at least is the theory of it.'

Should she congratulate him? She said with a laugh, 'Oh, I don't know. What you say may be very true of life in general, but difficult to conceive of lighthouses in particular. Still, out of very ignorance I am bound to believe.'

She glanced behind her then at Augustus. He had risen, and might join them, but chose rather to cross to the other rail and stare back at the islands. It was perverse of him, when every minute the lighthouse must claim more of their attention, and even Alfred abandoned him to watch.

They had come close enough to see the lightman's quarters perched at the top of the central column like an enclosed crow's nest on a mast. They could see quite clearly the men climbing over it, and the lighters bobbing on their long mooring ropes. A few minutes later the cutter was anchored just outside the rough water around the rock and the two officers were preparing to be winched aboard from the boat.

There was no time to watch them go, as Euphemia and the children did. She must sit apart from them all and apply herself to her drawing. She found her box. She sat in the chair Augustus had vacated and, frowning, began at her task: the central core, the supporting girders, the small splayed figures working on it; but it could not fill her mind as once it might have done. She strained her hearing against the baffling sounds of wind and sea and birds for his approach.

He came up behind her on the deck and leant on the rail, staring moodily down onto the water. She looked at him and then at the lighthouse and then at her pencil lines on the page. She dared not add to them. He distracted her. She wished he would move away, but when he did her attention was not freed.

After a time he came back and stood behind her, then

162

reached over her shoulder so that she felt the cuff of his coat catch slightly on her shawl. 'There,' he said, laying his finger on the drawing. 'It's wrong there. The perspective's not true. Do you see?'

'I shall correct it,' but she kept quite motionless.

'Yes, do,' he said. 'We don't want the whole thing falling down,' She gave an appreciative lift of her head. He said quickly, 'I thought Euphemia would never set you free. I have wanted an opportunity to speak with you.'

'Have you?' For it seemed he had not.

He took up his old position at the rail. 'I had thought of writing to you about it, but letters harden things so and are best left to pleasant matters.'

'And this is unpleasant?'

The light off the water accentuated the deep wrinkling of his face and caught at the pale pouching under his eyes. He would not look at her again, but hung over the rail. He said, 'What do you think of this place? Of the life I lead here?'

There was no time to consider. She said almost plaintively, 'You know I find it a beautiful place. You know that it heals me.' Then, collecting herself, 'You lead so useful a life here that it cannot fail to give you satisfaction.' She waited, looking at the flashing sea, very still at the centre of an agitated circumference, her hand resting on the page, her fingers stretched along the pencil.

'I'm thinking of leaving the islands.'

'Leaving?' For the way he spoke gave the word no weight.

'I intend to sell the estate.'

'But you can't do that.'

He smiled downwards. 'I can if I wish to. You seem to forget I am entirely free. I only hold the lease. As it stands, it will die with me.'

'Well,' she said, 'well? You have always known that. What has changed?' Then, without letting the question form first in her mind, 'Do you wish to marry?'

It seemed that she had said an intolerable thing. He would not answer, would not look at her. The light off the water played cruelly on his face.

He said, 'I have no intention of marrying.'

'But you should, you should marry and have a child. What is the purpose of all this if you do not?'

'That was never the purpose. Can you not understand that?'

'No,' she said. 'No. I cannot.' So sudden was her gesture of denial that the forgotten pencil fell from her hand. He stooped to pick it up and held it out to her. In an extreme of caution lest their hands touch, he pinched the top of it and she the bottom, between thumb and forefinger, as if the thing itself were composed of a dangerous substance.

He said, 'Of all things I do not want a child.' Then, turning away and altering his voice: 'The Duchy are attempting to change the terms of the lease: to demand more rental over and above the original fine. It is as good a time to break away as any.'

She began to speak very rapidly then. 'But surely they would not. Think of the example you have set here, to your own class, of selfless devotion, and to throw it all away. They must be made to see reason. Surely they will alter their terms when they take into consideration all that you have done here. They have an enormous debt of gratitude towards you, surely.'

The conviction in her voice gave her the courage to turn her face sideways to look at him hanging his head down over the water, with the wavering light moving across his mouth and cheeks as if it would cause his face to melt. It was quite expressionless. Nothing she said had meaning for him. But he had heard her for he said, bitterly, 'Will you not listen to me? I cannot continue as I am. I think it is destroying me.'

'That cannot be, you have everything still to live for.'

'I cannot believe that you are saying this to me.'

'But it is the truth. It is perverse of you not to see it.'

'It is affectation in you not to see I lack the one thing I have come to want.'

She laid down the drawing board. The pencil rattled off it onto the deck, but neither regarded it. She sat rigidly upright, thinking, in her frightened imagination, It

164

cannot be on my account. I have done nothing. Nothing.

She said, 'If it is on account of the lease, surely the Duchy can be approached. Discreetly, I mean.'

'They have been utterly unjust to me.'

Instantly her mind fastened on the word. Unjust. Unjust. For he had been unjust to her. She had never felt so agitated. She was aware that she turned the gold bracelet on her wrist first this way, then that, and that he glanced around with irritation at her hands. Instantly she let them fall to her sides, but a moment later felt again the hard little band of gold edge between her fingers. She began to speak then very rapidly, wondering where she had found such words; knowing she merely used them to ward off words from him that might damage beyond repair what she would not lose. For she had never for one instant meant wrong, thought to intrude herself upon the normal course of his life, intended him harm. He is unjust. He is unjust, said the voice in which she spoke to herself, while at the same time she heard, speaking on and on, the voice of the woman who had never meant to harm.

'But what will become of the people here? Think of the condition in which you found them and the remarkable improvement you have made in their lives and their morals. You cannot raise them up so and then simply let them fall into the first hands that offer you a certain sum of money. It would be wrong.'

He said, 'It has become intolerable to me when you are away. It is intolerable when you are here.'

'But you must not. You must not want anything of me.'

'I am unable to want anyone else.'

'That cannot be. That is perverse. You know how it is with me. You know I cannot.'

'I have not asked you to.'

'No. You have not.'

'I have merely said it is intolerable.'

The jarring of his legs as he strode on the planks seemed informed with anger. Almost immediately he crossed the narrow deck and must wheel away from the opposite rail, like some animal in a menagerie that paces to within an inch of its cage wall and wheels and paces back again, endlessly stating the terms of his confinement.

He would not turn back to her as he should and speak pleasantly. It would cost nothing to speak at least pleasantly, but he would not. He thought with hatred of her inadequacy to his need. The lack of understanding she had shown. He had lessened himself in reaching out to her. He had been drawn into saying more than he had any right to say. He had meant only to speak of the lease. For she of all people should understand his feeling in that matter of the lease. That he was abused in this. It was intolerable that she sat and continued to draw as if nothing had passed between them.

When Robarts and his second officer were aboard again, the cutter steamed back through the wild landscape of the outer rocks, towards the jagged outlines of the islands, wavering, but unmistakable as solid land. Behind the next mass of green water they shifted and vanished; re-emerged altered; floated unobtainable when the wave subsided.

His hatred spread itself. The sound of voices and people returning to the other chairs seemed to hold open hostility to himself.

He pulled his watch from his pocket and scowled at it. He returned to stare at her back, thin and upright in the chair, with the shoulders slightly pinched behind her as if in defiance. The soft stuff tied to her bonnet fluttered out, but she was stiff. He thought with hatred of the dry stiff thing in her that did not yield. What was it to her whether he came or went? He would go where he pleased. They would not dictate to him. He owed nothing. He would not be confined. No doubt but she wanted him here, where she might make of him what she would, drag out his soul at a distance, give nothing in return. She had aged. She was not as he remembered her. She hardened into age. She cared nothing for him, but dragged endlessly at his attention. What was this? What was that? Could she do this? Could she do that?

Still as she sat, he seemed to see her move like a shadow,

166

tall, supplicating, in her narrow dress, claiming his appreciation of her drawing. Then she would turn and give it to someone else. She wearied him. He would have her gone, but at thought of her absence his existence seemed lost to him.

There was no opportunity to speak until they were again on land. The tide was still out. They landed not on the quay but on the beach below the Abbey and each climbed separately across the deep pale sand. Augustus was ahead of her. The sand dragged at her shoes as she tried to follow.

She called his name, 'Mr. Walmer.'

Surely it was an intentional discourtesy that he did not immediately turn. His anger was directed at her. But when after an instant he stopped, faced her, said 'Yes?', the blankness and distraction in his eyes made it seem that he scarcely knew her.

On that impression her uncertain spirit fastened: that she was after all of little account to him, that her existence hovered at the edge of a life dense with activity and acquaintanceship, love even, of which she knew nothing. She saw her own life in its decorous course from house to house, from year to year. She saw him as still far behind, possessed of years that she had lost. It was absurd to imagine that in coming she had stepped aside from her normal course to bestow something for which there was a need: to suppose that the islands had in some way offered a landscape in which from time to time meetings with the insubstantial intimacy of letters might occur. She had been deeply misguided in this: the conviction established itself in the second in which he slowly turned and pronounced the query, 'Yes?'

A moment before, pronouncing his name, she had feared that she might inflict pain. Now she would penetrate his thoughts with any weapon to hand. Her face and voice would betray as little as his.

She said, 'Captain Robarts has offered to let Harriet and myself cross to the mainland with him.'

'But he goes tomorrow,' he said, as if she were mistaken.

167

'That is what he suggests. That we accompany him.'

'And what do you wish?'

'The passage would be far easier by steam. We could reach Tregilly by morning.'

'Then of course you must accept his offer.'

'I shall forgo a week here.'

'Well, it is entirely as you wish.'

'I told him I must consult you.'

'I should be selfish to inflict the packet crossing on you needlessly. Of course you must go. I shall go back and tell the boatman.'

It seemed he turned too quickly, with a particular motion of the shoulders that expressed relief of an unwanted burden, and walked back rapidly down the beach to where the cutter's boat was preparing to leave.

13

They travelled the brief journey from Westporth to Tregilly by chaise. Moonlight kept the sides of the road visible through the jolting window frame. Harriet dozed. Amelia leant her head against the upholstery and watched hunting owls hang suspended above the dusty hedgerows: short wings out-stretched, legs dangling. Knowing them to be predatory things, intent about their business, she nevertheless felt herself to be among them, pale, insubstantial, stretched against nothing, dispossessed. The insights of such bleak moments carry untold authority. She seemed to haunt a world in which she had no substance; which could take on no substance for her.

She had been happy on the island; there she had taken flesh. Rocking her head on the upholstered seat she thought with astonishment that she had exiled herself from that place. When she shut her eyes there rose behind them the glittering skeletal substance of the beach on which she had spoken her intention to go. If she opened them, the pale desolate owls hung over the hedgerows. Other images obtruded. She saw the scalloped shadow on the deck, the pencil rolling into the scuppers, she felt the reluctance with which he had turned. Sand dragged at her feet until she was forced to ask: What is it you want of him?

It is to be his friend, she pleaded, to be of comfort to him. You can see that he is lonely. 'Dear Saviour, comfort him in his loneliness.' She had fallen inattentively into prayer. And Pontefract? What of him? Why the proximity of this question? Had it come as an answer? She was tired of it all.

169

'Support me in my duty, oh Lord.' These phrases, like wardens, precluded thought.

She groped after her husband in her mind. Like some familiar object, noticed three times in the day, handled even, he evaded her. She would recall the drawing room in which they spent their evenings and shut her eyes and be instantly confronted by that mound of glittering sand.

For what have I done? she asked herself, freed of prayer. But there was no answer to that, and again the language of her faith caught at her heart. Support me in my endeavours to be more dutiful. She was able to recall Pontefract now. 'Are you warm enough?' she asked him. 'Why are your hands cold?' He filled her with fear. At the thought of him she felt an inner disintegration that made her tremble in the dark, and again the sand intervened: a substance of pale, glittering, disconnected things, the residue of minute lives ground and discarded by the sea that might not take a shape or find a boundary. At the thought of her husband this was her composition.

'Come, sit by the fire,' she told him. 'You are chilled. Shall I ring for wine? Shall I read to you?'

But it was not enough. Mild kind man, turning his long red hands as close as he might to the fire: he was the hedge in her maze, the rock on which she broke.

She remembered waking happy on the islands. 'Oh Lord,' she prayed. 'Teach me to love as I ought, according to my duty. Teach me to submit myself. Teach me to obey. Teach me not to resist or argue inwardly.' And felt each phrase draw down upon her its concomitant weight of failure.

A line of pain established itself between her right shoulder and her skull. She greeted it without dread. It was the concentration of something she would never need to name. She was often afflicted so. The way in which she held her head was a part of the stiffness and rectitude of her normal bearing. Pontefract would recognize it at once as she climbed from the chaise.

She would not close her eyes again. There was no need. The owls had vanished. A clear dawn was breaking and the glimpses of countryside through the hedgerows were familiar now. Slowly colour was absorbed back into the fields and trees. Familiarity tightened.

The chaise slowed and turned off the rough road onto their own smoother drive. The sudden sway and change in sensation roused Harriet, who moaned, stirred her shoulders irritably.

'Harriet,' said her mother.

'Yes?'

'We're home. We're at Tregilly.'

Her daughter smiled and looked out of the window. 'So soon?'

'We made good time.'

'Will Papa be up yet, do you think?'

'Not yet. It is too early. He does not expect us.' She watched her daughter so quickly awake, so pleased, staring, alert now, for the first sign of a living thing, a servant, her father, a horse, a dog, with an indiscriminate eagerness.

There were the turrets of the house showing above the trees. There were wisps of smoke: the early fires had been lit. All unchanged. As it had been on the first day that she was brought to it. As it would continue without her. There was a curve in the drive. The house rose starkly across the end of it. Early light flared from the ranks of windows and seemed to make the place impenetrable.

Harriet said suddenly, 'Oh, I am glad to be back for Sunday.'

'Why?' The statement disturbed something in the mother.

'I miss our church when we are away. The other is so new and unfamiliar. It feels wrong to me. Dear, dear, little church. I can see it now.' There was the low square tower, the dark canopy of cedar, but the words, it seemed, came from Harriet's sleeping mind and had no part of the day. Her strong plain face was flawless in its health and alive at this moment with joy.

'I did not know it meant so much to you.'

'Oh, but it does.' The quick voice seemed to gather in

171

her former words as if she had not really intended to utter them at all.

'We have not talked of it,' said her mother.

'No. I did not care to talk about it.'

She turned her face away towards the window again. 'They will not expect us,' she said happily. 'How pleased they will be.'

It was strange to ring at one's own front door; strange to give surprise to Pontefract's manservant who happened to open it. The statues in the hall were very white in this uncertain light. The clatter and voices of servants had a pleasure and urgency that would be hushed later. It was an hour quite unfamiliar to her. She breathed in its particular smell of damp and woodfires gone cold in the night.

'I shall go to my room,' she told Harriet.

She lay on her bed, but sleep did not come. Nothing went away. She rose and went into her boudoir. It was fully light now. She moved restlessly about the room, tugging the curtains back to let in more light, lifting and setting down the miniatures on her writing table – her mother; her father; she and Cissy; Pontefract, sent her before her marriage. Harriet when she was three. All sunk in various depths of absence. All unobtainable to her. And now the island too was taken from her. She did not suppose that he would write.

Suddenly, as if some engagement pressed and there were only moments left, she sat at the table, took pen and paper. *My dear dear friend*, she began. But could not go on.

Beside her on the cluttered table there lay her Commonplace Book bound in black calf and stamped with her initials. In it, day by day, she confessed to God her failings and wrote her resolves to act better. Now she lifted it reluctantly and laid it open on top of the unfinished letter. She dipped her pen in the ink and wrote: *Give me strength to perform my duties to the best of my abilities, Oh Lord*.

She rose then and went downstairs to the breakfast room where she found her husband.

*   *   *

172

'But this is a great and unexpected pleasure,' he said, rising, pushing the chair back, dabbing fussily at his lips with his stiff white napkin so that the next words were blurred.

He had straightened now, came towards her with his arms extended. Smiled. How pleased he was. Clapped his hands lightly on her arms. Kissed her on the forehead. He smelt of toast and soap. Then he held her from him in sudden alarm. 'You are ill? Why did you come away? Oh,' he cried, as if the pain had reached across and struck at him. 'Oh, your poor neck.'

'It's nothing,' she said, touching her neck with her hand as if she would hide some offensive thing. 'Truly, it is nothing. It grew stiff in the chaise. Sitting for so long. And are you well?' The taut thin skin of her forehead seemed to crease all at once like tissue in concern for him.

'Capital,' he said. 'Only I missed you. I missed Harriet. I could not believe it when I heard her voice. What a pleasure for me.'

'I do not know Harriet,' she told him, looking directly at him from over her cup.

'I beg your pardon?' Yet he had heard her, but wished her not to speak so.

She said again, 'I do not think that I know Harriet.'

He rose as he said, 'I cannot decide whether it is warm or cold. There she is!' he said at the window, affection causing him to drag out the words. 'What a charming sight. She has found Rob. I do believe he is her favourite after all. Will you come out with me?'

They walked on the terrace. It would be fine but it was cold. She could feel the summer falter for all the dark bulk of leaves of the great trees.

Below them Harriet threw a stick in a high spinning arch over the lawn. The dog arched its back as it ran. Harriet ran after it, bunching up her skirts in either hand. 'She's glad to be home,' he said with satisfaction.

'Yes.' But her discomfort over Harriet made her voice sound uncertain.

They had developed a habit of not looking at each other as they spoke, but staring outwards as if something in the

173

garden or on the facade of the house had caught their attention. She reached out to snap off a flower of lavender and roll it in her fingers, saying, 'I had hoped she might enjoy being with Alfred and Sarah, but she seemed to take so little interest in them.'

'Poor Harriet. They have never greatly interested me either.' Later he said absently, 'Wilcox was here yesterday.' He placed his hand over hers, which rested on his arm, as the stick whirled through the air again. The dog barked. The girl laughed at a little distance. It was all as he believed it to be.

'Your hand is cold,' she said. 'Shall we go in?'

'No, no. This is pleasant. I like to watch her.'

'What is it he wanted, Mr Wilcox?'

He gave out a groan. 'Poor Harriet, he wants her to attend upon him once a week for spiritual guidance. He feels we should set an example in this when it appears levity is rife in the county. Still, I suppose I am bound to ask her her feelings in the matter.'

'*Have* you asked her?'

'No. I must, I suppose.'

'She is too serious,' his wife said with a sudden vehemence. 'She should not go.'

'Well, I cannot forbid her outright.'

'It is not natural to want to listen to that man more than she must.' When he made no comment she felt driven to go on: 'She is too much alone here. She should be more in the company of young people.'

'That will come,' he said contentedly. 'She is still a child.'

When he noticed his wife's failure to respond, he said, 'You should ask Euphemia here. It is not far for her to come from Longridge. Have her bring Sarah and young Alfred. I'll give him some shooting and the girl can fill her head with all the right sort of nonsense.'

'I shall,' she said, towards a nasturtium in a stone pot. 'I could not sleep at all in the chaise. I lay down here but I could not sleep.'

'You should rest, then.'

'Yes.'

'And you will write to Augustus?'

'Yes.'

At her table she wrote:

Dear Mr Walmer, and would continue rapidly without thought:

I take up my pen immediately on my return to Tregilly to tell you of our safe arrival and our true gratitude for the days spent on your most lovely of islands. Sadly for us fewer than we had intended and without Pontefract, who sends affectionate regrets that he could not be with us, but will hear every detail of the many improvements you have effected since we first came among you. He does as you know take a lively interest in your experiment and hopes you may find time to call upon us during your visit to Longridge. It remains only for Harriet and myself to repeat our heartfelt thanks for your generous hospitality and the many acts which made our stay so comfortable and diverting.

Pontefract wishes me to send his love.

When she had done she did not read it through, but sanded it and folded it as carefully as a child might. Then she rang the bell for the servant to take it to the post.

From the autumn of 1848, only this letter survives. The Commonplace Book is kept scrupulously free of Augustus' name, and what evidence could there be that she thought of him when she wrote, in a style perhaps slightly more spontaneous than most entries,

It is sad that convention sets such limitations on friendship. To venture beyond the formalities is often to trespass. It must be intended that we confess our innermost thoughts only to One.

On 27th of September, 1848, she wrote:

I was guilty today of quarrelling in my mind with Mr Wilcox's sermon instead of sifting patiently through it all for some gleam of worth. I thought his text injudicious,

175

*and the example of adultery unseemly and extreme. No, I
committed the greater sin of quarrelling with the text
itself, for if the sunken ground of thought is forbidden us,
what room is left.*

Then she added,

*No room. That is His intention. I am sorely tempted to
delete this entry, but consider it my duty to perpetuate my
failings for what I may learn by them, rather than merely
forgetting.*

Never before had she been so intensely aware of the restlessness of autumn and a need to be out and moving. Especially when it was windy, she wrapped a shawl about her
head after dinner, and took her husband's arm and walked
with him; but never far beyond the terraces. It was as if
she feared winter might suddenly strike in her absence and
the house become unobtainable. It pleased him that she
came. How kindly he adjusted the shawl to cover her neck.
Occasionally they spoke. Such a plant must be sheltered
before the frosts, such a one pruned. Harriet should ride
more. But his voice was an interruption. She wanted to
listen to the sounds of drying and flight. Already blotched
crimson leaves had fallen from the virginia creeper and
scurried in the corners made by the projecting bows of the
dining room windows. Rooks rose with their disordered
shouting and spread in the wind like a skein of black wool
unravelling over the dark crests of the trees. These walks
along the terrace filled the intolerable hour between two
and three when the postman from the village walked up
the drive with his brown and white spaniel at his heels.

By three o'clock the warmth had gone out of the sun.
She would go inside, but among the letters laid out in the
hall none was addressed in his hand.

There was a fire in the drawing room. She was glad to sit
close to it rubbing her hands, in agitation rather than cold,
and looking about her. She would try to imagine Augustus
coming into this room. For he might call, though he had
not written. He would move between her and the Chinese

176

screen. Stand. Sit, perhaps, on the sofa opposite. He would speak. She would speak. She could not imagine the words. She had no image of him left except as a shape moving rapidly and impatiently, sending for his boat, striding to the quay, pacing the deck of the steamer. It could not be fitted into this room. He had chosen not to write. He might choose not to come, and if he did it would be when other matters prompted him. He would go as he wished. It seemed to her that other people's lives were united in this progress while hers had become in some way detached. Strong motives would propel them forward. Harriet would wield her new weapon of goodness against which she had no defence; Pontefract, his selfless devotion. Each threatened in its way.

Her mind was weary with it. She must not sit moping by the coals, but employ the last hour of light.

She rose quickly then, as if she must snap something restraining her, and moved from the warmth of the fire to her drawing table by the window. When she might she worked here, copying and perfecting the little sketches she had done on her visits, adding to them tiny human figures as she had been taught to establish the scale of the scene. She drew these figures rapidly, with little regard to the rest of the sketch. In one there was a sailor clinging to the pile of rocks in the lower right hand corner as desperately as if the next wave might claw him from his hold, yet the sea in that little sketch was calm. In another a woman's figure was caught by a gust of wind and dashed, pinned, crushed against the standing rocks in the foreground, yet the smoke from the cottage chimneys rose straight up into the air. Afterwards she noticed these small inconsistencies but could not bring herself to alter them, fearing to destroy what few virtues the drawings had.

On this afternoon, when she folded back the baize covering, the sketch on the table was that of the lighthouse. It was the least satisfactory of the collection. She had been distracted as she drew it and the obligation to have it mechanically accurate weighed upon her. The figures, too, were not dashed out of fantasy, but were supposed to

177

depict the men performing actual tasks on the structure. They did not convince and were all slightly too big. She bent without pleasure to her task, and often found herself looking out of the window for the sight of Miss Christian and Harriet returning from the vicarage. In a little time she would ring to have the curtains drawn, but not until she caught sight of them coming through the yew hedge, hurrying up the lawn.

Her thoughts could not fasten on what she did but must revert to the first time she had traced these lines, the words that had been spoken then. Her flight. His abrupt turning back to a life of which she knew nothing. It was that to which Euphemia had alluded on the cutter. It was that which now tormented her; not the thought of Augustus' angry loneliness but the possibility of a goblin love. A creature of the islands. She conjured up that thing – cretinous, but possessed of arts unknown to her – and shook her head in anguish to rid herself of the vision. She tried to pity him then, to feel in her the power to redeem him, but was as reluctant to imagine those scenes in which the softening of the voice, the extension of the hands, the soul's ambivalent desire to soothe became as fearsome to her as that squat and leering figure that might possess the islands in her absence.

So she sat with the pencil still between her fingers, alternately beset by thoughts she must disown, listening to beyond the silent room for the message of footsteps coming and going across the hall. At that time of year it is all too easy to leave the drawing of the curtains and the sending for lamps too late. Daylight deadens on the lawn before it should. Something malign comes in at the windows and enters the spirits. The clock on the mantel chimed five. Who would have thought to send for the lamps so early? Her eye was drawn to the trees outside, bared, it seemed, within the week. They did not seem, when she looked at them, like trees at all. The branches were tortuous and of a bright acidic green. The evening light had taken on a similar thick unhealthy quality. Large birds ferried themselves from branch to branch, then squeaked and gibbered as they crept about. She must cross the room and pull the bell; send for light and order the curtains drawn against a sudden fear of madness.

'Doesn't it get dark early?' said the maid, setting her tray of lamps on the table. She spoke in a scandalized tone, as if she had brought back some tale of outrage from the village.

'Too soon,' she said. 'Far too soon.' She was filled with a great impatience to snatch at the curtain and jerk it forward. Instead she took up a lamp and carried it herself to the little table by her chair near the fire. Lifting her needlework, she forced herself to sit and stitch, for no hour of the day should go unaccounted for. The brass rings clashed on the curtain rail, armour against the dark.

'Is Miss Harriet not back?' she asked the maid. It frightened her to think of those hurrying figures outside in a world grown obscure and shapeless.

'Miss Harriet is not usually back until six.'

Yes. Yes, she thought. Of course it is the dark makes me think it is later than it is.

'But the master came in a few minutes ago. He will be down shortly.'

'Yes,' she said, easing her neck against her hand. Only when the maid was at the door did she say hurriedly, 'Send John to the vicarage for Miss Harriet and Miss Christian. It is too dark for them to walk alone.'

She looked at the clock. So few minutes had passed. Why does he not come? she thought. He is usually down by now. Ten more stitches, she told herself, and then you may change to the pink. Listening for her husband she was stretched taut, by an inadmissible dread of his approach; his demand that she could not meet; her failure to love him as she ought. So that when she pricked her finger and, drawing it from under the canvas, was able to press from it a bright drop of blood, she felt punished and so relieved.

Her neck ached wretchedly as she sewed. I am ill for him, she thought. I am ill to provide for his need to care for me. We deal in illness. It is our language. If he were never ill, I should not know how to be good to him.

179

Stabbing the needle in and out of the canvas, jerking the wool, she studied the composition of her goodness: that it subjected itself to her daughter's stronger will, that it fed upon her husband's health, that it hoarded her pain from him to deny him goodness in return. Her mind, baffled by such clarity, looked here and there for some action, some gesture that would alter anything, but there was none. She could no more conceive of herself as anything but good than she could wilfully disrupt the pattern of her sewing by working seven pink stitches instead of ten.

She heard his footsteps cross the bare marble hall; always it seemed he stopped outside the door and prepared himself to enter. He would take out his gold watch and twirl it in his hand and whistle under his breath, entering as if swept forward on some current of life that did not require her.

'How dark it is,' he said. 'So early. Where is Harriet?'

But he must know. For three weeks she had gone every Friday as well as every Tuesday. 'She went to the vicarage.'

'Again?'

'Again.'

And now he stood still and they both looked at one another in the perfect understanding that they both thought these constant attendances at the church defiant and even sinister: that each felt powerless to oppose it. What court in heaven or earth would support their plea? She smiled at him then.

But could he understand at all her fear? He was walking to and fro again between her and the Chinese screen, whistling softly, swinging the gold watch delicately between his thumb and forefinger. Would he understand her fear for her child, that some vital thing in her already withered, when she looked so young and fresh? Surely in another year a kind of beauty would take temporary claim and make its demands with all the urgency of a brief stay. But would that man use the tasteless enthusiasm of his faith to rouse in her – she was always strong – the strength to resist; to cast out beauty even before it deserted her, to

180

reprove and abash its lovely clamour? Did Pontefract understand any of that, pacing up and down, lifting his watch to frown at it and saying, 'I do not like to have her out so late,' as if it were of no more consequence than that.

'I have sent John to meet them.'

'Well,' he said, dismissing her effort, 'but it is dark now. Surely there is no need to keep her so late. Wilcox should have more sense.'

'I shall speak to her,' she said to comfort him. But could she say to Harriet: You do not know how soon it goes. If you turn away from it when it comes, it will not come back. Look at Margot Whitlaw. Look at Mary Dell. Oh, but he was wicked. He did this for some end of his own.

'I believe he keeps a tally of souls,' she said bitterly.

'No doubt. No doubt.'

They were in perfect accord. There was no need to say of whom they spoke. It was safe to cry out to him as she could to no one else, 'With what nonsense does he fill her head?'

'I cannot imagine. I find him the most dreadful bore.'

'I think he must bewitch her.'

But could she tell him her real fear? Could she say outright to him: What if she loves him? Can she be in love with him?

That was unthinkable.

Yet she had thought it. Had spoken the words in her mind. But it was unnatural. She thought of Mr Wilcox with his crumpled suit and the wart by the corner of his mouth, to which the eye must drift as he preached on and on. And his dreadful coarse wife who listened at the study door – at least you could be sure of that – as he talked on and on, groping at her child's soul, dragging it down to his narrow uncouth lair.

'You should put a stop to it,' she cried out to her husband. 'Really you should.'

That had been an error. Her voice was raised. It was the tone in which she spoke. He gathered up the chain in his hand and put the watch in his pocket. Turning a little from her he said, stiffly, 'You can hardly expect me to

181

order my own chaplain not to encourage my child in her Christian leanings.'

Now he paced in front of her again, surrounding her, hedging her in. Had she worried him more than she should for her own selfish comfort? But she did not think he worried about Harriet. She had only to voice her fear for him to push the whole thing from her and deprive her of her worry. Yet it must all be taken out again and faced. She said aloud to her husband, 'Do you think she might be in love with him?'

'Harriet in love with Wilcox?' he said, in such astonishment that she wanted to laugh and felt at once some evil thing banished from the room. 'Is that possible? To love Wilcox?'

'Mrs Wilcox may have managed.'

'Ah,' he said, 'that was providence. No one else would marry either of them.'

She even laughed with him then, but the next moment heard herself say, 'But what if it were so?'

'That is absurd,' he said. 'You know it is absurd.'

'I weary you.'

'No, no,' with infinite weariness. 'It is only that I cannot agree to what is patently untrue.'

'What if she says she will not go to London. What if she will not go to dances. How will she marry?'

'But of course she will, when the time comes.'

'But what if she does not?'

'There is no doubt that when the time comes she will.' He was speaking very clearly, without looking at her, as if patiently to overcome some flaw in her understanding. It seemed his certainty was a rigid weapon against her.

'How can you say that?' she asked him. 'How can you say that?'

'I think there is no purpose to discussing it further. It will weary us both to no avail.'

'I had known you were weary of it,' she said, moving to the bell, for to pull it would put an end to the dangers of not being overheard, but as she reached out for it she trembled with the bitterness that he wearied of her. Inside

182

her head there was a shaking that would not let her thoughts subside and cohere which presently made itself felt as a pain below her left ribs. For she had wearied him, when it was her duty to soothe. She questioned him when it was her duty to accept his judgment. She had said the thing she had determined not to say. Only the presence of the pain enabled her now to still her face, for that she did not intend to reveal. That was her own. He could not say she imagined it. She greeted it with cunning as a thing which she could withhold from him, so that a minute later she was able to say calmly enough, 'Forgive me. I am being absurd.' And when he gave her nothing by saying, 'There is nothing to forgive,' she carried her pain erect back to her chair and took up her sewing again.

'Something will drive it from her mind,' he said. 'Surely they change. It must be at that age they fall in love.'

'Yes, yes. Of course.'

'Sarah Walmer will put her up to all of that.'

'They come in a week.'

'Well, there you are.'

When the maid came to the door she could think of nothing to say other than, 'Tell Miss Harriet to change and join us directly she comes in.'

When she had gone Pontefract said, 'But it is right that you should talk with her. It is only right that she should know how we feel.'

'Yes,' she said. 'It is right that she should know we are entirely united in this.' The shaken feeling persisted, as did the pain. She thought, with a dull distaste for herself, What will I say next? She said, 'The windows rattle so in the wind.'

'Yes,' he said. 'In the east wind. Always. It was raining when I came in.'

14

The Walmer family visited Tregilly during the second week of October. Alfred was eighteen that year and about to take up a commission in his father's regiment. His desire to embark on this new venture consumed him, but in deference to his mother, who was deeply opposed to it, he must keep silent on the subject. The months since their return from the islands had passed slowly. Her sighs were often audible and he undoubtedly the cause of them. It was a relief therefore to be able to set out across the hard ridged fields with old Pontefract and feel free to talk at length about the new life ahead of him with only distant sensations of guilt. When the light failed they walked slowly back to the house. Indistinguishable women's forms hovered by the windows watching for them. The evening ahead was to be endured, but he was good-tempered with the exercise and freedom of the day and prepared to make himself pleasant to Mrs Pontefract and to Harriet, whom he liked rather than not.

After dinner he stood at the piano while she played and turned the pages in answer to her vigorous nod. He thought she played rather well and had noticed that she was sensible with dogs and less difficult to talk to than she had been in the summer.

The door from the music room opened into the library. No lamps were lit there. Only firelight faintly depicted Pontefract dozing in his chair and the two mothers deep in talk upon the sofa.

For their friendship, which had existed cautiously until now, seemed to have made a sudden stride. When

Euphemia had been helped down from her carriage they had found themselves embracing in recognition of this new kinship. All day they had felt between them a pleasing sense almost of conspiracy, which now in the uncertain firelight came into its own.

The faint tongues of shadow and light played without distinction over everything in the room, altering, making insubstantial. Seeing her friend's face robbed of that certainty and permanence that made it formidable, Amelia was able to ask, 'Have you heard recently from Mr Walmer?'

'Have not you?' said Euphemia quickly.

'Why, no.' How intently was she watched? She could not tell.

Euphemia said, 'Has he spoken to you of his intentions?'

'No, no. But he would not.'

'You are as close to him as anyone,' said Euphemia.

'Why, no.' And then to redress what seemed startled and insincere she added quickly, 'He spoke of leaving the islands.'

'When was that?'

'It was at the lighthouse.'

'Oh, he has changed since then,' Euphemia said. 'It has still to be settled, but he intends to stay.' She hesitated a moment. 'He is to make Alfred his heir once everything is made final. He has promised that.'

'You are glad?' asked Amelia. For she was glad. She was confronted with a joy too forceful to trust, and cast about for an acceptable cause for it: 'You must surely be glad for Alfred.' She thought: it is the promise of permanence, the promise that nothing there will change.

'Well, there is little enough surety to it even if the Duchy agree. He might change at any time. He is too erratic, too self-willed. I cannot trust him.'

'Oh, surely in this matter.'

'Besides,' said Euphemia, leaning forward so that she braced herself on one plump arm dug deep into the sofa cushions, 'where is the money to come from? His income from it by no means matches what he lays out upon it.

Heaven knows how much of his fortune has been lavished upon it. And Alfred, you know, has nothing.'

'Alfred will marry well when his time comes.'

'He will need to,' said his mother grimly.

'But he will, he will.' Her eye was drawn to the boy, who stood back with his arms folded, reading the music over Harriet's shoulder with a slight smile. It was in the fullness of the lips she saw most his resemblance to his uncle. 'He is a charming boy,' she said. 'A fine boy. I so admire –'

And instantly Euphemia took her meaning. 'Oh, it is no easy task to raise a son. Alone.'

After some moments Amelia said, 'But you have Mr Walmer.'

'Augustus!' with so tight a scorn that Amelia went on uncertainly.

'He is very fond of Alfred. I am sure of that.'

'In his way.'

'I think that can only be in a good and generous way.'

'Oh, he is generous enough for his own ends. He is to purchase Alfred's commission. Did you know that?'

'And that does not please you?'

'To have him go the way his father went? He uses it to divide him from me. That is his true motive.'

Emotion had caused her to raise her voice and they both looked about them to see if they had been heard. But Pontefract did not stir. The air from Harriet's piano ran on undisturbed. The doorway framed the lighted room. She looked over her shoulder and smiled and nodded. Alfred reached across her to turn the page.

Amelia said to her friend, 'It is sad they cannot always be so.'

'She plays so prettily.'

They both watched a moment longer. The tune, an old one, briefly drew its own words through their minds. Then Amelia said, 'You cannot imagine how I torment myself with fears for her. She is so innocent, so unworldly – for all her goodness, for all her strength. Still, not every young man would see that.'

'She is a dear, good girl,' said Euphemia, reaching for her friend's hand on the cushion with a quick touch of sympathy. 'No one who had come to know her could but be fond of her. Besides, surely she has sufficient prospects to be able to follow the dictates of her own heart – to marry wherever she finds love.'

'But will she mistake love?' said Amelia. 'She is so quick to trust in people,' and would in the next instant have mentioned Mr Wilcox had not some instinct halted her. Instead she said, 'There are many men unprincipled enough to take advantage of that. Believe me, I have no ambitions for her beyond a loving and an honourable heart. Someone she had always known for whom love might slowly grow.'

'Ah, they are perilous years,' said Euphemia. 'One longs so to guide them through.'

'Indeed, indeed.'

'We understand one another.'

'Yes, I believe we do.' They were silent for a moment, each with their own thoughts. Then, as if she contradicted someone, Amelia said, 'She is a dear girl,' and sighed. 'A dear good girl. So serious, but that will pass.' She reached across the cushions and taking her friend's hand pleaded, 'Tell me that will pass.'

Euphemia smiled a smile which the shadows deepened. 'Of course, of course. With marriage all that changes.'

'It is far off yet.' For there was still a year, a little more, for the change to occur.

'A year. Two years. It's not so far,' said Euphemia, and then, impulsively, 'Oh, my friend, if I felt I could safely open my heart to you. It would so relieve me.'

'Need you ask?' said Amelia, gripping the hand she had not relinquished. 'Surely we have gone. beyond talk of safety with one another.'

'It is Alfred,' she said. 'I fear for him. He needs steadying. There is something – I will not say weak – but erratic. I see Augustus in him. I have fought so long against it, but it is there. And now the islands too offer him the same temptations.'

187

'They are like,' said her friend slowly. 'I have seen that.'

'He must marry,' said Euphemia. 'He must marry young. I am convinced of that. Someone with strength enough to balance Augustus' influence on him. I am powerless – but a wife – a girl with character and principle. Oh, my friend, such a one would be the saving of him.'

The thought must have time to expand between them. They sat for the moment hand in hand, studying the picture the lighted room presented to them of Alfred standing back to applaud while Harriet bobbed to him and laughed her frank clear laugh. But there was nothing there; not yet. They were unabashed with one another. When they laughed it was separately and not together. But there was time, Amelia told herself. There was still time. It is extraordinary how conversation with another woman can raise the spirits and restore a sense of normality and purpose. For some days after the Walmers' departure Amelia felt cheered.

'Do you like Alfred?' she asked her daughter. 'And Sarah?'

Harriet said, 'I cannot entirely like them. They are so without seriousness.' But she smiled as she said it and added, 'They are pleasant enough.'

'We should have them again. It will be helpful to know more people when we are in London.'

There was no reply to that. The mood of optimism could not last.

The weather broke, but any hope that cold or wet would deter Harriet and Miss Christian from their visits to the vicarage soon faded. And still no letter came.

Indeed no letters from Augustus to Mrs Pontefract are traceable until after the New Year, and it is tempting to surmise that none was written. His preoccupations at that time are, however, recorded in a letter, not to Amelia but to his Prince, written on 12th of December, 1848.

Sir,

Frequent letters to your agent having met with no response, I take the liberty of addressing myself to you direct, emboldened by the memory of the many considerations shown me by your esteemed predecessor at the time when I first leased these islands.

The terms of the lease, as then prepared, took into account the extreme poverty of these islands and the failure of various large charitable sums to give anything but the briefest and most superficial relief to the inhabitants, many of whom exhibited, to those who cared to see, those very signs of sullen disregard of self-betterment which many landowners of that time had sorry cause to recognise as symptoms dangerous to their class. It was recognised that my schemes for improvement must be implemented cautiously over a long period of time: that above the normal fines, certain capital investments on my part would be necessary from the start and that it might take many years of careful stewardship before any yield might be returned to me.

His writing on the paper was as strong and assertive as ever. He took a little notebook from his breast pocket and began to copy from it the amounts of money spent on the pier, on the church, on the schools. He knew each figure well enough, but told himself he must be accurate and check it with the little book. The sight of his writing ploughing the surface of one page and then another made him feel more himself. The diffuse sense of ill-being that had plagued him lately took on form. He thought of all that he had done, and the ingratitude that he had met. Among his own people in the islands he could accept and understand it, for what they had was scanty and immediate. Interfere with that and of course they were resentful. And who would blame them if they did not understand the principles he worked on? It was his own kind he could not forgive, who thought as he did, who had read the same theories, who saw in their hearts the utility of what he did, but would give him no recognition. Still worse were his masters, who knew well the terms of the original lease. The old King had been generous and seen the need of the islanders for just such a man as he. But now that it was done. – the pier built, the church consecrated – all was changed from the old humanity to German precision.

He had made arrangements that, after spending Christmas at Longridge, he should go in person to London to speak with his solicitor and lay assault upon the Duchy's offices. Meanwhile he would have it all in words, first to his Prince, then he would write it all again to the secretary of the Duchy, then to his solicitors.

He wrote that he could no longer afford to maintain his position in the islands, that he would be forced to sell the lease to someone who would agree from the start to the newly imposed terms; who might be persuaded to continue the works he had begun in the islands with the same single-minded devotion that he had shown; who might meet with more approval and recognition than he had done.

For you will understand, sir, that the soil of these islands lies thinly on the rocks and neither my continuous efforts to conserve it, nor the many scientific advances in agricultural method our age has witnessed, will ever substantially increase its annual yield. Yet these rocks do breed – their chief crop if you will – a race of men, sturdy and independent, disciplined from birth by the harsh, erratic laws of storm and tides, but tolerant of other discipline; prepared to work and to work hard, but like all men, when work is denied, equally prepared to live by their wits and to throw their hopes for betterment not on their own exertions but on the vagaries of chance. Hence the flourishing trade in smuggling and the rumours of more nefarious practices that I found on my arrival.

As you must know, these evils are now entirely stamped out. By a firm policy of forbidding the passing of land to any but the eldest son, the numbers dependent upon the scant soil are gradually being reduced. The many building schemes I have initiated as well as the current boom in ship-building have provided work for some. For the rest,

entrance to the Royal or Merchant Navy, or the Revenue
Cutter service, has provided a livelihood suitable to their
talents.

Underlying these policies has been my belief, held since
earliest manhood, that the restraints our class puts upon
the poor, albeit for their own good, should ever be
matched by the gift of education which it is our duty to
provide.

It is my proudest boast that the children of the islands
are from the tenderest age not encouraged but coerced to
attend a course of study equalled by few similar schools
on the mainland . . .

His anger informed his writing. It made him restless.
When he had said all, and signed his name, he felt the need
to state the case again to himself. It was the ingratitude of
his peers he felt the most bitterly, for they had all entered
the decade of early manhood repeating to each other their
beliefs in the need to rescue England from terrible decay
and threatened upheaval, and which of them but he had
applied these early principles with anything like the same
practicality? There may have been a model farm here or a
Parliamentary resolution there, but he had seen to the
building of the pier: had helped build it on some days with
his own hands. Had it really cost him so much? He took out
the little notebook again and checked that it had. And so
the ships of deeper draught could anchor and at once it
had made a difference. But who was there to care about
one obscure man, without influence, trying to build something with his own bare hands? Who would they find in
this new peace-fattened generation to take on the work
with anything like his dedication? Well, that was their
concern. Because there was no more that he could write,
he began to pace about his study striking the back of his
boots with his stick, for he could not bear the wastage of
effort and of life itself. All his old grievances were felt
anew. If some of this ill-humour lingered from the bitter
but nameless disappointment of the summer visit, some
too came from a more immediate source.

He had, that very morning, been deeply upset by the contents of a note sent over from St Warna's by Wills:

I send this, Wills had written, *as I am laid up with an acute attack of rheumatism and cannot face the crossing – else would I have come to speak with you direct. News of a horrid circumstance has reached my ears – indeed may have reached yours by now – that old Jenkins of the Hill Farm, going apparently to St Warna's for the day, caught the packet to Westporth and journeyed from thence to Portsmouth – unbeknownst even to his wife – in the hopes of seeing his son Edward who is apparently stationed there. And indeed found his way to the lad's ship, where, either in confusion at the strangeness of the place, or in despair at parting a second time from the boy, he took his own life by casting himself violently into the sea. The incident is much talked about here and coupled with accounts of Jenkins' threats to you. As you spoke to me in confidence, I fear he may have boasted in the local taverns before his departure, and have his threats held up to him on his return. No doubt he will shortly be given some leave to visit his mother, and I cannot help but feel that if you were to advance your visit to the mainland, say by a week, much unpleasantness might be avoided. The old man was of course known to be an unstable creature.*

This final sentence with its note of cautious reassurance irritated him intolerably, for it was hardly his agent's place to exonerate him from blame that he had no intention of taking on himself. He had a deep contempt for suicides. Nothing but the man's inherent weakness could have prompted such an action. As for Edward Jenkins, he was entirely without fear of him. However hotheaded the boy might be, he could not hold Augustus responsible for his father's wilful self-destruction. And how dare Wills suggest to him that he flee from this boy, on the grounds that he had boasted of killing him in his cups? Remembering the actual incident, the boy's flushed face and his closeness to tears, his acceptance of the situation which he had had to disguise to his mother. Augustus felt nothing but pity for him, deprived as he had long been of the support and example owed him by a father. At first he resolved to delay his departure for the mainland until Jenkins was back in the islands, so that he might publicly convey his condolences. Then he thought of the folly of connecting himself with this event in any way. He had selected a date a week hence to leave, told his household of his departure and written Euphemia announcing the time of his arrival at Longridge. Nothing had happened which could in any way cause him to change his plans in one direction or another.

He sat heavily at his desk, took a new sheet of paper and wrote off to Wills, thanking him for his solicitude, instructing him to reassure the widow that the lease would be continued in her son's name, saying that he hoped Wills' rheumatism would be sufficiently recovered for them to meet before his departure in a week's time.

In that final week before Augustus' visit to the mainland it was commonly known that Edward Jenkins had arrived back in the Gweal, but he was seldom seen about the place. Augustus, far from avoiding him, found himself consumed by a wish to see this boy again. Not to express false regrets of the father's death, but simply to see the changes wrought on the son by the two years of constant exertion and flying motion about the world. In the evenings of that last week he took to walking his little dog along that path linking the rear of his estate to the village, and passing both the gateway to the Hill Farm and old Mrs Traherne's cottage. It seemed inevitable that he would catch sight of Jenkins working late in the farm yard, or setting out to one of the taverns in the village. But each time he passed the farm gate, picking his way across the slough of mud and slurry the cows had made in front of it, the thatched, huddled outbuildings appeared deserted. The life of the place seemed shrunk in on itself to the single glowing pane of the farmhouse higher on the hillside, where he might not intrude. He left at the end of the week

193

without seeing any glimpse of him.

As soon as he was away all such obsessions left him. He arrived late at Westporth, slept a few hours at the Anchor and early the next morning, regardless of the cold, set out to walk the twenty miles to Longridge, to celebrate Christmas with Euphemia and her children and deal with any matters needing his attention there before he journeyed up to London.

15

It was from London, at his house in Eaton Square, that he wrote to Amelia Pontefract for the first time since her departure in August:

My dear Mrs Pontefract,

You will have heard, I think, of the storm; its general path of destruction and the particular blow it struck at the islands. Wills writes that on the morning following he looked as a matter of course for the reassurance of the lighthouse's presence and found it quite gone: the sea being as content and enigmatic as the cat that swallowed the finch. The St Warna's men put out directly and found no trace of all those months and years of toil, but one twisted metal leg still bolted to the rock, and that broken off three feet above. Well, it was a great folly to confront the sea with anything so frail. I have written at once to Trinity House with a reiteration of my own belief that blocks of solid granite, interlocking and cut to lock into the living rock, alone can hope to survive. The work must begin at once, for though mercifully no lives were lost the work was abandoned for the winter months, and with each successive winter that the light fails to show more lives are put at risk.

My own affairs might be said to prosper, for on the very day that the islands were being lashed by storm agreement was reached whereby I can at least hand on my work there to whom I choose. So all hopes and achievements are not dashed at once and I return with a longing I cannot explain, knowing how recently I was anxious to be free of the place and that a scene of devastation awaits me.

I am saddened to hear from Euphemia of my old friend's recurring illness. I would come were I at Longridge and sit a few hours by his bed, but this wretched business has distanced me from the places where the mind takes its pleasures. He has my sympathy. A visit to London is a fever to me. I count the days until I can return to share my old friend's convalescence.

Yours sincerely,
Augustus Walmer

This letter reached Tregilly four days later. It was brought by a servant to Pontefract's bedroom where Amelia, through the past week, had nursed him through a feverish cold. A sudden absorption of light from the room caused her to take the letter to the window, where she read it with the slight sadness and disappointment that often attends something long withheld and unexpectedly granted. But when she folded it again it was with a deep relief of feeling. She was forgiven. Everything was as it had been. The lease was secured and by supposition Alfred made heir. It seemed that the island floated again within her reach, so that, looking up, she was confused for a moment by the scene presented through the window. The sky had turned a sickly yellow. The bare trees lined against it kept unnaturally still. The circle of lawns and fields crept and tensed itself before the coming rain, which presently fell with a quiet watery sound. A bird flew from one tree to the next, its shouts seeming part of the same mechanism as its beating wings. Within minutes the wind began to rise, the windows to rattle and the trees to sway woodenly.

It was a Wednesday. Harriet and Miss Christian had set out for the vicarage shortly after their dinner. Watching the approach of this present storm, Amelia was immediately divided between a fear of their being caught up in it and a more tormenting fear that they might be prevailed upon to take shelter at the vicarage for the night. Then, as she stared through the window, two figures came through the gap in the yew hedge and made their way up the lawn.

She could have cried out, 'They have come,' but remembered in time that Pontefract slept and stayed as she was and said nothing. The wind had disrupted their usual nun-like appearance. Both were nearly running, each with one arm raised to hold on to her bonnet, while their cloaks were blown out raggedly behind them and their skirts dragged at their legs. Amelia, seeing them at this disadvantage, like a pair of bedraggled birds hurrying to roost, suddenly realized the extent to which she had allowed herself to fear them. Nearly three months had passed since she had first promised her husband that she would speak with Harriet about the London season that lay little more than a year ahead. Yet she had shirked doing so. Now, with the hopeful letter in her hand, with so much at stake, she felt a sudden onset of courage and resolution. An instinct told her that this was the moment, before the storm subsided and the world returned to normal. Besides, Miss Christian, after enduring the indignities of the wind, could be counted upon to spend some time in her room, and Harriet could be spoken to without interruption.

She waited until she heard their footsteps and breathless voices leave the stairs. Then, without delay, she quietly let herself out of the bedroom door and crossed the landing.

She hesitated for a moment before raising her hand to her daughter's door, for why exactly had she come – except from a certainty that she must? Her rings struck on the wooden panel and made her knock more peremptory than she would have wished. Harriet's voice called, 'Yes? Who is there?'

She must know, thought Amelia, and would not call out who she was in the passage of her own home, but opened the door a little way and said softly, 'It is I, Mama.' She would not ask: May I come in? but made her entrance slowly, thinking that she had not crossed her daughter's threshold since their return from the islands.

The room in that interval seemed to have acquired a secretive air. Its extreme tidiness suggested hidden things,

197

or some fearful withdrawal, as if the drawers and cupboards might really be empty and everything packed for
departure. All traces of childhood had been removed:
surely the little chair with the dolls had been there only a
few weeks ago? It was like a room set aside for a guest and
Harriet, still in her wet bonnet and cloak, a silent visitor,
staring out at the darkening drive for the carriage to come,
all pleasure in the visit spent, about to depart to another
life. The candle stood unlit on the table. The room could
only be seen by the uncertain firelight and the uncanny
rapid sky beyond the window. It was impossible not to
say: 'Why don't you take off your bonnet and cloak?'
  'Oh,' said Harriet. 'Yes.' She undid the ribbons, lifted
the bonnet from her head and set it carelessly down on the
window seat.
  Her mother sat beside her and could not but reach out
and smooth her hair where the bonnet had disarranged it.
Harriet sat quite still. Since earliest childhood she had
sensed a quality of reproof and regret in her mother's
caresses.
  'And your cloak?' said Amelia.
  'In a moment. I am a little cold.'
  'We could sit closer to the fire.'
  'No, no,' said Harriet, and rather, it seemed, than be
drawn from her outpost by the window she began slowly
to undo the fastenings of her cloak. The fire flapped in the
abandoned room, as if trying consciously to bring life to it.
  'Was there something you wished to say to me?'
  'I wanted to talk with you,' said Amelia, but she had
prepared nothing, imagining the words to be natural
things that would come of their own accord. 'I was concerned about you.'
  'Why?'
  'You have seemed altered lately. Very quiet. I thought
something might make you unhappy.' She looked directly
at Harriet, doubting that the answer to this would be
direct, for she was of course convinced that she in some
way must be the source of her child's unhappiness.
  'No,' said the girl. 'No,' There had suddenly entered her

voice an ardour which made Amelia draw back slightly and watch her in alarm. Rain at that moment struck the window like a handful of gravel thrown by some malicious watcher in the dusk. It made Amelia start, but Harriet sat quite still, aware only of her own thoughts. Presently she went on in the same tone, 'I have never been happier in my life. I have at last found happiness. I have found happiness in Christ.' The voice of Mr Wilcox, flung out at the mother, who could have cried out, 'Not now. Oh, not now of all times.'

Harriet went on: 'I had not spoken to you of this before because I was not entirely sure, but this afternoon I was able to go to Mr Wilcox and assure him that his prayers for me had finally been answered and that I was prepared to give up my life to His cause.' There was no mistaking that she pleaded for some understanding. All the time the little frown of effort rested between her eyes. Already, when it eased, two tiny lines remained on the fine skin. It will mark her, thought Amelia.

She said coldly, 'You do not sound yourself.' For what did she mean: give up her life?

'Oh, Mama, are you not glad for me?' said Harriet, as if her mother had not spoken, and reaching out she seized Amelia's hands in a cold hard grip that seemed devoid of love. 'Say you are glad.'

'What does this mean?' said her mother. She tried to control her voice to a pitch that was both steady and reasonable, but trembled inwardly with a fierce vindictive hatred for Mr Wilcox, who stood between her and her goal, so that her words seemed in danger of being loosened and thrown from her without caution. I must not speak his name, she thought, I must not be tempted to speak his name.

'It means that from today I will be a new person.'

'Don't frown,' said her mother and reached out instinctively to smooth the frown from sight.

Harriet, seeing the movement of her hand, jerked back as if she expected to be struck. This gesture, so sudden, so exaggerated, was more than her mother could endure. She

199

lowered her head to her hands, shielding her eyes, stretching the loose skin of her eyelids with the pressure of her fingers. 'I did not strike her,' she said to God. Then, 'Let me not strike her,' for as soon as her child had flinched she had wished to strike her.

'Mama?' said Harriet. She spoke quite calmly.

Her mother did not look up but repeated from behind her hands, 'What does this mean?'

'It means,' said Harriet softly, 'that I shall not have a season in London when I am seventeen. I have renounced dancing. I shall stay at home and teach at the school until harvest time.'

'This is the work of Mr Wilcox,' cried her mother out of the flashing darkness created by the pressure of her own fingers.

'You are not to blame him. It was my decision.'

'But I do blame him! He has taken advantage of his position to influence you against the wishes of your father and myself.'

'He has influenced me for nothing but good.'

'For *his* good.' For his tally of souls. She knew. 'Not for your good. He has never thought of that in his pride.' The words rang out in the wretched emptied room.

'He is not proud. He is humble. He is good. You cannot understand what he is.'

'Oh, I very well can,' said her mother, dragged now by her anger. 'I have seen his kind often enough. All he wants is power.'

'He is the first person to have made me truly happy.'

She could not sit still under such a blow, with her face watched. She rose and went to the fire, stretching out her hands to it, turning her wrists this way and that. The odour of cruelty seemed released in the room.

'He has come between you and my duty towards you.'

'Your duty is towards Papa,' said Harriet, so quietly that her mother, twisting her wrists up and down in the firelight, went on without heeding her.

'He knows your father's wishes in this matter and he has deliberately defied him.'

200

But she had not escaped her daughter's words. They had lodged in her mind, even as she spoke, so that she broke off and, turning back, said almost in a whisper, 'What do you mean?'

'You know what I mean,' said Harriet still more quietly. Behind her the window rattled senselessly in the rising wind.

'But I do not.' For she would not condemn herself. Yet almost she would have the thing said to have its reality established in another voice.

Harriet held her frightened face quite still. 'I mean that Papa is ill and you must care for him.'

'You said my duty. You told me my duty.'

'Well,' said the girl sharply. 'Is that wrong?'

'Are you suggesting that I do not do my duty?' She turned and walked slowly back to the window with her head thrown a little back and her eyes narrowed in their intensity. She was terrible. She knew how at times to make herself so. The shift of fear in the girl's eyes as she watched her made her cruel. 'No,' Amelia said. 'No, I am wrong. I have wronged your Mr Wilcox. He is not making use of you. You make use of him. You use him to escape *your* duty. You never wanted a season. You are afraid.'

'No,' Harriet said. 'No.'

Seeing her so with the calm face suddenly drawn up in distress, the mother felt cruelty tighten like a band across her breast. What am I? What am I? she cried out to God, turning in fear back to the fire. For she had been within a breath of saying the thing which must never be said, that Harriet was too plain for the season to be anything but an ordeal for her. But it must not be. Alfred Walmer would be there. He would like her. He did like her. Only there he would see her in a different light and might be brought to love her. Her figure was good. She danced well. Her manner, when she was herself, was easy and natural. And he, for all the apparent lightness of his charm, was perhaps more sensible than his mother knew. The name, the family, the money, all might predispose of the unaccountable leap from liking to love. Only she must not flee from it. This must be stopped. Amelia had begun walking in extreme agitation. Sometimes seeing the fire. Sometimes seeing the dresser, thinking the words she must not say. I did not say them, she said to God. I did not say them to her. But she knew fearfully that they had formed in the mind and would lie there until in some further moment of rage she seized them and hurled them without compunction. What is happening to me? she thought. None of this would have happened but for that terrible man. She suddenly stopped and looked helplessly down at her child, saying, 'We must not quarrel. We must talk about this when we are calmer, but we must not quarrel.'

Harriet said, 'Mr Wilcox warned me that you would oppose my conscience in this.'

Persecution, sounded the voice of Mr Wilcox in the shaken room. He will have told her, thought the mother, that those whom she most loves will persecute her, for Christ's sake. She felt tired and confused, as if they had argued for hours instead of minutes. She did not think her daughter would love her again. And so, although she sensed the girl was cold and frightened, she could not comfort her. She could not cross from the fire and touch her. She was defeated. She felt the warmth of the fire on her face, and by a particular shrinking sensation under her eyes knew that she had wept and that the tears had dried on her cheeks. She knew that however often they quarrelled and wept, there would be nothing but defeat. Something in her child defeated her. Some power to exert the differences between them, when they were the same flesh formed in the same mould. She had no other. Would never have. She wanted to go now, but felt she must not go without saying something. Any silence between them would be a potent, terrible thing which might grow out of hand and never be broken. No words came to her.

Harriet said in a quiet, shaken voice, 'What will you tell Papa?'

'Why, nothing,' said her mother bitterly. 'He is ill. There is no purpose in distressing him before we need.'

'I should rather he knew, rather it were over.'

How pitiful she sounded, but Amelia could not go near her. She said, 'Do you wish me to tell him? Or will you?' Her voice had come to sound more normal. Something resilient in her spirit would ease itself of pain. For why tell him now, when surely she would change? There were six months yet. Suddenly she would hear the absurdity and ignorance in Mr Wilcox's sermons, would notice the mole on the lip and, with the sudden cruel revulsion of youth, want only to get away. 'No,' she said, 'no.' And as if released from a spell she could run from the fire and walk towards her daughter, stretching out her hands to her, though Harriet made no move to take them, saying, 'No. Neither of us will tell him yet. We shall talk again.'

'I shall not relent,' said Harriet, so easy was it to read her mother's thoughts.

'Well, we shall see.' Amelia, resting her hands on her daughter's shoulders lightly, kissed her hair. 'We shall see,' she repeated, out of the same superstitious dread of leaving the room in silence. Then, in defeat, she added, 'Shall I send Miss Christian to you?'

'Yes,' said Harriet. 'If you would.'

She was in the passage again, walking hurriedly towards the stairs, telling herself repeatedly that it was she who had suggested fetching Miss Christian. So that it was absurd to be hurt by Harriet's tired acceptance. That was her purpose: to climb rapidly the next flight of stairs to Miss Christian's room, with angry biting steps that would keep pace with the bitterly thought words and prevent their overwhelming her.

For whom have I wronged? she said. What harm have I done? Who has suffered except for myself? And pity for herself, drawn here, drawn there, by one person's demands and then another's, would not soften but made itself felt, a sharp painful grievance in her breast.

She rapped on the door and felt the accumulated years of dislike for Miss Christian hard on her knuckles.

'Miss Christian?'

No answer.

'Miss Christian. It is I, Mrs Pontefract.' Why had she climbed the stairs and not sent a servant? No answer. So she lay on the bed, that withered young woman. She stared at the ceiling. She heard the rapping, the suppliant voice and felt the full contempt of the virtuous. She raised her hand to knock a third time and lowered it, thinking, No, I shall not. Harriet must do without. And lest, after all, the door should suddenly be opened and she be found there, she began to hurry down but stopped on the landing, aware again of the existence of the storm which for the past minutes had been lost to her.

In these upper portions of the house rain could be heard drumming on the roof in the intervals of wind. Then gusts rattled the windows, and somewhere above her a door slammed with an irregular senseless violence.

She would not climb the stairs again. I shall go down. Send a servant up to shut it. It will wake Pontefract. For surely that dreadful sound echoed all over the house. Nevertheless she continued to stand by the landing window, breathing in the chill smell of the leading, watching the demonic trees sway violently from side to side, further, it seemed, than their natures might withstand without snapping. But they had been made with this capacity for storm. She felt she watched a secret thing they would not care for her to see, and would be unable to see the trees again entirely as they would wish her to.

'But I have done nothing,' she said in bitterness to God, locating Him now outside the window in the storm. 'I am what I have always been.' The door above her banged and then in rapid succession once, twice, again, but though she waited for the next report was then silent. She wrongs me. I have never failed in my duty. When he was ill, I nursed him. I fail because I am inadequate and through no lack of duty. All the time she watched the trees and marvelled that they were made so when the incidence of storm was so rare.

The thought came into her mind, spoken in the flat unpleasant tones of truth: All this is her revenge. It springs out of jealousy of your affection for Augustus. Was it God's voice, sounding like her voice?

I am to blame, she cried out to God. For what? she cried after Him when, not answering, now surely He turned from her with contempt. For what have I done? But her need for self-love scoured at her soul. Have I been less dutiful than I might? Have I not loved adequately? She was running down the stairs, for reassurance must be wrung from Pontefract, whether he slept or whether he woke. All these years had they withheld from her truth of the inadequacy of her love? Were there definitions of love of which she knew nothing? Only in ignorance had she trespassed. For I am innocent, she said to God. Then: of what? What have I done?

Nothing, she said savagely to God, who was her enemy in this. Nothing.

She had arrived at her husband's door, and now a true contrition struck her, that if he slept it would be wrong to wake him. Therefore she did not knock, but quietly opened the door, looking at once to see if he stirred or sat upright.

She saw a woman's figure bending over him, holding carefully to a candle which she shielded with a glowing hand so that the light would not fall directly against his closed eyelids. This woman did not move but continued to stare steadily down at the face of her husband raised on the pillow, exposed in sleep.

The unexpectedness of this sight – the sense of violation it conveyed to her – slowed greatly the duration of the minute in which she watched this silent scene. Rapid thoughts filled it. That here was some servant uncertain as to whether to draw the curtains and risk waking her master. That Harriet had come hurriedly to speak with him before her mother might. But to stare so long. Then the unnatural in this act transferred itself to him. Was he dead? Had death awed the watcher out of speech and motion? The shock of that thought brought recognition of Miss Christian's dress, Miss Christian's narrow buttoned back, the thin tight knot of Miss Christian's hair, the devoted greed of Miss Christian's posture over the bed.

At that moment lightning filled the two tall windows of

the room with a weird electric blue. It seemed that daylight burnt outside and night remained trapped within the house. Her own voice spoke out of a cold and angry calm. 'Miss Christian, go to your room.' Miss Christian screamed and dropped her candle. Amelia watched it slowly fall, not towards the bed-hangings but onto the carpet, where it guttered feebly against the leg of a table and went out. In the dark Pontefract could be heard struggling to sit upright. Miss Christian, audibly drawing breath for a second scream, ran past her. Thunder closed in with its sharp explosion.

'What has happened?' asked Pontefract in some alarm.

'Nothing,' she said firmly. 'It is only a storm.' He must be soothed so that she might be given time to form a more truthful answer to herself.

'Should we not do something?' he asked, but hearing the utter folly of his question sank back on his pillows.

His wife, who at moments was sharply delineated for him by the recurring lightning and at other moments was quite obscured, remained, silent. She had sat abruptly down on the edge of the bed, so abstracted in thought that she flinched neither at lightning nor thunder. For, despite her denial, something had happened. She had seen in Miss Christian's deplorable state her own: unsingular, observed, pitiful and absurd. She must, at last, as the unsparing light again penetrated the room, name to herself the thing that she wanted and perceive how little to do with virtue was her inability to reach out towards it.

That same light suggested, beyond the windows, areas she might not venture into that were limitless and strange. All her frightened wanting turned back upon itself and must be transformed before it savaged her into surrogate wanting for her child.

For the island still floating just beyond her reach might yet be unobtainable.

In the morning the daylight had that brilliant quality which often follows in the wake of a storm, with its nervous assurance that all is well.

206

And all was well. The trees stood upright against a motionless sky. Miss Christian joined her employers at the breakfast table, pale, but without any reference to her behaviour of the previous evening. It seemed that incident had taken place in a lapse of time which, having no reference to past or future, was powerless to affect either and might be forgotten. It would have been possible to believe that it had not happened at all, were it not that with every entrance of a servant into the room came more news of some local disaster: a certain elm had fallen across the road, a pig had been swept off its feet, a cottage chimney had crashed through its roof and narrowly missed killing the occupant.

There is always something ridiculous in these sudden reversals. The survivors at the breakfast table laughed, but were instantly contrite. Harriet, as if to establish that the conversation with her mother at least had never taken place, said that she and Miss Christian would go directly to the vicarage to make sure that all there was well and to offer their services to any of Mr Wilcox's parishioners who had suffered hardship.

'Why, of course,' said Amelia. 'You must let us know what we can give. Food? Blankets? You will tell me? John could take anything down in the cart this afternoon.'

'You could come with us now,' said Harriet, it seemed with an effort.

'No,' said Amelia quickly. 'I must stay here and see that Papa does not overtire himself.' It was as if they had written each other's parts in some harmless theatricals.

Amelia herself, when she had spoken with the housekeeper and seen Pontefract comfortably settled in the library to await any news of damage to the roof, put on a heavy cloak and, with a jar of chicken jelly from the larder, set out along the back drive of the house to a row of cottages where one old woman at least would be unable to venture out and might be short of food.

She walked briskly in the lane, surprised to notice under the calm sky all the alterations of the storm. The edges of the track were thickened with a mass of broken twigs and leaves which had clung on unnoticed since summer. A few branches had fallen across the path, but these she was able to drag aside. She had feared an entire tree might have fallen; even cut off the house from the village.

But there was no cause to worry. On her return she was overtaken by the postman, with his brown and white spaniel at his heels, coming as usual to deliver the post. 'I shall take it,' she said lightly, and smiled at him. None were addressed to her. But it no longer mattered. He had written. He had said that he would come and in due course he would.

She did not attempt to calculate when. There is no narrative in these affairs: and then he said . . . and then he came . . . and then, and then, as when the servants talk, but where there is no outcome, no progress is possible, there are no events, only a state of mind, continuous until exhaustion puts an end to it.

All that week the wind persisted. The sky was heavily overcast. Rain fell in sudden showers. It was impossible to go out. She had a fire lit in the drawing room directly after breakfast and the lamps brought well before dusk. Still the windows rattled ceaselessly, so that she failed to notice a distinct knock. When it came again she looked by habit to the door, supposing it to be a servant. Pontefract crossed rapidly to the window. She saw him part the curtains, then he gave out a cry, which, before she could interpret it, was lost in his casting up of the heavy window frame. He stood back, dragging the curtain with him. It seemed that he was replaced at the window by Augustus, standing with one foot on the sill, as if waiting permission to enter. Cold air blew into the room.

'Come in, come in,' said Pontefract, reaching behind him to close the window, but it seemed her permission he must have; for he stood staring at her with such directness that she wondered bitterly if he had spied upon them through the curtains, to know so surely where to seek her out. His hair was wild and stiffly blown about. His face was wet with rain. It seemed that he had dressed himself in the storm that he might present himself before her distraught, damaged, accusing like a thing in a dream. She said coldly from where she sat, 'Why, Mr Walmer, you are very wet.' She was quite still; quite sane, now.

'My dear fellow,' said Pontefract, clapping his hands onto Augustus' arms, 'you are soaked through.'

He laughed. He ignored her. Together they turned to pull down the window. 'I am on my way to Westporth. I take the packet in the morning.' He looked past Pontefract's shoulder saying, with a humility that must mock, 'Am I acceptable as I am?' The damp cold smell of the out-of-doors was still in the room. 'I have only come for the moment. I should not mind at all being sent away again.'

'No,' she said. 'You have made your entry.' The bitterness she felt astonished her. 'You had best stay.'

'Come to the fire,' Pontefract was saying. He crossed over to the bell and pulled it. 'You shall have brandy. Sit down, sit down.'

But he would not sit. He stood in front of her saying, 'I shall not take your hand. I am too cold.' Now that he had come into the lamplight, the fine moisture on his travelling cloak shone like a hoar frost.

'Why are you come on foot?' said Pontefract. He rang again impatiently. 'Surely you do not intend to walk to Westporth?'

'I thought I would. I sent my luggage ahead.'

Footsteps clattered in the hall. He went to the door and told the servant to bring brandy. Augustus stood opposite her. He looked about the room with a bright attentiveness, as if it threatened him. He did not speak. Nor did she. But hearing his stick tap against the inside of his boot she sensed in him that resistance, that irritable pulse that beat at variance with the rest of the world, and pitied as entirely as she had raged at him.

The servant came into the room with a decanter and glass on a tray. Pontefract must take his cloak and insist on his sitting. Throughout the ritual of pouring they talked to one another with such ease. One voice. Then another. About London. About the weather. Augustus sat forward on his chair; he must prove his intention of leaving. Pontefract stood smiling down at him with that odd protective love people retain for friends they remember as children. The warmth of the room and the sharp spread of the brandy in his chest seemed to draw upon him the fatigue of the journey and the long miles he had walked already. For a moment he lowered his head and pinched the bridge of his nose between his thumb and forefinger.

'You are not to go,' said Pontefract. 'You are to stop here tonight. You will exhaust yourself.'

'I intend to,' he said. 'Then I can sleep.'

'But here. You must.'

'No,' he said. 'They expect me. I go on tomorrow. I came to ask a favour of you,' he said to Amelia.

'What is that?'

'I remember that you drew the lighthouse. I came to ask you if you would make a copy of that sketch for me.'

'But you shall have it as it is.' She crossed quickly to the drawing table, released the pins and handed it to him, saying, 'I still do not have the men right, but you will want it as a record only.'

'If you will not stay,' said Pontefract, 'at least your cloak must be warmed.' This must be arranged. He went to the door and called after the servant. They heard him cross the hall and then his voice again receding further into the house, for he would see to it all himself.

She said, 'You have not written – until last week. I had your letter then.'

'Well, I have come.'

'Why?' she asked him. 'Why like this?'

'There are things I would take with me into exile. Your picture is one.' He stared at her as he spoke and she at him: both too versed in separation to suppose they might retain what they saw.

'I am surprised,' she said. 'I was under the impression that we quarrelled.'

'I did not quarrel, it was you that chose to leave.'

210

'You misunderstood.'

'I shall ask your forgiveness, then.'

'I shall give it; not knowing what it is for.'

The little clock on the mantelpiece fretted at the silence until she said, 'So you go back after all.'

'You wished me to.'

'But that is not why.' He rose then and stood with his face half averted from her, staring into the fire, rubbing his cold hands above the flames. The silences between them were shaped by things they might not say.

'There is more to do there than I supposed. The lighthouse too. Has Euphemia told you I have left it all to Alfred?'

'She said you had considered it.'

'Well, they agreed to extend the lease over three lives if I accepted their terms. It gives the place a future which I could not provide.'

'May I be happy for you?'

He turned to look down at her. 'Yes. I should like you to be.'

'It can be as it was?'

'If that is how you want it to be,' he said. And then, 'I believe it is.'

'Oh,' she said, 'I do not know about wanting.'

He sat in the chair again, leaning forwards, smiling slightly.

'Euphemia believes I am out to corrupt his soul – I believe she has settled on Harriet to save it for him – should you like that?' She perceived him as already gone.

'I think you know that I should.'

'I was not sure.'

'It is my dearest wish,' extending her hands, spreading them helplessly, letting them fall. 'It is something that I may wish for.'

He said, 'Then he may hope to have a kind of happiness there that I cannot.'

And she. And she. But all that was inflexible in her prevented her from saying so, although Pontefract could be heard in the hall and the rapid clock beat out like a metronome time still in her possession. 'Which is as it should be, for it was meant as a place to be happy in.' He rose as he spoke. She could tell by his voice that he would go now.

The actual farewell was got through in the usual bustle of arrangements and formalities: servants with the dried cloak and the drawing wrapped in an oiled square, a lantern lest he be delayed, dogs imagining that they too were going somewhere and getting in the way, Pontefract putting on his own overcoat to stand by the open door, urging him to keep warm, to take care, to come back. It was a drawn out affair but it ended quickly enough. He turned to wave once, but by then had taken on the guise of any traveller. Taking her husband's arm, she turned and walked back across the hall while the servant shut the door behind them.

Nothing stirred in the wintry landscape but a few starving birds in the hedges. Augustus walked with his head down, studying in the fading light the frozen ridges and hollows in the road, avoiding the thick crazed patches of ice set into the footsteps and hoof marks and ruts of wheels. If anyone else had travelled that day they had left no impression. He crossed a rigid land as if he, the only warm and moving thing, had escaped an enchantment and left nothing living behind him. He walked rapidly, all the more that he had a repugnance, on this occasion, for his own thoughts and a fear of their backward drag. He needed the cold to strive against or he might have doubted his own existence. He wanted the painful sensation of his cold legs striking the road to force his mind forward on the routes of this scheme and that – the lighthouse, the schools – ahead of him. Any weakening, any delay might cause him to question the importance, even the sanity of what he did: setting out on foot in the sullen light of an afternoon that would shortly fail, for a crossing he dreaded, at the wildest season of the year, to islands that could bear him no joy and would, in time, starve him of occupation. Each jarring contact with the frozen road drove home further attainment of the physical exhaustion that would permit him dreamless sleep. He walked with the greed of someone soon to be confined. His mind was now set wholly on the islands.

He reached Westporth shortly after dark and took a bed at the Anchor, where his luggage waited. When he was called in the morning he knew at once, by the quality of light on the whitewashed ceiling of the room, that it had snowed in the night, and looking out of the window saw that snow still fell in large wet wandering flakes onto the scant layer encrusting the rooves and ledges of the little town. Already the cobbles were trampled black and shiny. Still it persisted. The man who carried his portmanteau to the quay had unmelted snow clinging to his cap and beard. Their footsteps rang clear. Their breath was solid before their faces.

Had they had much snow?

No. This was the first fall. Hence the air of festivity, the children shouting and hurling in the lanes leading down to the harbour. He felt exhilarated and enclosed by cold.

The pile of bundles and baskets waiting on the quay was coated in snow. Two other passengers, hands in pockets, heads retracted into their coat collars, eyes lowering from under their caps, detested the cold, but he paced briskly up and down, thinking to keep warmer by moving.

When the church clock struck nine, the chimes reached the quay with odd clarity; the cold might have affected the tempering of the metal or the very quality of the air. He wondered, as he paced about, whether the excitement and expectation which pressed against his ribs like cold lungfuls of air were simply the effect of the snow, or whether the snow, with its curious alteration of things, accorded exactly with some change in himself. It was a bitter day to make the crossing. His sense shrank from it, but he gloried in the lack of alternative. He had cut himself away. He had no existence now until he arrived there.

Shortly after the last chime was silenced the captain appeared striding along the quay, dangling the mailbag from his hand. Augustus fell in beside him, his head bent down, the solid column of breath rising sideways above his collar. Here was a man who knew him. There was acceptance in the very curtness of his greeting. Together they led the way to the steps, with the two wretches defeated by cold shuffling behind. They sat side by side in the gig as the boatman drew out of the harbour around the pierhead. There was the *Lord Wellington*, her mainsail up, white against grey sea and grey sky. Behind, the snowy rooves of Westporth climbed like tortuous white steps up the granite town towards the smooth white fields beyond.

'Will there be snow on the islands?' he asked Tregarthan.

'Showers, maybe,' he said. 'I doubt it will settle. We'll be out of this in an hour or so.'

He stood on the deck amid the din of the cutter's boat being hoisted in and the foresail hauled up. Then the anchor. They were in motion. He began to stride around the decks with the false purpose of such a man at sea. He forced himself to walk into the wind, then felt its pressure on his back, behind his knees. The cold would not defeat him, but already he feared a moment when he must give way.

For a while longer he continued to stride against the cold on the rocking deck, bracing himself against the gleaming cabin's side, swinging himself under ropes with hands almost too stiffened to grip, drawing in great breaths of cold air that numbed areas inside himself he would not be conscious of; putting off for as long as possible that moment, which now he admitted must come, when the cold was too much for him and he must go below to the fumes of the cabin stove and the inevitable retching of his fellow passengers. Even when something more powerful than decision drove him inside; even when, soon afterwards, mounting nausea drove him to the cold privacy of the captain's cabin: some vestige of his early morning pleasure stayed with him. In the rattling, heaving darkness his eye saw the swift motion of the cutter forward before the wind and his consciousness just clung to a sense of darkened time slipping beyond control: so that, wretched as sickness made him, he experienced the necessary break in being between the mainland and the islands, and felt the relief of the fugitive who crosses water to destroy the traceable line of his scent.

When, at last, sudden easing of the ship's motion told him they had come within the island's shelter, he roused himself and went on deck with a sense of entire newness. The sight of the low islands, denser and darker than the dark sea and dotted with isolated lights, was now deeply familiar to him, but the journey had freed him from familiarity with himself. He seemed to issue out of something forgotten, with nothing to intervene between himself and each new event. Never had he arrived at the islands with such a sense of hope.

His boat was waiting at the *Lord Wellington's* mooring. Without landing at St Warna's he had himself rowed directly to the Abbey landing on the Gweal. From there he walked without a lantern. Although the dark was now profound, the white sand that drifted over the narrow channel of the path made its course just discernible. He would have walked faster, to attempt to drive some feeling back into his legs, but he feared the long strands of briar crossing the track might trip him if he did not watch carefully for their thin shadow. When the way seemed clear he allowed himself to look up to where the lighted windows of his study were visible against the dark hillside. Now that he was so near he let his mind dwell on the warmth of that room; the joyful reception of the dogs; the warmth of vermicelli soup, which would be heating for him now; all the pleasant sensations of being in that room with the windows closed, the curtains drawn, and with knowledge of the cold simplified distances spread around them.

16

It was his custom each February when he returned to set his mind to some particular task, so that he could see it through the early stages before his August visitors arrived; then hasten its completion between their departure and the onset of winter. This year his mind turned to the various improvements he wished to make to the island schools.

He had long since, as threatened, converted the upper chamber of the Customs House into an infant school, leaving more space in the old premises. This year he planned to attach an entirely new room to the schoolhouse on the Gweal, thus making provision for the younger children to be taught separately. While in London he had found time to consult his friend Turnbull, the educationalist, on the latest plans for such a structure. Several were available in those years when elementary schools were coming into being up and down the country. A copied plan with a few modifications of his own had already been dispatched to Wills, and he expected to find the foundation ditches already dug.

But less tangible foundations must be laid in the quality and efficiency of the teaching in these schools, and to this problem he now bent his formidable attention. Turnbull had taken him to several of the new training colleges set up in recent years, with a view to his enrolling three of his most promising pupil-teachers. If this scheme were successful it would solve the recurring problem of finding suitable schoolmasters on the mainland, and settling them and their inevitable wives into the alien world of the islands. Two young men from St Warna's had already

216

been selected for training. By the end of the year he planned to despatch Adela Traherne to the women's college in Chelsea.

He had meant to send for his boat on the very morning after his arrival and, after meeting with Wills, to inspect the schools on the main island, the two in the town and the one out in the country, but on waking he was filled with a desire to remain for this one day within the confines of his own domain. He wanted, too, to find out for himself whether Edward Jenkins had returned to the islands and whether he was still at the Hill Farm. But this thought he kept to the back of his mind, telling himself that as Wills had made no mention of the new schoolroom in his last letter it would be foolish not to check on the foundations at first hand.

Accordingly he sent the boatman away with a note for Wills, saying that as there appeared to be nothing of pressing importance he would delay his first visit to the main island until tomorrow. Immediately after breakfast he set out on foot along the long walk between the hill and the lake. At that early hour there was considerable activity. Birds glided onto the surface of the water, preened above their white shadows, sat still on nests among the soft pale rushes; but all this was so remote from any human enterprise, so noiselessly conducted, that it seemed a part of the rapid movement of light on water and merely added to a sense of serenity.

A shot rang out on the hillside above him. He heard the yammering of ducks and the beat of wings off the lake, then the harsh cry of one of his own peacocks from behind the wall and the excited barking of dogs from their stone kennels behind the house. At the curve in the path he saw the two gamekeepers knee-deep in bracken, with their rigid easy stance, the guns slanting downwards. The head keeper made one fierce gesture with his arm behind his back, to go no further, which Augustus instantly obeyed: bowing to the man's primitive authority, but at the same time fretting under it. There was violent agitation among the dead bracken. Then a wet spaniel emerged, sniffing in

217

a distracted circle. The gamekeeper gestured him on. He made no attempt to call up to him, merely lifting his hat, but the absolute intentness and certainty of man and dog irritated him, for what could they possibly be doing that was of any real importance? It was no part of his world. He merely kept them. Alfred, he thought, would enjoy that side of things, would go among these men more easily than he.

He went through the farmyard and took the track leading to the village. He spoke to the few people he passed, making as if to lift the visor of his cap with the tip of his stick. When Billy Bayliss passed him pushing a handcart, he peered inside and saw a stone.

'What's that for?' he asked him in his loudest voice.

'My wall,' Bayliss told him. 'There's a gap needs filling.'

They looked not at one another but at the stone. All the time they stood there the schoolchildren ran pelting past them: the boys snatching and tossing each other's caps as they ran, involved in some vehement conspiracy, the girls arm in arm, whispering, tossing and sly.

'Where did you find it?' he said to Billy Bayliss.

'Up Downs. I'd looked for days for one that shape.'

'So long as it came off no other wall,' he told him grimly, and walked on.

He stood by the door of the schoolroom, motioning Davies to go on as if he were not there, but the children turned their heads to stare at him. He frowned and pointed to the books with his finger until they bent their heads again. Adela Traherne moved silently between the desks, so quiet and withdrawn that she seemed to absorb all the restless sounds made by the children's boots and fists. Occasionally a chalk shrieked and they all turned to look at him again but he frowned and pointed to their books. He noticed how unconsciously the girl laid her hand upon the shoulders or heads of the children as she bent over them, and how some of them leant against her as she spoke, but she spoke so quietly that he could not make out her voice. He calculated that she was eighteen now. He thought she would do well in London, that it was an opportunity for her. Outside the window he heard the regular chink chink of the spades as the men worked on the foundation ditches. When he had inspected their progress, he resolved to go back past Mrs Traherne's cottage and discuss the matter with her.

As he began to climb the stony track behind the village he made out Mrs Traherne's small unbending form walking ahead of him, with her cloak fluttering behind her and a basket on her arm. He went briskly to overtake her.

Hearing quick footsteps gain upon her, Mrs Traherne turned patiently into the grass at the base of the low wall and waited for him to pass, scarcely looking to see who it was.

'May I walk with you?' Augustus asked. 'There is something I must discuss.'

She ducked her head with her habitual misleading humility of manner and began to walk at his side.

'May I take your basket for you?'

'That's kind of you,' she said, settling it on her arm, 'but it weighs scarcely anything.'

He was silent for a moment, trying to shorten his pace to hers without appearing to. She had aged recently and the hill grew steep for her. He would not have her hurried. He said, 'I am told Mrs Jenkins is a friend of yours. It has been a sad time for her, I fear.' He wondered if this woman would reproach him in any way. She said simply, 'He was of little use to her, but still she grieves.'

'It was the manner of it,' he said. Then, 'Is the boy back?'

'He has been. He was with her for a week. The other would be more comfort to her if she would let him be.'

'Yes. I should imagine that.' Silence came between them again. Finally he said, 'I wished to speak of Adela's future plans.'

'Oh!' Her tone of rather harsh surprise seemed chosen to establish that she held him apart from these.

'I spoke to you once before about the possibility of sending her to London to be trained.'

'Trained?' She would put off understanding as long as she could.

'To teach,' he said patiently.

219

'But she is teaching. Does she not give satisfaction as she is?'

He would not hurry her. He leant against the wall so that she was forced to turn and look at him. The bitter weariness and resistance in her eyes shocked him. 'With a certificate she could take over the infant schoolroom. She would be paid more. I should, of course, see that so long as she continued to teach there she had tenure of the cottage.' He did not say, 'After your death', but the understanding was instantly there.

'To London?' she asked, drawing out the word to a great distance. 'Is there nowhere nearer?'

'She will be well cared for. I have visited the place.'

'Oh, I dare say. But to travel all alone!'

'I thought you had wanted this for her.'

But she would not meet his eye. 'We have come a long way to this place,' she said, looking slowly about her from under her parched heavy lids. 'I've to thank you for that, but now to take her away again so soon!'

'It is not a question of taking her. I have no power to take her,' but it crossed his mind, as he spoke, that Mrs Traherne herself had not hesitated to take Adela and that now she did the child wrong. Instantly he sensed that this idea had conveyed itself to Mrs Traherne, who said stiffly, 'There are some would say she is not mine and I have no power to make her stay.'

He pitied her then and said more kindly, 'She will be well cared for. I can assure you of that.'

He sat on the wall. She stood squarely opposite him so that the disparity in their heights was done away with and they looked directly at one another. 'And what of the time when I am gone?' she asked him. 'Who is to care for her then?'

'She will marry,' he said, almost dismissively, for surely Mrs Traherne took too much upon herself.

'Ah, marry,' she said now in her most scornful voice.

'Don't you see,' he said patiently. 'If she is able to find employment here she will never have to marry. She will be able to suit herself in that.' But he thought of the girl and the child leaning its head unconsciously against her breast: of course she would marry.

'It worries me night and day what will become of her when I am gone.'

'Well, you must trust me in this – that this is the best thing for her. I thought you were in agreement over this. I am sure we have spoken of it.'

'Then it was a long way away.'

'But do you agree to it? If I promise to make myself personally responsible for her safety?' But under her steady look, and the force he sensed of her bitter convictions, formed by a life of which he knew nothing, he felt that the word had become a dubious thing. He felt the total folly of his promise and said immediately: 'Nothing, of course, is safe. I should like to think the child's gentleness and innocence would insure her protection in the world, but who can say? You must decide what you think best, but surely a respectable means of keeping herself independently is her best defence in life?'

'You are right,' she said suddenly. 'If I keep her with me she will have nothing. Very well, you may send her then.' And without another word to him, certainly with no word of thanks, she nodded and began again her slow climb to her own gate where she turned without looking back and went into her cottage.

Mrs Traherne's sudden resistance to the idea of Adela's going to London was voiced only to Augustus. And, indeed, once she had accepted that the girl must go, her old almost vengeful ambition for Adela came back to her. As she could not prevent this rupture in their lives she forced herself to want it, as proof that Adela could triumph in a world from which she had fled. Her fears for her, which were deep and tormenting, she kept entirely hidden.

As for Adela, this chance to obtain a teacher's certificate had been the height of everyone's ambition for her. She had come to accept it as an immediate goal which she was fearful of not achieving. So when the letter of acceptance came from the college she felt great relief, and was inclined to interpret her Aunt Traherne's pride and fierce pleasure as her own.

At first the strategies required to fill her small trunk were endlessly absorbing. Neighbours brought gifts, small things: a ribbon, a comb, a text. Not only Mrs Davies and Mrs Jenkins but a few of the more prosperous mothers of the schoolchildren, out of gratitude perhaps for Adela's gentleness, or perhaps fascination at the very thought of that remote city of which they knew nothing but the wildest untruths. A few of the older women may have chosen this moment to express a stifled regard for Mrs Traherne's steadfast keeping of her pledge, which they would never have dared to show in any more direct way.

All these treasures Adela packed and repacked in her trunks, laying them this way and that with great solemnity, as if she foresaw the need there would be to build her former world out of these small tokens in a place where her own precarious existence was not known at all.

The parting at the quay was solemn, too. Only on the last morning of all did the full sense of separation from her Aunt Traherne overwhelm her. Billy Jenkins had come early after milking to wheel her trunk in the farm handcart to the quay. They gave him a few moments' start. Then they set out. A dark drizzle fell. Cows stood on the hill, their hides patched and matted with rain; the sky was low and hopeless. Two or three other groups entered the empty lane and headed towards the quay, silent, bowed under the weather. As they passed the schoolhouse, kind Mrs Davies stood waving in her dressing gown. Adela held tightly to the old woman's hand all during the walk from the village to the harbour, and felt its hard grasp in return. When she glanced at Mrs Traherne's face it was set in its most resolute lines, but Adela sensed her desolation. Her farewells when they reached the quay were stern and brief. A moment later Adela was seated in the heaving gig, looking up at that lifelong figure, diminished already, standing a little apart from the other women, watching without flinching as her very existence was drawn from her. Adela felt intense pain, and at the same time fear and shame, for at the height of her feeling she perceived its impermanence and began to dread that moment when cold or hunger or excitement would distract her. She closed her eyes on that image, and held it as long as she might, but of course soon she was bound to open them again.

The boat had begun to move away from the quay towards St Warna's. She watched the group of off-islands and the standing rocks between them shrink and close in on one another, as if they instantly healed over any gap that she had left. Seeing them in the distance, crouched and shrunken above the jostling water, it seemed she had never truly been a part of them. It occurred to her then that perhaps she had now picked up the thread of that original journey on the *Severn*. All these years she had carried that event around inside her, unable to remember it, so that she must endlessly listen out for scraps of that legend until she seemed to see it as clearly and detachedly as some gull that had swooped past and with its predatory eye snatched up an impression of the woman dragged on the rope from the sea, clutching the white garments of the child, and then, wheeling back at dawn, the drowned soldier in his red coat on the rock.

Later, when the *Lord Wellington* tacked farther and farther out to sea, she chose not to watch the receding islands. In the long interval when neither islands nor mainland were visible it seemed she was released of that identity in which Mrs Traherne had clothed her nakedness, and that those two vanished portions of herself, her myth mother and myth father, reclaimed her. She felt for the first time their curtailed lives existing in her. She knew nothing of them, but then she knew nothing of herself, other than as a centre around which the island, familiar but alien, had spread itself. When next she tried to think of Mrs Traherne, although she could remember exactly where and how she had stood on the quay, no distinct picture would form, and the pain she felt at the thought of her was already a fugitive one.

Can it be? she thought. *Can I really be like this?*

She could see the stuff of her new plaid dress where her arms leant out of her cloak and rested on the rail. She felt its tight grip in the small of her back and the tugging of her bonnet in the wind. She thought of herself for the first time as something which other people might see and wonder at. Even the fears that beset her on that journey of managing her body in an unknown world, the anxiety about the next privy, the fear of sweating, were not unwelcome.

The rain had stopped. She ate the food Mrs Traherne had prepared for her on the deck, and drank a little water from the barrel by the mast. Then as the cold began to settle, towards mid-afternoon, she went into the cabin. Faces turned to study her, and there was a cheerful shuffling together to make room. She kept her eyes lowered and climbed past outstretched legs until she reached a narrow gap. Then, sitting herself cautiously with her back pressed against the wooden partition of the cabin, she pretended to sleep while she listened to the voices around her.

It disappointed her that they spoke of things she knew. There were five men in the cabin, all farmers from St Warna's taking the last of the potato crop to Westporth. They spoke of the price of potatoes and Mr Walmer.

'I wouldn't trust him further than I could bloody throw him,' said one. 'And I couldn't throw him far at that. He's a terrible bloody belly on him these days.'

'Yes,' said another. 'He's a miserable bastard, but I don't mind him.'

The voices dragged her back out of her forward journey. She was impatient with them. Once, when she allowed her eyelids to waver open, she saw the farmer opposite staring at her without animation or inquiry. Quickly she shut her eyes again, but a moment later was aware that the older man beside her had turned in her direction.

'Do you feel the motion, Miss?' There was amusement in his voice, as if he knew well enough that her sleep was a pretence.

'No,' she said, opening her eyes. 'I feel quite well, thank you.'

They all watched her now, bright-eyed, with smiles just withheld as if they planned some sport. She was afraid of them.

'Will you take a little piece of barm bread with me?' said the older man courteously enough, holding out a slice of cake on a spotlessly white napkin which fell down over his hand.

'No, thank you, I've eaten,' said Adela, more out of fear of depriving him than reluctance to eat it, for it looked very good.

'Very well, then,' he said, withdrawing the cake. Her heart contracted with fear that she had offended him. 'It looks very good,' she said, 'but I have eaten.'

One of the other men chuckled and muttered under his breath to his neighbour, who drew the back of his hand slowly across his mouth and said, 'Do you travel far, Miss?'

'To London.'

'To visit?'

'To train at Whitelands' college.'

'Well, fancy that. What will you be at home, then?'

'A teacher.'

'Oh. I'd a teacher once,' he confided to his friend. 'She never looked like her.'

'There. You'll cause the young lady to blush if you go on like that. You pay him no heed, Miss.'

She smiled at them uncertainly, wishing that she might close her eyes again, to avoid theirs and to avoid the need to speak. For she had no idea how to speak to them. The formal exchanges between Mrs Traherne and her neighbours were of little use to her now. It seemed some statement was expected of her which she had failed to make. As if she had not known the words of some childish chant and so the game had swept past her, leaving her standing by the edge of the playground tormented by her own ignorance. Still, as in the past, in the rough grass outside the school, she was in her heart relieved not to be swept away into a game of whose purpose she was ignorant. She sensed it lay in an area at once unpleasant and exciting, and wondered if she might close her eyes again, or whether

225

that would bring down comment upon her. She sat, therefore, with her head bowed slightly over her gloved hands folded in her lap and wondered if they still watched her.

When their conversation was expended the men grew restless and stirred audibly on the hard wooden benches. Finally the heavy-set man opposite sighed, rose, stood, rubbed his hands and said, 'Well, I'll take a turn on the deck.' He pushed open the door of the cabin. One by one they rose and followed him until the cabin was quite empty. She felt immense relief, stretched out her legs, looked at the shining toes of her new boots, but almost immediately feared that some inadequacy of hers had caused them to go out into the cold when they might have stayed chatting cosily along some lines unknown to her in the warm close cabin. She could see them through the little window in the cabin door, walking against the wind, their hair driven upright from their lowered heads, shoulders hunched, hands in pockets, as if they had set their bodies to describe the wind and the comfort from which she had driven them.

A raw unprotected feeling she had known in the intervals of studying at school descended upon her, but was soon dispelled when one of the men opened the door and said quite naturally to her, 'Come and look, Miss. We're close into land. You won't find it too cold.'

He held the door for her; walking through it, she found herself facing the high solid rise of the mainland out of a quiet sea. It disappointed her that she was capable of seeing so little of what she knew to be so great in size, and that only in the height of the rough brown cliff and the brilliance of the green fields laid upon them did this land greatly differ from what she had left. Then she allowed herself to believe that perhaps what seemed familiar rose out of memory of that childhood existence she had lost, that this was indeed recognition of a domain that was her own; and so everything new, the smell of woodfires, the din of the cobbled streets between the close-packed stone house fronts, she absorbed as easily as a lesson learnt, but forgotten, which would soon be called to account.

The Reverend Mr Jameson met her on the quay. She spent that night at the vicarage, eating with the family and sleeping a sleep of sheer exhaustion, as if she had walked all day against the pressure of the wind.

In the morning she was taken to the station and seated in the carriage of a train. There she sat staring for the next hours through the window in a trance at all this new world, which was proffered and then endlessly snatched from her by the confusing speed of the train.

17

At Paddington Station she waited by her trunk on the platform as she had been told, and presently a little lady in a black bonnet approached and asked if she were Miss Traherne. Adela said she was.

'I am Miss Lawson. I have come to take you to the college.'

Side by side they swayed through the dark street in a cab. Miss Lawson asked if she were cold, if she were tired, if she had eaten. To all of which Adela answered, 'No.' But she could scarcely find the courtesy to turn her head from the window. In the dim street lights the pavements were thronged with people. Windows were lit on the tall house fronts and dark figures moved and stood in their separate lives behind the invisible glass. Everywhere the surfaces of staring faces seemed thrown up to her from the edges of the street. Once they passed a crowded market and here the faces, garishly lit by flares, were like masks caught in moments of excitement open-mouthed. She could not free herself of the impression that each and every one was of some significance to her. For why else at that precise moment, should they and she pass one another? A coincidence so remarkable must form a bond. In all this vast sampling of humanity she must find something to recognize and claim as her own.

Presently the little woman beside her said, 'We are nearly arrived.' They had left the crowded streets behind them and moved down a road where the patterned facades of the lighted windows stretched unbroken on either side. Suddenly they heard the cabman call over their heads as he drew in his reins, and the intensified clatter as the horse broke its trot. The cab swayed to a halt. 'We are there,' said Miss Lawson, with a certain drama. 'Mrs Watson will have waited up for us.'

'Who is Mrs Watson?'

'You do not know who Mrs Watson is? Why, she is the superintendent.'

They climbed down by the gate of a large stone house like the others Adela had glimpsed. An iron railing barely divided it from the pavement. Through the carved transom over the imposing door candlelight showed, but the rows of windows above were entirely dark. 'The girls are all asleep now,' Mrs Lawson told her. 'You must go into the dormitory very quietly so as not to disturb them, but first Mrs Watson will speak to you.'

They were met in the dimly lighted hallway by a tall gaunt woman, who said, without smiling, 'I hope you had a good journey, Adela.'

'Thank you, Miss.'

'Mrs Watson.'

'Mrs Watson.'

She held a lighted candle in a holder and now, advancing it to Adela's face, raised and lowered it, staring at her all the time through its haze of rays. By the same light Adela must inspect the superintendent: a long sallow face that did not care for what it saw but took its time in looking. At last she reached out her free hand and, pinching a fold of Adela's skirt, held that up to the candle light. 'I suppose you think your clothes very pretty?' she said unpleasantly. 'Very fine?'

Adela said nothing.

'Presumably that is not your only dress. You have another more suitable.'

'I have my old skirt I teach in.'

'And no other?'

'Only this.'

'Well, the skirt must do while you sew a dress like the other girls'. You do not, I hope, suppose you will be able to send for a sempstress in your new calling.'

'I should have no need.'

'Do not answer back, Adela.' Then, speaking only to Miss Lawson, she said, 'As the plaid is so dark I think we might permit it on Sundays once all the braid is picked off.'

The cost of the braid, its brave extravagance, the sense of conspiracy with which she and her Aunt Traherne had bought it from the little shop on St Warna's, the tedious hours spent stitching it along the line of the plaid, all came vividly back to Adela, but they were powerless charms. She had lost on the instant all pleasure in this dress, which, like that original white one she and Mrs Traherne had sewed together, had seemed not so much a covering as a bark that would carry her safely through elements of which she was incapable. Now at the start it had failed her, and with a cruel disloyalty she thought of Mrs Traherne's ignorance of what would do.

It appeared that a letter had been sent – but never arrived – specifying the nature of the green rifle dress that must be worn on weekdays. Two must be sewn; a letter was despatched at once to Mr Walmer, asking if he would pay for the stuff. Until his answer came she might not even begin but must make her way among this mass of knowing girls in her old teaching skirt and her patched blouse. When the stuff was produced she was set at once to sew in her recreation times, half an hour after breakfast and after lunch, and after tea when the other girls swayed and leant together as they walked up and down the path of the garden behind the house.

A table was drawn up to the window of the low, panelled parlour, and here Adela sat, sewing as quickly as she might, for she longed for the dress to be complete so that she might take on its drab colouring and be like the other girls.

Outside, the world pressed upon the little room. The window overlooked a street where traffic constantly clattered and rumbled and the soaring birdlike cries of street sellers could be heard. There were other sounds, especially in the early morning, the straining cry of cocks, and the sound of boats' hooters. She let herself imagine that the long hours of travelling had not existed, that the harbour and the countryside around Westporth were still within her reach. That if she could once be out in the street she might follow the hurrying figures she could see through the iron fence and find herself there. She knew this was not so. Yet she listened with a kind of passion, frowning with effort, as she sewed, to hear these fugitive sounds above the immediate clatter of boots on the uncarpeted floors, the ceaseless chatter of the girls, the insistent clamour of the handbell.

By the end of the second week the drab green dress was complete, but wearing it scarcely decreased Adela's sense of separateness. Heavily as this bore down upon her she recognized an aptness in it, and had perhaps always suffered from a sense of dislocation; so that her late arrival, her odd clothes, her unfamiliar dialect all seemed expressions of a truth disclosed.

She was deluded into believing that everyone else had attended the college for at least a year, that they had formed intimate and exclusive friendships with one another, that they shared an instinctive knowledge of what to do and watched, aghast, her ignorance. The many shy kindnesses shown her during her first weeks she took as signs of pity. The reticence induced by her beauty and her air of slight distraction she supposed to be disappointment in her. She said very little; speech had never come readily to her. Almost she feared their smiles, their requests that she join them, through a certainty that anything they appeared to recognize in her was a delusion, that on knowing her better they would find her dull and tire of her, and that friendship offered and withdrawn would pain her more than the belief that it did not exist.

She went about trying to remember her way, trying to remember, when the handbell was rung, where she should go next, trying to absorb all that was told her, all the time conducting in her head a rapid senseless argument in her own defence: I could not have the proper dress, coming from so far. There was no time to have it fitted when I came. So deep was her anxiety that her lips moved. 'Are you praying?' one of the girls asked her.

Her waking day was filled with inordinate fears of making some mistake which would reveal her ignorance of what was correct. Nothing was too trivial to fear, for it seemed that the slightest flaw could be enough suddenly to release upon her the bottled malignity of the world.

Day followed day, each with its minute distinctions. Monday, Tuesday, Wednesday, each was a separate territory with a separate range of hills to toil over. She saw time as a week now, laid out in the timetable, ruled with black ink, and she like a speck of dust on this or that part of it. To have laid these ruled segments end to end and made a whole year of them would have been quite beyond her imagination.

Only Sunday, with its ritual of difference, gave some impression of an outer world. On Sunday she put on the dress which she no longer loved, then, two by two, they walked to the church farther down the road. Because she had arrived alone, because her sewing had kept her separate in the recreation times, there was no one for Adela to walk with. If she hung back, usually someone was left single at the end, as glad perhaps for her as she was for them. Yet they would scarcely smile at one another as they took their places side by side on the pavement, and talked little as they walked through the still, hushed Sunday street to Early Communion, shamed at the friendless state the other mirrored. Some instinct warned her not to befriend these other solitaries lest she never be free of them.

The church was big and newly built. So few people had died since that only the north side of the churchyard was broken by graves marked with new unweathered stone. To the south a patch of roughly scythed grass lay waiting; here they were allowed to walk and play between the early service and matins. She stood leaning against the wall, not wanting to appear alone, near but not part of a group of girls.

'Did he kiss you?'

'Let me be. I don't have to tell you.'

'Come on. What was it like?'

'What did it feel like?'

'All goosey.'

'Oh, I wish. I wish. I wish.' Round and round she whirled,

hugging herself with her own arms. That girl was Miriam Archer, who slept in the next bed. Who had waited for her on the first morning.

On Sunday the girls who had crinolines might wear them, but they must have only one colour ribbon on their bonnets, no flowers or feathers or bead trimming, neither pink nor red trimming. She had learned these things, but feared constantly that she would forget. The soldiers' voices were very deep in the church. The singing made her back shiver. But you could not see their faces. When they took off their caps their heads were cropped. Their necks were red; they had boils on them.

On Sunday there was cold roast beef and after lunch they might go to their dormitory. Miriam Archer lowered a penny on a string from the window into the road and the bunman took the penny and tied a bun to the string. He came every Sunday. They all clustered by the window with their crinolines poking up. In the evening they marched again, two by two, to the church for evensong. But, look as she might, she could see no explanation for the crowing cocks, the booming hooters, and dared not ask for fear she met a look of blankness or a denial that these things existed outside her own imagining.

Only in the classroom was her burden of ignorance lifted from her. There she forgot herself in the pages, thick, soft, and slightly greasy with use, of her text book; in the black columns of figures, in the difficulty of pressing the steel nib against the ruler's side without its suddenly spreading and spluttering. Every sensation, the smell of the ink, the feel when she dipped her pen of little pellets of blotting paper at the bottom of the inkwell, the cut of the desk's edge into her forearm as she wrote, the ceaseless grating of chairs, the smell of sweat in the airless room, was intensely familiar. Most of her life had been made up of these things. In all the lesson hours she was in a world she knew, safe because its perils were known. When questions were asked she raised her hand fearlessly and when, sometimes, the teacher looked at her and then away, she felt it cruelly that she might not always answer. At those times she was unaware of the other girls in the room, but when the hand-bell in the corridor was rung an emptiness like hunger seemed to press outward from inside her. She was at a loss then. Immediately the other girls came alive around her. A whole stream of separate existence seemed loosened in the long windowless corridor leading to the dining room. She feared them. She had always feared them. Other children. An alien breed, who must ultimately unite against her as soon as she made an error. It was March now, but Adela had no sense of winter's passing. She scarcely knew how long she had been here. The time before. Who she had been seemed a legend now. A thing read in a book and told over in the head until it is neither real nor unreal.

The bell had rung. She was hurrying to join the line to go into dinner. It was a Wednesday. There would be boiled mutton and potatoes and cabbage. She could smell it in the passage. A girl said to her, 'Are you Adela Traherne? You are to go to Mrs Watson's room right away.'

'Ooh,' said Miriam Archer, sucking in her narrow cheeks. 'Whatever have you done?' She rolled her eyes and meant it as a joke, but even after all these months it seemed to Adela that the extent to which she might be wrong was endless and unknown. Unknown to her but not to that grim woman waiting behind her door. One by one, she had no doubt these inadequacies were shortly to be named to her.

Reading the neatly written sign, *Knock before entering*, she knocked. Mrs Watson's voice said, 'Come.' Adela entered a small room as austere and comfortless as any of the dormitories. The superintendent watched her from behind a little desk. There was a chair, but Mrs Watson gave no indication that she was to sit in it. It seemed with an effort that she raised her long narrow face as Adela came closer. 'Good evening, Adela.' The woman watched her from under heavy, haggard lids. 'I hope you are happy with us, Adela.'

'Oh, yes, Mrs Watson.' For the purpose of speech was to say what would not anger her.

All the time the superintendent held an open letter in her long fingers, rubbing it meditatively as if the feel of it might yield up some secret not apparent in the words. 'I have a letter concerning you.'

From whom might such a thing come? She stood still waiting.

'Do you know a Mr Walmer?'

'He is my patron,' said Adela. But the question filled her with a sudden fear that Mrs Watson would next disclaim all knowledge of him. That the reason for her being here had been forgotten.

'That is Mr Augustus Walmer. The sender of this letter is a Mr Alfred Walmer.' She spoke as if someone attempted to dupe her.

Adela was silent. The matter had moved beyond her ken.

Mrs Watson sat watching her. 'He says he is Mr Augustus Walmer's nephew. Is that the truth?'

The truth was a thing like a sword. Mrs Watson had access to the handle.

'Yes, it is,' said Adela with the sudden vehemence of a child who has been accused of lying.

'You are not to speak to me like that, Adela.'

'I am sorry, Mrs Watson.'

'Well,' she said next, 'don't you wish to know what the letter says?'

Adela merely moved her lips. Mrs Watson went on. 'It appears he wishes to see you. He says his uncle has asked him to check on you, on your well-being. I trust you have not been complaining about your treatment here?'

'No, Mrs Watson.'

'You have no cause.'

'No, Mrs Watson.'

'You have not written then, to either Mr Augustus Walmer or this Mr Alfred Walmer, soliciting their sympathy?'

'No, Mrs Watson.'

'Mr Alfred Walmer is a young man, I presume?'

Again she scarcely answered, confused by her memories

235

of him as little more than a boy, and by the sense he had filled her with, as he shouldered his gun and walked with his uncle, of being infinitely older than she.

'He is coming here on next Monday afternoon. I shall let him see you. Not alone, of course. He can ask you whatever it is he wishes to ask and then reassure his uncle.'

Adela had sat abruptly on the chair and, covering her face with her hands, burst into senseless tears. She felt them trapped wetly against her cheeks. She felt them well up without control from some part of her that had lately been denied voice. Their reality astonished her. They removed Mrs Watson, who could be heard at a distance asking harshly, 'Why do you cry, Adela?' They filled her with sudden shaken pleasure. She could see the terrace of the house and the boy standing in sunlight in the doorway with his gun bent over his arm. Something at least had been given back, retrieved. Something that she might see within her head existed also in the streets outside the house.

Mrs Watson said, 'We do not behave like this here, Adela. We do not inflict our emotions on other people. You must have complete mastery of yourself before you attempt to undertake the important calling offered you.' Yet it seemed to Adela that the grey eyes watched hers less with disapproval than with a bitter curiosity. 'Have you no handkerchief, Adela?'

She said, 'Yes.' And finding it in her sleeve began to wipe her eyes. She had no explanation for her tears. She was still too shaken to speak clearly, but she stood up and managed to smile uncertainly at Mrs Watson, who said, 'You will be ready and in possession of yourself when he calls.'

'Yes, Mrs Watson.' She had backed to the door. Her hand already groped for the handle behind the small of her back and she was in the passage as she heard Mrs Watson formally dismiss her.

She stood crushed towards the end of the line of girls waiting to go in to dinner. At such proximity their wiry hair smelt rank as foxes. She was jostled from behind. She felt the unpleasantness of their fists in the small of her back, their breath on her neck. They talked incessantly, but with such din and rapidity that what they said meant nothing to her. Constantly she was jostled. A monitor called silence and the great sibilance of words faded and rose again. The doors at the head of the stair were thrown open. She was pushed along with them into the dining room.

Here each class had a table, but at it you could sit anywhere you pleased. She feared arriving early, lest no one take the place beside her. But if she arrived late, as she did now, she feared going boldly beside another girl who might want the chair kept for her friend. Sometimes they tipped the wooden chairs against the table to show that they had a friend coming. Sometimes, when she asked if she might take a certain seat, the girl turned rudely and said, 'No. It's for someone else.' She felt then that they disliked her but did not understand why.

But today, when she reached her form's table, Miriam Archer patted the back of the chair next to her and said, 'Come and sit here.' She said it as if it were no concern to her whether Adela said yes or no.

Adela smiled at her. She felt grateful that the problem was settled for this one meal. But still the unreasoning voice in her head said, 'You cannot sit with her every day. You must not make her feel she must always have you. She will not want that. She will tire of you.'

Miriam Archer smiled her quick bright smile. She said, 'What was it, then? What had you done? You've been crying, haven't you?'

'Nothing,' Adela said. 'It was nothing like that.'

She thought Miriam Archer was disappointed and so went on, with a halting importance, 'It was that Mr Alfred Walmer is to call on me on Monday afternoon.'

'Who's he when he's at home?' Her hair grew in a mop of curls all over her head, but beneath that soft shapeless mass everything about her was very thin and quick. She seemed to know exactly what she was about. Her narrow face came to a sharp point at her chin. She had an old face. Already the skin around her eyes was wrinkled and shadowed. It made her look surprised but knowing, like an owl. Still, she was very bright. She chatted all the time, so there was no anxiety as to what to say to her.

When Adela told her about Alfred Walmer she said in a saucy voice, 'Well, I don't know about you. I'll have to keep an eye on you.' And that Sunday they walked to church together.

18

At four o'clock on the Monday afternoon a messenger came to the Biblical History class and handed the mistress a note. Adela allowed her eyes to rise only a second to see this transaction and bent her head at once over a page of meaningless words. The mistress said, 'Adela Traherne is to go to the Visitor's Room.'

She rose a little too quickly, as if to a cue. There was a withdrawal of sound, a suspension of work that caused her boots to tap after her as she walked between the desks to the door. She felt the pressure of their interest not unpleasantly – especialness had always seemed her due – and walked down the corridor to the room where visitors were received. Miss Lawson waited for her outside the room and whispered, 'You have a caller, Adela.'

'I know,' Adela said, but the sense of well-being that had possessed her as she rose and walked from the classroom was suddenly replaced by an empty uncertainty. Miss Lawson reached around her and opened the door, at the same time pushing her forward to face Alfred Walmer's back.

In the small cell-like room reserved for callers the window was set above eye-level. As he waited he had instinctively turned towards it, tilting his head so that he might feel the spring sunlight on his face. At the sound of the door opening he turned, extending his big gloved hand, smiling stiffly at her. He said, 'You may not remember me, Miss Traherne.'

She said, 'I am called Adela here,' and watched the abruptness and awkwardness of the reply register on his face. It had grown thinner, but not entirely hardened. She would have known him, in any case, though not perhaps if she had passed him in the street. Now he seemed to look past her to Miss Lawson for assistance.

Miss Lawson said, 'Of course you are to be called Miss Traherne by anyone to whom you are not related. Won't you be seated, Mr Walmer?' But in the moving and turning that this occasioned Adela found the young man smiling at her in such a way that the gift might not be intercepted by Miss Lawson. She did not smile back, fearing to be forward, but sat on one of the chairs placed around the walls, quite unaware that she should speak, merely waiting for him to deliver the message he had come with.

He too sat, without embarrassment, watching in curiosity her vacancy of spirit. A shaft of dusty spring sunlight had found her out, perched on her chair, quite remote from him, quite complete. Yet, passive as she was, she dragged into this uncompromising room her small store of associations. He saw quite clearly the governess' hasty punitive handling of her hair on the sunny terrace, the fluid brilliance of the world they had moved out to in a boat. The excitement and the newness of the islands came back to him so forcibly that for a moment he was confused as to why he was in this room designed to frustrate meetings.

Watching her stillness surrounded by sparks of dust soaring and falling in the slow channel of sunlight, he was filled with lethargy and a reluctance either to move or speak, so that he started when Miss Lawson gave a little cough and said, as she might prompt a faulty lesson, 'Are you staying in town, Mr Walmer?'

'No,' he said, tilting back his head. 'I am studying at Woolwich. At the shop. Mathematics. I must go back by the five o'clock steamer.' He watched Adela to see if the sound of his voice affected her in any way. She sat as if the occasion she waited for must follow his departure.

He thought he could have drawn her, and imagined the pencil following the full curve of her breast and her cheek

240

and the chin held at just that defensive angle that showed she knew she was watched and half feared it. He thought how beauty is a kind of disfigurement. He thought how Adela's lay somewhere in the odd, wide, slightly irregular setting of the eyes and that one might never tire of watching her and speculating whether it were beauty or irregularity. The mass of dark hair trapped light and burnt away the line that divided her from the surrounding air.

It was extraordinary to see her so. To have come with no picture formed in his mind between one concern and another, at someone else's bidding, and find this person he had seen once as a child. He wondered how one spoke to her, if it were possible to make her smile.

He said to the woman, 'I have recently heard from my uncle, asking me to call and hear at first hand whether you were satisfied with her progress.' It was not what his uncle had said at all.

The woman smiled eagerly at him and said, 'Miss Traherne does very well here. She is a little silent, as you can see. Really, Adela,' she added, 'you must find your tongue.'

He said quickly to help her, 'Do you enjoy being in London, Miss Traherne?'

Adela looked up then without reserve; patience rather than shyness might have caused her to hang her head. 'I have seen very little,' she said. 'Only coming from the train and between here and the church.'

'The girls are kept very busy, sir,' said the woman.

'That is a pity,' he said to Adela, who looked at him swiftly then, in eagerness or alarm he could not tell. There was a bare quality in her face that cautioned him, for he had almost suggested that he might visit her again. Now he asked himself, did he really want to give up another afternoon in town to charm her into speech? He thought not. He would be late now if he did not rouse himself and bring this to a close. But even as he thought these words he heard himself say, in a curious, persistent voice, 'When I was a boy, I thought you very brave to go out onto that rock with my uncle to see them build the light.'

'You wanted to go, too,' she said.

241

'Yes. I remember.' He must go now. He would miss the steamer if he delayed. 'What am I to say to my uncle?' he asked, smiling at her, tipping back his chair and reaching down for his hat. 'I must write to him tonight.' He thought it would be a pleasure to do so, to try to find words to describe her. 'Well?' he said. 'What shall I say to him?'

'That I am very well.'

'And grateful for the opportunity given you,' prompted Miss Lawson.

'And grateful.'

'Oh, I am glad to hear that,' said Alfred very gravely. 'I am sure he would have you grateful.'

She looked dumbly at him. He was standing and she too must stand. She might take his hand now, but then he must go. He was smiling pleasantly at Miss Lawson. At the door he said, 'I think my uncle intended from his letter that I should visit Miss Traherne from time to time, when I'm in town. He cannot, you know, but feels she should be visited. You must accept me in lieu of him, I fear.' And he walked quickly out into the corridor and out into the street.

'I doubt he will trouble to call again,' said Miss Lawson when he had gone.

'He said he would.'

'He will not if you do not trouble to make yourself pleasant, Adela. Really there is no call for such sullenness. In your position you will have to accustom yourself to speak with the gentry. You will have to give a better account of yourself than that.'

As soon as Alfred was in the windy street he felt astonished that he had spoken those words when, expressly, he had decided not to; but a sense of her abandonment had brought an intolerable pressure upon him. Perhaps, too, the oddity of the meeting required to be put right. At least he had not committed himself to any exact date for his return. He had three weeks' leave due at Easter and might postpone calling again till his return. It occurred to him then that the wisest course would be to relate the little incident to Harriet Pontefract while he was at home. He would surely see her and hint to her that she and her mother might take this task upon themselves when they came up to town for the season in May. Harriet, with her sweet seriousness, would better deal with the girl than ever he could. He wondered with sudden irritation why his uncle had not thought of that for himself.

That night he wrote to Augustus, saying simply:

I called on Miss Traherne today as you requested and found her to all appearances well, although she is so very silent I had only her pretty face and the remarks of a sheeplike attendant to go on.

As for the sketch he had thought to amuse himself with, although her posture on the chair had haunted him throughout the darkening journey to Woolwich, try as he might, once he was alone in his room he could not conjure it up in his mind, let alone get it down on paper.

A week later, with no very clear explanation to himself of what he was doing, he took a river steamer from Woolwich early one Sunday and paid his fare to Chelsea Reach.

It was a cold, blustery March day. A squall of rain struck the steamer at Westminster but by the time he had walked ashore at Chelsea the sky was clear again. He went briskly up through the quiet Sunday street towards the spire of the new church. The clock chimed the half hour as he approached it and the rapt, quiet air of the building led him to suppose that the communion service was already in progress. He walked restlessly up and down in the street wanting, he decided, only to exchange a word with Adela, so that he might feel free of the foolish commitment to visit her again, which she by now had, perhaps, entirely forgotten.

When the three-quarter hour struck he took up his position leaning against a tree roughly opposite the church door, which, a few minutes later, grated open to release the congregation. Then he caught sight of the troop of girls in their dark dresses and bonnets going out by a side door into the empty burial ground. There, slowly, they progressed up and down in pairs and little groups. Some clustered in the corners of the walls for shelter from the wind. He saw with alarm that some of them were veiled against the weather and wondered if he would ever recognize Adela, but almost immediately he thought he did and fixed his eyes on that one figure walking slowly with another girl, arms around each other's waists, and now she seemed to him entirely unapproachable. It had been sheer folly to suppose she had wished him to come again. They walked towards him without seeing him, then away, before he could be sure that it was she. Then, as they approached a second time, he walked rapidly up to the wall and said in a low, hurried voice, 'Miss Traherne, I was passing and thought I should tell you that I am leaving London for a while.' He could see the movement of her eyes but the shadowy veil prevented him seeing if his appearance had startled her. 'I had said I might call on you again at the school and would not want you to think that I had forgotten.'

'Oh,' she said simply. 'I had not supposed you would come. They said you would not.'

'Well, I have not,' he said awkwardly. 'Only to explain that I must go away.'

'Will your train not go without you, then? You seem in such a hurry,' said the friend, but the mixture of impudence and resentment he sensed in her only fretted the very edge of his attention.

He said irritably to Adela, 'Won't you lift your veil? I can't see you.'

All her movements were slow and uncertain. She raised the veil but lowered her eyes as she groped carefully with a pin to secure it to the brim of her bonnet. The lift of her arm, the tightening of her breast, the fumbling of her fingers all filled him with impatience. 'To tell the truth,' he said, 'that room in the school is so grim we cannot talk there with any pleasure. I wondered if you would care to walk with me by the river. Your friend, too, of course.'

'Oh, we could not,' said Adela, looking around with alarm. 'They watch us here. You should not be speaking with us now.'

The friend said slyly, 'I could ask her home with me Saturdays. No one would know if she walked a different way. They trust us, you see.' And she slipped her arm with an odd little proprietary movement through Adela's.

'At what time?' he asked her.

'Two in the afternoon. From the school.'

'Are you sure they'll let her go?'

'You'll have to wait and see, won't you?'

'It's not worth my coming unless I know.'

'That's your affair.'

'When I come back, then,' he said carelessly.

'When will that be?' Adela asked. She alarmed him then.

'A few weeks. Late in April. I'll come if I can.' And he turned and walked rapidly away from them.

'Well,' said Miriam Archer, 'you're a dark one.' Her voice seemed to rob and pry. 'Who is he?' When Adela said nothing, 'As if I didn't know. He's Mr Alfred Walmer, isn't he?'

'Yes.'

'He's taken a fancy to you.'

'Why, no,' said Adela, as if she really would not have it so. She began to struggle to unpin the veil again.

Miriam Archer laughed. 'Why, of course he does, if he waits in the street for you.' She stood very close to Adela, pushing aside her hands to release the pin herself and tug the veil back again.

'But he does not,' Adela persisted, knowing that it could not be so. There was a partition in her mind between his being there and that possibility. In a sudden rush of feeling, of which the source was confused, she tightened her arm around Miriam's waist and leaned her head so that the straw brims of their bonnets grated and made her shiver. She said, 'Well, I do not care for him at all, any more than if he were Mr Walmer himself.' But already, it seemed, a clock had been set in motion inside her. She had become the anxious measurer of time until his reappearance.

*   *   *

Alfred spent a fortnight at Longridge, but although he saw Harriet Pontefract on several occasions he found no opportunity of mentioning Adela to her. Once he was at home it did not seem that she existed. Often he told himself: I have not thought of her today.

For the final two weeks of his leave he joined Augustus on the islands. He went on two such visits a year now: in April, on his own, and in August with one party or another. Although nothing was ever stated, the April visit especially was spent instructing him in the running of the estate.

He came leaving the mainland ragged with new growth, expecting to find spring present in the mild climate of the islands, but it was never so. Only the gorse that Augustus had planted over the years bloomed. A few willows by the lake sent out sharp green leaves. Otherwise the spring seemed to have receded at its most hectic time.

When, a fortnight later, he returned to the mainland, its sudden acceleration astonished him. He sprawled back in the railway carriage experiencing a strange sensation of being dragged along a rope to his source. His uncle had made no further mention of visiting Adela and he had not brought up the subject. Any mention he had made to the girl of coming again would surely be forgotten now. He felt quite free of her. Nevertheless, the first Saturday found him boarding a steamer for Chelsea. He told himself he could prove nothing of how little he felt if he were not put to the test of seeing her again. By the time the church bell struck two, he was standing in the street by the college watching the front door.

When Adela and her friend issued arm in arm he walked after them on the far side of the street, constantly having to slow his pace so as not to overtake them. Then, when they were safely round the corner and out of sight of the college, he crossed quickly over and spoke to them.

'Oh, we had forgotten you,' said the friend. 'We did not expect to see *you* again, did we, Adela?'

She had no veil today. It had moved her to see him. She did not know how to hide it.

'Will you walk with me?' he said. He was careful to avoid looking at the friend, who might come too.

'I'll be on my way,' said Miriam. 'Be here by four if you don't want to make us late.'

'Oh, no,' said Adela, gripping her hand, 'won't you come with us? We could walk that way. We'd scarcely be late.'

He watched her confusion cruelly.

Miriam said mockingly, 'Do you want me, Mr Walmer?'

'No,' he said to her. 'I do not.'

'There you are. You see?'

'Don't go,' said Adela.

'Oh, but I must. He wants to have you to himself. Four o'clock!' she said to Alfred.

'I don't like her,' he said. 'Will she always come?'

'She's my friend. I only come out because she asks me.'

'Do you mind being alone with me?'

'I cannot stay long.'

'Would you like to walk?'

'Where shall we go?' she asked.

'Where would you like to go?'

'I know of nowhere. Do you?'

He said, as if it did not concern him, 'It's up to you where we go.'

'Where are the boats?' she asked him shyly.

'By the river.'

'May we go there?'

'Very well,' he said.

She stood quite still in the road, so that he laughed and said, 'Don't you know which way to go?'

'I hear the hooters,' she told him. 'I want to see it, but we always go another way.'

He put his hand on her elbow and propelled her forward, walking, he knew, too quickly for her, but wanting to be away from the college.

It had been right to take her to the river. It pleased her to see the boats and the water. She wanted to walk out to the end of the wooden pier and there, silently, they watched a fisherman lounge against the rail, staring at the narrow curved tip of his rod until it began to dip and spring. They saw him crouch down on one knee with his hand held in a suspended clasp an inch from the handle. Adela watched the tip of the rod for its account of what was hidden by the thick brown water as intently as if all her interest lay there, but he did not think it did. He thought some of it at least lay with him, as he leant back against the opposite rail with the sun on his face and watched her through the blur of his half-closed eyes.

Suddenly the fisherman seized his rod and jerked it upwards. He began to wind in the line and far out in the stream they saw a small sparkle of disturbance. Then a bright thrashing fish appeared, drawn along the surface of the water. She turned back to him, her mouth a little open with excitement, but immediately the bell in the old church chimed the half hour past three. He said, 'We must go back. You'll be late.' And she moved so quickly from the rail that he thought she was relieved to know that the time was up and felt that the afternoon had been wasted.

He was careful not to mention coming again. Probably he would not. In any case he would not come next week, whether to cause her pain or to establish in his own eyes that he was entirely indifferent to her would have been beyond him to say. He imagined her coming down the steps of the school looking for him in the street, walking slowly lest he had been delayed.

But the next Saturday was a wretched day for him. By evening he was tormenting himself that she was indeed as withdrawn and indifferent to him as she had seemed, that she had walked the dingy streets laughing and clinging to her friend, taking tea with her parents above their shop, glad he was not there. The following Saturday he took the steamer again, and after that gave up all pretence, at least to himself, that he did not come every Saturday for the hour he might walk with her.

At two o'clock she came out of the college. Without a word

now Miriam hurried away from her up the street. He was waiting. He watched her as she came towards him.

She liked most to walk by the river. She would lean beside him on the wooden railings, watching the boatmen work on their upturned boats, or a fisherman cut up his gleaming bait on the river steps, or some oarsman, in his full white sleeves, dart quickly past against the green hills on the farther bank. He had no idea at all what went on in her mind.

One afternoon in June he took her into the gardens at the end of the tow path.

'Do you like it here?' he asked her.

'Oh, yes.'

'Do you know why you like it?'

'It's pretty?' Even of that she sounded uncertain.

'Well,' he said. 'Is it? Don't you know? Can't you tell whether you are happy or not?'

'I told you I was.'

He got to his feet then in one movement and walked a little away. He leant his elbow against one of the trees and stared at the river, all the haste gone out of him.

Even so slight a movement affected her now like the withdrawal of a tide. She could not look at him. She could not speak to him. She could not accept his reality as something that came and went at will. He gave to her or drew from her as he moved towards or away. There was no limit to his power of going. At any moment thoughts she could not see might direct him away into that world she could not imagine, for she would not have it exist.

The church clock struck the half hour.

He said, as he was bound to do, 'I must take you back.'

She took his arm. He kept his head lowered and said nothing. The street leading from the river was empty. All sound seemed exhausted from it. They paced out their silence.

He said, 'Well? Shall I come again?'

'Yes.'

'I'll come on Saturday.'

He had come now for six weeks, but he had never before

promised to come. She thought of her wealth, that all week she might be sure of his coming, and looked at him so intently that he laughed his rather harsh flat laugh, pushing back his hat, taking both her hands in his, as if he would swing her around in a game.

With the opening of the season he came more often to London. His mother and Sarah were staying in his uncle's house in Eaton Square and in June the Pontefracts rented rooms there. Sometimes he walked, sometimes he took the omnibus from Chelsea and changed and shaved before accompanying them all to evening parties. Then he slept an hour or two before taking the dawn steamer back to Woolwich. It meant that often when he arrived at Chelsea he was carrying a case with his dress uniform for the evening. He felt foolish carrying this as they walked along the river bank. Once he hid it by some barrels, but worried constantly that it should be stolen and the evening be spoilt with explanations and reproaches. Adela herself never asked what it contained, nor where he was taking it. He wished sometimes that she would ask. The divide in his life troubled him. When he walked with Adela under the shifting shade of the elms by the river, breathing the river smell and the tarry smell of the beached boats, he would think suddenly of the coming evening, the stifling rooms, the crush, the discomfort of his uniform, the effort to talk, all with a profound weariness as things he cared nothing for. But when he was again caught up in the midst of it all, the still reflections of the afternoon seemed to have no rational place in his life.

One evening late in July he sat with Harriet Pontefract by the open windows of his uncle's drawing room, watching the other couples dance. Lately he had taken, when he could, to sitting out the supper dance with her. Then he might take her in and not be obliged to make conversation with anyone he knew less well.

She asked him, in the tone of playful reproach established between them that summer, 'How did you waste your time today?' For she thought him very idle, very careless. He must improve no end before she would ever consider him. It would have been easy enough to say, 'You could not in a hundred years guess with whom I wasted it this afternoon.' But he did not. It had passed beyond that now. He would keep his time with Adela to himself, and relish withholding it from these people who had the ordering of his life.

Instead he smiled at her, and feeling a sudden compassion pleaded, 'Won't you dance? Just this once? Surely your scruples need not count with me. I dance so badly it would be more like a penance.'

But she was true to her word and would not, although he knew she wanted to.

'You should not trifle with her,' his mother said, when he had gone again into the dining room to fill his glass. 'She's half in love with you already.'

'Not Harriet,' he said with a laugh. 'She has more sense.' But that was what they wanted. He knew that well enough.

'Oh, but it is cruel,' said his mother only half reproachfully, 'if you intend nothing.'

'Well, there is time for that,' he said, for he was to be posted abroad within the next year, by Christmas, perhaps. Later in the evening, to make obscure amends, he sat down by Harriet again and asked her, as earnestly as she could wish, if he might bring his dog over to Tregilly before he went away and let her care for him while he was gone. Then, seeing the furtive joy in her acceptance, wondered if that too had been wrong of him.

He set a little chair for Adela by the river, where the sun fell through the leaves of a great elm. Then he sat on the ground with his back against the tree trunk, trying to memorize the way she sat. She looked past him to the bright activity of the boats on the water. There was a drought that summer. It had not rained at all during the weeks he had come to visit her. The turf was brown and harsh under his hand, like the bristles of a brush. Day after day passed like this, with the sky flawless and unaltering.

251

It blurred the passage of time. It seemed that nothing would change out of the trance of exhausted heat that rose off the nearby city.

'You are to talk to me,' he said, smiling at her. When he sat, he was quite still, as if he would never move again. He was smiling at her. He said, 'I like to hear your voice. I hate London voices.'

'What am I to say?'

'You are to tell me something. Talk about yourself. I know nothing about you.'

Nor did she, but she must speak or he might become impatient and turn away. 'I sat an examination before the inspector.'

'Did you? I am very impressed.' But he did not seem to mock. He spoke as if he wanted her to speak again. She began to tell him about the inspector and the questions he had asked. How she had feared for Miriam Archer, who had not prepared as carefully as she, how she had known the answers to his questions and how pleased and kind he had been. But as she spoke she feared what she was saying. She feared herself in it. The words seemed jerked from her and full of boasting. For she knew she had done well and it would not be permissible to say so to another girl, but surely it was safe to him. She watched to see if she displeased him. His face seemed set in a quiet smile. His eyes watched her face and she turned away again. She did not think he listened to more than the sound of her voice. She did not think it mattered what she said. Her voice broke off and she had no recollection of the words she had been using. He sat with his legs stretched easily in front of him and his ankles in their dusty boots carelessly crossed. Sunlight on the side of his face sparked on the stubble of his cheek and lip. She felt his pleasure and half knew that she caused it. But he watched something other than what she perceived of herself, as if he had found pleasure in something through misunderstanding it.

When she fell silent he roused himself. 'Is that what you want,' he said, 'to do well in examinations?'

'But I must.'

'Why?'

'There is a certificate.'

'And then?'

It had seemed so absolute an end. 'It is so that I can teach in the school.'

'*The* school?' He made a sudden harsh sound in his throat. 'Is there only one school?'

'You know he has paid for me to come here.'

'And you will go back?'

'But I must,' for there had never been an alternative to that.

'You do not think that a waste?' When she did not answer, 'He doesn't own you. You could pay back what he has spent on you.'

'But I want to go back. Where else is there to go?'

'There is everywhere else,' he said angrily, 'but you don't know that.'

She kept quite still. She would not be forced out of the present with its enormous certainty.

He said, 'Anyone will employ you, once you have your wretched certificate. You could keep yourself in London.'

She said shyly, 'If I do well, they will ask me to stay on here another year. If he will pay for that, I might stay.'

'Well, he must pay. If he will not, I shall.'

'Why you?'

'Because it will all be mine. I've as much right as he.' He was aware of an ugliness in what he was saying that he had not intended; aware, too, that he had not mentioned that he himself was to go away. But there was August yet, September, October, November even. The thought of her not being there was intolerable to him. And nothing was official. It was all rumour. They might never go. He said almost harshly to her, 'When can you know if you are to stay?'

'When the results come.'

'But when?' For even that uncertainty was hard to bear.

'Soon,' and she gave a little shake of her shoulders as if she feared to know the results, which seemed to him affected, for of what importance were they?

'Then you'll write to him immediately and ask? You promise me that.'

'Yes. I promise.'

But he must ask her again. 'You're sure that you will not put off writing? You will not forget?'

In the following week, the first in July, the results of the inspector's examination were pinned up in the corridor outside the dining room. Adela had done very well. She was to be awarded a first class certificate and she must decide whether to return to the islands or to stay in London to study at the college for another year. She told Mrs Watson that she would like to stay. The superintendent said that she would write to Mr Walmer to see what his wishes were. Adela was to write to Mrs Traherne, but the days went by and she put off doing so. In her last letter her aunt had mentioned being unwell. She had not heard from her since. How, possibly, could she write now to say that she would not be returning as promised in August? Yet he would be there on Saturday. He might be angry if she had not written. He wanted her to stay. She knew that if she did not write the letter to Mrs Traherne before she saw him again she might lose all desire to return at all.

It was Friday evening. While she stood in line to go in to evening prayers in the parlour, a girl had handed her a note saying she was to go to Mrs Watson's study directly the service was over. She felt stricken with guilt, as she knelt down to pray, that she had not written the letter and did not want to return to the islands. She was aware of the girls settling into their chairs, dragging their heavy green skirts about their knees, whispering apologies, forced by a certain grimness of atmosphere into wretched paroxysms of coughing and laughing that must be stifled in their arms in the pretence of prayer. All around was the thin sharp odour of girlish sweat. Miss Lawson shuffled music at the small upright piano and then launched into a voluntary that gave no hint of ending. There were footsteps on the

254

bare floorboards. Mrs Watson lowered herself stiffly onto her prayer stool. Her long arms were propped upright on their elbows. Her head was buried in the crook of her arms, as if it had been struck down by a blow on her bared neck. She was quite motionless except for the raised hands, which twisted together as she prayed in a constant dry tormented motion. Finally she rose to a sitting position and signalled to Miss Lawson, who plunged into a hymn tune, followed by the rapid breathy voices of the girls. Mrs Watson prayed aloud again. Then there was another hymn. An open door pressed against the agitated room a bright rectangle of innocent garden. Hard blue sky appeared above the opposite wall, and, at its base, wall-flowers emitted their smell of consummate sweetness, which Adela was to mistrust all her life.

She stood in front of Mrs Watson's desk. The super-intendent sat behind it holding a silver paper cutter, the point pressing into the tip of one forefinger, the knob against the other. All the time they talked she tilted and turned this little implement, sometimes catching the light on it. Adela watched it rather than her eyes.

She said, 'Do you know why you have been sent for?'

Adela said hastily, 'I have not written the letter. I meant to, but I have not had the time.'

Mrs Watson gave a quick irritable frown. 'What letter was that? Did you intend to write to me?'

'To you?'

'To whom did you intend to write, Adela?'

'To my Aunt Traherne. We spoke of it. You were to write to Mr Walmer. I was to write to her. About my staying. We spoke of it last week.'

'Well,' she said, the little knife suddenly still between her fingers, 'you have saved yourself the trouble of writing, have you not?'

'What do you mean?'

'Don't trifle with me, Adela. You know very well I cannot keep you here.'

'But why?' she said, refusing to know. 'Why?'

'Because you have behaved deceitfully and dishonourably, as no girl from this college should.'

'What have I done?' And still she would have herself believe that the thing she had done lay unrecognized in the dark confused thickets of correctness and error within the school, rather than in the sun-scoured streets, where she might feel rightness and even, at the prospect of tomorrow, joy.

Mrs Watson would not have it so. 'You have betrayed my trust in you. You have betrayed the trust and friendship of Miriam Archer. You have disgraced your patron. You are a wicked girl. A wicked, deceitful girl.' As she spoke her voice took on the rhythmic quality it achieved in impromptu prayer, as if the words had come alive and must endlessly multiply and give birth to others until the world was overwhelmed by these things. Her eyes never left Adela's. There was excitement, even pleasure, in them. So that when Adela cried out again, 'What have I done?' they had triumphed over her. She no longer protested, merely asked, knowing what it was, for her sin to be named so that all might be over with.

'You have been meeting with Mr Alfred Walmer.'

She said ferociously, for all that she almost whispered the words, 'There is no harm in that.'

'Can you be so ignorant as not to know the harm?'

But Adela would give nothing.

'If a young woman of your background meets secretly with a young man of a very different background, there is only one interpretation can be put on the thing. He will be aware of that, even if you are not.'

'I do not think of such things.'

'It is high time that you did. Surely you are not so ignorant as never to question his motives in meeting you like this?'

'He has been told to by his uncle.'

She made a sound of harsh impatience in her throat. 'He would have come here then honestly, and rung the bell, not arranged meetings where you might be compromised.'

'He does not arrange. Sometimes he is there in the street.

256

Sometimes he is not.' But she realized, as she spoke, that he had always been there. She had simply feared that he would not.

'And when he is there, what passes between you?'

'Nothing.'

'Nothing! Would you have me believe you stand like posts? You do not walk? You do not talk?'

'Yes.'

'And what is the subject of your talk?'

But no word of what was hers would she give away. She said, 'I tell him what I have done at school.'

'And that is all.'

'That is all.' Indeed, there was little enough more for Adela to speak with a fierce certainty, so that even that grim woman faltered and pretended to play with her little knife.

'Well,' she said. 'Well, I would not think you sly, Adela. But I must give account of you to Mr Augustus Walmer. I cannot keep you here. It is impossible to trust you and so the responsibility is too great. You must be sent back.'

'When?'

'On Monday. If I could arrange for you to be met sooner I would, but I cannot.'

'And I cannot come back?'

'There is no question of that now.'

'But you said that I could. I wanted to. You said that you would write to Mr Walmer.'

'And what would you have me say to him, Adela?'

She was silent then, watching the slow gyrations of the little knife, until Mrs Watson said quietly, 'Perhaps you see how my generosity in allowing you to keep your certificate. In not informing Mr Walmer. If it were not for the delicacy of the situation, that you have misbehaved with his own nephew, I should be bound of course to say. You mentioned that your aunt was unwell. That will be given out as your reason for going. What you say when you meet him is your own affair. I would simply be rid of you, Adela. You are to spend the next two days quietly in the sickroom, and pack while the other girls are attending

257

church. In that way you will draw the minimum of attention to yourself.'

'I am not to say goodbye.'

'No.' She thought of him standing in the street, watching the door.

'But Miriam. May I tell Miriam, at least, that I am going?'

'There is no need for that.'

'But she will wonder what has happened.'

'She knows,' said Mrs Watson.

At two o'clock on the following afternoon Adela let herself out of the sickroom and walked softly to the head of the stairs. The building was very quiet. Some of the girls who had certificates had left already. Some, like Miriam Archer, visited their parents and took friends with them. Those who stayed behind kept to the dormitories to savour their hour of idleness. She walked slowly down the stairs, looking about her, expecting at each moment to be intercepted. In the hall she saw Miss Lawson propped on a chair, on watch perhaps, for Mrs Watson, she knew, kept to her room at this time. Adela stood quite still on the bottom step watching the little woman, waiting for her to turn and cry out, and then saw that she slept as she sat, bolt upright.

Adela slipped past her, opened the door as softly as she might, and began to run down the steps. The shrill sound of Miss Lawson's voice was so real in her imagination that she could scarcely believe she did not hear it.

It was raining. She had brought nothing to wrap about her lest she be seen on the stairs. He was waiting a little way up the street holding an umbrella. He came quickly towards her, too agitated to smile.

'Well,' he said. 'Have you heard from him?'

She said, 'No.' She walked with him under his umbrella. Even in the knowledge that she must go, she was entirely happy. He held his arm tightly around her. Two girls running and laughing on the shining pavement stood aside to let them pass. He walked very rapidly, without speaking, so that all her thought must go into keeping up with him. It did not seem important now that she must go. It seemed there was as much time as there had ever been.

'Where shall we go?' he said.

She turned without a word down the street towards the church, drawing him with her. Once she slipped slightly on a wet leaf on the pavement and he said irritably, 'Oh, I go too quickly.' He stopped then, but she pulled him on into the green still churchyard. On the porch he turned her towards him. His face was blurred and foolish with smiling. She shut her eyes against it. He kissed her then. She stayed quite still, not knowing how to respond to him. When he held her from him his face wore the same rapt and vacant look, as if the features had been smoothed away. She did not know him.

He said, 'Do you love me, Adela?'

'No,' she said. It was wrong that she should love him. She watched his eyes to see if he minded when she said that, but nothing altered his smile.

'I think you do,' he said. Then he went away from her quickly so that she wondered if she had displeased him. His voice was strange, solemn, almost formal. 'What are we to do then, Adela?'

'I must go home.'

He did not seem to understand her.

'I must go back to the islands.'

'But you said you would stay. You promised you would write and ask if you might stay.'

She said, 'My Aunt Traherne is ill. I must go back.'

'When?' But he spoke less in anger than wonder at what was happening.

'On Monday.' The words had no meaning for her.

'You'll come back,' he said. 'When will you come back?'

When she did not answer he reached out and turned her face towards his with the warm palm of his hand. He said, 'It is on my account that they are sending you away, isn't it?'

'It doesn't matter,' she said. 'I am bound to go to her. But she will get well. She will not die, will she?' Her voice, close to his face, was suddenly shrill like a child's.

He felt her distracted from him and said, 'No, no. Of course she will not.'

'I might come back when she is well.'

'You will not,' he said, stroking her cheek with his finger as if it surprised him that she was still within his reach. 'Once you go back you will never leave.'

'You don't know that.'

'Oh, I know,' he said. 'It is what you want, to go back there.'

She turned her face into his hand, smelling his skin, saying quietly against it, 'You will come there. You will be there soon.'

He said, 'That will be different.'

'How different?'

'You don't understand,' he said. 'It will be different there.'

But she could not imagine a difference.

He kissed her. There were areas of dark and warmth in which she felt entirely safe. She could not understand why he said, 'What will become of you?' as sadly as if they had already parted.

'It is all right,' she told him. 'They won't tell him why.'

He went to the edge of the porch and, staring out into the rain, said with the same sadness, 'Is that all that matters to you?' But when he turned back to her she smiled at him as if nothing mattered.

He said, 'I must take you back.'

'You are not angry?'

'No,' he said. 'No, of course I am not.' He pushed up the umbrella and pulled her against him again. They began to walk back the way that they had come. He held her tightly against him. And even now nothing could diminish her happiness. It seemed an indestructible thing. She did not believe they would reach the college. She did not believe that the present, warm and swollen, would come to an end, and the moment when it did had no distinction for her.

19

Only when she was sitting in the carriage of the train did it seem to Adela that something of magnitude had befallen her. Then she did not doubt that they had parted. She had no longer imagined that they would meet again. Those circumstances connected with the tree, the river, the church porch, the small accumulation of words spoken, were all now crowded intolerably inside her head. It seemed they would not be released again. She felt the weight of her hands in the lap of her skirt and, looking down, saw them lie patiently there. Her body seemed to have taken up an attitude of waiting.

When the track curved and the carriage swayed she looked through the window and saw, through the sudden dispersal of smoke, the engine ahead. It dragged her forward on a line dictated. Somewhere else he too moved along some track, some passage, some road, but she could not know where. She possessed all that she might have of him now within her head.

The next day, the next hour, the next minute pressed immediately against her eye as the dark can on overcast nights. She could not penetrate it. She could not think ahead. It frightened her to sit so still as this.

There were people to meet her at Totnes and the same kind family housed her at Westporth. She thanked them. She walked slowly and carefully over the cobblestones leading to the quay. She was careful to keep her voice low. Everything seemed too fragile for disturbance. If they thought her odd she could not help it.

The sea was very calm. Once she had knotted her shawl

about her back she did not feel the breeze. She stayed on
the deck, walking up and down in the warm sun, more to
avoid the eyes of the other passengers in the cabin than for
anything she saw of the sea. She was without agitation.
The sensation of stillness continued to surprise her.

She watched the islands approach, but as the ship
turned on its final tack she crossed to the other rail and
stared again out to sea. When the anchor rattled over the
side and she heard the cries of the boatmen she felt no
haste. There would be a boat. Someone would tell her
what to do. She was filled with a great compliance, like an
invalid ashamed of the trouble she caused.

She heard her name and, looking around for the person
who had called, saw by the rail a young man, bearded,
holding her valise. She walked slowly across the deck until
she stood in front of him and said, 'I am Adela Traherne.'

'Indeed you are,' he said. 'I could not make you out in
the crowd but now I know you. Do you know me?'

'I do not think so.'

'Why, you did once. Have I changed so? I am Edward
Jenkins.'

'Yes,' she said, smiling. 'I thought you might be, but I
was afraid you might not. I did not like to say.'

'I knew you, Adela, once I'd made you out. You've not
changed. There'd be no mistaking you.'

'Haven't I?'

He was awkward then. 'Well,' he said, 'you've changed.
Of course you've changed, but not in yourself, I think.'

When she would say nothing to help him he added
abruptly, 'I've brought the boat. I'm to take you there
directly.'

'How is my Aunt Traherne?'

'She is not well,' he said, looking at her in a way that
made her suddenly afraid. 'She is not at all well.'

'Is she in bed?'

'Oh yes. They have not told you much, have they?'

'No,' she said uncertainly.

'Well, she would not write. She would not have you
anxious on her account, but my mother's with her,' he

said. 'She's with her night and day.'

The solemnity behind his words made it difficult to talk. 'Will you take in the rope?' he asked her when they were in his boat. He was distracted from her now and spoke to her as he would have spoken to anyone. She took off her gloves and wound the rope, while he settled to the oars and began to manoeuvre out of the flotilla of small boats clustered about the *Lord Wellington*'s hull, working one oar and then the other, with his head turned over his shoulder away from her. When they were clear of the harbour and he faced her again, pulling steadily at the oars, they spoke like strangers.

'It was flat calm by the looks of things. Couldn't have a better day to cross.' But the tone of death that terrified her had returned to his voice.

'Yes,' she said. 'It was very smooth.'

She asked if this were his own boat, but he said no. He didn't have one now. He'd borrowed this off Johnny Bishop. She would have insisted, as she had to Alfred Walmer: she will get better, she will get up again. But the set of his face as he pulled at the oars with his head thrown a little back, perhaps with the exertion, perhaps to avoid meeting her eye, made her know not to. She would have asked him what she should do, but he would not know. He had simply been sent to fetch her in the boat.

It was late. Summer evenings in the islands seem reluctant to fade. Long after the sun is down behind the western rocks some light holds, too faint to give colour, but keeping just visible the shapes and outlines of the land. And these drew Adela in among them by their endless appeal to recognition. The face opposite grew indistinct. The increasing darkness made speech unnecessary, so that turning to one side she might watch the steady encroachment of the dark islands as they grew larger and settled about her. They damaged the bright recollections in her mind, which seemed now to have lost all touch with even a past reality. The quay stood dense and black in the water. Almost she expected, despite what she had been told, to see Mrs Traherne's stiff form, static in that very place where she had watched Adela go. But of course she was not there.

When he had tied his boat at the quay and helped her up the steps Edward Jenkins went back for her valise, and then came scrambling up with it balanced on his shoulder. She said, 'What do I do now?'

'You keep your spirits up,' he told her. 'There's little enough any of us can do, but the sight of you will help her more than anything. She pines for that.'

Had he told her outright that Mrs Traherne was dying he could not have made his meaning more clear. Adela stood where she was and began to cry, helplessly, with her heavy hands hanging at her sides.

'Don't do that,' he said sharply. She understood that she placed too great a burden on him and found that she was able to stop crying at once.

'We'd best get along now,' he said.

'Yes,' she said. 'Yes, of course.' She reached into her sleeve for her handkerchief and dried her face with clumsy childish gestures. He did not look at her, but settled the valise on his shoulder and began to walk vigorously forward. Adela followed a pace behind, which he acknowledged by turning back from time to time to ask, 'Can you make out the path?' 'Can you see your way?' Once she asked him how long he would be staying in the islands and he replied that he had only a week or so now.

They walked along the track inside the harbour wall. The low close cottages pressed together behind their walled patches of garden, each with its glowing square of coloured curtain. The sea made only a soft predictable sound. Their steps rang out above it. Dogs barked distantly in the Abbey kennels. They climbed the hill. The fields, the rocks, the sea were there but scarcely to be made out now, so pressing was the dark. She heard Edward Jenkins' boots slip on the rough path. 'I should have brought the lantern,' he said. 'Can you see at all?'

'Yes,' she said. 'I know it well enough.' Her eyes had grown accustomed to the dark. The path sent up the faintest glimmer. It was easy to follow him, but she dreaded what she was going to. When at last the faint patch of light from Mrs Traherne's front room was visible above the rise of the hill she ran forward, brushing past him in the narrow lane, holding up handfuls of her skirt, stumbling in her haste.

'Easy, now,' he called after her. But at the gate she stopped and waited for him, staring fixedly at the window. He came and stood beside her, lowering the valise to the ground, as if he were not free to move until she spoke.

'Are you to come in?' she asked him.

'No,' he said quietly. 'Mother's made herself a bed in the room. She'll stay tonight, lest you're tired from your journey. I'll just take your case to the porch and be off home.'

She was grateful that he made no move to hurry her. Instead he said, 'I am sorry if I spoke roughly to you. I could not bear to see you cry so.'

'I stopped soon enough,' she said, as if to discredit her tears.

He said, 'You must be anxious. About what's to become of you. But Mother and Billy and I will see you right. You know we will.'

But it was not that that troubled her. She had not thought of that. She feared what she would find when the door opened directly into the room where Mrs Traherne slept. Death seemed to her a great embarrassment. She did not know what to do. Still he stood patiently beside her, making no move to urge her forward, until she drew in an audible breath and, catching at his hand in a hard wretched grip, pulled him after her down the narrow path and pushed the door open almost violently, without knocking.

She saw Mrs Jenkins rise from her chair. She felt the quick touch of her hand on her arm as she went past to her son. Heard the murmur of their voices by the door, but could make out nothing that they said. She knelt by the bed and took Mrs Traherne's hand carefully in her own. It was cold, but for an instant she felt the sliding bones tighten, then it lay limp and small in hers. Her eyelids, carved so starkly in their sunken sockets, made no move to open.

'It is Adela,' Adela whispered, but Mrs Traherne gave no sign of hearing.

She seemed to have wished herself away. She was always tiny and spare in shape but now it seemed she scarcely weighted the pillow or raised the bedclothes that lay loosely over her. All that Adela could see was the pale narrow head with its white springing hair bent awkwardly against the pillow. The white skin seemed tightened and smoothed. It was as if, in a final determination to ask nothing of her neighbours, she had consumed herself and forestalled decay. Adela was reminded of the little bleached collections of bone found lying in the spring between the grasses in the dunes. She had always found them beautiful and without implications of horror. Now she cautiously reached out her free hand and stroked the old woman's forehead at the line where her hair sprang surprisingly stiff and strong. She smiled then, a simple, slack smile. Mrs Jenkins, who had returned and stood beside her, said quietly, 'She knows you.'

'She thinks I am you.'

'No, no. She has waited for this. I thought you'd not come in time.' She went and sat heavily in the chair, rolling her head against the back of it as if to relieve herself of pain.

Adela did not think that she was known. It did not seem to matter. The sensation of stroking seemed to give pleasure: a fearful pleasure to her, too, for she would never have ventured such an intimacy to the real Mrs Traherne whom she had loved. A hard defensive grip of the hand was all the expression that love had found in touch between them, an occasional quick kiss on her forehead, proprietary, almost ceremonial, never moved by impulse. It seemed a legacy, but even as she thought so she was filled with pity for the woman in the bed, whether for what she had become or what she had been was beyond her to tell.

20

Augustus, of course, was well aware of Edward Jenkins'
presence on the Gweal. All comings and goings to the
island were related from one person to another and eventually penetrated the Abbey. He had never taken seriously
the boy's angry threat and felt nothing but scorn for the
rumours that Wills had seen fit to relate to him. Still, he
imagined that some blame for the old man's despair and
death might attach itself to him in their minds, and out of
respect for this, rather than any fear of them, he treated
the family with reserve. This, and his old sense of
involvement in John Traherne's death many years before,
led him to take no part in Mrs Traherne's austere funeral,
although normally he would have paid some sign of regard
to so long-standing a tenant and one for whom he had
always held a private respect.

There was, of course, some controversy as to what form
this ceremony would take for an avowed unbeliever. No
one questioned that it should be of the simplest, but should
it take place at all? Mr Peters declared that the service was
intended as much for the comfort of the living as the dead,
and that as Adela and Mrs Jenkins were both regular
attenders at his church he had no qualms on that score. But
the question of the actual burial was more vexed. Was
sacred ground in order? It was pointed out that although
her son had shared her scepticism no one had questioned
his claim on the diminishing space in the old graveyard.
But then the manner of his death had lifted him above
considerations of who or what he was. Mrs Traherne had
merely died. Eventually it was agreed that she should be

buried in the new churchyard at the end of the town.

I do not care to look too deeply into this compromise, Augustus wrote to Mrs Pontefract, *but at least she doubles the number of occupants and will make me better company than just Miss Christian's skeleton, who may, for all we know, be an unpleasant old pirate given to rambling stories of his deplorable past.*

He was saddened by the old woman's death and concerned for Adela. He would have liked to make some gesture of generosity towards the girl, but reminded himself that he had provided her with both a livelihood and a dwelling, without which she would have been quite destitute, and beyond that there was little that he could practically do. Although he felt moved to do so, therefore, he hesitated to call upon her, thinking that once she resumed her work in the school there would be chance enough to speak to her.

In the same way, although he took no steps to visit the Jenkins family, he hoped that he might meet Edward by chance and show in some way his interest and goodwill before his short leave expired. It was scarcely a conscious wish, any more than it was by a conscious decision that he took to walking along the back lane of the estate in the evenings. He would have said that both he and the dog were in need of exercise before they slept, but undoubtedly some instinct, as it had on a previous occasion, drove him to the very gate of the Hill Farm where he and Edward Jenkins might meet, if they met at all, alone and in the obscure light of the September evenings, he with no protection other than his stick and an ageing dachshund.

One evening, about a week after Mrs Traherne's burial, he saw a man come through the farm gate. The light was failing rapidly but he knew at once, by the man's regular stride, that of the two brothers this must be Edward. Yet he did not call out. Instead he drew back into the side of the lane, holding the little dog tightly under his arm, even placing his hand across its narrow muzzle, and watched Edward Jenkins make his way along the lane in front of him. He carried two buckets of water on a yoke across his shoulders and went carefully so as not to spill their contents. Augustus might easily have overtaken him, but he did not. Only when the young man was nearly out of sight did he feel compelled to follow him. The path rose up. Augustus followed at a distance, quite openly, although he continued to hold onto his dog. Any sound he made was probably masked by the slight creaking of the bucket, and the yoke made it unlikely that Jenkins would look around.

At the top of the rise he saw the young man turn into the gate of Mrs Traherne's cottage and there lower the awkward yoke from his shoulders. He thought at first that he was calling on the girl and felt shame for his spying, as well as some painful feeling he would not acknowledge as jealousy. Then he saw that Edward Jenkins had merely laid the buckets by the door, and understood that he carried water from the well to save the girl, and left his offering there without intruding upon her. He would come back now. There was no means of hiding from him on the exposed hillside. Nor would he wish to do so, but moved out into the centre of the path and stood waiting for him. But Edward Jenkins never saw him. When he came out of the gate he propped the yoke against the low stone wall of the cottage garden, where he might collect it later, and set off walking briskly towards the village. Augustus could have called out to him but did not. Instead, he waited until Edward Jenkins was out of sight, and then went quickly towards Mrs Traherne's cottage and, turning in through the gate, went up to the porch and knocked on the door.

He heard Adela's voice call indistinctly. She would suppose he was Edward Jenkins, who perhaps came every evening. He set the dog down in the porch and ordered it to stay. Then he opened the door slightly and said, 'It is I, Augustus Walmer. Will you forgive me for calling so late in the day?' Before she answered he let himself into the room.

Adela did not move towards him, rather away, reaching behind her back for the warm rail across the front of the stove which she gripped tightly, leaning back against her arms, watching him stoop as he came through the door, then straighten, too large for the small room whose quiet life he seemed to disrupt before he had said a word. His boots on the bare floor, his deep voice when he did speak, seemed to him to be insufferably loud. He reached out his hand awkwardly as if he would take hers, but she stayed where she was, gripping the bar.

'My poor Adela,' he said. 'I fear you are very much alone.'

'Yes,' she said, 'I am.'

'I feel to blame in this,' he said. 'Won't you sit down? I should like to sit and talk with you.'

She leant forward slightly, smiling to show that he might sit.

'I feel to blame,' he said again, 'that I sent you so far away. I had not understood until very recently that she was ill.'

'Nor had I,' said Adela rapidly. 'She would not say that she was ill. None of her letters until the last said. It was for that they sent me home.' She looked at him swiftly in the midst of her grief to see if he would accept this lie.

She began to cry then, as she had not since the night of her arrival, openly and uglily.

'Oh, don't do that,' he said to her in distress, in distaste. He got to his feet and came to her, putting his hand on her arm. She felt his kindness. She let him help her into the chair, although she did not want to leave the warmth of the stove. It occurred to her that she might cry whenever she liked, that the tears on her face would look the same whatever their source. They would think she wept for Mrs Traherne and for her alone, would approve and ask no questions. She sat now and he remained standing concernedly behind her, with his hand pressing without awkwardness between her shoulders as if he would weigh down the sobs. He fumbled in his coat with his free hand and gave her a handkerchief. She cupped it in her hands and lowered her face into it, smelling its alien smell, greedy for it because it belonged to Alfred Walmer's uncle.

'Shall I leave you?' he said. His voice seemed to startle her. 'Shall we talk another time?'

'No,' said Adela quickly. She drew in sharp little breaths, and rubbed her face dry. She kept the handkerchief gripped in her hand.

He drew up a stool and, sitting close to her, said, 'I came to tell you, Adela, that you need have no fears about this house. I have spoken to Wills about it and he agrees that so long as you are employed at the school you should have a right to a cottage of your own.'

She said distractedly, 'But what if I go away? What if I should go back to London?'

'There is no need for that. You have your certificate.' He was frowning at her, leaning towards her with his hands turned outwards on his knees. His big hanging face watched her with consternation. He did not know whether her words had any significance or whether they broke disjointedly from her grief and should be ignored. He said again, 'There is no need to go to London. Your place here is quite secure.'

She shook her head slightly, in bewilderment at not being understood.

'You can stay here,' he repeated patiently.

She understood then that he expected to be thanked. 'It was good of you,' she said, 'to enquire after me in London.'

Cautious, patient, confused, again he failed for a moment to follow her thought. Then he said, 'Oh, you mean Alfred.'

'Yes, it was good of you to send him.' But the words seemed to demand something as a question might.

'I'm sure it was a pleasure to him.'

'Yes. He said nothing to you?'

'On what subject?'

'On no subject.' Said with such a sigh that involuntarily he raised his hand from his knees as if he must steady her, but let it fall again at some barrier. He said, 'You are reassured, then, about the cottage and about your security here.' He would go now. He had said what he had come to say.

'But if I should want to go? If I should want to go to London?' She was quite fearless of him, but she spoke out

271

of the shreds of courage, for it seemed now that the precarious extent of warmth from the stove, the circle of lamplight, the strange intense sensation of his concern formed some powerful centre which drew her in. The outer world, which voiced itself in the hollow moaning of the chimney, was too perilous, too chaotic to contemplate. Had there been such a place as London? Had she laid claim to some existence in it? The substance had gone out of past time. It was a ghost of itself. She no longer believed, perhaps had never believed, that she would return to that place. It was imaginary. Turn her magic eye from it, it was not there.

'I could go there,' she told him. 'I could find a job in a school there.'

Suspicion taunted him briefly, but found no clear form. Why did she suppose then that he had paid for her training? He could not suppress annoyance that she had taken so much and now spoke without any awareness of his own feeling in the matter. He said, 'But that was not our understanding.'

The effrontery of it astonished him, as did her unconsciousness of herself as she leant towards him. Her hair was loose, blurring the edges of her face. The thin anxious smell of sweat came from her dress. Thoughts he could not grasp seemed visibly to move the young unprinted skin on her throat and by her lips. Her lips were parted with the effort to speak.

'Are you rejecting what I offered you?'

She stared at him, as if pleading for him to speak words she herself had no command of.

He said almost harshly, 'What do you want, Adela?' All that was moist and uncomprehending in her disturbed him unbearably.

'Want?' she said loudly. 'Want?'

He thought then she might be a little mad. But immediately she was quiet again, sinking heavily back against the cushion in the chair. He thought, I must go. I must go now.

She watched him reach for his stick and hesitate, staring

at her. He said in answer only to himself, 'You must not fear being alone, Adela. No one will harm you. We will speak of this later, I came too soon.' He had risen. He had made up his mind to go and moved as he spoke behind the chair and let his hand move now onto the pile of her hair, partly out of compassion, partly out of curiosity and a simple desire he had always had; to feel it warm and springing under his hand.

She did not start nor did he move his hand, for he feared now the ambiguity of any gesture he might make towards her, but let it rest there, telling the warmth of her head through the palm of his hand. He had lost the course of what he was saying. He was saying now, 'Do you remember when you were a child? I took you to the rock, and caught you up out of the boat.' He felt the movement of her head under his hand, nodding. 'You are quite safe, Adela. Do you understand that?' He rocked her head slowly with his hand. He knew he must go. He said, 'You may stay here as long as you want, as long as you teach in the school.'

His hand, in falling, brushed past her cheek and penetrated the dark warm space behind her hair, touched quickly and deftly the little knob of bone on her neck. He remembered then the necklace that had haunted his imagination many years ago. His fingers spread in search of it, but encountered only the solid warmth of her neck and shoulders.

He said, 'I must go,' and walked quickly out of the door, stooping through the low porch, stumbling so that he might curse to his relief at the little dog whom he had forgotten and who now forced his way between his feet and ran eagerly up the path towards the gate.

But Augustus turned aside and stood in front of the low square window. He had to stoop a little to see directly into the room to where she sat. She had not risen when he left, but sat motionless where she had been, holding something white. With a sensation of strangeness he remembered that he had given her his handkerchief. It was that she gripped and pressed against her cheek like a bandage.

Each second that he stood there filled him with a deep sense of peril, for he was convinced that she had made nothing of his strange behaviour, but if she were to look up now and see him that could no longer be. He seemed to see his own face, heavy and lined, severed by darkness from his body, pressed absurdly into the small space of glass. At any second she might raise her eyes and, seeing him, start up in fear and revulsion.

For I am old, he cried in rage to himself. To her I am older than I can imagine. But he did not move, and watched now in a new terror that by some unconsious movement she would reveal something of herself he ought not to see. He fought against a longing to lean his forehead against the smooth cold pane, for then surely some sound would penetrate her obscure thoughts and she must start up.

He heard the little dog move restlessly in the dark, coming back towards him from the gate to see why he delayed. Only then did he start away like a guilty thing at the fear that its bark or whine would reveal him. He began to walk swiftly towards the gate. Perhaps she had heard something, because the faint projection of lamplight was suddenly snatched away and, when he turned, he found that she had drawn a curtain so abruptly that there was no glimpse of her, other than in his mind, leaning towards the little window with her arm raised.

21

Early darkness and the approach of the hour when Harriet might change into her evening dress were slow in coming. It was her twenty-first birthday: a strange day that seemed more securely joined in time to the long succession of previous birthdays than to the days that had preceded and would follow it. She could remember each, if she tried, as part of a separate scheme of time made up entirely of birthdays. Each had held, as this one did, an almost superstitious feeling that the day must succeed without flaw, lest some irreversible harm might be dealt her and all of them. So precarious was this time of change, when, having been one thing the day before, she was, without any sensation of change, something else. It was impossible to do anything but to wait in the guise of one occupation or another for darkness to come and the party to begin. Several times she went and stood at the end of the passage leading to the kitchen, merely to hear its sounds of warm reckless activity.

Around the rest of the house cold intensified. In the expectant rooms it had a sound of its own: a minute crackling on the very boundaries of hearing. The sky was dull and still. The men bringing firewood from the spinney said that it would snow. She was aware of unaccountable feelings, chill and tense, that could hardly be called pleasure, although minute by minute she willed time to the point where she might slip her arms through her dress, and dreaded at the same moment the sharp access of cold to her skin. That Alfred Walmer must be present in the house. That she might stand on the landing and hear his voice distinct from the others, that he must speak to her, that he must hold her when they danced – for in so small a party he must dance with everyone – was certain. It required only the passage of time for this to happen.

The rest of his family were already here, staying in the house as well as the Railston cousins, Aunt Cissy's children, with whom she felt embarrassed because Aunt Cissy had died. Alfred would come from the depot at Exeter. He had promised to bring no less than three officers to make up the couples. Tommy Railston was too young to count. Sarah shared her room; they would dress together. They would be friends then, sisters, even, in their need, but all afternoon it was best to keep apart, resting their frail liking for one another for the sterner trials ahead, when each must look at the other in the final lamplight and venture down the stairs to offer themselves.

She had told Mr Wilcox that she would dance at this party. She had meant to explain to him that her conscience had directed her to; that it would cause pain if she did not, with Mama ill and Alfred Walmer so soon to go to Sebastopol. But in the end she had told him hastily, as she left the room, so that he could not argue with her. She had not been to see him since. Yesterday she had written to say that she was needed at home and could not come.

After lunch she said that she would sit with her mother, so that Miss Christian might be free to help Betsy Railston with the neck of her frock. She was glad to be free of them for a while. She gathered together her sewing basket and the little nosegay of wax flowers and evergreen she wished to bind and wear on her dress and knocked softly on her mother's door. Miss Christian partially opened it, with elaborate care, and seemed to fold herself through the little space allowed.

'She's asleep,' she said. There was a knowingness in her whisper, an invitation to conspiracy which Harriet would avoid.

'Betsy needs you,' she said in her normal voice. 'I'll sit with her for a while.'

'Are you sure?'

'Of course.'

'She'll have a lovely sleep now and be fresh for this evening,' said Miss Christian. They did not admit yet that Amelia, for a week, two weeks, had slept so every day in the afternoons, but continued to exchange these explanations as if each day's sleep were exceptional.

Harriet sat by the bed. She began to unpick with sharp small scissors the wax flowers which had last been worn in the summer, in London, as a crown, and bunch them together with sprigs of rosemary. The smell clung to her hands. She frowned her stern frown of concentration and only glanced occasionally at her mother's face on the pillow, smoothed and still and rendered harmless.

Once, as she looked, the eyes opened and her mother said, 'What are you doing?' The ease with which she slipped in and out of shallow sleep was frightening; it seemed to draw no distinction between the two states. Harriet held the nosegay shyly towards her.

'How pretty,' said her mother. 'Will you wear it tonight?' It was as if thought had never broken behind the thin closed lids.

'At the neck,' said Harriet, holding it against her grey dress.

'Yes. That will relieve it. Freshen it. Has anyone come?
'The Walmers are here.'

'I know that.'

'And Mr Walmer.'

'Oh, when?'

'An hour ago. He's out with Papa.'

'I must dress,' she said, sitting upright. 'I am so slow. I must speak to Pontefract. We must see that he does not keep the young men talking in the billiard room. They must dance.'

'No,' said Harriet. 'Not yet. It's early yet.' It disturbed her to hear her own voice speak so and her mother's restless disappointed sigh, like a child's at the slow passage of time.

'When does Alfred come? And his friends?'

'I have no idea,' said Harriet siffly. 'Sarah seems to think they'll come, but it's very cold.'

277

'They'll come,' said her mother. 'Has he written to you at all?'

'No. Of course not.' In double irritation that her mother grew clumsy.

'He is fond of you. I'm sure he is.'

She got up then and walked to the window, saying in a low voice which her mother might or might not hear, 'I know you want him to be.'

'Only for you,' said her mother. 'I only want what you want.' Then, when Harriet said nothing. 'You do like him a little?'

'A little,' said Harriet, but the word came out with a curious irony, so that she added quickly, as if it were she that defied her mother's wish, 'but he will not like me. Not enough. I'm sure of that.'

'He scarcely knows you yet.'

'He's going away.'

'Well, he will come back. He will be older then. He'll value you all the more.'

'You will not say anything to him. You promise me that.'

'No. Of course. Of course. I shan't even speak to him.'

'I would never see him again, gladly, if it meant he would return from Sebastopol alive.'

'Don't say that. You don't mean that.'

'But I do.'

'It's dangerous to say that,' said her mother. 'What good is he dead?'

'Harriet, beloved, keep still. Keep still,' Miss Christian called from the landing when she went downstairs again. 'You will tire yourself before this evening.'

'Yes, yes,' she called back impatiently. Then, looking through the landing window, she saw the snow. For a moment she stood quite still, with her arms folded tightly about her and twisted in her shawl. She watched its ceaseless movement drive the flat pressure of the dusk back from the windows, hollowing out spaces, drawing the light from the downstairs windows onto a thin white coating of snow on the stone terrace. How silently it had come.

Perhaps only she had noticed it.

She began to run downstairs, calling, as she pushed open the door to the drawing room, 'It's snowing. Look.' But already Sarah and her mother and the Railston cousins stood together at the window holding back the heavy curtain and peering out.

'Oh, Harriet,' said Sarah, turning to her with her too observant eye. 'Oh, Harriet, the dreadful snow. What if they cannot come and it is all spoilt? Oh, my poor Harriet.'

'But they must come,' she said. Never in all her life had she made a statement of such conviction. 'It will not stop them. They must come.'

'Well, I am sure they will make every effort,' said Euphemia. But she was vexed by the snow. She came and almost absently took up Harriet's hands, shook them, let them drop, in a kind of distracted sympathy.

They all hoped Alfred would marry her. She would not think of that. She would not let it spoil this evening. For he would not, of course. But must come this evening. That could not be taken away. Unless the snow deepened. Unless God were angry with her, that she had defied Mr Wilcox and run from the room before he had a chance to reason with her. That had been cowardly, ungrateful. Once when it had snowed, last year – the year before – her mother had said at breakfast, 'But you cannot go, I forbid it.' The light reflected off the white cloth had shown her face as plain and worn. Harriet had thought then, she is old. She does not know how to be happy. For it had been folly to think that the beautiful pure snow might form a barrier between her and Mr Wilcox. If anything it had been a medium through which she might join him in their separate prayers.

She had said to him, 'Tell me when you pray, so that I may add my prayers to yours.'

'At six in the morning and again at six in the evening. You will give me strength.'

'I will?' Had she really felt so?

'I shall know I am not praying alone.'

Was it possible that was a year ago? Now she shrank

inside from him when he spoke to her in that stifled room and he knew that and smiled at her in a begging way that made her cruel. She knew what he would say before he said it. When he spoke she watched the mole on his lip with horror, lest he forget himself and reach out with his tongue and lick it. She thought with astonishment that once she and Miss Christian had schemed to go an extra day to the vicarage. They had hurried arm in arm. At the sight of the vicarage chimney through the hedge her heart had moved so violently that she feared Miss Christian must feel it through her cloak. How could that be? She watched the mindless circling of the snow, desolate at what it had the power to take from her, and prayed now, 'Let it stop and Alfred Walmer come.'

Papa and Mr Walmer were in the room. She went back to the warmth of the fire, smiling at them, wretched. Mr Walmer's poor old dog lay by the fire, its naked stomach exposed to the flames. She knelt and, lifting its soft ear, whispered, 'I love him. I love him.' No one paid the least attention to her. The little dog twitched upright and began to bark. Euphemia Walmer said to her, 'I detest that creature more than I can tell you. The other dogs are shut away. Why can't it be? He was absurd to bring it.' Already she might be drawn into the family disloyalties.

But now that it was time she delayed. It seemed that the longer she took before she slid her arms out of her warm sleeves the more she might appease the snow. She sat by the window while Sarah Walmer changed her dress. 'Ah, your hands are cold,' she cried out when Harriet fastened her back. 'Do hurry.'

'They're sure to be late,' said Harriet. 'If they come at all.'

'The water will be cold.'

'Yes,' she said dully. 'That's true. There's no purpose to waiting.' She shivered as she washed herself in the tepid basin. She seemed to dwindle and shrink in the cold until there was nothing left of her. She accepted that he could not love her.

'You look so pretty,' she said to Sarah Walmer, who stood smiling thoughtfully at herself in the glass. She said nothing to that, but leaning her head towards the glass frowned, licked her finger, dabbed at her eyebrow. She knew just what she was doing. In other rooms the cousins would do the same, intent upon their separate mysteries.

'Do you know Alfred's friends?' said Harriet, keeping interest from her voice.

'I don't know one from the other. He brought some to us once. They were pleasant enough.' She did not care. She was younger than Harriet. She was to come out in the summer. They said she was pretty but Harriet did not care for her face.

'Does he like the army?'

'I don't know. He never says a word to me.'

'He must.'

'Why?' said Sarah Walmer.

When she sat shivering in her dress Sarah Walmer brushed out her hair for her in a long tail down her back. When Harriet had twisted it into a knot, Sarah helped her pin it up. 'It's lovely hair,' she said, as if it were something she considered buying, but laid it aside. In the glass Sarah assessed her without smiling, forgetting that it gave her face to Harriet just as it gave Harriet's to her.

'Is it snowing still?' Harriet asked. She had not the heart to look herself.

'Poor Harriet,' said Sarah Walmer, unkindly perhaps, from the window. 'It's very deep.' And then with a sudden burst of excitement, 'What if they do come? And we're snowed in? They'll be here for days and days. We'll all be engaged by the end of it. Even me. Even Betsy Railston.'

It was necessary to laugh even though it was unkind. It was necessary not to be alone.

'Let's go down,' said Sarah Walmer, catching at her cold hands. 'Oh, let's go down.'

'Am I all right?' Harriet asked her, although she had meant not to.

'Oh yes. Yes. You look very well. Your dress looks very well.' And they kissed each other suddenly, excitedly, but stiff too with caution for their flounces. For the very sounds they made running hand in hand along the cold landing were of excitement and anticipation, only to be shared between themselves. Not even with the Railston girls.

Above them Miss Christian hung over the balcony calling, 'My beauty, my beauty,' in her queer cracked voice and snatching kisses from her little pouting mouth.

'She's mad,' Sarah Walmer whispered in her ear. 'I think she's mad.'

'God bless you. God bless you,' cried Miss Christian and shook a Union Jack over the banisters like a duster.

Up the stairwell came men's voices: the deep confident voices of old men and the brief gruff answers of young men.

'They've come,' whispered Sarah.

'They can't have done.'

'Can't you hear?'

'Is he there?'

'I should think so,' said Sarah indifferently. She began to drag Harriet by the hand to the stair rail.

'They'll see us.'

'Well, they must see us.'

They were looking down onto the stone flags of the hall, all wet with melted snow, seeing the tops of the young men's heads and the bright shoulders of their blue regimentals. Short bursts of deep nervous laughter came up to them. That Alfred was alive and real and standing there seemed unaccountable.

'Come on,' whispered Sarah in her ear, but Harriet would have held back for fear of spoiling something. Her mind was never to shed its seriousness. It seemed to her as she walked slowly down the stairs that Alfred, who could not want to marry her, would be killed outside Sebastopol and that she, by having a birthday, by asking him to come to it, by making him ride across the snow in the dark, consumed excessive amounts of the time left to him.

He called her by her name. He smiled as if he were pleased to see her. She had known him since she was ten

282

and they had gone in the boat for a picnic. Three summers ago, her first in London, he had come to the house in Eaton Square. She had seen him nearly every week. Then, that Autumn, he had brought his dog over to Longridge and left him with her and a month later embarked for the Cape.

'Are they dancing together?' said Amelia, leaning from the corner of the sofa where she rested. 'Yes,' she said contentedly, 'they are.' The drawing room was lit by firelight only, but through the open doors of the library they could see the four couples stiffly following the pattern of the dance.

'Does he like her, do you think?' she asked Euphemia.

'Oh, I am sure he does.'

'She has changed. She is now how I once supposed her to be, but then she was not.'

Later, when the dancing had stopped and Euphemia gone to see to the supper, she watched Augustus come into the room and sit in the chair drawn up beside her with his old dog laid across his knees. They sat in silence for a minute or two. Then she said, leaning back and looking up at the ceiling, 'Don't you think the firelight very pretty?' When he only nodded, she went on. 'When I am alone I lie here and watch it and gossip to myself. I am grown suddenly very old.' She spoke as if the fact were a relief to her.

'You look very well,' he told her.'

'Oh, I am well enough for what I now am.'

He said, 'It is so long since I was last here,' and realized when she was silent that he had made some sort of an answer. She rested against the cushions, staring up at the erratic movement of light on the ceiling. Perhaps he tired her but did not find it painful to sit with her in this altered state, each wrapped in separate thoughts, in the ease of this exhausted but enduring friendship. Ten years ago she had been a fine woman. He had liked the lack of fragility in her then. He could remember how, on her first morning in the house, she had walked so eagerly to the window and raised her arm above her head to hold back the billowing curtain. He could remember little that they had said to one another, but supposed that over the years he had told her most of the acceptable things about himself.

She said, 'I tell myself the old stories about people I have known. I seem to have known a great many people. You must have known many of them too. It is curious we never talked of that. Did you know Cissy, my sister Cissy?'

'No,' he said.

'She died before she should have done.'

'You wrote me that.'

They heard Pontefract call out, 'Miss Christian, Miss Christian. To your post. To the piano.'

The dancers had reassembled in the adjoining room. Miss Christian played a few bars. Stopped. Began in earnest. The close shuffling and stamping of feet released them from the need to talk. Instead he sat a little back and watched her, as she turned her head on the cushions and stared eagerly into the lighted room for reassurance that Alfred danced with her child, for on that he saw her heart was set. And he, too, not wanting to think deeply into the past, which was gone, wanted it for a kind of justice.

In the years when they had written their unchanging letters she had wasted away from him into something bony and fragile. There had been no trace of it in her handwriting, nor in anything she had said, but then he had never told her the things that might give pain, and all that time this transformation was taking place. He thought of the creatures that he had collected one summer and kept in an aquarium in his study, with their skeletons in the form of transparent scales, their disproportionate dark eyes. They seemed fashioned so that they might vanish in the sea without trace on the instant of their death, and she, too, seemed to achieve a great modesty and economy in what she chose to keep of her life. He had loved most in her what was most spare and distant. He thought of Adela, who did not love him, whom he could not affect, could not damage. She is my survivor, he thought, and smiled.

Amelia supposed he smiled at her and, reaching out, touching his hand, asked for water. There was a glass on a

284

tray. When he gave it to her, she held it in both hands and drank it in little sips. She lay very still when he had taken the glass from her. He felt he watched a mystery and was awed by her. For it seemed less by illness than by an act of will that she had regained this spectral childhood, freed herself of the soft weight of woman's body and returned to this thin spare thing in which she had begun life. Out of the full face of her womanhood, which he could scarcely remember, had risen this thin bony childish face. He had a miniature of the dead sister Fanny, done when she was twelve. A charming thing. He could remember the painter coming to the house. He often looked at it. Taken as if she had been arrested in running after something. As startled and timid as now Amelia Pontefract, when the log fell at one end between the fire irons. When Miss Christian attacked the Dashing White Sergeant and the two lines of dancers formed again, she strained forward to see if Alfred stood opposite her daughter.

He sat with her, staring at the fire, repeatedly lifting and pulling the dog's soft stiff ear, but his thoughts were quite distracted. He was remembering playing in the rhododendron plantations at Longridge. Hiding from someone. Robert, his brother. Some visitor. They could hear his loud threatening steps in the next tunnel. Fanny crouched beside him with her skirt drawn over her knee, laughing with terror. She bit his shoulder to stop laughing. He could feel the circle of her teeth through the stuff of his shirt and the patch of cold and warm where she breathed. The light was dim in the tunnels like evening, but if you looked up there were bright flecks of sky. The sun burnt between the leaves. Flowers lay on the soft brown earth as bright and mysterious as jewels. They had hidden too well, he remembered. The voices and footsteps of the other children had receded and finally gone away, so that in the end the sense of triumphant secrecy was spoilt and they had come out and gone back to the house. It seemed now that if Fanny had lived and married and given birth to children, she would in the end by choice have returned to that state where he had lost her, and all the bitter grieving at her death was after all mistaken. Had he ever spoken of that, or written of it to Amelia Pontefract? He thought not, but it was odd that a moment later she should say, 'I met your sister Fanny. Did you know that she came to my wedding?'

'She wrote to me. I remember.'

'She was just a child. Why were you not there? Surely Pontefract would have wanted it.'

'I was in Ireland.' He had gone that summer through Connemara looking for land. 'I remember I could not come.'

'I remember her so well. Her face had no caution in it. And then to return from Italy and hear that she had died. She danced. I'm sure I remember her dancing.' And immediately she turned her head restlessly back on the cushions towards the dancers in the lighted room. Harriet was playing now and it was one of the other young men who turned the pages for her, and not Alfred Walmer.

When Euphemia came back into the room Amelia reached out her hand to her and asked anxiously, 'How are they? Are they enjoying themselves?'

'Yes, yes,' said Euphemia decidedly. 'I have never seen your Harriet so animated.'

'She is happy, then?'

'I think very happy.'

She let herself lie back and closed her eyes for a moment. When she opened them Augustus had risen and was leaving the room.

There was a commotion. The dance broke off midway. There was a sound of raised voices and laughter coming from the hall and the room was suddenly vacated. Euphemia went to the door and came back, saying, 'It is some bother with Miss Christian. She says there is a squirrel in her bedroom. Really, I think she is a little mad.' Somewhere in the house they could hear the frantic yapping of dogs and from overhead the clatter of running feet across the bare floorboards and thin carpeting of the upstairs passages.

*   *   *

286

For Harriet, after all, the dancing had not been the ordeal she had feared: not here, among her friends. For even Alfred's friends, whom she had never met before, seemed hers. As they passed her again and again in the figures of the dance their faces became printed on her mind, so that years later she could recall them at will: Henry Kirkbride, Sam Mayhew, who married Sarah in the end, though that night they hardly spoke, William Duff, Tommy Railston, who wore his hunting jacket because he hated being the only one not in uniform. When she must play she wished she were dancing, and when Sarah Walmer came and said that she would play she stood up very quickly to dance again, but Alfred danced with Betsy Railston and she must dance with Henry Kirkbride who had turned the pages for her.

But whether he danced with her or whether he did not, there came a moment in every dance when he must take her hand, and it was only courtesy to look at him and smile. Only she must remember not to look ahead or behind her to where he was, but look and smile at each one the same. She knew the dances. She had learnt them as a child, staying with the Railston cousins when Aunt Cissy was alive. Then they were like a game of remembering, and if you made a mistake you felt ashamed. And now she linked arms with him and he swung her round fast, but she was strong and sure-footed. He could not make her lose her footing.

'You will not be able to lecture me now,' he told her. 'You have grown quite as lightheaded as I am. What will become of my morals, now that you have taken to dancing?'

She laughed at him and swung onto the next arm and the next. And the dance was still like a game because none of them were as they really were, but that did not matter. She did not think Alfred Walmer would ever love her, but that did not matter now. Never had she felt so happy. 'I am so happy,' she told Alfred when next he swung her round and whether he heard her or whether he did not, or what he thought she meant by it, did not seem to matter at

287

all. When Miss Christian had run in saying there was a squirrel in her room and that it would bite her, she had wanted to cry out, Oh go away. You always spoil things. You and Mama with her illness. She pretended for a moment that she had not noticed her.

Betsy Railston said, 'Oh, it will go away, Miss Christian. It must be the cold has driven it in.' And she turned again to William Duff.

'But you must free it. It is terrified. It tried to bite me,' Miss Christian persisted.

'We'll chase it away, then, shall we?' said Tommy Railston, who was bored with the dancing.

'Where is it?'

'Oh, very well then,' Harriet said, for suddenly this bright room seemed to have exhausted itself, and lifting her skirt she ran past Miss Christian without even looking at her, out into the hall where her father stood staring rather helplessly up the stairwell. The dogs' bodies could be heard thudding against the gunroom door and low whines which Harriet found distressing came from behind it.

'Can't we let the dogs out, sir?' asked Tommy Railston. 'We could hunt it.'

'Oh, let them out, Papa. They do so hate being shut away.'

'Very well,' said Pontefract. 'We cannot have Miss Christian terrorized in her own boudoir.'

'But the poor little creature,' cried Miss Christian, now holding up her hands in some vaguely directed prayer. 'I'm sure it only showed its teeth because it was frightened. I did not mean to set the dogs on it.'

'They probably won't catch it,' Tommy Railston told her quite kindly. 'They'll just chase it about a bit. They very seldom *catch* anything.'

But in any case it was too late. The door to the gunroom had been opened and the dogs poured out, four or five of them yapping and showing their lean stomachs as they leaped up. Augustus' dog came shuffling in to join them from the billiard room.

'Come, boy,' said Alfred Walmer, sinking his fingers into the thick curling hair under Trouncher's collar. The dog lay low on the stones, its ears cocked. Its brown eyes turned up to him, waiting command. He rose quickly with his hand on the dog's collar and, stooping, ran with it at heel to the foot of the stairs. Everyone, even the dogs, was silent for a moment. He said softly, 'Go seek him,' and the dog, with one swift look back at him, began to bound up the stairs. Immediately the others raced after him, dogs and young men.

'Away halloo,' shouted Henry Kirkbride.

Tommy Railston made a hunting horn of his fist and blasted breathily through it.

Harriet, not even looking to see what Sarah and the Railston girls would do, lifted her skirt well clear of her slippers and began to run too, up the shallow stairs, two at a time, as she had not done for years.

'Your shawl,' shouted Miss Christian. 'You will be cold without your shawl.'

She pretended not to hear. The warmth of the dancing still glowed on her arms. The cold could not touch her.

On the top landing there was some confusion, as the dogs had rushed down the corridor and no one was certain of the way in the dim light that rose up the stairwell. Harriet pushed past them and took the lead. But when she came to the door of Miss Christian's room and heard the frantic racketing of the trapped creature on the far side of the door, she hesitated. Someone reached past her and flung it open. Immediately the dogs poured in and almost immediately out again after the still powerful and terrified squirrel, who was somewhere ahead of them in the corridor. For one moment as it leapt past her its desperation touched Harriet. She was awed by the plight it was in. She thought of herself at the very edge of life, knowing that her strength must fail and that stronger things opposed her. Then, needing to do violence to that thought, she began to run again with the young men down the corridor. There was no light there. They stumbled against one another in the passage.

'Where is it?' she called over her shoulder. 'Where did it go?'

'Up,' shouted Alfred. 'Is there another floor?'

'No. It couldn't get into the attics.' She scarcely had breath to make him hear, but ran ahead down the passage towards an uncurtained window. There she stopped for a moment, struck by the sight of the snow, which she had forgotten. They came up behind her, Alfred and Henry Kirkbride.

'Can you hear it?' said Henry Kirkbride in a whisper.

They stood, all three, just visible to one another in the chill reflection of the snow, listening for the frantic scrabbling of the squirrel. Not a sound.

'It must have gone down.'

At that moment they heard the sudden clamour of the dogs on the floor below and Tommy Railston's breathless cry, 'Yonder he goes.'

'Which way? Which way?' asked Henry Kirkbride in an agony of excitement, but had already begun to run back down the passage. He shouldered roughly past but Alfred stayed behind her. Once he caught at her bare arm, but she laughed and jerked it free and ran laughing ahead of him. On the stairs he was right behind her, sliding his hands on the banisters so that they pushed hers forward. At the landing she swung round, laughing at him. He caught her then and swung her round so that he went ahead of her, but she ran behind him with her hands on his shoulders until he broke away from her. Ahead of them in the passageway there was a final crash of dog clamour followed by dead silence. They stopped, then, and walked towards the dark group at the end of the passage.

'They've got it,' said Henry Kirkbride quietly. 'It's run up the curtains.'

One of the dogs jumped up and, sinking its teeth into the hem of the curtain, began to worry it this way and that.

'Careful,' said Tommy Railston. 'He'll tear it.'

'Get away there. Get away there,' said Henry Kirkbride. He seized the curtain and shook it, but the squirrel only clambered higher. When it moved they could see it indistinctly against the dark stuff of the curtain.

'Get it by the tail and wrench it off,' said Alfred.

'By God, it's bitten me,' said Henry Kirkbride in a shocked, blurred voice, for he had stuck his finger in his mouth.

But he must have shaken it free, for they could tell by the savage growling of the dogs that it had fallen.

'Get away there. Get away there,' shouted Tommy Railston. He went in fearlessly, cuffing them with his sleeve gripped over his fist.

'Whoohoop,' shouted Alfred, very loud and close to Harriet, so that she put her hands over her ears but leant a little back against him.

Tommy Railston held up the tattered bit of fur in triumph. She was glad it was too dark see it well, but she felt exalted by its death, as if it were in some way auspicious.

'Have you a knife?' asked Henry Kirkbride. 'Any of you have a knife? I want the brush, after a run like that. Here, give it me.'

Tommy Railston had a knife. 'Don't let it fall,' he said. 'They'd make a fearful mess of it.'

'Give it here,' said Henry Kirkbride. 'I'm having it. It was me got bitten.'

Alfred said to her, 'You should be blooded for being such a sport.'

She shut her eyes quickly and a moment later felt with curious excitement the stroke of its still warm flesh against her cheek. The dogs were yapping frantically.

'You must let them have it,' said Tommy Railston.

'You can't let them have it here.'

'Well, take it down and throw it out on the terrace.'

And Henry Kirkbride began to run downstairs again, shouting and twirling the dead squirrel about his head, with the dogs leaping up at him and occasionally tumbling on the stairs.

'Whoohoop,' shouted Tommy Railston, running after him with the others.

Harriet stood leaning over the banisters, watching them

open the door. Alfred's warm arm lay like a weight across her shoulders.

They watched Henry Kirkbride fling the squirrel out onto the snow on the terrace, shouting, 'Whoohoop. Tear him. Tear him,' to the frantic dogs.

After a moment, when Alfred seemed to have forgotten her, she stirred a little as if she would go, but he turned her face towards him then and gravely wiped at her cheek.

'Oh,' she said, putting her hand there. 'I had forgotten. I might have gone down like that. Is it all gone?'

He took her chin in his hand and, turning her face to the light, studied it, perhaps for no more than traces of blood: for he dabbed at it again with another part of the handkerchief. He was flushed and he laughed. She was not sure of him. Then he said, 'Do you think you could ever marry me?' He threw back his head defiantly. 'Would you marry me, if I were to come back safely and ask you then?' But he had asked her. There was no going back on it.

'Yes,' she said, without smiling. 'Yes.'

He had taken her hands quite hard in his and began now to pull her towards the stairs. 'We must tell them,' he said. 'We must tell them straight away.' And, dragging her by the hand, he began to run downstairs.

She woke early in the morning with a feeling of great strangeness. It was almost possible to fear that none of this had happened. But it had. They had all known that it had. She dressed and went downstairs to a house in which the very air and light and sound were altered by snow. No one else was about. She walked from room to room. Each had been restored, as if the previous night had never been. The cold light through the windows seemed to exalt and empty them. Happiness surrounded her like an element which she alone breathed. When she stood by the window, feeling the cold breath of the glass against her face, the bright simplicity of the world delighted her. She tried for one moment to think of the dark tangled things waiting to re-emerge, but the world was made of snow. The great bare trees were transformed by it. Under the clinging snow

292

the black branches seemed the shadowed underside of a fragile airy thing made only of snow. Had she struck at them with a stick, the great oaks which had towered over her childhood would have shattered at her feet. It seemed they would not move again; that they had taken up a final form. Shadows lay across the lawn, very long and narrow and blue, and at its edge a lighter line of snow was cast up against the hedge like a line of frozen surf.

She stood watching it, knowing that something irreversible had happened. Before long the house would begin to stir and one by one they would be heard on the stairs, would enter the room, and reaffirm the extraordinary truth of what had happened. She was glad then that Alfred had told them, although at the time she had wished he would not.

22

In the spring of 1856, Alfred Walmer visited the islands for the first time since his return to England. As the new packet steamed into the harbour he noticed at once all the boats were decked overall and festooned with coloured streamers. A large crowd was gathered on the quay. A band struck up, flags fluttered. A banner was raised on two poles and stretched against the buffeting of the wind until he could read the words: Welcome Home. With a dismay he would disown he realized this reception was for him.

When the steamer reached the quay a great cheer went up, making him shiver slightly through emotion, or discomfort, or memory of other occasions when men's voices had shouted in the open air. He stood at the head of the gangplank staring down at the upturned faces, his uncle's among them, smiling foolishly more from embarrassment than pleasure; he felt a sensation, oddly repugnant, that he was being drawn back into a past existence for which he was no longer fitted.

Augustus climbed half way to meet him, clapped him firmly around the shoulders, said, 'Come on. Come this way.' He too was moved and showed it, but more, Alfred thought, at the goodwill around him than at the sight of his nephew.

They walked arm in arm on an inspection of the local dignitaries. The faces, aged and forgotten over the four years, seemed suddenly to move into focus, proffering names and laying their claim upon him. Wills, of course, he knew: stooping and greying at forty as if the winds had got to him. There was Hall, the chief magistrate now. He and his uncle, who had detested each other for all these years, spoke with the heartiness of old friends. The oldest tenants pressed forward, each holding the banner of his trade: shipwrights, tradesmen, pilots, fishermen, reaching out their free hands to catch at his. Augustus pressed Alfred forward with his fist clenched in the small of his back, shouting names he half remembered into his ear, for the outbursts of cheering continued.

Then he was steered to the head of a slow procession. The magistrates, the last surviving veterans of the French Wars in their scarlet coats, the band and the tenants fell in behind. At the end of the pier a triumphal arch had been adorned with flowering shrubs and streamers whipping the wind. When they turned into the main street he saw another one by the Customs House.

'Was all this really necessary?' he said to his uncle without turning too obviously towards him, for they smiled away from each other and lifted their hands from time to time as they walked along.

'Well,' he said, 'it was put to me when they knew you were coming. They've done it all at their own expense. It was gratifying that they should, don't you think? Peters says a service of thanksgiving is in order – very brief.'

'You love it, really,' said his nephew out of the side of his mouth. 'You're grown as feudal as the worst of them. I wouldn't have believed it of you.'

There was something primitive and proprietary about the thin cheers along the stone street: the rejoicing that he had returned with all his flesh intact. He did not care to think that they owned him yet. He looked sideways at his uncle and saw him stride along, his cap drawn down over his eyes, his chin held at its most provocative angle, the half smile that accepted these cheers as his due, but rejected so defensively any possibility that they spoke of affection. He's good for years yet, he thought, and felt a motion of painful love which he knew well enough would turn to irritation before the day was out.

'We owe them something,' Augustus was saying, 'since

you'll not be married here.'

The service was brief enough and, for all its solemnity, never entirely shook off the festive air of the street outside. There was a constant fidgeting in the back pews. No one had thought to take the flags from the schoolchildren before herding them into the church.

Afterwards, in the churchyard, the band struck up again and Alfred found he was to unveil a simple granite cross bearing the names of two islanders, sailors who had died hauling guns up from Balaclava. He remembered that a letter had come from his uncle some months after their deaths, and that before he left he had managed to find the grave of one of them and draw a rapid sketch of it. Now he was led over to shake the hand of this boy's mother, who said, with tears in her eyes, that the drawing was her dearest treasure. He felt her warm dry hand fumble with his and feared she would never release him.

They stayed afterwards talking with Peters, while the band led the crowd away. Alfred looked around the bare churchyard and said, when his uncle was free, 'I see you've at least one companion for the poor skeleton.'

'Yes,' said Augustus with a short laugh.

'Who was it?' asked Alfred.

'Mrs Traherne of the Gweal. She died, oh, it must be five or six years ago.'

He went quickly down on one knee, peering to read the headstone. There were flowers on the grave, a little hand bunch of wild garlic. He imagined the indistinct form of Adela placing them there and said, without looking up, 'And the girl? What became of her?'

'She's married,' said Augustus shortly, as if that were enough.

Only later did Alfred say, 'You did not tell me who Adela Traherne married.'

They sat before dinner with the lamps unlit and the curtains in the library undrawn. Alfred, with his capacity for infinite stillness, stretched on the sofa. His uncle sat upright on the desk chair, twitching his stick between his ankles. His dog, a new one, perched on his knee.

'I don't believe I did. Do you remember her? She married Billy Jenkins of the Hill Farm.'

'Isn't he the lame one?'

Something in his tone made Augustus say defensively, 'It's not a bad match for her. He's a good enough fellow.'

'No doubt she could have had her pick.'

'No doubt,' said Augustus. Then, supposing the question must have arisen out of a dearth of things to say, he went on quickly, 'You must find it very quiet here. Very small. Very dull, after all that has happened to you.'

When Alfred said nothing he got restlessly to his feet. With his back turned, he said, 'I thought when you were a boy that you would be happy here when I am gone.'

The control in his uncle's voice, the stiff withdrawal of his attitude by the window, all cried out for comfort. But Alfred, distracted for a moment by the thought of Adela, and still disturbed by a sense that his newly returned life might be consumed by this man's obsessive concern, could find no acceptable way of giving it. He loved him, did not love him, and said in the end, almost brusquely, 'You're good for years yet.'

Augustus shrugged and looked out of the window. Presently he said, 'You haven't seen the light yet. It has become a kind of superstition with me to see its first circuit.'

It was an invitation. The least he could do was to rise and stand beside him and a moment later saw the red light make its first probing sweep between the western rocks. It seemed that so deft a movement, so intense a gleam, must generate some sound, but it stroked the sky quite silently, and passed and must be waited for again.

So that he turned impatiently back into the room saying, 'You could stand and watch for it all evening.'

'I do at times.'

'Well, that's not like you. You should not.' He flung himself down on the sofa. The sense of assumptions made for him, of a disregard for his own separate life, made him suddenly irritable. In the gloom of the unlit room his uncle followed and lowered himself, it seemed with exaggerated stiffness, into the chair opposite. The little dog rattled after him and jumped back on his knee. 'You shouldn't let him do that. You spoil him,' Alfred said.

When the windows had lightened and faded again, Augustus said, 'You did not care for that performance this morning, I think. I hope you are not angry with me. It was incredibly well meant.'

'I was simply unprepared for it.'

'I'd have warned you, had I known. But you were on your way before I knew myself.'

'I didn't mind. I enjoyed it in a way.'

'Well, it was necessary. You know that Trinity House are trying to limit the number of licences for the pilotage.'

'You said when you wrote.'

'It would fall very hard on a lot of them. I want them to know that I am absolutely behind them in opposing this, in seeking protection for them. That, in just a little part, added to the cheering, I think. I wanted them to associate you with all of that.'

'But why? Surely it will blow over.'

The carelessness of his tone was almost offensive. Augustus said, 'Still, it is important to show that we are both as one over this. There is no harm in that, surely.'

'No, but you are so inconsistent,' said Alfred, laughing in a very ecstasy of irritation at this man he was bound to love.

'What do you mean?'

'When you came here it was all self-help and utility. If a man could not earn his own living he must go. And you sent him. They still hate you for that. And now, when the rest of the country threw the idea out years ago, you talk of protection.'

He got restlessly to his feet and began to pace up and down in front of the windows, waiting, in spite of himself, for the light. 'Then you were all against the old order. Oh, I've heard all about it. And I sensed it, even when I was a boy, that you despised my mother's people and dear old Pontefract, because they were a part of all that.'

298

'No, no,' he said. 'Not despised. You know that.'

'Well, you thought yourself a better man than they. And you were. And you are.'

'No, no,' he said again, distressed.

'You are. I can say it. You've done infinitely more with your life than either of them.'

'It was there. It needed doing. I had no other purpose.' This humility and resignation goaded him on.

'But look at you now. Everything you said and did then was entirely radical. You wanted to change everything. To prove that the old ruling class had had its day and that you and your class knew how to put the country to rights. But look at you now. You've made this place your own. It was to be just an experiment. You were to take your ideas back to the mainland and shake them with the proof that they had worked. But you never left and now you want everything to remain the same. No one can have any ideas that contrast one particle with your own. Protection! My God, it is absurd!'

'Well,' he said from behind the desk, 'I have done what I understood. If it is to be done differently after my death, that's your affair. I can do no more than I have done. Anyone clings to what is slipping away from him.'

'And all this talk of death! You're not dying. You've never looked better. Besides,' he said, 'I doubt if I'd have done so very differently. It's just that it's all done.'

'All what is done?'

'All that you ever set out to do.'

After a moment he said, perhaps not in answer, because the light again had intervened, 'It is impossible to make people happy. To believe that by making their lives more comfortable and safe would make them happy was my error as a young man. I tell you that because I do not wish you to be misled when you are here. Nothing you do, nothing will achieve that.'

'It's the same with the war,' Alfred said. 'It achieved nothing. Nothing changed.' Then, knowing that he answered his uncle's need with one of his own, he broke off and said, 'Of course you make people happy. Your friends.

299

Here. I can remember standing in that door on the first morning I was here in a kind of wonderment of happiness.' Though later, he remembered, it had all been spoilt.

'Yes,' Augustus was saying. 'Yes. It is kind of you to say so.' But the words, meant as a restitution, seemed to have saddened rather than pleased him. A moment later he said almost shyly: 'There was something I've wanted to put to you but I scarcely know now whether this is the moment for it.'

'What is that?'

'It occurred to me that you might consider handing in your commission, settling here with Harriet for part of the year – oh, I'd keep out of the way – taking some of the burden off Wills.' Of course it was not only that he wanted, but something less defined, insatiable.

Alfred said harshly, 'But it's too soon. Surely it's too soon. I had not thought for years yet.'

'No, no. It was wrong to mention it. But the offer is there. I thought with Harriet, army life might take you away too much. With a family you might want to settle down. But you must have thought of all that.'

'Of course,' he said. 'Of course – and it's good of you. But so soon. Really, I had not thought.'

'Well, think then. Take your time to think.'

It must end there. They waited for the next passage of the light, as if agreed that it would mark a decent interval. The dinner gong, too, allowed them to speak differently, more comfortably. As they walked into the dining room Augustus said, 'I'll let you go over on your own tomorrow. You can tell Wills anything he needs to know.' For Alfred had promised to give his advice on the blasting of a pile of rocks that blocked the entrance to the harbour on the main island. It was the week of the neap tide. He had wanted since childhood to walk between the islands. At the very thought of it the sense of oppression lifted from him. He asked, almost eagerly, 'When is the tide out?'

'Five?'

'Could I come back on foot then?'

300

'Oh, yes, there's an hour at least on either side of the tide.'

When they had inspected the rocks and decided where best to put the charges, Wills directed Alfred to the headland at the far end of the harbour. From there he could make the shortest passage across the sands back to the Gweal.

'How long do I have?' he asked him, taking out his watch, as did Wills.

'An hour – an hour and a half. You're quite safe.'

Nevertheless he climbed up the headland first and stared across to the island. The sand flats stretched wide and gleaming like a wet skin just bared by the sea. Black rock piles lay scattered about them. He plotted his course between these, along the palest stretches of sand, and committed their shapes to memory. Here and there the deeper channels glittered, disturbing his eye as his ear was disturbed by the great withdrawal of sound. Something that he would set aside played at his reminiscence. He imagined his solitary figure receding deeper and deeper into that emptiness and felt a sudden reluctance to set out. Then, with relief, he saw walking towards him along the beach beyond the headland another figure: a woman, by her loose blowing clothing, moving outwards to the edge of the dry sand, as if she intended to cast herself off on the same course as himself. He would follow, keep her in sight. Then, long before he could make out her face, he recognized Adela.

Since his arrival he had been wary of meeting her, imagining that they might suddenly be brought face to face, but now, watching her at this distance, seeing her pushed obliquely towards him by the wind as if she were the last living soul on earth, he was reminded too forcibly, not of her, but of that unscathed young man from whom events had deeply divided him. He remembered his tormented restraint, his generosity towards her, the pain of letting her go, the intensity with which he had dared to feel. So that it seemed the figure drawn along the beach, both towards him and away, still kept possession of parts

301

of him that he had since lost. He began to climb down the
headland, abandoning the twisting track, but striding
from foothold to foothold on the stones among the worn
heather until he reached the sand. He wished that she
would turn so that he might see her face and be certain
that she knew it was he. He thought she did – she seemed so
little startled when he spoke to her – but stood regarding
him without welcome, nor any reference in her eye to
what she must remember of him. He said, 'Don't you
know me, Adela?' in an odd mournful voice. 'Have I
changed so?'

She looked steadily at him. Strands of her hair blew
across her face. It seemed wrong to him that she was as she
had been. She said, 'I cannot see that you have changed.'
And began to walk on.

He kept pace beside her, saying, 'Where have you been?
What have you been doing?' For it was absurd that they
should not speak naturally to one another. Without his
intending it, his voice had taken on the childish tone he
had used to penetrate her remoteness all those years ago.
He saw now as the wind blew her dress against her that she
already carried Jenkins' child.

She said, 'To the churchyard.'

'I saw some flowers on your aunt's grave. I was sorry to
hear about her.'

'Well, they were dead,' she said flatly, 'I took some
more.'

'I hear you are married now. My uncle told me.'

'Yes,' she said, and unconsciously her hand strayed
across the curve of the child.

'You know I am to be, next month?'

'Yes.'

'You remember Harriet?'

'Oh, yes. I am glad it is she.' She was silent then.

'Are you walking to the island? It is too far for you,
surely.'

'I know how far it is. I've often done it.'

'I'll go with you.'

'As you like. It's nothing to me.' As if she had bidden him

302

goodbye, she began to walk rapidly from him out onto the sand. He stood where he was, watching her go. But the very way in which she moved seemed to him reckless and wasteful. He could not leave her so. She paused a moment, stooping down to pick up the hem of her skirt. Then, without looking back, she set out across the tight ribbed sand of the channel bed.

He walked at a little distance, making no attempt to overtake her as she kept resolutely on, further and further out on the colourless brilliance of the sands. Bright flotillas of light were caught here and there in the emptying hollows. His eyes were dazzled by it. Her small form seemed corroded by light. A terror filled him that he would see her disintegrate, and that he was in some way the agent of that destruction, for his own images of death, gleaned before the walls of Sebastopol, were universal and grotesque. He must see now the bone, the very spine visible through the fragments of cloth and flesh. It seemed to him that he followed her with a need to speak that had little to do with the past but was present and pressing.

When he came up to her he put his hand roughly on her shoulder and said, 'You are to listen to me. You never listened. I never knew whether you listened or not.'

'What have you to say to me? Nothing that I want to hear.'

'I want to know what has happened to you. I want to talk to you.'

'Nothing has happened to me.'

'In six years?'

'I don't count the years.'

'Won't you walk along with me?' he said. 'Take my arm as you used to.'

She slipped her arm through his, then, but never stopped walking forward, forcing her swollen body against the wind as if she feared the tide might sweep in at any moment. At wide strip of water separated them from the next sand bar. 'Do you want to turn back?' he asked her.

But she splashed into the icy water, feeling it seep into

303

her boots. The pressure of the current on her ankles made her lean against him to steady herself. As soon as she was on the sand she drew her arm free of his and began to walk across a landscape increasingly strange.

The wide sand flats shone like metal. The water between them was very blue, presenting a shallow mirror to the sky. Gulls' white breasts reflected white splinters down into the sand. Birds' footsteps trespassed everywhere across the bottom of the sea. Only a few feet away a gull broke through the fragile shell of a sea urchin with its harsh beak and gorged itself. She heard him run heavily behind her, and fragments of his voice, but any words were dispersed by the wind. When he took her arm again he bent his head close to hers and said, 'You'll fall. What is the matter with you? Don't you care what happens to you?' He thought of the child in a kind of horror, unable in its frailty to make her hold to life.

'What's that to you?'

'You know I am bound a little to care for you.'

'That's not true,' she said.

'Don't you remember why I came? All that time. All that way. Is it possible that you've forgotten?'

She said, 'You went away.'

'It was you,' he said quickly. 'I wanted you to stay.'

But she repeated, 'You went away.'

He threw back his head then in irritation at her. She shouted in the wind, with her face streaked across with hair as if it had been roughly cancelled out.

'You don't understand me. I don't care whether you understand me or not.'

'What purpose is there for me to understand you? You must know how it is with me. You know I cannot choose what I do. What I am.'

'Oh, but you could,' she said. 'You do. You do what you want. That's what you do. You could always come when you wanted and go when you wanted to. Whenever you wanted to you could go.'

'Listen to me.'

'I can't hear you.' Shaking her head and her hair as if she would shake his words from her.

'You know it is all set out for me. That when I leave the army I must come here. That I must live out my life here. You must know that.'

'That won't be till he is dead.'

She had said something that he did not wish to understand, but put it away, saying angrily, 'Can't you remember what was good?'

She could see by his mouth that he was shouting at her, but the wind took all the force out of his words. It dragged strands of her hair across her eyes and, when she raised her head, her mouth. She did not know whether it was the wind that made her eyes weep. She shouted too, 'What good is it to me to remember?' But the wind distorted everything. She could not know if he had heard. She turned away, stumbling and splashing onto the next sandbank, and then began to run on heavy painful feet down its length. She flung back her head and shouted, 'You've no business coming here. You should have left me alone. I was happy enough.' But the wind took all sense out of the words. 'I don't care about you. I don't,' she shouted, but the wind took the words away. She rubbed her face on her sleeve and dragged the hair clinging to it back behind her ears, turning slowly around in search of the landmarks, the beach, the rocks, but they were gone. Nothing was familiar. She was caught in a hollow of sand rising on all sides. She could not see out of it. When he came towards her she began to shout again, 'I can't see where to go.'

He pointed with his arm as if he threw something from him. He was near to her now. She did not believe that he was here. She did not believe that it was possible to talk with him. He was shouting, too. 'That way.' He took her hand and made her put her arm through his. He bent his head and said severely, 'You will fall if you run like that.'

'No, I won't.' The water from her eyes dried cold and stiff on her face. She said, with a force that frightened him, 'It's not real, this. Can't you see? Where we are. It isn't meant to be. It's the bottom of the sea. It's an inside thing. It's not meant to be, here, with the light on it and us walking on it. It's no place. No place at all. I don't believe it's happening. I don't believe it's true.'

'Don't,' he said. 'Don't.' And, gripping the thick hair at the base of her neck, he would have held her against his shoulder so that she could not speak, but she twisted away from him, saying again, 'I don't believe it's true at all. If we stayed in it we'd drown. It's like being drowned. Like being under the sea. Like not understanding it. And you take the sea over you to be the sky and you fancy you walk about because you can't believe you're dead. And you shout and shout but the other person cannot hear you. You think it's the wind, but really maybe it's the water pouring down your ears. Because you're dead. You're dead.'

'Stop that,' he said, holding her from him, by the shoulders, shaking her slightly. 'You can't go on like that. I shouldn't have spoken to you. I've upset you.' But he held her again to comfort her, saying, as if they were words of comfort, 'I know it is quite wrong of me. I know it is wrong.'

And she, gone suddenly quiet, said, 'Nothing matters here. It's no place at all.'

'Then it is the place for us, Adela,' so quietly against her ear that it seemed even she must not hear it.

'I want to stay here, then.'

'We can't,' he said. 'You know we can't.'

Then, feeling her stillness, as if all life had stopped in her, said, 'I'm sorry. Sorry for it all.'

'It doesn't matter. It's not your fault.'

He said slowly, 'It's not his child, is it?'

'That's no concern of yours.'

'No,' he said. 'Of course it's not.' But had his answer in part at least.

They had begun to walk forward again, forced into collusion by the wind and the need to ford another channel.

'Only tell me he's good to you. You are all right? Is there anything you need?'

'No, it's all right.'

'It's not,' he said. 'You know it's not.'

He began to talk rapidly then, because what was

306

between them seemed suddenly exhausted, because of the need to press forward to the beach, because of the sense of time and space dwindling. For they had climbed imperceptibly out of the trough of the channel. The beach stretched ahead of them, apparently very close. Looking back, the shallow expanses of water had widened. He said, 'It was like this. I was thinking that before I saw you. Only dust, but glaring like this, day after day. Their trench and then their wall, no farther than that. Let me tell you. I want to tell you. When they left in the night, the guns stopped. You couldn't think what it was. It went silent like this. So that all the time your ears strain after sound that's gone. I thought I was dreaming. To be able to walk over that ground towards that wall and nothing – nothing – quite alone. And all the time listening for the bullet that must kill me. Watching the top of the wall for some movement, some flash.' It was that that had disturbed him in the glittering passages of water. His eyes narrowed in the glare, looking about him as if by speaking of these things he would make them reappear. His arm was close about her, half dragging her towards the beach which no longer seemed the beach. 'I climbed over the parapet. I seemed to see myself climb over it, as if I were someone crouched down behind it. Do you understand what I'm saying? I seemed to see myself in my blue jacket standing there and I thought: Now they'll shoot. But all the time I was looking down inside the redan and they'd gone. It was empty. I began to climb down. I was looking for him. One of the guns was gone. You could see where they'd dragged it out, and through the gun port you could see our trenches and our battery where he had taken aim. Next to it was his room: his table, his chair, an empty bird cage. He'd thought to let it go. But he'd left all the rest. Flute music, letters. He'd lived there. I'd killed him, I think.'

'Did you see him?' It startled him when she spoke, as if he'd forgotten her.

'No. I looked for him but he wasn't there. But I feel he was dead. I feel I killed him.'

They were on the beach now, climbing the hard, wet

sand. He pulled her round with him, so that they both stood staring at the land they had walked across, which already shone and crept with the incoming tide. He said, 'I feel he was me. Can you understand that?'

They did not look at one another but out at the vanishing sand. Birds flying to and fro in flocks close to the surface of the shallow water let out their easy automatic cries, and altered colour as they wheeled.

She said, as if it surprised her, 'You killed me, too.'

'No,' he said, holding her roughly to him so that he could not see her face. 'That is not true. I never harmed you.'

'I think you did,' she said, as if it were of no importance.

'No one can kill you.' He began carefully to wipe the strands of hair from her face with his cold shaking hand, saying, 'Look at you. Look at you. If anyone's alive it's you.' He kissed her where he had moved away the hair, insisting, 'There. It isn't true. None of that is true.'

'Oh, it's true,' she said.

But he might not have heard her. He was saying, 'When will I see you? When will I see you?' and when she had no answer: 'In August. I'll be here in August.' Unable to think for sadness and confusion what it was he was saying.

When Alfred had changed and come down for dinner he found Augustus waiting for him in the study. The room was dark when the sun was off the terraces. No lamps had been brought. Nor were fires ever lit in the summer. He would have been glad of one, for the walk had chilled him and he still shook inwardly with cold and misery.

I shall live and die in this house, he thought.

Augustus, stout and commanding, seated out of habit behind his desk, his thick ringed hand laid on it like an heraldic paw, made a focus for his wretchedness. He scarcely spoke to him but crossed the room ungraciously and stood staring out of the window, propping himself with one arm against its frame. 'It's quite light out there,' he said. 'Why is it so dark in here?'

Behind him the room remained silent. The little dog seemed to have been banished. He did not turn but continued staring out. Dense as the garden had grown in his absence, nothing in it was of a height to obscure his view of the beach and the passage between the islands, quite lost now under the water.

He heard his uncle say, 'Did you enjoy your walk?'

'Yes, very much.' But the tone he said it in seemed a surly enough denial.

When Augustus spoke again it was with a slow caution that acknowledged something was amiss. 'I made you out. I think. If it were you, you had a companion.'

Alfred, staring at the empty altered view, could only wonder what he might have seen or surmised. He turned back into the room and lowered himself onto the sofa without taking his eyes from his uncle's face.

'I crossed with Adela Traherne – Adela Jenkins.' When Augustus was silent he said stiffly, 'I could hardly let her cross alone.'

'No. Of course you could not. It slipped my mind, when you asked me about her, that you had made her acquaintance in London.'

'At your suggestion. You asked me to visit her.'

'Indeed.'

He said abruptly, 'The child is not Jenkins'. She said as much. Did you know that?'

'Well?'

'Well?' he repeated. 'You mean what concern is it of mine?'

'Did she complain of her treatment?'

'No.'

'Then it need not concern you at all,' and would have left it there rather than risk a quarrel neither could afford.

But the tiny darkened image of Adela, like something trapped at the back of Alfred's eye, receded endlessly onto the sand. He seemed to feel the primal injury done her – done, he would claim, to himself. He said abruptly, 'Was she your mistress?'

'You have no right to ask that,' said Augustus. He had braced his hands on the edge of the desk and pushed himself back from it, so that his face was almost indistinct in the shadows. But the question had come as no surprise.

'Surely I do? At least I am asking you direct. Presumably such things don't go unnoticed in a place like this. If I asked anyone they'd tell me soon enough.'

Augustus said very quickly, 'It is not generally known. Not known at all, I think.' Then, 'I see no reason to discuss it. It is quite over if that's what troubles you – if you were reluctant to bring Harriet here on that account. She never lived in the house, in any case.' So far had that been from Alfred's thought that he let out a single harsh laugh.

'It amuses you?'

'I am surprised,' he said, the more grimly and tightly that the mention of Harriet galled his own guilt and wretchedness.

'Oh, come,' Augustus said. 'Surely you are not. There were others before her. Your mother has had her suspicions from the start. I'd be most surprised if she'd kept them to herself.'

'That was different,' he said, and felt he had betrayed himself.

'If it's the child that worries you, I've no intention of acknowledging it. There's no question of that. Everything's as it was regarding yourself.'

'It's not the child,' he said with contempt. 'It's her. It's what's been done to her.'

'To Adela?'

'Well, you have wronged her. To take her like that as if you owned her and then cast her aside when it suits you – married off to anyone who would have her.'

'You do not understand at all. She married of her own free will.'

'Oh, that's absurd. What freedom does she have – does anyone have here?'

'The child will be well provided for. Jenkins is good to her. There's no question of that. They grew up together. They are like brother and sister.'

'And you would tell me that is what she chose for herself – out of the whole of life?'

'You do not understand. You do not know her. She is not

310

hurt by all of this. Adela's a survivor. She was dragged out of the sea to survive. Did she tell you that? Besides, no one has the whole of life to choose from.'

Alfred said, with a curious disgust, 'You speak of her as if she were a parcel of land.'

'Well?' said Augustus.

The appeasement in his uncle's voice, still more the smile that had appeared for an instant on his heavy face when he spoke of Adela, made him grasp his rage, as a raft, as a weapon. He was shouting now. The servants might hear, but the thought of their hearing confirmed him the more in his need to believe that he was Adela's protector and this other man her destroyer. 'My God, but you are arrogant. You think because you own this place – because you bought it – you can work out your will upon it and no one opposes you. No one has ever had the strength to do that. You take people's lives and do what you want with them. Well, if that's what having all this means I haven't the stomach for it.'

The room was silent then, measuring the weight of this blow, until Augustus said, in his most austere tone, 'Well, you will do what you want with it when it's yours. I'll not be here to oppose you then. Whatever it is you want, you'll do.'

'Oh, for God's sake.' For he was tormented beyond endurance by what he wanted, and the knowledge that in his turn nothing would oppose his getting it.

They observed one another without moving. The light had made its first silent sweeping intrusion on the sky but neither of them watched it or alluded to it, though Alfred, seeing the brass of Augustus' aneroid gleam and fade, was aware its time had come. He said, with a sudden resolution he scarcely believed in himself, 'Well, you will not do it to me.'

'What do you mean by that?'

'That I do not intend to resign my commission. Even if you order me to, I shall defy you in this. Even if the money that bought it is yours.'

'And Harriet, have you thought of her?'

311

'Do you imagine I have not thought of Harriet? That I have not thought and thought for years what was best for her and for everyone? What everyone expected of me? How everyone thought my life should be led?'

His uncle had thrust himself up from his chair and began to pace agitatedly back and forth between his desk and the bookcase. 'It cannot be best for Harriet to be separated from you. For you risk being killed. There is no need for it. It is pure wilfulness. When you could come here. When I need you here.'

Alfred said: 'I do not think that I can.'

'While I live, you mean? You do not want it till it's yours?'

'I did not say that.'

'What, then? You do not want it at all?'

'Really, I don't know.'

'After all,' he said, but was too proud to reproach him with ingratitude.

They had reached an end.

In a moment they must face the lamplight and the impassive scrutiny of the servants. 'Perhaps I should take the steamer tomorrow. It might be for the best.'

'As you wish.' A moment later he said, 'The will stands. What you do with it after my death is your affair. I do not wish to know. We will not speak of it again.'

'I am behaving intolerably towards you,' Alfred said. 'I know that – just let me have longer.' The inner shaking had intensified until he feared it must be apparent. The aneroid's brass gleamed and faded. He felt the light's persistent presence as a great defeat. Nothing he had said or done would alter its course. It seemed it had been set in motion to measure out his life. He could go to the ends of the earth and would know it silently paced out the time till his return. He could see the pain and uncertainty he had caused. He could sense its futility. The dinner gong sounded in the hall. The little dog was scrabbling at the door. They rose with one movement and Alfred followed his uncle into the dining room.

23

That May – the week before he had intended to set out for
the mainland to attend Alfred's wedding – Augustus fell
from his horse while riding across the moorland on the
northern end of the Gweal. He had little recollection of the
fall, other than the sudden shriek and flight of a bird, a
tern, he thought, rising off its nest directly at his horse's
feet. He lay on the heather staring up at the clear blue sky
in full consciousness, but at first unable to collect his
faculties or move. He was in no pain and curiously free of
distress, other than a fear that someone might have seen
him fall or might come across him lying there. He did not
know how long it took him, first to roll over, then to sit,
then to rise. The horse had run off but presently returned
and stayed patiently beside him. He knew he would be
unable to mount it again and made his way slowly back
leaning against its flank. Clearly, he had broken nothing,
but waves of nausea and dizziness kept him fearful that he
might fall again. He had brushed the broken twigs of
heather from his clothes as best he could, and skirted the
village by the road leading past the ruins of Mrs Traherne's
old cottage.

Had anyone questioned him he planned to say that his
horse was lame – though this was patently untrue. As it
was he passed no one, but was, of course, observed and his
plight much commented on. All the more so because
Edward Jenkins had arrived in the islands, presumably
on leave, on the very day before – and would now know –
as indeed was common knowledge – the nature of his
brother's marriage. The myth of his old grudge against

Augustus took on new life, but any substance to these rumours would have been impossible to find.

Augustus remained in ignorance of them. He was wretchedly stiff for a week following the accident, and plagued more by recurring bouts of dizziness and nausea, which caused him to cancel his visit and miss the wedding. The fall had taken a toll of his health and spirits he could not account for. It was noticed, even by the Abbey servants who saw him every day, that he had taken one of those imperceptible strides into age. His touchy fear of showing any physical weakness in public caused him to go about less. He kept to the house and gardens, following the gardeners about as they worked, countermanding orders he had given the day before. He was constantly irritable with Wills over matters he would formerly have overlooked. His mood was not improved by a letter from Alfred, written shortly after the wedding, saying that he was to be posted immediately to Hong Kong. The honeymoon was to be cut short: all plans to receive the couple on the islands cancelled. Augustus was bitterly disappointed, for he had hoped this visit would erase the ill-feeling of the last. Certainly Harriet's presence would prohibit any allusion to it; with the air of optimism and futurity that clings persistently to brides she might unconsciously have set things back on their original and proper course. Now, when he felt more mortal than ever, he was plagued afresh with uncertainty about Alfred's intentions and deep anxieties about his very survival.

Wills came more frequently to the island, no doubt to spare him. Early in June he mentioned, with a tactful caution that riled Augustus, that Billy Jenkins had again applied to Trinity House for a posting on the light and had already embarked on a probationary tour.

'Why wasn't I told of this?' said Augustus loudly, although the agent sat no further from him than the width of his desk. The news, the manner of telling it, made him suddenly angry.

'I only heard of it myself yesterday.'

'Well, it is intolerable,' he said, slapping his hand down

314

on the cluttered papers. 'He needn't think he can run the farm as well. Surely he can't have gone off and left his wife with the heavy work at this time?' For he knew the child must be born shortly.

'It seems they had it all worked out. The brother's back on leave and working the farm while he's gone.'

'Edward?' he said. 'Edward back in the islands? Why wasn't I told?' But he could guess why; Wills had shirked telling him. So he said, all the more irritably, 'It's intolerable that Trinity House should continue to interfere with my tenants behind my back. If they want him they can have him, but they needn't think that I'll go on supplying him with a roof.'

'That's just the point, sir. He came to speak with me yesterday, on his way out to the light. It appears that they won't take him without this trial run to see if he's suited to the life.'

'That's his risk,' said Augustus. 'He's made his choice. He didn't consult me about it. I'll not have him back.' But he thought of Adela and the child and knew as soon as he had uttered the threat that it was hollow enough.

Perhaps Wills knew, too, for he said now rather primly, 'He seems quite confident. He's slow of speech, but quite intelligent.'

'Oh, I daresay.'

'His leg's a drawback on the farm. I think he'll feel it less out there. He's always been a solitary sort of fellow. It should suit him well enough.'

'It had better,' said Augustus grimly.

'The point is,' said Wills, 'he wants the farm given back to his brother. If all goes well, that is. It seems that between them they've scraped together enough to buy him out. I think this is what they both want. They're very close in their way.'

It occurred sourly to Augustus that some of this money would have come from his own pocket, to ensure the well-being of Adela and the child, and that it would have given the Jenkinses some pleasure to spend it in this way. Wills was saying, 'I think he's always felt he did Edward an injustice.'

'That I did, you mean.' He got up as he said this and went

315

over to the window. He still walked stiffly from his fall. Wills, turning in his chair, said quietly, 'I think it would be as well to comply with him. Unless, of course, you don't want Edward in the islands.'

'Why should I not?' swinging round at him, so that the agent faltered and said, 'I'm sure he cannot still bear a grudge,' but something in his face made Augustus suspect he knew well enough the fresh grievance they might be supposed to bear.

'Nor should he,' he said indignantly. His voice, too loud for the little study, silenced the accusation Wills would never have the courage to make. 'I've done more for both of them than ever their father did, but if they want to cast all that away and tie themselves down that's their affair. I did what I could for them.'

'Shall I say you don't oppose them, then? That all things being equal, you'll consent?'

But he would not be made to agree so easily and said, 'Why cannot he come and speak to me about it himself?'

'But he is on the light by now.'

'Not him, Edward. It's Edward I want to see.'

'Oh, there's no need,' said Wills quickly.

'Do you think I fear him?'

'No, of course not.'

'Then tell him I would see him.'

Wills was with him again when, two days later, a servant knocked at the study door to say that Edward Jenkins was waiting on the terrace. Augustus rose without hesitation from the desk and went out to meet him, leaving the agent to follow uncertainly behind.

'Good day to you,' he said rather loudly to Edward Jenkins. He felt after all no fear for him, but watched him with the strange love and longing that such young men are bound to provoke, standing so squarely with the healthy flush rising above his black beard. He held out to Augustus a little plant with its sharp green leaves just showing above the dirty canvas in which it was wrapped. 'I brought you this, sir. I'd have come sooner had I had the time.'

316

'The Agave Salmiana,' said Augustus, taking it into his hand and running a finger gently along one of the spiky leaves. 'Oh, I cannot tell you how pleased I am to have one of these,' and he turned with a look at Wills as if to say: What did I tell you? He holds none of it against me.

'You know about it?'

'The Salmiana? Indeed, indeed. Simpson will be most interested to see this.'

'They say it doesn't bloom in a hurry.'

'Yes,' he said, 'yes. I'll not see it bloom. But you will,' he said, turning his severe smile onto the young man. 'You'll come to the garden and see it in bloom. I'll make sure they tell you.' He looked hard at Wills as if setting him this task.

'You'll be gone, then,' said Edward Jenkins. 'Or,' he said with a sudden laugh, 'you'll be a very grand old age.'

'There's always plenty of warning,' said Augustus. 'I've read about them. You can see the bud form some weeks before. They'll let you know.' All the time he had walked as rapidly as he might along the terrace, with Jenkins keeping pace beside him and Wills at his heels. 'I don't know when you last saw my gardens,' he said. 'You'll find it all changed.' For in recent years it had altered out of recognition. The boulder piles were covered with Mesembryanthemums and crowned with Agaves. Cactus and succulents clung to the rock faces, protruding green untender leaves. Down at the base of the hill, in the shelter of a hedge of Escallonia, he could see Simpson and two of his lads working in the smoke of a pile of burning leaves and branches. The sharp aromatic scent of Eucalyptus carried up the hillside.

'Simpson,' he called, loudly enough to start an echo. 'Come here, will you?'

Immediately the man laid down his tool and began to climb the long flight of steps.

Jenkins said quietly, 'There's no knowing whether you'll be here, then – or me, for that matter. How far off I'll be.'

'You like the sea?' said Augustus, seeming to watch the gardener. 'You're happy with the life?'

'I think you know, sir, that I wish to leave the sea. I

317

think Mr Wills here has told you that already. That I'm set on taking the farm again, if Billy can be sure of a living on the light, and if you'll allow me.'

Augustus turned to look at him shrewdly, but the young man continued to watch the approaching gardener, as if he measured out the time left for what he had to say. Yet he would not speak again until Augustus did.

'I see no reason why you should not, if no one suffers from it.'

'If you mean Adela and the child, sir, I'm the last person that would harm either of them.'

'Quite so,' said Augustus. He wondered if the child had been born, but could not bring himself to ask, calling out to Simpson instead, 'We should have come down to you. Then I could have shown Jenkins our Australia. It would interest him, I think. Look what he's brought us. The Salmiana. Isn't that splendid?'

The gardener took it into his hands with a slow smile of pleasure. He said quietly to Edward Jenkins, 'I heard your news. I hope all is well.'

'Quite well,' said Jenkins. 'Quite well, thank you.'

'What's this?' said Augustus.

'I was to tell you, sir, only we spoke of other things. Mrs Jenkins – Adela – was delivered of a child last night.'

'That's splendid,' said Augustus. 'Splendid.'

'A little before its time, it seems.'

'They are both well?'

'Quite well. It's a boy. They call it William after its pa.'

'I am delighted.' And watched him without wavering.

'They thought you should know. I was to tell you.'

'And your brother?' said Augustus. 'Does he know yet? He's on the light, surely.'

'We fetched him home yesterday. Charlie Bayliss took his place. She wanted him with her. I take him back this afternoon. I came to say, sir, would you care to come with us? I know you take an interest in the light. My brother thought you had not seen it lately. They'd have the winding gear set up for Billy. They'd as easily winch you up, too. If you feel up to it, that is.'

'Why not?' he said. 'Why not?'

'Oh, I should not, sir,' said Wills, coming quickly to his side.

'Why not?' said Augustus again. 'It's the perfect chance. I've done it often enough before.'

'But you had not intended it.'

'Well, the opportunity had not arisen. When do we go?' he said to Jenkins.

'Noon? A little after?'

'We couldn't have a better day for it.'

'That we couldn't, sir. I'd have taken my poor old mother out on such a day.'

'Until noon, then,' said Augustus, as if the parting must be postponed. 'You must come again. Simpson will let you in and show you where we put the Salmiana. Down there behind the hedge in what we call Australia. You'll do that, won't you, Simpson?' Then, when the gardener made no move to go, he said, 'It should be put in the earth as soon as possible.' But the old man continued to stand there quietly and patiently while the young man said, 'I must be off now. Until noon, then?'

'At the quay,' Augustus said. 'And thank you for this.'

'You should not go with him,' said Simpson, when he was out of earshot.

'You should not, sir,' said Wills.

'Why do you say that?' But, challenged, neither would speak plainly.

Simpson said, without meeting his eye, 'It's a terrible place out there.'

'Not today. Besides, I've been there often. I've been there on worse days than this.'

'Well,' he said, 'they're a rum lot, those Jenkinses. Feeling people but close, so as you'd never know. The old man was like that for years. Then suddenly he ups and kills himself.'

'Yes,' said Augustus. 'There's no telling with anyone. You can go now,' he said. 'You'd best get that into the earth. You too,' he said curtly to Wills.

*   *   *

He went into the house and rang the bell in the hall and ordered his dinner delayed until he came back. 'I'm going out to the light this afternoon,' he told the servant.

'Do you want the trap brought round, sir?'

'No,' he said, 'I'll walk.'

He took out his watch, put it back, walked restlessly about the room. Then he took his long-neglected journal down from the bookshelf and laid it on the desk. He began to write, bending his face close to the page so that the words blurred slightly. The rapid marks he made seemed to have no relation at all to what was in his mind. His hand slid along the page. He felt the unaccustomed pressure of its downward strokes. He continued to write.

> . . . *There was one came up to my garden this morning, bringing me a gift. I have long impressed on all my lads the need to stock my garden and I suppose it has become among them a tradition, a safeguard, to please me with some token of the Antipodes. Still, it is something that all those thousands of miles away my existence came into his mind. He remembered his home and the opportunity I gave him to leave it and return, a man, bearing a gift; his bearing as he gave it to me was all that one could wish for, respectful without the slightest loss of manliness. He is tall, the steady blood apparent in his cheeks. His mother had that fine colouring. His father was a big man too, but dissolute, weak, with a sullen deference that was like contempt, but even as he held it towards me and I recognised the particular spiked leaves of the Salmiana the thought came to me that he must know it would not bloom in my lifetime. I have no son. I cannot be sure of Alfred's intentions towards this place. The Salmiana is likely to bloom in a wilderness of neglect.*

He shut the book without reading these words and slid it into place in the bookshelf.

He stood on the quay, propping himself against the wall that sheltered the eastern side of it, waiting while the men stacked provisions for the lighthouse into the gig. Behind

320

him the sea came and went in a rocky cove. He did not turn to watch it but stood quite peacefully, smiling into the sun, thinking of nothing, hearing the repeated dash of the wave and then its sad exhausted withdrawal, dragging with it pebbles that sounded. He must listen again; until he was reminded of laughter. And there again when the wave withdrew. He did not think it pleasant laughter.

They helped him down into the gig. He took his place in the stern and watched them, as he had for years on these journeys from place to place, gauging their hostility or acceptance, once with hope, then with indifference. I was fortunate, he thought, to live among people I could not expect to know, could expect nothing from.

The course they steered between the rocks was familiar enough, but even that, he told himself, was their secret. They had some knowledge of bars and channels; the sandy anatomy of the land between the islands that was a mystery to him, hidden, even from his imagination, by the bright beaten surface of the water. And they too, perhaps, were never entirely sure of it. For the shape of that landscape responded every winter to the great violence enacted above it. He knew nothing of all of that – never would. He watched, through eyes narrowed by the sun, Edward Jenkins' beard jutting upwards as he strained back on his oars. Effort at that moment contorted his face, but as it eased and came towards Augustus it gave no hint that he thought at all, of love or hate or birth or killing, of anything beyond a constant flicker of images of rock and hidden shapes of sand through which to steer.

He turned to look away from him and saw the islands float innocent and unobtainable in the benign circle they formed within the treacherous and bitter landscape of the outer rocks. He had thought to alter them. They had not resisted but reformed themselves around his granite structures. They had used him to their own ends. Too much of his purchased world had been made of volatile substance. Even the rooted rocks changed constantly in appearance with the fluctuations of the water, with his own restless movements from place to place. They mocked him as surely as they had mocked the doomed passengers of the *Severn*, waving and cheering their belief in the islands' salvation until the very moment of their drowning. And in that moment had anything been revealed to them of the true nature of the landscape spread out around them? He thought not. He thought they were swept away believing still what they wished to believe.

He stared at Edward Jenkins' straining face and thought, is it possible that my death is conceived there? But he could see no indication of such a thing, and felt no fear. He had known at once when the trip to the rock was mentioned that the way to rid himself of fear was to cast himself off into these men's power, onto this outermost rock. The instinct was immediate and strong. He trusted it implicitly and stared ahead now at the lighthouse on its crest of rough pink granite, darkened with barnacles and hanging with seaweed, like some strange excrescence that had always been there, towering largely above them.

They could see the three men waiting with the rope on the off-set, high above the point where the shaped granite was interlocked with the natural rock. Even on so calm a day the sea made snatches at them, hurtling up out of clefts in the rock and then streaming out white through crevices, as if forced from jets.

One of the men threw the rope. It twisted for a moment in the air and then fell into the sea. The men craned over their oars, watching intently for the float at its end. 'There.' They rowed towards it, but the swell was heavy where the divided sea rejoined around the base of the rock. They lost sight of it and spotted it again a number of times before it was retrieved and fastened to the gig. Then they manoeuvred in as close as they might without being drawn into the turbulence of the breaking waves. The harness was lowered down the rope.

'Would you go first, sir?' Billy Jenkins asked him.

'No,' he said, 'you go. I'll follow.' And he watched him from the heaving boat swing and dangle in the air as the men on the tower wound him steadily upward, and his brother steadied and slackened the rope from the boat.

They cheered him when they hauled him onto the off-set. Perhaps on account of the child.

When it was his turn it seemed he was shot suddenly upwards, for the boat fell away beneath him into the trough of the swell and he was left spinning in air, unable to see the boat he had sprung from, nor, from the angle at which his head was held by the harness, the tower to which he was going. Sea and sky circled. All that preserved him from the waves or the rocks was the delicate tension of the rope held by the unseen hand on the winch, Billy's, perhaps, and Edward Jenkins' far below in the boat, playing it out lest it grow taut and snap and hurl him into the sea, or taking the strain onto his own arms lest it grow slack and Augustus be hurled against the rock. And so he dangled, a helpless inanimate thing at the mercy of that man's touch. See how he preserves me, he told himself in triumph, and heard them cheer again above the racket of wind and breakers as they dragged him onto the narrow off-set and pulled the harness from his back.

He climbed the dog steps hand over hand, with his face kept resolutely to the smooth grey face of the tower, and he would keep on, he told himself, this time to the very top. He would not permit himself to tire.

'You'll want to see the cracked optic,' Billy Jenkins said to him in the gloom of the entrance floor. The other men had stayed below on the off-set to winch up the supplies.

'Indeed I do,' but already he was short of breath.

The young man said, 'It's a steep climb.'

'You go first,' he said. 'I'll take my time.'

'Would you wait a bit first?'

'No, no. Go ahead.'

Determinedly he began to climb the iron stairs circling the store rooms, and then, higher still, stone steps imprisoned in the walls themselves. Billy Jenkins disappeared ahead, not dragging himself by the rail as he did, but bracing his hands on the ceiling and climbing agile as a cat despite his lameness. Occasionally his voice echoed down, 'You all right there, sir?'

'Yes,' he said, 'yes.' And forced himself stubbornly upwards.

He was winded when he reached the foot of the final ladder leading to the light and leant against it, struggling to catch breath, but no breath he drew was deep enough to ease the tight hollow in his chest. When he glanced up he saw that Billy Jenkins waited for him. His face, with its slight distortion, like some sad comment on his brother's, hovered over the gap in the floor.

When he had helped Augustus up he said kindly enough, 'It's a steep climb.'

Augustus nodded but would not risk his voice. His own weakness sickened him.

Now Billy Jenkins was saying, as if to a total stranger, 'Here's the cracked optic, sir.'

Augustus studied it, struggling for breath, longer than he need, imagining the great wave coming solitary out of the sea; its long slow curve up the column of rock until it dashed on these windows a blow still powerful enough to crack the thick glass of the lens. Outside the window now there was nothing but sky and the wheeling shapes of gulls. When he could control his voice he said with wonder, 'It came as high as this.'

'Keeper says he's never known a night like it,' said Billy Jenkins. 'He says it won't stand up to another night like that. But I tell you something, he says the worst was the next day. He went out there on the gallery and it was clear and still as this, but, he says, you could hear the boulders cast up by the storm grinding against the base of the rock here. It's a terrible sound, that, he says. A sinister sound. As if it meant to get you in the end. You couldn't help but think of that, he said.'

Augustus said, 'Can I go out there?'

'I'd not advise it, sir.' He would not say that if he meant him ill.

'You go. Surely.'

'About once in the day.'

'Well, surely it's calm enough today.'

'You'd be surprised, sir. It's never still there. You'll keep a good grip of the rail. There's one spot the far side, there's shelter from the wind. We'll work our way round there and back again.'

When they reached it, and the racket and strain of the wind was abated, he found he could not see the islands at all, only the great arc of the sea, and that seemed meaningless enough, with no hint of what it was or what it did or even a distinct line where it ended. Only a quivering surface that caught the light: a trick of light that hid the nature of the thing was all he saw.

A week later he wrote:

My dear Mrs Pontefract,

I am laid up, if not positively done for, and at such times miss the presence of friends who are as present in my thoughts as if I heard them move about my house or in my garden, though to be honest I would not have them in the room to see the state I am reduced to. It seems I slipped and fell on Thursday coming down from seeing the damage to the light, dazzled I think by light and a certain dizzying sensation of solitude. And so I lie here unable to think myself as anything but alive, but equally unable to think myself onto my legs again as I would be: going down to the quay with my boat waiting to take me across to meet the old Lord Wellington. *Where forms stand by the rail, I recognize them long before I read their faces or guess the purpose of their visit. To know that you will handle this page, and read the scrawl of my hand upon it, gives me as always the most profound comfort. I could wish that Alfred were safely returned to ply between us with the news I have not the strength to write.*

> *Yours sincerely,*
> *Augustus Walmer*

My dear Euphemia,

You must forgive me for not receiving you since your arrival in my house, but I am still somewhat tired and best keep company with myself. The enclosed is all I can manage for a sketch of the simple granite slab to be taken from Peninnis Head. Wills knows the very stone I long ago selected to mark my grave, and will take you to the spot. The bare record of my existence is to be placed upon it. I desire to be buried at dawn and would have no public ceremony beyond the few close friends who truly grieve. For I do not believe I shall yet be so long dead not to sense the presence of those whose image has been so real in the long periods of separation that have marked my life – death being little more.

Augustus.

3rd of July, 1856

My dearest Amelia,

We have found your letter of condolence most affecting, but will not hear of your making the crossing. Harriet in her condition must not. And for you to make it without her would be excessive.

It is agreed the funeral will be on Friday. You will understand that in the circumstances we shall limit numbers to members of the immediate family. It was my dear brother's wish that it should be very quiet.

The response of the islanders has been most gratifying. Signs of respect, and recognition of the sacrifices my poor dear brother made, pour in upon me and I have found it all I can do to maintain the composure so necessary on these occasions when every eye is upon me, both as the chief mourner and the mother of the new incumbent.

Your devoted Euphemia.

24

Adela Jenkins walked by the harbour each evening in the summer with her little boy running eagerly ahead of her. Her second child was due to be born towards the end of the month and she followed with the slow self-absorbed movement of women at that time. She and the child always walked this way at dusk, to see the first sweep of the light. The boy, who was six now, had been taught to believe it was a message of greeting sent especially to him from his father, and fretted if it rained and he could not walk to one particular rock below the Abbey farm to wait for its coming.

Neighbours returning from work in the garden, or setting out to visit lobster pots, or merely strolling along by the harbour wall to watch the alterations of the fading light on their known world, were accustomed to look out first for the child and then Adela in the white dress she always wore. The air of careless authority her condition gave her, combined with her habitual reserve, made their greetings cautious, for it was uncertain whether or not she would respond. Still, she was, as she had always been, an object of speculation and interest. The baby, according to the women, had fallen lately and must be born soon. Which of them had not in secrecy calculated the likely date of its birth against Billy Jenkins' last but one shore leave? But such sums are complicated and difficult to perform in the dark, in bed, between waking and sleeping and preoccupations of one's own. No conclusion was reached, nor much pursued, for Adela inspired little malignity among her neighbours.

The evening was warm, and when she had walked beyond the farm and was unlikely to meet anyone else she let her pale shawl fall back from her head and shoulders and walked more freely. Presently she heard the rattle of the old dog cart and the clip of the pony's hooves. She called out her boy's name, 'Billy,' and stood back herself into the thick weeds at the base of the wall, watching the cart approach. It carried Mrs Walmer, whom now she hardly thought of as Harriet, as utterly was she what she had become.

The groom stood holding the reins and behind him Harriet and a young nurserymaid sat facing one another. The maid held the youngest child, a baby still. A little girl and a fair, rather frail boy sat on either side of their mother. As it drew closer the cart slowed to a halt. The groom jumped down and, lowering the back board and the steps, helped Mrs Walmer onto the road. Then he lifted down the little boy. With a quick nod to Adela he climbed back and, taking up the reins again, set out along the Abbey drive with the nurserymaid and the two younger children.

Harriet, holding her little boy by the hand, approached smiling, saying, 'I shall walk with you if I may.' And then, as if she needed to explain, 'It is such a very lovely evening. Do you not think so?' she persisted, when Adela merely smiled.

'Yes, I do.'

'Shall we walk?' But Adela hesitated where she stood and pulled her shawl up over her head again, aware less of this women's graciousness than of some intention behind it.

'Which way are you going?' Harriet asked her.

'We go to see the light lit.'

'Wouldn't you like that?' Harriet said coaxingly down to her child, who looked steadily up at her. 'Take Billy Jenkins' hand there and he'll show you where you can see the light. It's his papa lights the light, you know. That's clever of him, isn't it?' And, lifting her head, she smiled warmly at Adela to include her in her pleasure at her child. 'Yours will be born soon,' she added kindly.

'At the end of the month, I think.'

'Will Billy be home by then?'

'Yes,' she said.

'You must ask me if there is anything at all I can do.' There was a concern in her voice which Adela felt to be a form of courtesy and to lay upon her other pressures she would resist. She said quickly, 'Oh, I have all that I need, thank you, until then.'

'Don't you grow lonely?' Mrs Walmer said presently. 'I could not bear to be so alone.' She began to walk forward, following the little boys who had reached the rock and stood side by side, staring at the gap between the outer rocks where the central eye of the light would first appear.

'Well, I am never alone,' said Adela, smiling in their direction. Lately the child's constant activity and demands for notice had irritated her, and this evening walk, when he ran ahead, absorbed in the promise of the light, gave her rare moments of peace. Now these were interrupted and the effort to respond to this woman, who had made the gesture of climbing down out of her cart and must expect something to come of it, wearied her. She feared Mrs Walmer too, a little, for nothing in the blandness of her look and speech would ever change with what she might think or even know about Adela, so that her kindness held no comfort.

Adela's silence seemed not to affect her. If she regretted her gesture of remembered friendship she did not show it, but fell into Adela's languid pace, watched the two children, felt the loveliness of the evening as if in sympathy. Presently she said, as Adela had known she must, 'Do you remember when we were a little older than that?'

'I remember Miss Christian.' Harriet was startled at her laugh.

'Poor Miss Christian.' But she too laughed softly, noncommittally, for some contact must be made.

'Poor old Miss Christian,' said Adela, the laughter quite gone.

'Papa has her with him still, of course,' said Harriet

329

quickly. 'We could not let her go, after such loyalty.'

To laugh at? To be good to? thought Adela. She would have been left alone and sighed restlessly, wishing the light would come and put an end to this.

Harriet said, with her controlling kindness, 'Are you happy now, Adela?'

'Now?'

'Now that you are married? Have children?'

'Why, yes.' But it surprised her that this woman, whose superior knowledge of things she had accepted since she was a little scowling child, should speak of happiness as if it were a static, central thing, even a normality one should attain to.

But if Adela's tone were careless or dismissive the other young woman chose to ignore this and went on in her light rapt way of speech, 'I often think of old Mr Walmer when we are here, how he would tell us to be happy. And now I am – beyond my dreams.' She turned to Adela with this fact, beaming upon her as if she bestowed a gift.

'I am glad,' said Adela, as indeed she was.

'I did not care for Mr Walmer when I was a child,' Harriet went on. 'And when I grew up he seemed forever telling people what they should do and how they should live. I know he was resented here – misunderstood, for I am sure he meant kindly – hated even. But wrongly, because he meant so well and did such good. It seems almost unfair that Mr Walmer and I reap the benefits of all that he did and that we are loved and he, I think, was not.'

What did she ask? Adela said, 'He was a kind man.'

'You found him so?'

'Always.'

'I know he left you provided for,' said Harriet softly. 'Mr Walmer told me.'

What had they exchanged? Where, if anywhere, did it leave them? Neither knew, but turning from each other noticed with relief that the light had begun its silent pacing.

The two children stood side by side on the rock, motionless with awe and waiting. So that Harriet's cry of, 'There!

330

Look, Christopher! It is the light. Do you see it?' seemed to intrude upon and dissipate something. She walked quickly ahead of Adela, and leaning over her child said, 'Well, you have seen it now. We must go home to Papa. You must say goodbye now.'

She had come too late to hear Adela's child whisper to him, 'It's my Daddy's eye. It's my Daddy's big eye upon you.' But this thought was still enormous in his mind. He looked vacantly towards his mother, as if waking. Then he took her hand and said goodbye and came along eagerly enough.

'Goodbye,' he said to Adela, staring up unguardedly. She was known to love and draw children to her. She reached down now and touched his hair, watching him in silence, then smiling her sudden rather secretive smile.

'Goodbye,' he said again.

His mother said, 'We shall talk again. Do you go back now?'

'No,' Adela said quietly. 'We go on a little way from here.'

They separated, Adela and her child to walk farther along the shore, presumably to the very wall of the estate, Harriet and hers to follow the drive up to the Abbey. It was a long walk for him at the end of the day. She wished, before they reached the gates, that she had not so impulsively taken him out of the cart. She sent him directly to the nursery, saying to the maid, 'Bring him down, just for a minute, when he has had his supper. He must say goodnight to Mr Walmer.'

For Mr Walmer, the servant had told her, was in the garden. He loved this time of day and spent it in the summers wandering about the lower terraces and garden beds, which extended now beyond view of the house and were beginning to take on the tangled secretive look they have today. He had recently begun his collection of crepuscular moths; on these walks he set his traps and made his observations as to which pale blooms the creatures visited.

Because of the serious nature of the thing Harriet never accompanied him. She herself found these summer

331

evenings oddly sad. She remembered that it was a time of day her mother had never cared for. For the reason, or because of the dulling light, or for the uncertainty of waiting that her husband's evening strolls imposed upon her, she always set about some useful task to distract herself. This year it was to finish the set of kneelers for Augustus Walmer's church that her mother had been working on when she died. They were, her daughter knew, intended as a memorial. Now, with a slight revulsion she would not admit to, and which was surely nothing more than the association with her mother's poor dead hand, she picked the last but one of these from her workbasket, and, drawing the light close, began to work upon it.

When the nurserymaid brought the little boy down, she was surprised to see how dark it had grown. 'Run out and find Papa,' she told him, first checking to see that his woollen wrapper was knotted securely about him. 'He must be coming back by now.'

'It's not too cold for him, is it?' she asked the maid, when he had gone running out through the open window onto the terrace.

'No, madam,' she said, looking wistfully after the child. 'It's very warm tonight.'

She worked again at her sewing, making herself complete two rows of little sloping stitches before she raised her head again to listen for them. No sound, only the strange heavy scents of the garden came in through the windows. She would not rise and look out. She would not have him see her anxious. For what could possibly befall either of them in a place like this? Nevertheless, half way through the next row she set the work aside and, walking through the open window, leant on the balustrade and called, 'Christopher! Christopher!' Knowing that it was to her husband she called.

Then she heard the child's terrified crying. Even before the shock of the sound had made itself clearly felt she saw Alfred striding up the flight of steps with the boy in his arms. She ran towards them, calling out, 'What is it? What is it?'

332

'It's nothing,' said her husband. 'He's had a fright. It's nothing.' But he was upset, too. He walked so rapidly along the terrace that she could not keep pace with him, but hurried behind them towards the lighted windows, saying, 'What has made him cry like that? What frightened him?'

Inside, he set the child on the floor, stroking back his damp hair and saying almost angrily, 'Stop now. Stop. I tell you it was nothing.' When Harriet knelt down and took the child in her arms he left them abruptly and went to stand in the open window, staring down into the obscure garden.

'What is it?' she said, rocking her child against her, half laughing, now that she had him safe. 'What can have frightened you so?' She held him from her, lifting up his hair, turning his hands over in hers, parting his wrapper to see if he had fallen on his knees, but he was quite unmarked.

'What is it?' she said, holding him again.

Against her ear he said, 'It is his eye. It is his eye.'

'What does he mean?' she asked her husband. But seeing, at that moment, his form darken against the arc of light outside the window, and feeling the child's arm tighten around her with fear, she said with relief, 'Oh, it is the lighthouse. We were looking at it earlier. It must be that. But why should it frighten you tonight? You love the light.'

'It will see me,' he said. 'It will tell them I am there.'

'Tell who?'

'The people in the garden.'

'What people?' she said, frowning quickly up at her husband.

'I saw no one.' He had turned to watch the boy intently. It occurred to her that he might be angry that his son had been afraid and she held the child defensively to her.

With his hot wet face pressed between her shoulder and her neck, he whispered, 'There was a man. And a woman crying. And someone else moving about. I was hiding, but the eye came and found me out.'

She looked up again at Alfred, saying sharply, 'There should be no one there at this hour. Did you know them?' she asked the boy, holding him from her now so that she too might watch him as he answered.

He stared blankly into her eyes, seeing instead the pale hooded shape of the woman in the white dress, hearing the movement of the leaves. Already the woman's weeping voice, the sad unseen presence of the man, even the sound of that other hidden boy creeping closer, were like a remembered dream. Butting his face into her neck again he whispered, half-ashamed, 'Maybe they were dead people.'

'*Dead* people,' she repeated in alarm.

Alfred gave a single harsh syllable of laughter. 'Perhaps it was Miss Christian's skeleton.'

'How odd,' said his wife, raising her small startled eyes. 'I was speaking of her this evening to Adela Traherne. She laughed too.' But she was distracted then by the child's body tensing with fear against her. 'What is it? What is it? she murmured.

He clung tightly to her, knowing that in an instant the light must penetrate the room in search of him. 'It was the eye,' he told her, hopeless of making them understand. 'It was the eye that saw me.'

When it had gone he raised his head, blinking. His father had come close and smiled down at them, saying, 'It must have been the leaves he heard. The wind's coming up.' Then, going down on one knee, he said to his child, 'It was nothing, do you hear? You imagined it all. In the morning we will go down there and see. You'll see. There will be nothing there.'

THE END

The Doctor's Wife
Brian Moore

'One of the outstanding works of fiction of the year'
PETER TINNISWOOD, THE TIMES

Sheila Redden is on her way from war-torn Belfast to the south
of France where her husband Kevin will join her in a few days
to relive their honeymoon of fifteen years ago. But Sheila had
not reckoned on meeting Tom Lowry and finding her life
transformed. *The Doctor's Wife* is a brilliant portrait of a
woman who is suddenly confronted by the devastating power
of passionate, erotic love.

'Nightmare images of tanks cruising down empty night streets,
feverish erotic couplings with a stranger in foreign hotels; a
married woman with one son from a provincial backwater
breaking out on a trip abroad; a concerned sibling observing a
rebellious young sister; the palpable absence of God in the
central characters' lives and the notion that art and sex might
replace Him . . . the principal ingredients of Brian Moore's
fine new novel . . . a splendidly bracing experience'
NEW STATESMAN

'The erotic force of the love scenes is considerable'
THE GUARDIAN

'The most alluringly complex adulteress to come along in print
for some time'
TIME MAGAZINE

'It is uncanny; no male writer, I swear (and precious few
females), knows so much about women'
JANICE ELLIOTT, SUNDAY TELEGRAPH

0 552 99109 0   £2.50

BLACK SWAN

Mrs. Pooter's Diary
Keith Waterhouse

'The whole book is a bundle of fun . . . it is ingenious and it is
immensely entertaining'
DAILY MAIL

"The Laurels"
Brickfield Terrace
Holloway.

I have discovered (although he does not yet know that I know!)
what it is that my husband does in the quarter-of-an-hour
before retiring each night. If he may entertain hopes of
publishing a diary, then so may I – after all, it is not as if my
dear Charlie were a 'Somebody' whose thoughts and
impressions are any more profound or worthwhile than the
next person's. He is, alas, thanks to the good nature that holds
him back, no more of a 'Somebody' than is –
Mrs. Charles Pooter

THE DIARY OF A NOBODY is one of the great classics of
English humour. MRS. POOTER'S DIARY is more than a
brilliant homage to the original, it is a wonderful comic
creation in its own right.

'Mr. Waterhouse does it brilliantly . . . had me in stitches'
AUBERON WAUGH, DAILY MAIL

'What Waterhouse has managed is to re-create the whole Pooter
world, as if in a three-dimensional model, and then show it to us
from a quite different perspective . . . Most readers like the
Pooters, and I suspect quite a few of us admire them and even
envy them; Waterhouse has left that affection intact'
SIMON HOGGART, OBSERVER

0 552 99117 1   £2.50

BLACK SWAN